I0647190

Goodnight, Sweet Prince

Chris Davidson

A Tale of Elsynvaal

Published by
Best Global Publishing
PO Box 9366
Brentwood
Essex CM13 1ZT
United Kingdom

First published 2009

http://www.bestglobalpublishing.com

'Now Cracks a Noble Heart

Goodnight, Sweet Prince

And Flights of Angels

Sing Thee to thy Rest'

Wm Shakespeare
Hamlet - Act 5 Scene 2

Acknowledgments:

"Freezing" (p47)
Lyrics by Suzanne Vega
Music by Philip Glass
Recorded on "Songs from Liquid Days"
CBS; MK 39564

Also: My thanks to John Lakeman,
D.M. Extraordinaire,
without whom Elsynvaal would not exist

Dramatis Personæ:

Elsynvaal:

Horatio talMerios – a Mage of Elsynvaal
Hamnet – Prince, heir to the throne of Elsynvaal
Polon – The King's Chancellor; a Mage of Elsynvaal
Ser Loren – Polen's 16 year old son
Serra Olivia – Polen's daughter
King Hamnet
Claude – the King's brother; Prince Hamnet's uncle
Master Will Shaksper

Glasgow, Earth

Emma Campbell
Martin Paterson
Maggie Walker
Jeff Zimlinsky
Milo Diaz
Mhari McLeod
Duncan McLeod

5

Part One

Dreams and Schemes

Chapter 1

A world away from Elsynvaal's unfolding drama, a girl lay asleep, dreaming.

A laugh catches in her throat as she urges her horse onwards. Her long jet-black hair comes loose and whips around her face as she looks back over her shoulder at the rider behind. He is gaining on her. We'll see about that! Smiling, she leans forward across her horse's neck and urges the animal on even more. Her laugh rings out. Behind her a midnight-blue cloak billows out as she and the dark-haired man gallop across meadows filled with acre after acre of summer-bright flowers that dance and wave in the breeze. Over to the left is a copse of trees, to the right blue lake the shines under the clear blue sky. Not far ahead is the outcrop of rocks that is the race's finish line. She glances back again. Damn, he's still gaining on her. Come on, baby, she urges the horse. You can do it.

Then something darts out from the undergrowth across their path, forcing the horse to break its stride. She pulls on the reins, showing the horse down. The young man with unruly dark hair and smiling hazel eyes draws up beside her, and grins. They draw their horses to a walk and he reaches over, laughing, to touch her face...

Only a dream. Only a dream. Emma fought to cling on to it even as it faded. Such a lovely dream. But who was he, this dark haired stranger? She rolled over on one side and her eyes fell upon the framed photo on the dresser. Immediately, the sight of the photo made her feel disloyal to Martin. Here she was, dreaming of some stranger instead of him.

She pushed the duvet back and glanced at the silly Mickey Mouse alarm clock her little brothers gave her last Christmas. She read the time and collapsed back against the pillows. *It's far too early to be awake,* she thought. But she was awake now, whether she wanted to be or not. *Why can't the damn birds sing their blasted songs later - once decent folk are already awake?* The early morning light streamed through the window. She'd forgotten to close the curtains again. She licked her lips. *I need a drink.*

She reached for her dressing gown and went to the window to close the curtains. The loud swish startled a large snowy-white bird perched on the decorative iron railings outside the window. It turned its sleek head and regarded her with hooded eyes before abruptly flying off.

Emma frowned a little, then dismissing the bird from her mind she turned away.

Absentmindedly re-plaiting her waist-length hair, she opened her bedroom door and trotted across the living room to the tiny kitchen area of the flat she shared with her fellow student and oldest friend, Maggie. Lifting a sheet of Maggie's music from the floor as she passed, she dropped it onto the overflowing pile of books and manuscripts beside the digital piano.

She poured herself a cold drink of good Glasgow water, and leaning against the sink as she drank it, thought again about the dream. *Who is he? And why do I keep dreaming of someone I have never met?*

Twice more in the ensuing week she had the same dream, but then things took a turn for the worse. One Saturday while shopping in Sauchiehall Street she stopped in at Starbucks. Idly stirring her latte, she glanced casually around and met the eyes of a man sitting alone at a table near the door. A young man with hazel eyes and unruly dark hair down to his shoulders.

It was *him*.

She turned away at once, her heart thumping from fear or possibly even anticipation, but could not resist glancing back again a moment later. She casually shifted in her seat and peered at him through the curtain of her hair.

He'd gone.

She looked all around, but he was no longer in the coffee house. The table by the door was now occupied by a middle-aged balding man reading the 'Glasgow Herald'. What the hell? He had been there. She was certain of the fact. She'd seen him, with the same tantalising half smile on his lips. Or had she conked out for a minute, long enough for him to leave? But no. If she'd fainted or something, someone would have noticed. But how could he just disappear like that? And where had the balding 'Herald' reader come from? She lifted up her coffee to try to calm herself down. Her hand shook and the cup rattled against her teeth.

Two days later it happened again. She walked into the lift in the College and turned pressed the button for the second floor. But just as the lift doors were closing, she saw him again, standing in the corridor she had just left, just beyond the doors. But he hadn't been there before she got into the lift. She was sure of that. She would have noticed him, surely. Could he be a student here in the RSMD College?

Was he stalking her?

Once she'd voiced the stalker thought, the idea took root in her mind. She began seeing him at odd times, sometimes in a crowd at college or in the street, but he always disappeared again before she could do anything. But what *could* she do? Talk to him? Demand to know why he was stalking her? *If* he was stalking her.

Things continued to get worse. She spotted him one day in Argyle Street, standing on the opposite side of the road. Heart in her mouth, she dashed across the road, dodging cars. Keep him in sight. Don't lose him. Then she was standing in front of him, gripping his sleeve. But now it wasn't *him*. Not her hazel-eyed stranger. Dumbfounded, she spluttered apologies to the blond man he'd inexplicably become.

Am I going mad? Hallucinating?

The final straw was one evening about four or five weeks after the first dream. Emma had been looking forward to a cosy evening in with Martin. Just the two of them, because Maggie had gone out and they for once had the flat to themselves. Sitting close together on the sofa with romantic music in the background and a glass of wine in her hand, she opened herself to Martin's kiss, and saw in her mind's eye the laughing eyes of the dream stranger. She drew away and opened her eyes and for several seconds, instead of Martin's face, it was *his* face that she saw inches from her own.

Oh my God!

The hallucination faded almost immediately – the hazel eyes changed to blue and the face reverted to Martin's. Emma pushed him away, her eyes wide with shock. The glass fell from her hand and her eyes dropped to the red stain spreading like blood over Martin's shirt. She raised her head and met Martin's eyes, only to flinch at the puzzlement and confusion in his eyes as she backed away. *When the hell is this going to stop?* she thought frantically, as she backed away from him and watched him futilely wipe at his shirtfront with a pile of paper tissues.

"I'm sorry, Martin. I'm sorry. I don't know what happened. Are you okay? Your shirt is ruined. Red wine stains are terrible to get out." She knew she was rambling and making no sense at all, but she couldn't face the look in his eyes when she'd flinched away from his kiss. And every excuse she used to avoid his anxious questions only made her feel worse. But how could she tell him what had happened? She didn't know herself.

***

Over the following days, Martin watched as Emma's attitude towards him changed. After that inexplicable evening in the flat when she covered him in red wine, she had became distracted, as if distancing herself from him. Now it was Friday – the last rehearsal before the Autumn Concert. He was in one of the practice rooms at the College, with Jeff Zimlinsky waiting for the others to arrive. Martin, uptight and nervous, paced the room, gnawing at his knuckles.

Worrying.

About the Concert.

About Emma.

He knew he had to talk to her, to straighten out what was going wrong between them. If not, the concert tomorrow could be a complete washout – down the drain and flushed into the River Clyde before you know it. And there was so much riding on a good reception for his two new compositions. He couldn't allow a break with Emma to interfere with the concert. It was too important.

Jeff settled himself on a chair, placing his bad leg carefully in front of him. "Sit down for God's sake, Martin. You'll wear out the floorboards. They'll be here soon enough. Look, see. Emma's already been in." He nodded towards the cello case lying beside the piano.

"Yes, I know. She's got a lecture this evening and is coming straight to the rehearsal room afterwards." He paused, glanced at the cello case and added, "At least she's remembered."

Jeff frowned at him. "Be reasonable, Martin. Emma hasn't forgotten a single rehearsal in the eighteen months since we've all been together. She's every bit as reliable as she's talented!"

Martin dropped into a chair and scowled. How would the group function if she and he split up? Jeff had been right. He should never have asked her out. The minute he and Emma became an item, the professional relationship they'd had up until then changed. *But damn it all,* he thought, *I love her!*

Jeff nudged his elbow. "Lighten up Martin," he said. "Drop the tortured-composer-on-the-eve-of-a-premiere look."

The mocking tone was counter-balanced by the twisted grin that suddenly appeared on his scarred face, the legacy of a car smash when Jeff had been fifteen.

"Well, that's what I am!" Martin retorted, but the smile he tried to paste onto his face slipped away too quickly.

Jeff got up painfully and limped to the piano behind Martin, to hit a few keys.

"Do you miss playing?" Martin asked.

"Yes, I suppose I do, but there's no use in playing the *'What if...'* game. I can't play with hands like these." He looked down at his stiff and scarred hands. "I'll be content with my voice. At least I was left that."

Martin leaned back and punched him on the shoulder. "Who's getting down now?" But there was respect in his voice for the way Jeff managed his disfigurement. As he put his folder on a music stand, Martin's thoughts wandered to the little that Jeff had told him about the car accident that had ended his hopes for a career as a musician. Black ice. Smashed car. Fire. Martin shuddered.

Jeff's voice broke in on his reverie. Martin turned round at his mocking tone and caught the look in his face. "Okay," he said. "I'll forget about the situation with Emma for tonight. I'll wait until after the concert tomorrow. Hopefully she'll open up. Anyway, I've enough to worry about in making sure these pieces sound right. The trio will be fine, but I am a little nervous about one or two bits of the rondo. Milo almost fluffed up the end section last practice."

"Ah, well it is a fiendishly difficult tenor entry. It's almost atonal the way it clashes with Emma's phrase, *and* it's high in pitch for a tenor. But Milo's up to it. He'll be fine. I suppose we could suggest he wears his tight trousers!"

Martin laughed. "That would be one way to make sure he hit the high notes. My God. I think I've aged ten years in the last fortnight!" He lifted up a wad of music manuscript and looked at it. His smile faded. "I'm still worried about Emma." He raised his hands in supplication. "I know, I know. I said I'd leave her out of it, but her concentration these last few weeks has been up the creek What if she mucks up the whole thing?"

"Listen to me, Mr Patterson. Emma's fine. Okay, so she's obviously got something on her mind at present. Even I've noticed that. But so what? She's too much of a professional to allow

13

whatever's bothering her to interfere with her work. Something you're not managing too well right now, I might add."

Martin turned away and snatched up the sheets of music. Jeff shrugged and stood up to begin setting out the music stands and chairs ready for the others arriving.

Finally Martin spoke. "Zimlinsky, why is it you're always right?"

"See, Patterson, I'm looking from outside. It makes a difference. Look, man, I know what you feel for her. You're worried and uncertain about where it's going. But, as you have just said, for the good of the music group you have to set all of that aside, at least until after this damn concert tomorrow."

Martin laid his hand on his old friend's shoulder for a moment, and gave a wry grin. "Okay, I'll give it my best shot. Let's get moving. Maggie and Milo will be here soon. And Emma's lecture's due to end about now."

"What of the other two? Milo was picking Maggie up, wasn't he?"

"Yes. So we'll have to hope his car's up to the job. It broke down again yesterday. He spent nearly two hours on the hard shoulder of the M8 from Cumbernauld waiting for the RAC to arrive."

"What was it?"

"Something caught in the carburettor, he said." Just then they heard the sound of voices, and the door opened. Maximilian Diaz, darkly handsome in leather jacket and jeans entered with Maggie Walker at his heels. She stalked into the room and shed her jacket and violin case before announcing that she was going to the canteen to get a glass of water.

"That's the last time I travel anywhere in that apology for a car!" she exclaimed. "The stench of petrol fumes has completely dried up my throat!" The door slammed behind her.

Milo shrugged. "She's in prima-donna mode, unfortunately. The car's not *that* bad." He caught an amused glance between the other two. "What's going on?"

Martin waved him away. "Nothing, Milo, nothing at all."

Milo perched on the back of a chair and swivelled his dark Italian eyes round the room. He shrugged out of his jacket and tossed it onto a nearby chair, then gestured towards the cello case by the piano. "Where's Emma?"

14

Just as Martin was about to reply, the door opened again and the girls entered. Watching them, Martin marvelled once more at the dissimilarly between them in appearance. Maggie was quite good looking, he supposed, with a face that was open and friendly, framed by shoulder length mid-brown hair. She smiled often. But Emma, his Emma, was simply strikingly beautiful. Her Japanese ancestry showed in her high cheekbones and clear dark eyes. Normally she wore her hair tied in a thick plait down her back, but today it was a jet-black cascade falling down her back as far as her waist. Martin looked at her as it flowed across her shoulders and longed to run his hands through it. He turned abruptly, and utterly missed the sad look on her face as she turned and looked up towards him.

"Okay," Jeff said. He clapped his hands together in an attempt to dispel the mood. "Let's get tuned up."

Martin had written two pieces for the group to perform. The first was a trio for strings, which they had performed before, but the second was his new composition. *"Friends: An Introduction and Rondo for unaccompanied voices"*, was a piece Martin had written especially for the music group. He'd sweated over it, and each of them knew it. The rehearsal began well enough, and even to Martin's critical ears the trio sounded good, with Maggie on violin, Milo on viola and Emma on cello. Jeff the critic, perched on a stool to one side, agreed.

The problems began when they began the new unaccompanied piece. First Emma came in late at the beginning of the rondo, and then in a very exposed alto section she missed an entry completely. By the time they reached the end, her voice was ragged and despondent. It sounded awful and Martin could see from her eyes that she knew it. But no-one said anything, not even Milo, strange in itself.

Emma snatched up her copy of the music from where it was lying on a nearby chair, rifling through it for the missed entry.

"It was bar 32." Martin failed to keep the ice out of his voice.

"I'm sorry Martin. Can we go through it again? Once I have had a look at the score it'll come back to me."

"The concert is tomorrow, Emma. If you don't know it now you'll never learn it in time."

Emma's flinch at the criticism tore into his heart. "I *do* know it Martin," she said. "It's just a lapse in concentration. I'll be fine tomorrow. Please - let us try again."

When the others went along with her, Martin gave in and the four singers stood ready to begin. The *Introduction* had a medieval feel to it with overtones of plainchant, which with a smooth musical transition moved into the second section – the *Rondo* movement, a circular movement with the voices overlapping and counter-pointing one another. Maggie's soprano rang out clear above the others while Jeff's warm and resonant baritone added depth. Each voice was exposed in solo at least once and although they reached the end together, it sounded rather more ragged than it should have been on a final rehearsal. Emma's indecision and lack of confidence had infected the others. Martin played the chord of C minor. They were a full semi-tone flat.

"Oops!" Milo murmured. Maggie looked at him, daggers in her eyes. "Well," he replied to her. "You know what they say about a bad dress-rehearsal – a good performance on the night." Emma gave a wan smile, but Martin glared at Milo. It was just like him to try flippancy to lighten the sombre mood.

Martin's face remained stony. "We'll do it again. Jeff, watch bar… 24, I think it was. Yes, that A sounded a little sharp. Emma, use the music this time, and sing with more confidence. I could barely hear your line on bars 46-50. Maggie. Watch the sustained top A in the penultimate bar. Right, let's take it from the top." He played an E major chord and Jeff's warm baritone began the *Introduction.*

Halfway through, Martin allowed himself to relax a little. Emma's exposed entry was flawlessly executed, and as the piece progressed towards its climax, he could feel their confidence grow. They were good. They all knew it. He caught Emma's eye, allowed himself a small smile. Then watched incredulous as her voice faltered and faded and her eyes widened with shock as she stared at him. The others continued gamely on, eyes flicking towards Emma, and finally stopped abruptly as Emma let out a groan and covered her eyes with her hands. Maggie was there immediately, taking her hands and whispering to her as she slipped to the floor. Martin covered the distance in seconds and crouched down beside her. Her head whipped round and her eyes went wide once more.

"No!" she shouted. "Go away, Martin. Don't come near me. Don't let me see you."

Maggie looked up in consternation. "Best if you leave now, all of you. I'll see to her. Go to the pub and we'll come on later."

Milo shrugged and headed for the door, looking over his shoulder at Martin and Jeff. Martin looked shocked. Jeff took his arm and steered him towards the door. As the door closed behind them Martin stopped.

"I'm not going," he said. "I'm waiting here. They might need our help."

"I'm okay with that," Milo said. "Anyway," he added, "our instruments are still in there." Jeff threw him a dirty look.

Inside the rehearsal room, Maggie guided Emma to a chair and sat with her, waiting for her to speak.

"I'm frightened, Maggs. I think I'm going mad!"

"Sshh, lass. You're not. Tell me what happened."

"It was the man in the dream. Martin turned into the man in the dream again."

"Wait a minute. What man? What dream? Why don't you start from the beginning?"

"It was the dream. Five, no, six weeks ago it started. I'm out riding across fields and I'm dressed in weird gear, and there's a man with me, with hazel eyes... I should have told you about it!"

"Sshhh lass. It's all right. Tell me now."

"It keeps coming back."

"The dream?"

"Yes. And it's got worse. I see him now when I'm awake. I saw him last week in college and then later in Argyle Street. Only it wasn't him, only someone like him... I think. Then just now... that was the second time..."

"What was the second time?"

Silence.

"Emma?"

She lifted up her head and looked at Maggie. "Just there - during the rehearsal, Martin looked at me and smiled and his face changed."

"What?"

"Martin's face changed into the stranger's. Didn't you see anything?"

"No. I saw nothing. What did you mean the second time? Has this happened before?"

17

"Yes. Tuesday night, at the flat." She clasped Maggie's hands, crushing them in her anguish. "I'm scared. If you didn't see anything, Maggs, it means I'm hallucinating. Am I going mad?"

"'Course you're not! But I think you'll have to tell Martin at some point. Do you feel up to it?"

Emma was still feeling shaky and dazed when they joined the boys outside in the corridor. As they left the College building and headed towards George Square, she could hear them chattering.

Jeff's voice: "Milo, don't be stupid. If you're driving you're not drinking."

"Don't worry, Jeff, he's not driving," Maggie replied. "The bloody car broke down again. We had to walk all the way across town from St George's Cross." Maggie sounded annoyed, even now. "It would have been quicker for me to walk to Kelvingrove station and take the subway."

"Away wi' you, Maggie. You know you enjoy my company."

"Says who?" she retorted.

Emma almost smiled. The bickering between Milo and Maggie was so much a part of their relationship that listening to it gave her a perverse feeling of normality. She wondered once again if it masked some deeper feeling between them. On the other hand, what could happen to the cohesion of the group if she and Martin…?

Her introspection was brought to a standstill as Martin came up beside her, her cello case hanging from his shoulder and banging against his leg.

"You all right?" he whispered.

Emma turned away to avoid looking at him. "Yes I'm okay, Martin," she whispered as they followed Jeff and the still-bickering duo to their local, a pub in a side street near George Square that they often dropped in to after rehearsals.

Being a Friday night, the bar was crowded. Milo held out his viola case in front of him, and like the prow of a ship, created a narrow path through the crowd to the bar. Minutes later he was passing glasses of amber liquid back to the others.

"Not much chance of a seat."

"Trust Milo to state the obvious. What about sitting outside?"

They pushed their way back through the crowd to sit on the cobbled pavement outside.

"Good idea," Jeff commented as they settled themselves on the ground. For late October the night was remarkably warm. Maggie pulled a rain jacket from her huge shoulder bag and spread it on the cobbles.

"Ever-ready Maggie." Milo could not resist making a comment. Maggie tried to cuff him, but missed and spilled some of her drink instead. Milo laughed.

"We won't be able to do this much longer," Jeff remarked. "It will be too cold soon. It's been a lovely autumn this year."

From her perch on a parking bollard, Emma could see the statues that adorned the Square. Maggie noticed her glance. "Remember last New Year's Hogmanay party in the Square? What an atmosphere there was. The fireworks, the singing, the music, the laughter. That was…" her voice trailed off.

"…it was when Emma and I first got together," he finished for her. He looked over in Emma's direction and slid closer to her. "Look, Emma," he said quietly. "I don't know what happened back there but I do know there's something wrong. Won't you tell me what it is? You've been so aloof and unapproachable recently. What has happened?"

Emma glanced round before answering. "It's nothing. Nothing you've done. It's just that there have been some strange things happening to me recently. I can't explain it… I've been having dreams."

"Nightmares?"

"No, they're not nightmares. Actually in themselves they're quite pleasant, I suppose, what I can remember of them."

"So what's the problem?"

By this time the bickering duo had shut up and everyone was watching them. Emma looked round at the faces of her four friends and smiled sadly. "I'm sorry Martin; I ought to tell you this alone." Martin shifted away a little and his face took on a rigid look.

"Tell me what? Do these dreams affect us - you and me?"

"I don't know. I'm all mixed up. It's getting like I can't be with you without it happening. Perhaps we'd be best to discuss it later."

"No," he said. "You may as well go on. You've got their attention now."

Emma gasped in shock.

Maggie reached out a hand to stop Martin but he pushed her arm away. "Go on, Emma" he repeated, his eyes riveted on her face.

"All right then! I'll tell you. I keep having this dream. It's always the same with the same man in it. I can't remember much of the dreams themselves – only the man's face."

19

"Who is he?" Jeff asked glancing at Martin who was suddenly stony silent.

"I don't know who he is. But the frightening thing is that I've starting to see his face during the day – when I'm walking along the street or along a corridor in the College, and then he's not there any more. I can close my eyes and his face is there, painted on the inside of my eyelids. Lately even when I'm going to sleep his face is there, inside my head."

"No wonder you dream of him then." Jeff was matter-of-fact. "Do you know him? Can you describe him?"

Emma looked at Martin, who refused to meet her eye, and then at Jeff. "He is a stranger. I've never seen him except in those dreams. Anyway what does it matter what he looks like?"

No-one spoke. Emma looked around from one face to another. Maggie was looking at her hands clutching her glass, her eyes hidden by her fringe of hair. Jeff looked quizzical; Milo was smiling.

"I knew you would not understand. Am I going mad? Listen. I'm talking to somebody," and here she glanced at Martin, "and suddenly instead of that person's face I see his. It's uncanny, and it's scary. That's what happened back there. Martin's face changed and became this stranger's face instead!"

When Martin finally spoke his voice was quiet but heavy with underlying emotion. "That's what happened Tuesday night, at the flat?" Emma slowly nodded.

"It's not my fault, Martin," she tried to catch hold of his hands, but he pulled away.

"Interesting." Milo as usual had to make a comment. "So this is why you're forgetting notes and phrases? Interesting indeed."

"Shut up, Milo!" Maggie retorted. Then she turned to her friend. "Can you stop it happening?"

"I don't know how. The dreams are not frightening in themselves. It's just this... seeing. It almost feels as if this man, whoever he is, is somehow drawing me to him."

Jeff leaned forward. "What do you mean 'he's drawing you to him'? Is there a connection? No, Martin," he said waving Martin back, "just shut up just now." He turned back to Emma. "Do you think he does want to get in touch with you?"

Emma shook her head, confused. "I don't know what it's all about. In the dreams he's not threatening, or doesn't seem to be. It's the hallucinations that scare me."

"You need to see a doctor," Milo said.

But Jeff could be very tenacious. "Emma, do you want to get in touch with him, to find out what's going on?"

Wordlessly, she nodded. "I just want it to stop."

Jeff leaned over once more and covered her tiny hands with his larger, scarred hand. "I don't know if you'd be willing to try it, but I have an idea of something that might help you." He cleared his throat and threw back his long hair, exposing the burn scars on his ruined face and neck. "After this happened, a Ouija board put me in touch with my parents."

"Oh go on, Jeff. Ouija boards are a lot of crap." Milo was scathing.

Jeff leaned forward towards Milo. "It sounds to me as if something or someone needs or wants to get in touch with Emma, and one of the things the board can do is to contact those who want to contact us."

"But we're not dealing with someone who's dead," Emma said.

"We don't know who we are dealing with. That's the problem," Jeff said.

Maggie was aghast. "It's too dangerous. Who knows what could happen? She's already affected by all of this."

Milo laughed. "Of course we know what would happen, Maggie. Zilch! Nowt! Nothing! A big fat zero!"

Emma turned to Jeff. "Do you think it would work? That we would be able to contact this man and find out who he is and what he wants?"

Jeff's eyes were sombre. "We could try. It helped me. If we do it tonight it might help your concentration for the concert tomorrow. Mhari McLeod would do it," he went on, referring to a friend who was a notorious dabbler in all things arcane – tarot cards, palmistry, graphology, biorhythms – and Ouija boards. "She would set up a board for us."

"I'm not sure about this." Martin's voice was quiet and his face had gone deathly pale.

"Please Martin," Emma pleaded. "I need to know I'm going to be able to perform tomorrow. This concert is important to us all. I don't want to mess it up."

"If you want to you'll be all right. Just – just don't look directly at me. You were fine in the practice until you looked at me. Put it down to Dress Rehearsal Syndrome. But don't do this Ouija board thing, Emma. I don't like it."

"It'll be all right, Martin. And anyway we don't even know if Mhari could set one up."

"I think she would. I'll call her." Jeff took out his mobile phone and began flicking through the address book.

Within minutes it was set up. They drained their glasses and set off back to George Square. Emma stopped and looked back. Martin had not moved.

"I'm not coming," he said as she approached him.

Emma turned to him. "Please Martin. Do this for me. I need you to be there."

"What? So you can see him instead of me again? Is he very handsome, this dream stranger? Does it give you a buzz to see his face while making love with me?"

"For God's sake, Martin. So that is what's getting you! It freaked me out! Don't you remember? You're jealous of someone who might not – probably doesn't – even actually exist." She stopped, her face clouding. "Maybe this is all just a figment of my imagination. Maybe I *am* going mad. If I was, would you abandon me then?"

"No."

"Then why now? Come with me Martin. I need your support."

The two stood in the dark street, holding hands and facing one another. Her head was tilted up slightly to meet his eyes. Then, subtly, gradually as she watched, the colour of his irises changed from blue and darkened to a green-brown hazel. The shape of his jaw squared, his lips changed shape, becoming slightly thinner. His hair was no longer short and spiky on top, but unruly, wavy dark brown that fell over his collar and framed his face. The face looking at her was no longer Martin's. Emma gasped and stepped back, thrusting Martin's hands away.

"It's happening again, Martin. Help me!" Swiftly the illusion changed again, and Martin was once more gazing at her, his blue eyes filled with concern.

"He's gone now," she whispered. Martin put his arms around her and hugged her to him. He could barely hear her whisper. "I'm scared, Martin."

"Okay," he murmured into her hair. "Let's go."

As one, they turned and hurried after the others, Martin's arm around her still-shaking shoulders.

Neither took any heed of the large white hawk perched on a rooftop overlooking the pub. It gave a low squawk and ruffled its feathers. Then it spread its wings, and took flight.

Chapter 2

Horatio talMerios, Council Mage and Companion to the Prince Hamnet of Elsynvaal, closed the door of his apartments and poured some wine. Swirling it around in the goblet, he stood by the window absently gazing outside. Candle light lit up the windows of the King's apartments across the quadrangle from where he stood and shadows crossed the glass now and again. *Is Hamnet arguing again with Claude?*

He sighed and turned back into the room to sit by the fire blazing in the hearth. Relishing the fact that for once he had some time to himself, he lay back in the chair and closed his eyes. His body relaxed, but his mind remained very active. The intensity and drama of the two months following Prince Hamnet's return to Elasyn Castle had kept him continuously occupied. Each passing day left him more confused than before. It was rare luxury to be alone to relax and gather his thoughts. He leaned back and allowed his mind drift back, reliving the events of the past two months.

***

There had been no warnings, no disturbances in the Ether to alert him to the event that was to rip Elsynvaal apart; a fact that later was to make him very uneasy. Loren's telepathic hail from distant Elasyn Castle came as a complete shock.

Horatio was relaxing in the late-afternoon quiet in the grassy quad of Deighford University, in the shade of the ancient banda tree, tutoring two students on the intricacies and pitfalls involved in Ether-Crossing.

"But you have done it, haven't you, Horatio?" one of the boys said. "Crossed the Ether to another world?" His was rapt with curiosity and wonder.

Horatio nodded, a smile twitching at his lips. "Yes," he said, "I have."

"What was it like?"

"Very unpleasant indeed, I tell you. The Void is dark and dank, and can even be dangerous. A single instant can subjectively last a day, so a mage must concentrate continuously so as not to lose his way."

"Has anyone ever got lost?" the boy leaned forward, his eyes bright.

Little savage, Horatio thought but he smiled as he replied. "None that I know of, but that doesn't mean it has never happened."

"Have you ever brought an alien back through with you?" the other edged forward, eager to get his question in.

"An alien?" Horatio smiled. "The inhabitants of the three known worlds are no aliens. They are as human as we are. But to answer your question, I have not returned an other-worlder with me, though it has been done."

"Who was it?" one of the boys began to say, but at that instant, Horatio felt a familiar tingling on the back of his neck and held up a hand.

"It's a di'speak contact," the other boy murmured. The two boys looked at one another and lapsed into silence.

Horatio leaned back against the warm trunk of the banda tree and opened his mind to receive the mental hail from Elasyn, two days' hard ride away. He could receive only aural: the signal was not strong enough for visual. A wave of incredulity hit him as he recognised the voice in his head. He frowned and clenched his jaw tightly.

<Loren?> Horatio's mental voice betrayed his disbelief. It was unheard of that the pampered son of the King's Mage should be able to create a contact. He was no mage and completely untrained in di'speak, untrained in fact in any metafunction. Horatio's head spun at the possible implications. *<How have you managed to do this?>*

The reply was faint and distorted. *<I will explain later. I don't know if I can hold this contact. Please listen, Horatio. Prince Hamnet must return immediately to the city.>* There was a pause as the young man's mental voice wavered. *< His father the King has died of a brain seizure.>*

<Loren, this is a poor jest indeed!>

<No, my Lord Horatio. It is no jest.>

Loren's tenuous contact was threatening to collapse. Horatio could still receive no visual. Only his panic-stricken voice. He strengthened the link between their two minds, and gradually the boy's panic lessened. As the link improved he achieved a visual image. Loren was pale, his eyes frightened and darting uneasily from place to place as he described the events at Elasyn Castle. He was obviously under considerable stress.

<Why has your father not contacted me?>

<The King's brother ordered him to wait. But there's something that is not right, Horatio. The Prince, the new King, should be here in Elasyn Castle! You must bring him.>

<I will, Loren. I will bring him.> Horatio's mental voice was intentionally soothing and calming. *<The Prince will return as soon as possible, but in the meantime it might be best to say nothing to your father about achieving this contact with me. It was a brave thing to attempt.>*

Horatio saw him frown. *<Yes, I suppose.>*

<You have done well, Loren. I will speak to you when we reach Elasyn.>

Contact broke, and Horatio leaned forward, his mind whirling. His two students were watching him, curiosity and fear written clear on their faces. *And what did my face tell them?* He wondered. The mage looked at each in turn.

"Go to the common room," he said. "I have had things to do."

Eventually Horatio found Hamnet in the gymnasium with some of his fellow-students. When the mage called him out of the game, his first reaction was one of laughing good-natured frustration. But on seeing the look on his friend's face, his laughter faded.

"Horatio. What's wrong?"

"Sire…" Horatio said. He got no further. Hamnet gasped. The nineteen-year-old Prince knew that only with his father's death would he be addressed as Sire. He gripped the mage's arm, his eyes narrowing.

"Sire?" he whispered. "What has happened, Horatio? Why do you address me in such a manner?"

"I am sorry, Hamnet."

"My father… is dead?" All colour had fled his face, and he staggered on his feet. Horatio put out a hand to steady him.

He nodded. "I'm sorry, my Lord. I had a contact from Elasyn a few minutes ago. I came to you immediately."

"What happened?" the young man asked.

"Come through here, where we can be alone." He gently guided the new King to a small room nearby, usually used for student-tutor interviews. A table stood in the centre of the room, flanked by tow straight backed chairs. A padded couch stood over by the empty fireplace.

Hamnet collapsed onto the couch and stared up at his friend. "For the god's sake Horatio, tell me what happened! Was it an accident? It must have been an accident. He was in such good health! What happened? And why?"

The final quietly spoken question encompassed disbelief, fear, longing and grief in a dark intensity. In all of the years Horatio had known the laughing Prince and watched him grow from a mischievous boy into the bright-haired handsome young man he now was, he had never before heard such passion in his voice.

"It was a brain seizure. That is all that Loren could tell me."

"He can't be dead, Horatio. It is not possible. Only last month we were in Elasyn and he was in excellent health."

Horatio nodded. "I remember."

"A brain seizure, Loren said. But what does Loren know? He's just a boy."

"He's less than three years your junior, sire."

But Hamnet would not be distracted. "Did the physicians not see any dangerous signs? Lord Polon is the King's Mage – was he negligent? Tell me Horatio!"

Horatio had no answers. In times of suffering, we all need someone on whom to lay the blame. He lapsed into silence, thinking of what now lay in store for this boy. The dreadful responsibilities of ruling a Kingdom. All Hamnet's life he had known this day would come, but its suddenness had taken the young prince utterly by surprise, and left him vulnerable and scared.

"We will leave at first light," he said.

The University was still and quiet as the two young men saddled up and left Deighford, riding flat out up the Coast Road before heading east towards the mountain pass. Only one person knew of the reason behind their sudden departure, the Chief Reader of the University, though rumours soon abounded among Horatio's students.

***

The horses broke free of the trees and raced across the open plain, their riders' cloaks whipping out behind them. When they joined the road, they urged their mounts to even greater speed. There was little to slow their progress. Prince Hamnet kept his eyes on the distant horizon, oblivious to all but his need for speed. His companion kept pace, occasionally leaning forward in his saddle to whisper encouragement into his horse's ear.

Eventually the two slowed down to a walk, aware that the horses were lathered and their breathing little more than laboured gasps. The second horseman drew alongside the first.

"We won't make Elasyn tonight, Sire," he said. "The horses have had about as much as they can take. There is a hostelry is only a short distance away, at the crossroads with the Great North Road. Perhaps we should spend the night there and continue in the morning."

"Perhaps so. It is unwise to continue on the road after dark. Yes, we should stop at the hostelry." The young man leaned forward and stroked his horse's lathered neck. "Poor girl," he murmured into the horse's mane, "I've been pushing you too hard, haven't I?" He straightened up, glanced across at Horatio, and frowned. "Do you think they'll know? At the hostelry, I mean." He sounded like a young, frightened boy.

Horatio glanced across the gap between them, his concern clearly written on his face, but Hamnet was no longer watching him. He was staring ahead at the hostelry buildings now visible on the horizon. "Perhaps, but I think it unlikely. I have had no further news from Court, so I doubt if any official announcement has been made yet. It is worrying, I must admit. The sooner we return to Elasyn the better." He glanced up at the sky. Diminu moon was rising, but without Principa also in the sky there was not enough moonlight to trigger the ley-lines. Had the two moons been in the sky, they could have been in Elasyn by now.

They walked the horses forward towards the hostelry, each wrapped in his thoughts. Then Hamnet broke the silence. "You know, Horatio, this is probably the last time I'll be able to ride free like this, alone. After all, the King cannot go abroad without an escort, can he? My father," he paused, and Horatio could hear the damped-down emotion in his voice, "...my father hated the loss of independence the throne brought him." He trailed off, uncertain, and lapsed once more into a silence that continued until they clattered into the forecourt of the hostelry.

After a restless and fretful night, they set off again, making good time on the clear roads. Then, several hours into the afternoon, with the sun well past its highest, they crested a hill and laid eyes on the city of Elasyn, capital of Elsynvaal and main residence of the King. It lay in a valley, a walled city that had in recent years burst beyond its curving narrow streets. Clusters of white dwelling houses now sheltered beneath the walls. Their new thatched roofs still glistened golden in the afternoon sun.

Beyond the narrow river and towering over the crowded houses, the stone walls of the Castle stood formidable and proud. A flag hung at half-mast, limp in the still afternoon air. As they drew closer and entered through the gateway, they saw cliques of people begin to gather. Many had black strips of cloth tied around their left arms, a sign of mourning. The news has broken, Horatio thought, so why has Polon not contacted me?

As the two riders approached and were recognised, a murmur rose and moved with them as they progressed through the streets towards the Castle. "It's the Prince. The Prince has come." The two young men exchanged glances. This is not as it should be, Horatio thought. Something is wrong. It was difficult to read his friend's face. Hamnet seemed completely rigid. Horatio's fears were realised when they reached the Castle gates.

The drawbridge was up.

Hamnet stood in his stirrups before his Castle gates and demanded entrance. Long minutes passed before the drawbridge, creaking loudly, slowly descended over the moat. The two dusty travellers, tired faces now shorn of youth, clattered across the drawbridge, under the portcullis and into the castle courtyard. People milled around, and from the crowd a slight, girlish figure moved towards them across the courtyard. Hamnet slid from his horse and took the girl's hands in his.

"Fair Olivia. I am pleased to see you."

"And I, you, my lord Hamnet. But would that you had been here yesterday."

Horatio dismounted and moved to his friend's side. The murmuring had ceased and the crowd now stood very still, listening, waiting. Hamnet's hushed voice was chill as he and Olivia moved off to one side. "What more has happened? My mother the Queen – is it she?"

"No, my lord, the Lady Queen is well."

"Then what? Tell me, Olivia!" His still quiet voice grew colder.

"The King's Will was read yesterday and his brother was named as his successor. My lord Hamnet, you are superseded. Claude, your Uncle, is King…"

"My father changed the succession? Disinherited me?"

Horatio watched helplessly as his friend gathered around him all the dignity he could muster. With head held high, the Prince walked into the Castle that had been wrenched from him by treason. For only treason could have caused this turnabout. But who was the traitor? And whom could he now trust?

Serra Olivia followed him inside. The murmuring restarted as the couple passed up the wide stone steps leading to the anteroom of the Great Hall. Horatio handed the horses' reins over to a stable boy and followed as numbness spread through his bones.

No good can come of this, he thought.

**

Horatio shook himself and brushed his hand across his eyes. He glanced at the guttering candle and knew he should go to bed, but tonight his mind seemed to be incapable of shutting out the memories. The first confrontation between Hamnet and his uncle had been remarkably subdued, despite the news Hamnet had just received. Horatio remembered following Hamnet as he strode from the courtyard to his Uncle's apartments, where Claude had welcomed him with smiles, exuding counterfeit warmth and fake apology.

Claude lounged on a plush couch, a wine goblet in his hand, and plates of discarded sweetmeats on a table beside him. He did not rise to greet his nephew, and showed little grief at his brother's untimely death. Horatio considered the differences between the two royal brothers. King Hamnet had been scholarly, tall and lean of frame, while his brother Claude was broader in stature and preferred weaponry to books and learning. Now, at the age of forty, Claude was still at the peak of his maturity.

After his nephew burst in unannounced, King Claude laid aside his goblet and glanced towards the man sitting close beside him – Polon, the Lord Chancellor. Horatio looked closely at the Court Mage, once more wondering why Polon had not contacted him by di'speak. Then his attention was caught by the dialogue between the uncle and nephew.

"My dear Hamnet," Claude said, "I knew absolutely nothing of the changes your dear Father made to the Will. The honour granted to me was totally unanticipated."

Horatio tuned out the words, and focused on exerting a minor probe to test the truthfulness of his statements. He was only mildly surprised to meet a protective shield. A glance at Polon showed that the old man's face wore the intense look usually present only when he was spell-casting. That would explain the *how* but not the *why* of the shield.

Hamnet demanded to see the Will, which Polon produced with a flourish. *He's in on it, whatever it is*, Horatio realised.

By the time they left Claude's apartments, Hamnet was bowed under with grief and despondency. Even a meeting with his mother did not ease him.

Nothing of consequence had come from that initial meeting. Nor indeed from successive confrontations. The usurper was calm, composed, and certain of his actions, while Hamnet was young and inexperienced in coping with deep grief.

His future was blurred. Polon had apparently thrown in his lot with Claude, as had most of the Castle's populace. Hamnet's supporters consisted of Serra Olivia, her brother, Loren, his personal guard and Horatio himself.

As for the Queen... Horatio shuddered as he recalled Hamnet's reaction when he discovered only a few weeks after his return that his mother was to marry her brother-in-law. An ancient law from the early days of colonisation was cited, whereby a man was not only legally *allowed* to marry his brother's widow, but was encouraged to do so.

Hamnet had raged wildly for an hour without a break and then collapsed across a couch, convulsively weeping. Nothing he, Horatio, could do could ease the pain her betrayal to his father's memory had caused. It was after this episode that he had begun to suffer bouts of depression, often condemning in strong words the inconstancy of a woman's love. His manner towards Serra Olivia began to change. Often he abruptly sent her away when she would have offered comfort. At other times he was rude and unkind to her.

When the time came for his mother's wedding, he refused to attend, spending the time instead in a brothel. When he returned several days afterwards, he was outwardly calm, but cold towards both his mother and her new husband. Horatio watched helplessly as the Prince cultivated the severe, unsmiling and suspicious mask which he wore continuously from that day on. In a way, that mask became his refuge.

Only when they were alone was Horatio allowed to see through the mask to the disillusion that simmered beneath Hamnet's outward chilly mask. His moodiness and introspection increased, alternating with periods of intense, even manic, activity.

In an attempt to distract Prince Hamnet, Horatio proposed a journey through the Ether to another world. Polon acted as anchor and eventually they found a link on the world the denizens called Earth. The time differential that existed between the two worlds allowed them to spend several weeks in that world, making friends with one whom they eventually brought back to Elsynvaal. A poet and writer, Horatio hoped he would serve as further distraction for the Prince. Now more often than not, Master Will was found somewhere close to the Prince, forever sharpening his quills, for he refused to use normal writing implements, and scribbling furiously. Horatio had to admit that the man was talented, and the Prince had taken a strong liking to him.

Horatio lit a new candle, refilled his wine goblet and stared into the fire. Sleep was far from him and his worries continued to plague him. Worries like the sudden change in popularity of the new King.

The old King had been widely respected for, despite his bookishness, he had been a king whose audiences and judgements had been universally recognised as impartial and just. Claude, however, was rarely at Court. His youth and middle years had been spent in foreign lands and he had returned to Elsynvaal only recently. As far as Horatio could tell from his fleeting visits to Elasyn with Prince Hamnet, Claude did not command the respect his brother had won from the people.

Now, though, it was different. Whenever Claude went out riding with his hawks or in his carriage, he was cheered enthusiastically wherever he went. His popularity seemed to know no bounds. To Horatio in his watchful state, this *volte-face* was very disturbing. The situation reeked of magic at work, but he could find no evidence whatsoever of sorcery. Neither could the Watcher Wizards of the Council.

Then to add to these worries, there were the dreams. For several weeks now, Horatio's sleep had been disturbed and punctuated by a recurrent dream. He should have been able to discern their origin, but could not.

Horatio worried at the problem unaided, for these were dreams he could not discuss. Not even with Deveron, his old mentor, much less the Wizards' Council. The former would laugh; the latter scorn. And the reason? Almost every night for the past two weeks he, Horatio, stout of mind and whole of heart, in the depths of slumber had dreamed of riding out across open fields with an unknown girl with long hair streaming like a black banner behind her.

Suddenly restless, he stood up and went to his desk. He lifted up a framed picture, a thought-painting he had himself produced. A smile touched the corners of his lips but his eyes were wistful. *Who are you?* he silently asked of the girl in the picture. Standing there by the desk he began to feel the touch of cold as someone attempted to di'speak him. Still holding the framed picture he eased himself into his desk chair and closed his eyes.

<Ho!> he thought, readying his mind for the long-distance conversation. *<Who calls?>* As the link solidified the semblance of a face was etched on the inside of his closed eyelids. Deveron di'Caledon, Master-Mage, Antriantara of the Wizards' Council sat at a paper-covered desk in a wood-panelled room. His iron-grey hair, instead of standing in an abundant halo around his face, lay flat and lustreless, and worry was etched on his face. His eyes, almost hidden within the folds of laughter lines were devoid of their normal sparkle. *<Deveron? Is it you?>*

<Indeed, Horatio, 'tis I. Am I so changed that you failed to recognise me?>

<What's happened?>

<Oh this and that - Council business, as ever, my boy. I will enlighten you when I see you in person.>

<Then you are coming to Elasyn?>

<Yes. We will be with you soon. In time for the Coronation. In the meantime I have a task for you to perform. . . Are you alone?>

<I am.>

<Then listen carefully. I believe that there is something in the offing. There is a disruption in Elsynvaal's Ether. Be very watchful Horatio. I believe the disturbance emanates from your vicinity.>

<The only magical use I can discern is my own and Lord Polon's. There are no other mages in the Castle.>

<Watch for a disguised aura. There have been scryed warnings from the god.>

<Disguised?>

<Be vigilant, my young friend. You could be in danger. Now, the party with whom I am travelling will arrive on the day of the Coronation celebration. I will speak to you further on this matter then.>

<What do you want me to do?>

<Watch, my boy, and listen. Contact me if anything untoward happens.>

<I will.>

<Remember what I have told you. Be vigilant.>

<I will, Deveron. Farewell.> He broke contact and opened his eyes. The picture frame was still in his hands. *Are you connected with this?* he unaccountably asked the beautiful black-haired girl of the picture, then immediately thrust away the thought as absurd.

Suddenly the door to his apartment was thrust open. He casually stood and replaced the frame on the table, and turned towards his visitor.

"Ho! My Lord Prince," he said.

The Prince replied in kind, but seemed somewhat distracted. "My uncle has come up with a splendid notion, Horatio," he continued, wandering over to the window, idly watching a snowy-white hawk wheel gracefully in the quadrangle before landing on Horatio's window-sill. "By-the-bye it was my lord Polon who thought of it, but what's the difference? If one coughs the other sneezes. So here's the rub – you are to cross the Ether to Master Will's world and obtain the services of some entertainers for the Coronation festivities. Polon will anchor here."

"I see."

"Polon has already gone downstairs to begin preparations. There are only a few days in which to accomplish this, so you must come now."

"But my Lord Hamnet, you yourself are aware that it is not always possible to make contact. The time differential seems to fluctuate. It took four days of searching to make contact when we brought Master Will over."

"Both Polon and the King are convinced that you can manage it – a mage of your calibre." Hamnet turned to the set of foils on the sword-rack and lifting light rapier, cut a few neat quarters. "In fact what they actually said was less complementary, but you do not need details. You are as aware as I that we two are not the most popular in inner court circles. Come. We must away and prepare." Replacing the sword carefully, he headed for the door.

Horatio glanced fleetingly once more at the image of the girl in the frame and turned to follow his Prince.

Beyond the window, the white hawk spread its wings and lifted off from Horatio's window sill. It circled once and flapped away across the rooftops and battlements of Elasyn Castle. North it flew until the lights of the town were far behind. Only then did it swoop down to land on the scrubby grass. As it did, the form of the bird wavered, grew and metamorphosed into the form of a small dark-haired woman dressed in a long dark gown. She stretched once, and then sat on the ground, her knees drawn up under the gown and her chin resting on her knees. Her hands wove a sigil in the air and gradually the image of a middle-aged man formed floating in the air a few feet away. The figure regarded the bird-woman with narrowed eyes.

"Father!" she cried out.

"What is it?" he responded. "Does this call mean that you have succeeded?"

"I have indeed! Even now the link is being forged!"

"You are certain it will work?"

"It will, Father. It will."

"Good. Now leave me now. I am busy."

The image faded and the bird-woman was alone once more. She sat for a moment, frowning; then she laughed aloud, leaping to her feet. She re-formed her wings and feathers and took flight once more heading north, towards the forests and the ice.

Chapter 3

It was only an hour since Jeff's phone call to Mhari, but the séance was about to begin. As she climbed the stairs where Mhari had the Ouija board set up, Emma's feet grew heavier, as they had every step of the journey from the pub to where they now were – Mhari's home just off Byres Road in the middle of student-land. She walked in to the low-ceilinged attic room and saw an oval table set up in the centre of the room, surrounded by a collection of motley and mismatched chairs. She sat down in the nearest, unsure if her legs would hold up much longer. Each passing minute only served to convince her that this was a bad idea. Why ever had she allowed Jeff to convince her to do it?

She looked around the attic room as the small group of people settled in various seats around the table. She barely heard Milo as he made his usual witty banter. None other than Jeff knew Mhari MacLeod very well – she wasn't a music student like the rest of them. She was studying psychology, which Emma supposed could possibly have some kind of a tie in with the décor and paraphernalia dotted around. Dim and claustrophobic, it was lit only by a pair of five-branched candelabrum. Fabric in various purple and pink shades hung in swathes from a centre point above their heads, caught up at the point where the sloping roof met the walls. Astral charts adorned the walls, along with runic charts and posters of fantastic creatures. On the bookcase just beside her titles like 'Mind over Matter' and 'Palmistry – a study of Personality?' sat alongside 'Behavioural Psychology' and several of Piaget's books on child development. Over in the dim recesses of the far end of the attic, cardboard boxes of various sizes and shapes crouched, concealing God knows what. Eerie shadows jumped across the charts on the walls and the folds of fabric with each candle flame flicker.

Emma glanced at the person behind this bizarre room, seeing her on her home ground for the first time. When Jeff came off the phone to Mhari, he said that he'd taken her totally by surprise asking her to set up this session, but Mhari seemed to be totally in her element, sitting at the head of the table, calmly laying out the lettered cards.

As if feeling Emma's gaze on her, the mystic looked up and smiled, possibly in an attempt to reassure her a little. Emma was far from reassured though and swiftly dropped her eyes from Mhari's to the table. In the centre sat an object resembling a magnifying glass minus its handle. It had a rim about half an inch wide, under which were a number of tiny ball bearings. Emma stole a glance at Martin sitting beside her. His face was still, rigid even, his eyes fixed on the table.

Just as Mhari completed the circle of cards, there was a sound at the door. The door knob turned and the door eased open. Jeff Zimlinsky stuck his head round the door, the ever-present quizzical look on his face. No-one laughed. No-one ever laughed at Jeff's damaged face, a marked contrast to his voice, which was a deep and pleasant baritone. "Sorry I'm late. Everything ready?"

"Come and see," Mhari invited.

He moved into the room, his tall form lurching as he came forward to peer at the table. "Yep, all ready. Good of you to organise this, Mhari."

"No problem, Jeff. Long time since I've had a go at something like this."

He pulled a chair up between Milo and Maggie and sat down.

"Now, are we ready?" Mhari said, looking at each in turn. "Emma?"

Emma looked up sharply, her breath catching in her throat. She felt her blood drain from her face. She glanced sideways at Maggie, who gave her a smile. *Maggie's not afraid, so why should I be?* she asked herself, trying to calm her fears. But she remained very aware that she was the reason that they were here. Part of her was still absolutely terrified of what she could find out about the man in the dreams. He was handsome, attractive no doubt, but… mightn't he be dangerous too? She frowned, and looked down, away from everyone's prying eyes. She took a long breath. Yes, she was scared. Nevertheless, she had agreed to this fiasco. She nodded uncertainly to Mhari.

"Milo?"

Milo Diaz tossed his hair back out of his eyes, took a drag on the cigarette in his hand and with a grin, nodded to her. Nothing ever seemed to faze him.

"Maggie?"

"Sure. Let's go."

"Martin?"

"Yes."

"Now," Mhari said, "I think you are all aware of how this works. The cards spread out around the perimeter of the table each show a letter of the alphabet. The ball-bearings," she laid a finger gently on the magnifying glass and ball bearing object, "allows the spinner to move easily. Okay, now everyone, place your index finger lightly on the spinner. Exert no pressure. And there's to be no pushing at all. We must allow the spinner to move of its own accord. I'll do the talking. Any questions?"

"Yeah." Milo's arrogant voice broke into the silence. "How do we know if someone is pushing?"

"I'll know," Mhari replied. "Now let's go."

Mhari stretched out an elegant ring-covered finger and placed it lightly on the rim of the spinner. One by one the others did the same, Emma reluctantly last of all. No-one spoke. How she regretted allowing herself to be talked into this fiasco! For that was what it certainly seemed to be. The six sat in silence, fingers lying lightly on the spinner, and nothing happened. Then Milo burst out laughing, and lifted his finger away from the spinner. "This is stupid. There's nothing happening. Come on, let's just forget it."

"No Milo," Mhari's voice was quiet and calm. "Put it back, Milo." Unsure why he complied, Milo did. A minute passed. Then Mhari gave a small gasp. "I can feel something. Quiet now." A pause. "Is anyone there?"

"Good God, Mhari. Can't you think of a better line than that?" Milo's voice was scathing. Once again he snatched away his finger from the spinner, and at that moment the spinner shifted, very slightly, and then stopped.

"Someone pushed it!" Milo accused.

"Put a sock in it!" Martin's voice was tense. "No-one pushed. Now just shut up and be still."

Mhari repeated her question. The spinner shifted a few inches in Emma's direction then changed its path. "It's moving. It really is…" Emma's voice was faint. The spinner shifted slowly across the table and round the perimeter of the table.

"Searching. It's looking for the right card."

Suddenly with a sudden jerk, the spinner scraped across the wooden table to the card on which was written the word "YES".

Milo pushed his chair back and stood up. "Who's cheating?" he demanded.

No-one paid him any attention. Five pairs of eyes were locked on to the spinner's movement as it returned to the table's centre.

"Are you willing to talk with us?"

The spinner shifted back again to the word "YES".

"Are you a spirit?" The spinner swivelled round the perimeter and stopped at the card with a question mark on it. "Are you dead?" The spinner swivelled and shifted to the "NO" card.

"You're alive?" A shift to the "YES" card.

"Who are you?"

The spinner's movement was uncertain, searching for letters as it moved. "Quick, Milo, write this down. It's spelling out something... H-O-R-A-T-I-O-T-A-L-M-E-R-I-O-S."

"That's not a name. It's just gibberish."

"Let's see it." The spinner had stopped at the edge furthest away from Maggie and her arm was stretched across the table. She pushed her chair back slightly and twisted round to peer at the paper in Milo's hand. "Of course it is. The first bit spells out 'Horatio', you know, as in Horatio Hornblower, or Admiral Lord Horatio Nelson, hero of Trafalgar and lover of Lady Emma Hamilton. The Talmerios bit must be a surname of sorts. Sounds like Greek or something."

Mhari addressed the spinner again. "Is your name Horatio?"

"Yes," came the answer. Voices burst out in commotion.

"Quiet!" Mhari hissed. "We have to find out more." She turned back to the object on the table. "Where are you from?"

Mhari called out the letters to Milo. "E-L-S-Y-N-V-A-A-L"

"Was that a double 'A'?" Milo asked.

"Yes, I think so."

"What was it? Elsa's Valley?" Emma asked.

"No," Milo replied. "The letters spell out Elsyn Vaal. Never heard of it."

"South Africa?" Martin suggested. "Isn't there a Boer word *vaal* that means *field* or *grassland*?"

Mhari addressed the spinner again. "Please tell us – where is Elsyn Vaal?"

There was no response. Then just as Milo was gathering his breath for another caustic comment, it began to move again. "F-A-R-A-W-A-Y"

Milo snorted. "Great! This sounds more and more like a trip to Narnia, as in *'From the town of Wardrobe in the county of Spare Room'*!"

Mhari gave him a cold stare. "Maybe it would be best if you left," she said.

"No way. Not when it's getting so..o..o interesting. But I'm cool, I'll shut up."

"You'd better." She turned back to the table. The spinner was lying still in the centre of the table. "Please tell us – why have you responded to our call?"

The spinner moved slowly round the table. But the movements were more confident now. It knew now where each letter lay and moved directly between the letters. Emma watched as her finger was dragged around from one letter to another. She caught the first few letters "H-E-L" but then lost track.

"H- E-L-P- U-S - Helpus?" Milo's voice was puzzled.

"No. It's two words - 'Help…us'!" Martin's voice cut across the uproar. "He's asking for help."

"But who? Where? Oh God, I wish we'd not started this." Emma sounded scared. Martin reached over and gave her free hand a squeeze. She held on to it and looked at him. He smiled but she couldn't.

Mhari was paying no attention to them. "This is wonderful," she said. "The best Ouija board I've ever seen!" She turned her attention back to the spinner. "How can we help you, Horatio? Milo, get ready to write it down."

The spinner had already begun moving.

"What does it say?" Mhari was impatient.

"It reads as 'It is a long tale. Are you ready to hear it?' Well are we?"

"Yes." Mhari was adamant. "We are ready, Horatio. Tell us."

The spinner shifted, twisting and turning, moving surely across the table surface. Arms began to tire, brains too as they tried and failed to make sense of the message. Minutes passed, the only sound Mhari's voice calling out letters and Milo repeating them as he recorded them. Eventually the spinner ceased its frantic spell-out and sat quiescent in the centre of the table.

Jeff looked at the letters Milo had recorded, mentally inserted spaces and punctuation, and then sat back, removing his finger from the spinner.

"Well?" Mhari asked. "What does it say?"

Jeff sighed, and his voice was very quiet when he spoke. "He says he's from another world. An alternate reality."

"*That is it*!" Milo cried out. "That takes the biscuit! We now have all the proof we need of how stupid it all is!"

Jeff held up his hand to stop the flow. And read out to the others the complete deciphered message. "I think this has gone far enough for now. We'd better stop there."

"How can we stop there?" Mhari cried out. She turned her

attention to the spinner. "Horatio. We need time to think about this. If we try to contact you in a day or two, would you respond?"

"YES."

Mhari turned to the others. "Tomorrow night?"

"The concert is tomorrow."

"Sunday afternoon then?"

"WAIT!" Emma cried out. "You haven't asked about my dreams! That is why we did this!"

"Sorry. With everything else, it slipped my mind."

Strangely enough it was Milo who turned on her. "How could you forget, Mhari? Don't you realise that this is important not only to Emma but to the rest of us as well? Didn't Maggie explain?"

"She spoke of someone contacting Emma through the medium of dreams, and that she's suffering from a severe lack of concentration. But please realise, Milo, that these things take a lot of psychic energy to make them work, and if I try to keep going much longer I'll lose the connection altogether."

"So you say. I say we ask," Jeff's voice was quite reasonable.

"All right then. Here goes. Horatio, we'd like to ask something of you. If you cannot answer, we will understand. Will you listen?"

The spinner swung to YES.

Mhari took a breath. "One of us here has been having dreams which have been rather disturbing and frightening. Can you tell if these mean harm or good?"

For a full moment there was absolute stillness. Emma's finger, resting on the spinner began to tremble. She was about to remove it when the spinner began moving, swiftly spelling out a reply.

L-E-T-O-N-L-Y-T-H-E-O-N-E-W-H-O-D-R-E-A-M-S-T-O-U-C-H-T-H-E-C-O-N-E-K-T-O-R

"Emma leave your finger on the spinner. Everyone else, back off. Okay, Horatio we're ready."

Emma closed her eyes as the spinner moved gently across the table. No jerks this time – only a smooth, continuous movement for what seemed to Emma to last for a very long time. Then it stopped. She removed her finger and sat back.

"What does it say?" she asked in a small voice.

Milo read out the reply. "It says: *Do not fear. No harm is intended. All will be explained in time.*"

Emma snatched her hand away. Martin put his arm around her.

Mhari indicated that they should all put their fingers back on the spinner. Once they had, she addressed the bodiless entity conversing

41

with them. "Thank you Horatio. We will contact you in 36 hours. Would that suit you?" An affirmative. "All right then. We'll let you go now."

The spinner moved in a small circle and tipped over on to its side with a clink. The ball-bearings rolled across the table and clinked onto the wooden floorboards.

"Who did that?" Milo again.

"Oh give it a rest."

"Someone pushed it."

"Forget it Milo." Maggie sounded bored with him. "Why can't you just accept what you've seen with your own eyes? Some things in this life just cannot be explained in sentences simple enough for your brain to comprehend."

"Say that again, will you? I didn't quite get it," he asked, seemingly serious. Maggie laughed.

"Well, well, well." Martin commented into the silence that followed. "At least something has come out of this fiasco, Emma. According to our disembodied Horatio you have nothing to fear."

"Yes, Martin. I'm sure I'll be fine."

Jeff was re-reading the message from 'Horatio' frowning a little as he did so. "Well, this is something, isn't it?" Jeff commented. "Not every day we get invited to a royal bash. What do you make of it?" He threw a glance around the table.

"I think it's all rubbish!" Milo, ever the first to speak. "Someone was pushing the spinner just to take the Mickey out of the rest of us. I don't care who it was, but I for one am not taken in by the joke."

Maggie jumped in. "No-one pushed the spinner, Milo. We would have felt it. The spinner was moving of its own accord."

"I've seen it happen before," Mhari added. "Often."

"Auto-suggestion then. One of us unconsciously pushing it."

"Give over Milo." Jeff turned his full gaze on the other. "All of us were confused about what words the letters made. None of it made sense to me either until I saw the message written down." Then in his beautiful baritone, he once more read aloud the message from 'Horatio'. Nothing less than an invitation to sing at the Coronation of a King!

"So what do we do?" Mhari was like a child promised a treat. "Are we going to do it? Do we go?"

"I think we should sleep on it." Jeff – the voice of reason.

Maggie looked over at his scarred face, and watching her, Emma was reminded inexplicably of something she'd recently said about Jeff. About how much she admired him for the special courage he showed when standing up in front of an audience.

"Now that is a gig. An extraordinary gig. "

Emma, confused and even more anxious, barely heard Maggie's words, or her small laugh. She tried to listen to the discussion.

Milo as always was negative and sceptical. Jeff was guarded, determined to 'sleep on it'. Mhari was desperate to go. Maggie seemed to be seriously considering the option. And Martin? Emma looked at their entwined hands. Martin turned towards her, a questioning look on his face. She looked away. Should she go? Perhaps it's the only way she was going to find out what was going on here. He did seem to know something about the dreams. Maybe he could tell her who the stranger was.

She said, "It would only be for a weekend. He said so."

Martin said nothing, but Jeff shook his head. "Look at the facts, Emma. None of us has ever heard of the place. Is Elsyn Vaal a city or a town? Some tiny African state no-one's heard of? And if it is, then how can the trip possibly be only for a weekend?"

"He spoke in English," Maggie offered.

"He, if it was a 'he', *spelled* out words in English."

"Don't be obtuse, Milo. Okay, the wording is a bit old fashioned, but it was the English language."

"Okay, Maggie, point taken. Now, look at it another way. Do you really want to go rushing off to a place you've never heard of to a gig with a KING as audience?"

"Why not? It would be a unique experience."

Martin spoke for the first time. "Hold on. Just cool it, both of you. I think Jeff's right. We should consider all the facts we have. This – *Horatio* – told us nothing more than that his country, Elsyn Vaal, was celebrating the wedding and coronation of their new King and that he was to organise the entertainment. Okay? But, and this is the hard bit, he said he heard the Ouija board call on the *Ether* – his word – and contacted us *somehow knowing* that we sang and played together. *That* is what I find difficult to get to grips with."

Jeff inclined his head. "We need more information."

"Agreed."

Milo stood up abruptly, the scrape of his chair on the floorboards loud. "I can't believe what I'm hearing. You are actually considering doing this mad thing! Well you can count me out. Find yourself another tenor." He strode across the room to the door, his boot heels sounding sharp against the bare floorboards.

"Milo, wait!" Maggie was on her feet, striding towards him. "Stay a while. We're not going to do anything rash. Why don't we all just think about it, as Jeff says, and meet up again tomorrow after the concert? If you really don't want to take part in the discussions then, that's fine. Agreed?" She turned back to the four still seated round the card strewn table. Each responded with a nod. Milo looked across the dimness of the attic room and nodded.

"Okay. Till tomorrow." He left and they listened as he clattered down the steps. Eventually the sound of his footsteps receded.

"Time I was going, too," Emma said glancing towards Martin. "I'm suddenly very tired, and I want to get some sleep tonight. To be ready for tomorrow."

"I'll take you," Martin stated.

"I'm going too," Maggie added. "Can you give me a lift, Martin?"

"Sure. No problem. Jeff?"

"No, I'll hang on here a bit I think, and walk home. We're not far away, after all. Don't wake me if you're late getting back to the flat."

*   *   *

In the car, Martin brought up the subject they'd avoided so far. "Could that have been the stranger in your dream, Emma?"

"I don't know. How can I? Nothing is ever said in the dreams. It's all visual and emotion. Silent. All of this tonight was verbal. No emotion, no feelings. No visual input." Martin had no answer.

"*All will be explained in time,* he said," Emma mused.

Martin felt a shiver of foreboding. "That makes you feel better?"

"Maybe. I think I'll be all right for the concert tomorrow, if that's what you mean."

"Good." Martin said, but to Emma's ears he still sounded unconvinced. "That's good."

Conversation after that became somewhat stilted. Martin drove in silence, concentrating on driving and his own inner emotion. It began to rain again. Emma sat beside him watching the sudden downpour, offering little more than monosyllabic answers to Maggie's comments about the rehearsal – *was it really only earlier this evening?* – and the Ouija board events.

Then Maggie changed tack. "Even if Milo does decide against going," she stated above the labouring car engine as it took the steep road leading to the tower block where she and Emma shared a flat, "*we* could still do it. You could sing, Martin."

At that, Martin had to laugh. "I'm no singer, and well you know it, Maggie." He pulled in at the edge of the kerb and switching off the ignition, turned to Maggie as she opened the door to get out. "I'll think about it. Though they want a singing group so it really is only the four of you that are invited, isn't it? You two plus Jeff and Milo. Not even poor Mhari, who I think would desperately want to do it!"

"But you are the pianist, Martin. You'd have to come."

"How do you know there would even be a piano for me to play?"

Emma spoke then. "Let's leave it all for now. I'll see you tomorrow, Martin. No, stay where you are. It would be best if you didn't come up tonight. Maggie and I both need some sleep before dawn comes." She leaned towards him, and kissed him lightly on the lips. Martin raised a hand to draw her to him, but she'd already turned away to open the door of the car.

"Goodnight, Martin. Come over about five. We'll feed you before we head for the concert. Jeff too, if he wants."

"OK. We'll do that. Goodnight, Emma." She could feel his eyes still on her as she ran through the rain to catch up with Maggie. When she reached the glass entrance doors, she turned back and waved to him, then watched as he drove off. Then she turned back to Maggie, her smile evaporating.

"I don't want to talk about it," she said even as Maggie opened her mouth. "At all."

***

The rain-slick back streets of Kelvingrove were empty and silent.

As he drove, Martin mulled over the evening's events, trying to rationalise all he'd seen and heard. He still hadn't succeeded when he pulled up outside the Victorian tenement building where he and Jeff had shared a flat since they'd come to Glasgow as students. He glanced up at the third-floor living room window. It was in darkness. Martin parked the car outside the tenement building, giving thanks that there was a space, locked up and headed upstairs to the flat. His footsteps, as he climbed the stone steps, bounced off the tiled walls and echoed up the stairwell. Taking out his key, he unlocked and pushed open the door. The flat was is complete darkness. He switched on the hall light, and moved quietly to Jeff's bedroom door. He pushed it open wide enough to see Jeff's empty bed. Closing the door behind him, he turned to the kitchen, where he filled the kettle with water ready to make coffee.

He was sitting on the floor of the living room with an empty coffee mug listening to Monteverdi's Vespers, when he heard Jeff's key in the door. "I was beginning to think you'd decided to stay over at Mhari's place," he called out. "I made some coffee, but if you want some you'll have to boil the kettle. The water will be cold by now."

But when Jeff came into the room he headed straight for the drinks cabinet. "I need something stronger than coffee," he said, pouring out a large whisky. Glass in hand he sat down on the sofa, knocking half of the drink back in one go. Martin turned to look at him. Jeff's voice sounded strange.

"What's up?"

Jeff stood up and limped to the window. He jerked the curtains closed, as if to shut out the night. Then he turned back to his friend, gazing across the book-lined room at him. "After the rest of you left, Mhari and I tried the board again."

"And?"

"We got through again. I'm doing it, Martin. I'm going to Elsyn Vaal."

***

Milo Diaz lay fully dressed on top of his bed, staring at the ceiling. He could hear the television set downstairs, and the muted sound of his flatmates' voices. His ex-girlfriend's voice was louder than anyone else's, as usual, sounding almost abrasive to him now. How was it he'd never noticed it before? His mind shunted back to the pathetic scene over dinner last night, when it became patently clear that their relationship was over.

I suppose it all comes down to the fact that she's just not a lady, he thought. *She has no class, and definitely not worth hanging around for.* He sighed. *I suppose I'd best begin searching for new digs.*

He rolled off his bed and pulled down the soft sports bag he kept on the top of his wardrobe. Inside was the fencing gear he'd not touched for months. *I'm out of practice,* he thought as he ran his hand lightly over the linen jacket. Reaching in, he pulled out the padded white fencing jacket, the gloves and the mask. The jacket fitted like a second skin, comfortable and pliant. Pulling tight the buckles of the jacket and slipping on the soft gloves, he crossed to where the paired foils hung on the wall by the window.

Standing back, he squared off and began some feints and ripostes. But it was no more than a lethargic workout, and did little to take the edge off his tensions and dispirited feelings. With a curse, he sheathed the foil with a determined thrust and stripped off the padded jacket. He tossed it onto the bed, leaned over to the hi-fi and flicked it on.

The music masked the strident voice still holding forth in the room downstairs.

Milo lay back on the bed, shut out thoughts of his ex-girlfriend and gazed up at the ceiling again, thinking instead about the events of the evening – the disastrous rehearsal, Emma's disclosures, all he had seen and heard in Mhari MacLeod's attic room. Everything within him told him to concentrate on the concert tomorrow and forget the whole absurd business; scepticism was the key. And disbelief. Then he corrected himself, trying to be honest. There was a small part of him that wanted, even needed, to know more. He closed his eyes and let the music from the hi-fi flow across him, soothing and stilling him.

> *'If you had no name / if you had no history /*
> *If you had no books / if you had no family'*

The singer's pure voice lit up the room, soaring and weaving. But as he lay and listened to the lyrics of the song, Milo suddenly and inexplicably felt a shudder run through him. He grabbed the hi-fi remote to shut off the sound, but the words echoed within him.

> *'If it were only you / Naked on the grass /*
> *Who would you be then? / This is what he asked /*
> *And I said I wasn't really sure /*
> *But I would probably be / Cold /*
> *And now I'm freezing. Freezing'*

Chapter 4

"Just take deep breaths," Maggie whispered to Emma. "We're all nervous."

Martin's slot in the programme was about half-way through the second half, following a flute and piano duet by two second years. So, for the first half of the October Fest Concert, Emma had sat as part of the audience with Maggie and Martin, while Jeff and Milo sat in the row behind them.

As the applause for a string quartet of third years ended, Maggie turned to Emma. "That was really good, wasn't it?"

"Uh huh. High standard this year."

"The standard's always high," Martin put in from her other side. "And it's not because of the grade we could get. This concert is a showcase – the only time in the academic year when students perform in public."

"Of course. That's why it's so competitive to get a slot in the programme."

"Milo said he saw some paper reps here," Martin went on, "critics who could open doors with a good review."

"Really?" Maggie leaned across Emma and hissed at Martin. "That so takes the pressure off! Thank you for that."

Emma laid a hand on the arm of each of them. "Sshhh. Here's Colin and Mary."

Martin and Maggie subsided back into their seats. Emma watched as the duo took the stage. She and Mary had the same the singing teacher. But even that fact was not enough to keep her mind on the music. Over and over again, last night's events played in her mind, along with the questions of whether or not she should go to Elsyn Vaal, and what the Horatio person knew of the dream stranger. Nothing probably. What were the chances? Millions to one.

Emma did what Maggie suggested. She took long deep breaths to remain calm.

***

After the interval, they went backstage. Emma watched Martin as he moved restlessly around the performers' area, never sitting still for more than a minute at a time. But she was unsure whether his restlessness stemmed from the perfectly normal nerves before a performance or from memories of last night's disastrous rehearsal and the ghastly séance that followed it. So she sat, uneasily aware of Martin's anxiety, trying to not think about the part she had played in it all.

Glancing round, she realised that the only one of the group who seemed to be at ease was Milo. Ebullient, irrepressible Milo. Emma caught a glance from him, a look that emphatically said "No worries". Emma smiled. He was right, she thought. Forget the dream-man. Forget the Ouija session tomorrow. They would perform well, she told herself, because Martin deserved their best effort.

As time went on, the 'holding pen', as Milo called it, became quieter, as groups of people took their turns on stage. Finally the flautist and pianist were called.

They were on next.

They each collected their instrument and after high-five slapping and grins of 'luck', they filed out of the door on cue.

"Deep breaths," Maggie whispered in Emma's ear. "We'll be fine. No. We'll be great!" Emma squeezed her hand and followed Martin's lead along the backstage corridor under the orchestra pit. Another few moments and they would be on stage.

Deep breaths. Calm.

Then Martin led his four friends onto the Concert Hall stage to face their audience – fellow students, lecturers, tutors, family, friends… and press. He took his conductor's baton to the podium and turned to introduce his two compositions.

"Ladies, gentlemen and fellow students. The two pieces we will perform for you tonight are my own compositions. The first is entitled *Trio for Strings*, and is played by Maggie Walker on violin, Emma Campbell on cello and Milo Diaz on viola. For the second, entitled *Friends: An Introduction and Rondo for Unaccompanied Voices*, we will be joined by Jeff Zimlinsky, who will sing baritone."

Despite Martin's fears, both pieces went excellently well, as if the fates had conspired to soothe all misgivings and hesitancy. The trio was smooth and crisp, and received thundering applause when it ended. Turning back to the three of them, Martin gave them a nod of appreciation. Then he turned to motion Jeff onto the platform. The others laid their instruments down and rose to stand before him. Emma sang her heart out, feeling the sublime sound they were creating rise up to ring through the rafters of the Old Concert Hall. As he lowered his baton at the end of the piece, Martin nodded and grinned at his friends before turning to the audience's applause. *We did it!* Emma thought ecstatically. *We bloody well did it!*

After the concert ended, they gathered outside the performers' exit. Members of the audience, and other performers stood around, discussing and dissecting each others work, and handing out congratulations. The concert was an unqualified success. Martin's hand was repeatedly shaken in congratulation by people he knew and people he didn't. Milo said he was going to the pub for a drink to celebrate, but Emma and Maggie pleaded off. The after-effects of anxiety and nervousness and adrenaline rush had left both girls exhausted.

"I just want to go home," Maggie pleaded.

"Me too," Emma added.

Martin smiled. "Okay, I'll drop you off then," he told them. "What about you, Jeff?"

"I'll come too. I feel a bit beat. Sorry, Milo. See you."

But as they headed down the damp Glasgow street towards Martin's car Milo suddenly dashed after them and caught Emma's arm.

"Wait! Tell me, is it still on for tomorrow?" he asked. "The séance?"

Emma felt Martin turn and look at her. A flash of fear crossed her features as she nodded to Milo. "I think it has to be," she said before turning to Martin. "Take me home now please, Martin."

Martin laid his arm round her shoulders and led her away. Maggie and Jeff followed, leaving Milo to walk back to the crowd. A loud *caw* raked the air, and all four turned to see a large pure white hawk sitting on railings at the edge of the pavement.

"That bird!" Emma gasped. "I've seen it before…"

The White Hawk cawed once more and opened its wings with a snap before rising gracefully into the air to disappear in the darkness.

***

Monday evening. Once more they were back again in Mhari McLeod's attic lair. Emma looked around. The scene was set as for a gothic play – unseasonable rain battering against the sole window; lighted candles smoking in the candelabrum and the table neatly set out with letter-cards. But there was no-one sitting round the table.

Instead Emma and the others sat or stood around, sipping from the steaming mugs of coffee that Mhari was handing out.

Emma took her coffee from Mhari and then caught Milo's glance from across the room. She smiled and patted the chair beside her. He nodded and moved over to join her.

"I'm surprised that you turned up tonight," she said, "after yesterday's fiasco."

Milo gave a typical shrug. "Didn't have much on tonight, so I thought I might as well come. That way, if something does happen tonight, then all the time we spent trying to make contact with Horatio yesterday may not have been such a waste of time." He lifted his cup and took a gulp of coffee. "I did wonder if you would be here, though. Nothing much was said on Friday about your dark stranger, was there?"

Emma glanced at him, searching for the mockery. But for once, Milo had dropped the act. "I'm surprised at myself for coming. It's a waste of time, isn't it?"

"Good coffee, though. Remind me to tell Mhari that she could set up a little coffee house nae problem. Starbucks widnae hae a look-in." Emma laughed at his exaggerated accent, but noticed that Milo's eyes were not laughing. He was taking all of this seriously.

"Milo," she said, drawing his head closer, "I don't know what to make of this, but since the séance on Friday night, I have not dreamed the dream once. That's three clear nights. Nor have I seen the stranger. No vague sightings; no hallucinations. Is this a coincidence?"

Milo's eyebrows rose and his mouth moved into a 'O' shape. "Maybe. But perhaps not. Horatio may well know something. Maybe, if Mhari succeeds you'll know more. Nothing to do but wait and see. When is she going to try again?"

Emma looked around at the others.

Jeff was standing a little way off, still and silent, introspectively cradling his hot coffee. Maggie was on her knees leafing through the sheets of paper strewn around her on the floor, the hurried scrawled letters of 'Horatio's' words from the second session on Friday night, when Jeff and Mhari had reopened the contact alone.

Martin was sitting with Mhari. Emma tuned in to the conversation. "The thing is, Mhari, you would have to stay, in order to open up the way for them to come back."

"No! Can't you see what this means to me? I must be allowed to go. I can't be left behind!"

"Someone strong needs to be here for the return. That's you, Mhari. I couldn't do it. I'm not tough enough psychically."

"Jeff?" Mhari's voice was pleading.

His voice was sad. "True, I'm afraid. You would make the best anchor. Horatio spoke of it last time. Remember? If - *if* we go, we have to know there's a way home. I know. Believe me." Mhari looked at his scarred face, nodded, and turned towards the table.

"Surely all of this is academic anyway," Milo pointed out. "It's all moot if Horatio can't get through. He didn't come through yesterday, and you've been trying for almost an hour now. He might never contact again. Have you thought of that?"

"He will. I know it. How about we try again now? There might be some response this time."

In the silence that followed, Emma took her place at the table along with the others. "Ready?" Mhari asked. Heads dipped and were raised. "Will you scribe again, Milo?"

At his nod, five hands stretched out across the table to rest lightly on the spinner.

"Are you there, Horatio? Is anyone there? Horatio, are you there?"

Silence. There was no response. The spinner lay quiescent in the centre of the table. Minutes passed. After each unanswered call, the silence grew heavier.

Emma glanced towards the flickering shadows as they roamed around the packing cases and boxes, growing more unsure and afraid as time passed. Something was wrong. Something was definitely wrong. She jerked her finger off the spinner.

Martin caught the frightened look on her face. "It's okay, Emma. We just have to be patient. Put your hand back."

As she delicately placed her finger back on the spinner it began to move. But not in the tentative way of the previous session.

Mhari gasped. "Quick, Milo, get this down. A-P-O-L-O-G-E-S-F-O-R-M-Y-T-A-R-D-Y-N-E-S "

"It says: *Apologies for my tardiness*" Milo's voice, surprisingly, was clear and incisive.

"Is this Horatio?" Mhari asked. The spinner swung to the 'YES' card. Then it continued spelling out letters – so swiftly that Milo needed his full concentration to get the letters shouted at him written down in order. After the spinner stopped its wild motion, it took him several minutes to decipher the message.

"This is crazy," Milo said, looking at the letters he had written down.

"What does he say?" Mhari asked, squinting at the paper.

"He wants to come over to us, to make it easier to explain everything."

Chaos erupted. "No!" "How?" "Wow!"

Emma sat immobile, her heart racing.

Then Mhari gathered her wits and addressed the spinner. "Have you done this before?"

To Emma it seemed that the glass and chrome thing lying in the middle of the table had taken on a life of its own. A strange feeling of unease swept through her, making her light-headed and dizzy. Something was about to happen. Something momentous. She looked around. Everyone was focused on the spinner as the next message was spelled out. Emma sat frozen, except for the jerks that travelled from her finger up her arm as the spinner dashed crazily around the board.

"Tell us how we can help you to cross," Mhari was saying.

"*No!*" Emma's silent scream echoed inside her head. She tried to pull her hand away from the spinner but somehow couldn't. Not until the end of the message, when the spinner finally lay quiet and silent. As she drew her hand away, she noticed it shaking.

"What does it say?" she asked, her voice trembling. She felt Martin turn to her, but could not hear his words. Her world had shrunk to only Jeff as he read out the message from the alien being. For such Horatio was, she now had no doubt.

"He says: *I have visited your world before, and can ensure the crossing will be safe for both you and myself. I have aid here with me to enable me to return.*"

"Go on. What else?"

Milo frowned. "The next bit says: *Will you aid me to cross? If so I request the use of some clothing to wear as I am unable to carry non-living material through the ether. Tunic and breeches would suffice.*"

"Wow," said Maggie, only half in jest. "Just like in '*The Terminator*'"

"*Tunic and breeches*? This is a joke!" Milo stood up, rage and incredulity battling ferociously in his face and stance.

"Sit down!" Jeff's voice was strident, sure. "We have a decision to make. And it has to be made together."

The blood drained from Emma's face. "I'm scared, Jeff. This whole thing is just too weird. You don't know what this *Horatio* is.

It could be a demon or something out of legend. A vampire. A…a thing! How do we know it's even *human*?"

"You've been watching too many horror films," Mhari replied. "There are no such things as vampires and demons."

"You can't be sure of that! Jeff, you know more about all of this than anyone else here. Tell them it's too dangerous."

Jeff looked over to her and stretched out his scar-free hand to cover her white one. "I'm sorry Emma. I don't know exactly what's going down here, but I know one thing. Horatio is no demon." He turned and spoke to them all. "I say we help him cross. Who is with me?"

In the end only Emma dissented. Shocked and frightened, she stood up from the table, stumbled across to the end of the attic and crawled among the boxes. She could not be a part of this, but she couldn't leave either. Her heart was thumping; her throat dry and contracted with fear, but she could not leave, abandoning her friends to whatever it was they were calling out of the void. There must be some truth somewhere that would explain the vampire and demon stories. How do they know that they are not calling on that truth now? From her huddled position, she stretched out a hand to open the door a little. Homely electric light crept through the crack, making it easier to see the others as they made their preparations. At one point both Martin and Maggie came over to her, trying to soothe her fears, trying to understand her panic. But all to no avail. Mhari went downstairs, returning shortly afterwards with clothes belonging to her brother. No tunic and breeches, but a baggy T-shirt, a Scotland rugby shirt, a pair of joggers. "Safest," she laughed, "as we're unsure of his measurements."

Eventually the preparations were complete. Martin came to her, asking her to join them. She shook her head, numb. The five took their places round the table again and Mhari addressed the disembodied presence.

"Horatio? We are ready to help you cross. Come to us now."

***

Even from her hiding place Emma could feel the sudden drop in temperature. Her breath, shallow and rapid, was exhaled as vapour. She shivered. Between her and the table, a misty shadow was forming. The five at the table sat motionless, as if frozen in their chairs. Terror gripped her, as she tried to force a scream from between her icy lips. The shadow thickened, took form, coalesced

54

into a naked human body crouched on the floor, hands protecting the dark-haired head and dusky olive skin covering back, legs... Emma felt like a voyeur as she watched the beautiful young man pull himself up from the dusty floor and attempt to stand. He was facing into the room, his back to her. Then Jeff was there with clothes and a warm welcome. The icy cold had already begun to disperse.

Still in her hiding place, Emma watched as her five friends gathered round the new arrival, all talking at once, introducing themselves. *He* was a pool of stillness in the centre of their amazement and wonder.

Then he spoke. "There were six of you," she heard him say in strangely accented English. "Where is the sixth?" He turned in her direction and looked straight at her with his beautiful hazel eyes. Her shock was palpable. She tried to scream, but her throat was locked. "I am real," he said very gently. "No demon, no devil. A mere human, such as you. Horatio talMerios of Saravaal, at your service." He followed up with a bow that would have been a credit to any Tudor Lord.

Against her will, she felt her cramped legs unlock and stretch as she drew herself to her feet. "It's you," she said. *I'm in shock*, she realised. *I should be screaming my head off, but I can't make a sound.* Close up, she could see he was not as tall as she'd first thought. The rugby shirt was too big and the joggers fell in folds around his bare ankles. But undoubtedly it was *him*! "Duncan's much taller than you," she heard her voice say, then felt like kicking herself for saying such a stupid obvious thing.

Horatio turned to Jeff, dark brows raised in a question. Already there was a rapport there. "The clothes you're wearing belong to Mhari's brother," Jeff informed him. "He plays full-back in one of the local rugby teams. Big bloke." Then he turned to Emma, drawing her forward. "This is Emma Campbell," he said. Emma felt her hand taken lightly in cool fingers and watched numbly as he bent his head over to drop a gentle kiss on the back of her hand. Then he raised his head and their eyes met in a silent recognition before she felt Martin's hand on her elbow, turning her away from Horatio and back towards himself. She could feel Horatio's eyes on her as Martin led the group back towards the table and found an extra chair for Horatio.

"So this is England in the 21st Century," she heard him say, this stranger who was in fact no stranger to her at all.

The correction from Maggie came swift and sure. "You're not in England. You're in Scotland. It's the little country which is attached to England's northern border. More specifically, you're in the City of Glasgow."

"My pardon. When travelling it is sometimes difficult to get things absolutely correct. I hope you will forgive my errors and correct my mistakes. Now, to business. Lord Polon can hold the opening in the Ether for no more than two of your days, so we have that time to make our arrangements. That is, if you decide to come to Elasyn for the festivities."

"You said the place you come from was called Elsyn Vaal," Martin said.

"That's correct. The country is named Elsynvaal. Forgive me if I correct your pronunciation. It is but one word, not two. I live in the city of Elasyn, and it is there in the Palace-Castle that the coronation will take place in several days' time."

"You said something about a wedding?" Maggie asked.

"Yes. The King's marriage took place a few weeks ago."

"If we were to come with you how long would we be away?"

"Four or five of your days. Time runs slightly differently in Elsynvaal. If we leave in two days' time, I could return you home on Sunday evening."

Maggie looked thoughtful. "What about our classes?"

"Get the flu or something," Milo commented, the first time he'd spoken since being introduced to Horatio.

"All of us?"

"Only four, remember?" Mhari's voice was sad.

Horatio turned to look at her. "Poor Mhari," he said, "who will have to stay to be the necessary anchor." He reached over and took her hand in his. "Then it shall be you who will show me round your City of Glasgow in the time I have here, and I in turn will show you as much of Elsynvaal as I can!"

"How can you if I have to stay here?" Mhari sounded puzzled.

"I am what is known in your world as a wizard. A mage, a sorcerer."

"I knew it!" Emma's voice hummed in the sudden silence. "Evil. Evil. You have..." She pulled herself violently away from Martin's light hold, backing towards her corner with its friendly patch of light.

Martin quickly crouched down beside her, his arms tight around her rigid body. She resisted for a moment, trembling in his arms,

then she suddenly relaxed. Her head fell forward on to his shoulder. Martin looked down at her closed eyes and then glared over her head at the mage. "What have you done to her?" he hissed.

"She is overwrought. She will sleep for a short time and when she awakens, she will be calmer. It happens sometimes." His voice was calm and unconcerned.

"What happens, sometimes, exactly?" Jeff's deep voice asked, stepping forward. "You arrive here, and immediately you start throwing magic spells around?"

"I do not unnecessarily expend my energies. She was about to become hysterical and needed help."

"Unasked." By now Jeff was standing almost face to face with Horatio.

"Indeed," came the affirmation.

Mhari stepped forward between them. "Hold it boys. This is getting way too heavy. How's about we slow it all down, check Emma's okay, talk about it?" Her voice held a plea. Jeff took a step backwards. Horatio held up his hands, palms outwards. His eyes still on the mage, Jeff spoke over his shoulder to Martin. "Is she all right?"

Maggie had already gone over to Emma and was helping Martin to lay her down more comfortably. "She's breathing easily. She seems to be asleep." She looked up at Horatio. "Are you sure she's okay?"

"Yes, she is fine, I promise you. Perhaps I could explain a few things, ladies and gentlemen?" He paused, looked round at the group and taking their silence as assent went on. "This girl, Emma, is sensitive. Would you agree, Martin? Yes, I thought so. As a sensitive, she reacts to changes in the atmosphere. There was a dramatic change in the Ether as I was preparing to cross over, which is only now beginning to fade. Mhari, you also show signs of sensitivity. Did you feel anything?"

Mhari nodded slowly. "Yes, I could feel it. It suddenly became very cold." She looked around at the others. Martin and Maggie looked blank and Jeff said nothing.

Horatio smiled. "When I crossed over, Emma encountered something that is totally outside her experience," the mage continued, "and it made her panic. All I did was to cast a very small and harmless spell to give her the time to assimilate what we're discussing now."

"You mean she can hear what's going on now?"

"Not exactly. Her brain is storing the information, which she will then be able to access once she awakens, if she wants to. Otherwise it will fade and be forgotten."

"Like cribbing in your sleep? I could do with a spell like that for learning some of my theory!"

"Oh that's just like you, Milo!" Maggie's tone was sharp. Then she turned her back on Milo and spoke to Horatio. "How do we know you won't… that you aren't…"

"I can only give you my word. I'm not evil, despite Emma's rash accusation. I came to ask for your help, remember?" Silence. "How can I convince you I am not intending to harm you?"

"Christ!" The expletive came from Jeff. "You really expect us to *cross over* to wherever you come from while you're pulling stunts like this? I can't believe I encouraged this!"

Horatio's voice was mesmerising, soothing. "Jeff, if you'll just give me…"

"Don't do that. Don't try to manipulate me – or any of my friends. This has all been a big mistake. Perhaps you should just go back to Eslinvale, or wherever it is, and leave us alone."

Horatio held up his hands in supplication. "Everything I have told you is true. Yes I am a mage, unknown in your world, fairly rare but not unheard of, in mine. That means that I am trained in the use of magic, but at the same time am bound by the Wizards' Council to use my powers only for the good of mankind. In this and any other world I know of, Evil carries its own trademark that can be tracked down by Watchers and reported to the Council of Wizards. Offending wizards are dealt with in whichever manner the Council deems fitting. We mages live by a very strict set of rules. I will not harm you, nor will I allow any harm to come to you, should you decide to come with me to Elsynvaal in two days' time."

"This could all be a pack of lies." Milo remained sceptical.

"Much as I hate to admit it, it has a ring of truth," Jeff said slowly.

Martin, still unnerved by the spell laid on Emma, rounded on his old friend. "Are you out of your mind, Jeff? The whole thing sounds like something that has been dragged kicking and screaming out of some third-rate fantasy novel. So much for your *'Don't try to manipulate me'* bit! You've just been done, son."

"Nevertheless, I'm giving Horatio the benefit of the doubt. I might even go to Elsynvaal," Jeff said.

Chapter 5

Late afternoon sunshine played on the waters of the Kelvin River as it meandered through the park-land. Overhead the trees were just beginning to change to their autumnal colours. The wind that had been blowing all day had dropped and Emma thought it very pleasant to be strolling along the riverbank. Strange how it came about that she was the only one free this afternoon to show Horatio around. Usually at least one of the others had been free to show their very own ET visitor the sights and sounds of Glasgow.

He'd been soaking up the tourist sights of Glasgow – the Victorian architecture of the city centre; the Cathedral (Maggie had given him the full history); George Square with its imposing City Chambers; they'd taken him on a pub crawl and to the theatre. So it probably was good for him to just stroll like this, in silence along the side of a good-natured and peaceful river.

But how she would have liked someone else to be there instead of just the two of them. He made her nervous. Her feelings towards him were ambivalent. Beyond that initial look of recognition nothing had been acknowledged. Neither of them had mentioned the dreams. In fact, this was the first time they had ever been alone. It was true that he was very attractive with his dark hair and hazel eyes that seemed to smile independently of his mouth. It would be so very easy to be attracted to him. There was also the air of mystery that surrounded him. A wizard.

This was where the ambivalence crept in. She was wary, perhaps even frightened of him. Somehow he had been trying to contact her across the void by means of the dreams. But magic was something she simply did not understand.

The silence between them had gone on long enough, she decided. She stopped beside a park bench and sat down. He kept on walking, seemingly unaware that she was no longer beside him.

After ten paces, he stopped and turned to walk back to where she was sitting. "Sorry," he said. "I've not been very good company this afternoon, have I?"

She shrugged his apology off. "No problem. We all have things to think about. I don't suppose you're an exception."

He sat on the wooden bench beside her then leaned forward to pick up a handful of stones and began playing that old children's game where stones are thrown up into the air and than are caught on the back on the hand. She watched as he did it perfectly time after time. "Does that come naturally to you or are you magicking them not to fall? If there is such a word as *magicking*, that is."

"I have quite good balance anyway, but yes, probably I am cheating by exerting some influence on them. Without malice aforethought, I must add though."

"So you were influencing the movement of those pebbles without even really thinking about it? Making them stay on your hand without falling."

"One of the earliest attainment tasks of a mage apprentice."

"What else can you do?"

"Are you really interested Emma? Or is this merely conversation? Assuredly I am aware that there has been, shall we say, a measure of coolness between us since I arrived and I know that you are loath to cross over to Elsynvaal."

"I wouldn't exactly say loath, more unsure. Likes of - '*Is it really safe?*' Or '*Will we be able to get back?*' Little things like that."

Horatio nodded, and proceeded to throw the pebbles one by one into the water, skimming them neatly across the surface.

"You're showing off!" she laughed. "Master Mage – are you trying to impress me with your party tricks?"

He turned and looked into her eyes. He'd thought they were black, like her hair, but they were really a deep brown with golden flecks in them. He smiled wryly. "You are incorrect, lady. Why should I try to impress you with such ploys? You read too much into my actions, and see what is not there. I see it is impossible that you might one day cease to think of me as an evil magician attempting to whip you all away to a dreadful death!"

She looked down, abashed. "You must agree that this whole thing is not easy to accept. The first thing you did on your arrival was to slap me down with a magical spell!"

"It was a simple sleep spell to calm you down. It worked, didn't it?"

"Sure. But was there more in the spell? A little something extra perhaps?"

"Do you mean did I use magic to affect your feelings?" His voice had lost a little of its warmth. "Let me tell you a few things about my world and the use of magic. Elsynvaal has what you would call a pre-industrial society. But in contrast to your own feudal history, magic is tolerated there. I say 'tolerated' because we are strictly controlled. An unregulated mage could do a lot of damage to the fabric of society. We are allowed to use magic only for the good of others, and we are strictly forbidden to use it in furtherance of our own aims, wishes or desires. These strictures we all adhere to, as part of the vow we take when admitted to the Council of Wizards. So for me to lay a spell of that type on you would be totally against my Council vow."

"If you did make such a spell, how would they know you had broken the vow?"

"The magical Ether surrounds us all. Every spell when cast emanates the Ether, and Watchers are always on duty. Additionally every spell has a unique signature, just like a handwriting signature…"

"…so the Watcher knows who cast the spell."

"Correct. So how does it sound to you?"

"What part in particular, Horatio?" He watched as she tilted her head up so that she could look into his eyes. He discovered he was right. She *was* smiling. Then she looked away again. "I have to think about all of this. It's a lot for me to take on board, you must admit."

"You'll have to trust me. You're right to be wary of magic. It has been known to kill, if used by one not capable of holding the spell or power within himself. It's not only mage-apprentices who have died through trying a spell beyond their capabilities."

"And you? How capable are you to do this thing?"

"I can do it. There is no way I would run the risk of endangering you – any of you," he amended quickly. "Do you want to know my credentials? You smile. Magicians may have poor credibility here in Scotland in the 21st Century, but in my world to be a Creator, or a Seer, or an Illusionist is a wonderful thing. We do not crave fame or status. And once we have completed our training and take our oath we cannot turn our backs on what we have become. The power is with us wherever we go, forever."

"Go on."

"You want the whole of my CV?"

"Your CV? But of course. But who taught you that bit of jargon?" she asked, laughing.

"Milo. He also told me about mobile phones, internet dating and scuba-diving."

"I should have known. His mind is a cesspit full of useless

information."

"Not always, I think." He tossed the last pebble in his hand a few times before letting it drop at his feet. Then he turned back to Emma. "All right, Emma. You asked for my... CV. Well, here it is. I am a Council Mage trained in the arts of healing, defensive shields and di'speak. Also to a lesser degree in scrying, illusion and offensive weaponry. The spell I used on you was one of healing. These are my credentials. If you want me to, I could display some of them. It might help to ease your fears."

"What here? In Kelvingrove Park?"

"With the ducks as witnesses," he affirmed.

"Can you make something?" He could hear the smile in her voice. Much better.

"To a degree," he temporised. "I can do this... " A motion of his hands and a bundle of leaves seemed to be swept up into his lap, even though by now there was virtually no wind. And now his hands fashioned those dried-up wind-blown leaves into a beautiful white flower, not unlike a rose. He stood up and presented it to her with a courtly flourish.

"Thank you, kind sir," she smiled back.

"Unfortunately, the charm holding the rose together in this form will fade and it will revert to leaves. So it is not true Creativity, which is a truly rare gift, but Illusion, a much more accessible skill."

"How many kinds of magic are there? You mentioned Creators, Illusionists and Seers."

"You really want to know, don't you?"

"Of course I do. I want to know about you. I mean," she went on, looking away, "about Elsynvaal and what it's like there. After all – magic is part of it, isn't it?"

He smiled again, feeling more relaxed now that she was actually talking to him. On his arrival he had instantly recognised her as the black haired girl who had been nightly haunting his dreams. And for the last two days he'd been confused by the sudden and inexplicable feelings he'd felt towards this girl-woman, which was only compounded by her obvious antipathy towards him. Was she finally beginning to see him as a human being like her instead of an alien monster?

He began to tell her of Elsynvaal's magic, rare enough in itself, and the various forms it could take. He told of the skills of levitation, illusion and scrying, artefact creation, of di'speak and Ether-Crossing and the big one - Creativity.

"Di'speak is the ability to converse over distances with another mage – like your telephone. Ether Crossing is a very advanced form of di'speak. All of these skills can be developed to a greater or lesser degree, depending on the ability or talent of the individual mage. A mage must be able to hold the magic within himself or herself, and the ability to do this varies in individuals as much as a talent for music, or art, or logic."

"So the talent to learn magic is inherited?"

"That is correct."

"So mages marry?"

"Yes, of course. Some do marry, some do not. We are no different from other men and women. We have our desires, our dreams. Why do you ask?"

She gave a short embarrassed laugh and stood up, starting to walk again. He got up and walked alongside her.

"Don't know, really," she shrugged her shoulders lightly. "I suppose it's the old tales of Merlin and his entrapment and loss of power when he fell in love."

"An old tale from your past?"

"A myth. No-one knows if Merlin was a real wizard, or even if he actually existed. The story was not written down until several hundred years it supposedly happened."

"Tell me the story."

As she spoke she gazed across the slow moving water and unconsciously twirled the white flower in her hands. Horatio sat and watched the light play across her features.

"It is supposed to have happened in the dark ages of British history," she said. "There was a king, Uther Pendragon, who lusted after Ygraine, the wife of another man – the Duke of Cornwall, I think. Anyway, the King conspired with Merlin the wizard to fix it so that he could sleep with her. Merlin's payment was to have custody of the child born from that union. So one night when the husband was away at war Merlin cast a spell, which allowed Uther access to Ygraine disguised as her absent husband. Uther had his wicked way with her and Ygraine bore a son who become the legendary Arthur Pendragon, who himself spawned a whole host of legends. Merlin became the benefactor and later advisor to Arthur. Then much later, when Arthur was grown, Merlin met the nymph Nimue and fell in love. Nimue used his love for her to trap him in some kind of Everlasting Enchantment as punishment for his wrong-doing."

63

"An interesting story. Actually there are one or two parallels with Elsynvaal. Lord Polon is Mage-Advisor to the King, true, but wizards are not punished for falling in love. We do fall in love, and do marry. But for some reason we usually marry later than non-mages. Something to do with the long period spent in intensive apprenticeship perhaps. Anyway, I haven't done anything about a wife yet."

He glanced across at her. She was walking beside him with her head down, her incredible hair falling like a black waterfall over her shoulders and partially obscuring her face, but he thought he could see a smile through the cascade. He pushed the air around her head lightly to make the hair waft around and saw he was right. She *was* smiling. They walked on, the silence between them now companionable.

They drew close to the old Victorian building of the Museum and Art Gallery that bounded part of the southern edge of the park. They ought to go in, after all it was to visit the gallery that they'd come out walking across the Park, but Horatio hung back, reluctant to introduce external influences to the new congenial atmosphere between them. He broke the silence with a question.

"Can I tell you what was bothering me earlier?"

"Sure, Horatio. Anything I can do to help."

"I have a very good friend, who is finding life very difficult at the moment."

"Is this hypothetical, or real?"

"Pardon?"

"In this world, people who have a problem they want to talk about often begin by hypothesising that it is a dear friend who has the problem."

"No, no. The friend I mean is the Prince of Elsynvaal. He grieves his father, and cannot come to terms with the fact that he is dead. I know not how to console him. He worries me."

"Do you think he might do something to himself?"

"Suicide, you mean? No, I don't think he'd go that far, but he's in a poor state – full of jollity one day; in the depths of depression the next. He's but nineteen years old, and has been coddled all his life as the Prince and Heir. The King's death and now this business with King Claude has hit him badly."

Horatio suddenly became aware that he'd said more than he'd intended. Attempting to cover up, he rushed on hoping Emma had missed the reference to the 'business with King Claude'. "That being the case, I have to pay attention to the strange feelings I have been experiencing all day. There is something in Elasyn that I must attend to, and soon. 'Tis well that I return tonight." He paused momentarily. "Emma, will you be coming with me to Elsynvaal, alongside Jeff, Maggie and Milo?"

"I'm thinking on it, and it does seem *so very intriguing…*"

Then she dashed away, still carrying the white rose he'd created from autumn windfall, into the art gallery building. "Come on, Horatio. There are some marvellous paintings here!"

He laughed aloud and raced after her, somehow aware that her decision had been made. She would come. She wanted to be with him. He did not understand how she'd done it but somehow she *had* been calling to him across the darkness of the void. His own feelings for her were with each passing moment becoming less, much less, confused and his heart felt much, much lighter.

***

They wandered through the gallery, Emma pointing out various famous paintings, attempting to convey some of the history of art of humankind to this alien being. But it was obvious he was not really interested in paintings and sculptures. Eventually she said so.

He nodded in agreement. Then added, "But there is no painting or sculpture that can match the art form standing now beside me." She coloured a little, but said nothing.

"Tell me about yourself," he said.

So as they wandered through the sun-dappled balconies and galleries of art and artefacts, she did.

"My full name is Emasiyo Juliana Campbell. I was born at a very early age…" she began.

"How refreshing."

"…in Takamatsu, in Japan. Which infers correctly that I am part Japanese. My father's an engineer who used to work with a Japanese firm in Osaka. My mother was one of the bilingual assistants in the firm who dealt with outside contracts. They married, but when I was just over a year old my mother mysteriously disappeared. My father never found out what happened. He insisted that she would not have run off but if she *had* died, then her body was never discovered. The police interrogated him on suspicion of murder but he was cleared and shortly afterwards left the country, taking me with him. I'm not sure how my mother's family took it all - he never speaks of it and I've never been back to Osaka.

"So that is how I came to Scotland. Eventually my father married again, and I have two horrid little brothers who thankfully I see only occasionally. I suppose it's possible that they might improve with age. How's that?"

"Quite a story," Horatio replied. "So you are half Japanese. Is Japan far from Scotland?"

"Oh yes. A long way away, on the other side of the world. Though, in fact I'm actually only one quarter Japanese. Apparently my mother herself was not of full blood either. The story goes that she was born after my grandmother was raped by an unknown foreigner. Possibly by an American serviceman at the end of the War. But that's something few of my friends know. Except Maggie, because we grew up together." She stopped, suddenly aware that she was confiding in an almost total stranger. "Not that it's important, of course."

"Of course not," he agreed.

"Lord! I don't even know why I'm telling you all this. I don't usually…"

He stopped walking and turning towards her he lifted her chin, looking into her almost-black eyes. "Perhaps you trust me after all, mage and all," he said softly.

"Perhaps…" A half-smile, and she broke away and looked at her watch. "It's time we were going back. The others will be waiting for us and no doubt it will take you time to set up for the crossing." Then she reached out to take hold of his hand, and led him towards the exit door.

"You are coming, then? To Elsynvaal?"

"Why not? It might be fun!" The phrase echoed down the museum corridors and Horatio imagined he heard a laugh. But he merely shrugged and allowed himself to be led out into the sunlight and autumnal smells of the riverside gardens.

* * *

Two hours later in Mhari's attic the scene was set and they were ready to go. Mhari sat at the table, but the Ouija cards were no longer set out in front of her. Martin stood to the side of the table with Emma. His eyes showed his worry and fear, but his voice was quiet, pitched for Emma's ears only. "I am going to ask you for the last time, Emma. Don't do it. Don't go with them. Jeff may have his feelings of correctness and safety, if so then let him go. *You* don't have to go! Stay here with me. Let Mhari go in your place."

"She can't sing, Martin. Anyway, aren't you being a bit melodramatic? It's only for a few days. Just till Sunday."

"It's that spell he cast on you that first night when he came. It was more than a spell to make you sleep. Since you woke up you've been different somehow. It's too dangerous."

Emma looked down at her hands. In one hand she still held the flower Horatio had created for her, but Martin held the other so tightly that the tips of the fingers were white.

"Sometimes we all have to take risks." As she said the words, a shiver ran down her spine. She looked around at her friends, but no-one else seemed to have noticed anything. She gave Martin's hand a swift squeeze, leaned over and kissed him lightly on the lips.

But Martin caught at her and pulled her back towards him. "Tell me something Emma," he whispered. "Is Horatio the one you saw in the dreams and hallucinations?"

"Yes," she replied.

"Then why the hell are you going with him? Surely you can see that's why he came here – not this Coronation business, but to get you to come to Elsynvaal!"

"Martin, I believe in him. Something in here," she tapped her breast, "tells me it's right. That's why I'm going." She gave a small laugh. "After all, he is the man in my dreams. Sorry Martin. I didn't mean to be cruel." Then she turned and walked the few steps away from him to the centre of the room where Jeff, Milo, Maggie and Horatio stood with their hands linked. As she stepped between Horatio and Maggie she looked back at him.

"Goodbye Martin," she murmured. Martin glanced at Horatio who was watching him. His eyes were full of sympathy, which puzzled Martin until he realised the significance. They both knew Emma had already chosen.

***

Mhari sat at the table, holding the Ether-strands within her mind as Horatio had taught her. So much easier this way, she realised. She could sense the depth of the Ether, and could even sense the personality at the other end. If only she could have gone too. But Horatio soothed her frustration. "You now have the skill to hold open a way through the Ether," he had said. "At a later time you too will cross over and visit Elsynvaal. And then you can be trained properly." *Was that said merely to mollify her? Or was it possible that she could become like Horatio – a mage?* she wondered, fearfully.

Martin wasn't sure what he was expecting to see – his mind kept leaping to transporter room scenes in *'Star Trek'*. In the event, it seemed that between one blink of his eyes and the next they'd gone. Just vanished. The clothes they'd all been wearing fell into untidy piles where each had been standing. No afterglow, no rainbow image, no shimmer in the air. Just gone. He stood staring at the spot Emma had stood only a moment ago, feeling totally bereft. *Where is she now?* he wondered. *Is she all right? Four days until she returns. Four days. . .*

He reached over to lift the flower Emma had been holding. At his touch it crumpled into a handful of crushed autumn leaves. He drew his hand away swiftly, a shudder running through his body.

Chapter 6

The crossing took no time and a very long time.

Hold on tight Horatio had said. *Don't let go of one another.* Emma squeezed her eyes shut as Mhari's attic room suddenly disappeared, to be replaced with eerie cold damp darkness. She opened her eyes, but still could see nothing. Never had she seen such dark obscurity. There was very little sensory input – nothing but silence and blackness and a slight wind blowing from behind. They seemed to be moving with the wind but they were not walking. The cold was making her skin goose bump. She could hear Maggie whimpering. She moved a foot, touched the other bare foot. *There was nothing under her feet.* Her heart lurched within her chest. She gasped and clutched convulsively at Horatio's hand – and thankfully received a reassuring squeeze in return. She was reduced to an indefinably small speck in the vastness that surrounded her, while at the same time claustrophobia threatened to invade her senses. Time, relative at the best of times, slowed down and eventually stopped.

Then abruptly she felt Horatio slip forward and she too was tumbling forward, falling. She lost her grip on Horatio's hand. Light blazed in her face. Her knees gave way and she collapsed forward onto a cold floor. She felt a soft covering being wrapped round her naked shoulders. Gradually feeling crept back into her limbs. *We're here then,* she thought.

Turning her head sideways, she peered round the edge of the soft cloak and looked at her surroundings. Light came from flickering torches held in wall brackets. Bare wooden floor. Stone walls. Low ceiling. A single heavy wooden door strengthened with broad metal bands.

"Wow! I had a bad trip once, but that beat the hell out of it." Milo was on his feet, a heavy dark cloak wrapped around him, gazing around with a child-like wonder. A man, about middle age with a greying beard, was helping Jeff to his feet. Maggie was sitting wrapped in her cloak, shivering. A pretty young girl stood at her side, an intense look on her face. Through the thickness of the cloak she wore Emma could feel the warmth of Horatio's firm hand grasp her elbow as he helped her to her feet.

He turned to the young man who had brought Milo his covering.

"Loren, where are their clothes?" The youth grinned and turned to a chest behind him, but the older grey-haired man broke in before he could say anything.

"Everything has been attended to, Horatio. Olivia will accompany the two ladies, Loren will aid the men. We should leave introductions until all of you are suitably attired."

"You are too kind, my Lord Polon. Your servant." Horatio pulled his fur-lined cloak around himself, and made a low bow. There was a new sharp edge to his voice, but when he turned and spoke to the two girls, his voice was softer, gentler. A tiny smile curved his lips, and Emma, suddenly very aware of her nakedness beneath the cloak, clutched it more tightly around her.

"Emma, Maggie, if you go with Serra Olivia she will help you master the intricacies of the feminine dress." He bowed to them, confident and sure on his home ground. Emma found herself following Maggie and the young girl through the heavy oaken door into a passageway.

Lord Polon's imperious voice followed them. "Olivia. Remember, once our guests are suitably attired, you should take them to the Prince's library. We will meet there."

The girl turned back and dipped her head in acquiescence. "Yes, father," she whispered.

Up ahead, the short corridor ended in a spiral staircase. The light from the flickering candlestick Olivia carried cast eerie shadows that jumped around as they passed across the uneven stone walls. Emma caught hold of Maggie's hand and received an answering squeeze. Out in front, Olivia unhesitatingly led the way up the tightly curving stone steps. Several floors above, the stairs opened out onto a landing with three passageways leading away. Olivia led the two girls along one, passing several doors before stopping. Bending down, she turned the large wrought-iron ring in the door that served as a door-handle and pushed open the heavy door.

"This is to be your room. We thought you'd rather be together. It must be very strange for you – coming from a different world."

"Where will the others be? Jeff and Milo?" Maggie asked, looking around.

"These used to be the Prince's apartments, before…" she stopped, confusion wafting across her features. Covering her distraction she moved into the room. "Your friends will be close by. In the next room. See, here is the connecting door." She pointed to a door partially hidden among the woven wall coverings. "Now," she continued, a business-like tone deepening her youthful voice. "I do not believe you are familiar with gowns and kirtles. I am told that in your world women wear very strange clothes. Shirts and breeches, like men!"

Maggie laughed. "I suppose so. But it's to be gowns here, is it?"

"From what my father told me from his conversations with Lord Horatio, you have much more freedom than ladies have here in Elsynvaal. Is it true that you both attend the *University*?"

"Yes, we are both music students, at the College of Music." Emma answered while Maggie dropped onto the large canopied bed that stood on one wall opposite the connecting door.

"Here in Elsynvaal, only men and the mage-born attend the University. It is in Deighford, far south from Elasyn, on the western coast. But I think I would have liked to study there, if things had been different. However, let us to the task of dressing you." Her heavily embroidered gown swishing at every step, she walked to a large chest set against one wall. Opening it, she pulled out under-garments and over-garments of all kinds and gowns of varying colours and hues, while the two girls looked on in amazement.

"The Prince is holding a reception this evening, which requires formal gowns. I believe that this is all new to you. To begin with... this is a shift..."

Some time later, Emma and Maggie stood opposite one another, just looking. "You look as if you're going to a fancy-dress party!" Maggie said, laughing.

"Well, so do you!" Emma replied. Both were dressed in floor-length gowns. Emma's was of a pale lilac fabric, low cut at the neckline and gathered under the bust with a broad swathe of fabric of a contrasting shade. With each step forward, her petticoats rustled. Maggie was similarly dressed, in a gown of russet.

"Day gowns are much more comfortable. We wear fewer petticoats, for one thing, and no boning. Perhaps you will tell me about these jeans you..." Olivia broke off as a knock sounded on the door. She glanced once more at the two girls, and called out, "Enter!"

"It is time to join the others," Horatio said as he walked into the room, splendid in a dark suit of tightly-fitted jacket and trousers, lace at throat and wrists. Jeff and Milo followed behind him, looking very different from the guys the two girls were so used to. Jeff fiddled with the lace trim at his throat and looked very uncomfortable while Milo preened and grinned.

Horatio held out his arm and Maggie took a deep breath. "Let's go!" she cried, sweeping majestically past Olivia and taking his proffered arm. Daintily, she laid her hand upon his while laughing inwardly at herself. Emma stepped out into the corridor and smiled as Milo ironically bowed to her. Jeff brought up the rear with Serra Olivia.

They began walking in the direction of the spiral stone staircase. As she floated along, Emma's mind wandered. *It's just like being in a play or an opera,* she thought. Suddenly music winged through her head and she laughed. At the sound of her laughter Horatio broke off his conversation with Maggie and turned round to her.

She laughed as she replied to the unspoken question in his dark eyes. "I feel as if I'm just about to go on stage – complete with butterflies-in-the-tummy. I was about to burst into an aria from Wagner's *Tanhausser.*"

"Would that be Richard Wagner, nineteenth century operatic composer?"

Emma looked at him full in the face, noting his regular, even handsome features, the intelligence in his eyes. "You know a lot about our world."

"Curiosity is a fault of mine, I'm afraid. I have visited your world before."

Maggie stopped walking. "You mean you can travel to times other than the present?" She looked across Milo's head to Jeff behind. "Did you hear that, Jeff?"

"Time travel too. Well, who would have guessed?" Milo's voice was dry.

"Time is not linear," the mage said, as if that explained everything.

"In that case, Horatio, why pick on us," Emma said, "when you had all of human history to choose from? Why not have Handel perform for your King, or the Beatles? *Why us?*"

Horatio looked straight at her, his eyes drilling deep into her soul, but his voice was quiet and gentle, and pitched for her alone. "Because you called to me." Then he turned back and lightly gripped Maggie's hand. "Come, let us go. The Prince is waiting."

Emma felt Milo's eyes on her, but could not turn her head, staring instead at Horatio's retreating back. She could hear murmuring voices as she followed with the others, but her mind was in turmoil. *You called to me,* he'd said. *What did he mean? If anyone was doing any calling it was his appearance in my dreams!*

He's a mage. Surely it would be easy for him to do such a thing! But then she remembered what Horatio had said about the use of magic when they were walking in Kelvingrove. *"We are strictly forbidden to use it in furtherance of our own aims, wishes or desires"* But hard on the heels of that memory came another – the moment in Mhari's attic when he'd first appeared through the void and the first instant of mutual recognition before she'd freaked out and begun screaming at him. Her footsteps faltered. Milo glanced at her. Her smile was rather forced as she walked on.

At the top of the staircase, they turned along the central corridor and soon found themselves on a balcony overlooking a triangular hall. A raised dais occupied the apex at the far end of the hall. Along the wall below them temporary staging was partially set up.

"The arena for the Coronation celebration two days hence," Horatio explained. The Coronation will take place late morning, and then there will be feasting and festivities."

"And that's where we come in."

"Indeed. There are other acts of course – jugglers, story-tellers, even a mage or two, and troupes of actors and entertainers are coming from south and east. You will enjoy the spectacle."

He stopped at a door about halfway along the gallery and pushed it open. "The Prince's library," he announced.

Chapter 7

With the door wide open, there was nothing to be done but enter. The room was indeed a library – but the likes of which one none of the newcomers had used before. 'Dickensian' was the description that came to mind, though Emma thought it fitted in exactly with everything else they'd seen so far. A set of narrow wooden steps led from each side of the doorway up to a balcony lined – no – crammed with bookshelves. Emma craned her head round. Yes, the balcony went right round the room, ten feet above their heads. Richly woven tapestries depicting rural romps of various kinds hung from the walls, muffling sound and leeching light from the room. Doors led off left and right. Chairs and couches were dotted around the room occupied by a half-dozen men and women.

As Emma and her friends entered two men stood and moved towards them. The Lord Chancellor, Polon, they recognised from before, and the other had to be the Prince! *Do I curtsy?* Emma suddenly asked herself. She glanced at Horatio for guidance, but he was already walking forward to meet the Prince. Until this moment, she had not really thought about the royalty bit – and now it suddenly hit her that she was in the presence of *a Prince*. He looked very young. She remembered Horatio's words only a few hours ago in the gardens by the River Kelvin. He'd told her that the Prince was 'but nineteen years', not much younger than herself. He was dressed all in black, the only hint of colour being the very fairness of his hair. If his eyes were less cold and he wasn't wearing that haughty look, he'd be drop-dead gorgeous. Michelangelo's David.

The travellers stood together as Horatio introduced each to the Prince. Lord Polon, Court Mage to the King, stood slightly to one side, hands clasped together and a wearing a benign expression. Jeff hung back for some reason, standing side-on, as if unwilling to show his scarred face to the young and handsome Prince. Emma frowned. Surely he could not be ashamed of his scars? He'd adapted to the marks and as far as she was aware, never tried to hide them. Even when people stared, he did not back down. She'd seen him face down some pretty nasty prejudice – so what was going on here?

The Prince took hold of Maggie's hand, bowed over it while murmuring a welcome. "Welcome to Elasyn Castle, Mistress Maggie. I trust you had a good journey." His voice was light – a passable tenor, Emma thought. "Though I'm told it can be a little cold."

"Yes sir," Maggie was saying.

"Is that 'Yes it was good', or 'Yes it was cold'?"

"Both, I would say, sir."

The Prince gestured towards Lord Polon. "Is there nothing we can do to rectify the chilliness of the crossing? It really should be made more comfortable for our visitors." He turned back to the newcomers before the Lord Chancellor could form a reply. As the Prince turned to Emma, she caught a look in his eyes. Appraising? Speculative? Then his lips were brushing gently against the back of her hand and when he raised his head whatever she'd seen in his eyes had gone and he'd moved on to speak to Milo. Emma felt a hand on her arm and turned to find Serra Olivia at her side. "Come, both of you," she said, "sit with me."

Emma and Maggie followed Olivia to a vacant couch, where several of the richly-dressed courtiers approached them.

With the introductions over, the Prince turned round and held court. "He might look the part," Maggie whispered to Emma, "but he seems like a complete fool to me!"

His voice was haughty as he regarded the Chancellor. "My Lord Polon," he said, "thank you for your advice this evening. But I am sure that you have many other duties to attend to. We would not keep you from them. No doubt my gifted uncle has use of your services."

The Chancellor moved towards the door, obviously aware he was being dismissed. "As you say, my Lord Prince, my duties are weighty, and never give me rest. I bid you adieu, Ladies, Gentlemen."

But before he left, he turned back to his daughter, and spoke in an undertone to her. Emma watched as a flush crept up the cheeks of Serra Olivia. She glanced quickly in the Prince's direction before dropping her gaze to the floor. Lord Polon gave a small bow and left the room.

The door closed and it was as if a fog had lifted. The Prince immediately dropped his haughty demeanour and gave a short laugh. "Now we can relax. My apologies, Olivia for the insult to your father, but even you think of him as a pompous old windbag! I gather the parting shot was aimed at me?" Olivia looked down at her hands, silent. "Well? What has your good father been saying about me now?"

Olivia glanced around the room, as if uncertain as to how to reply. The Prince sat on the sofa at her side. "I'm sure we don't have to hide anything from our new friends here. Come – what has he been saying? Told you to stay away from me?" She dropped her head, and gave a nod.

"He has forbidden me to speak to you alone."

The Prince's smile wavered slightly but his voice was firm as he replied. "Well, he was right. You should not. But we are not alone now my lady, so come, smile and be of good cheer. Be hostess to our newly-arrived and very welcome guests." Then he stood, pulling her with him. Serra Olivia looked at the Prince, her lips curved into a smile that did not reach her still wary eyes.

"Come," the Prince continued, "let us eat. See what sweetmeats and wines we have for you to sample! You must be hungry." He snapped his fingers, and as if by magic a number of servants appeared bearing trays piled high with delicacies of all sorts, some familiar to the Scots newcomers, while many were not. A courtier approached, and Olivia introduced him to the quartet. After a few minutes desultory talk, Jeff excused himself and moved off.

After some time spent being introduced to one courtier after another all showing an interest in their journey across the void a dark-haired boy appeared at their side. "Are you recovered from your journey?" he asked.

Emma frowned, struggling to remember where she'd seen the lad before. But Serra Olivia merely took his arm and smilingly introduced him to the girls as her brother, Ser Loren. *That's it*, Emma thought. *I remember him now.* He was the boy who'd been with Olivia and Polon in the cellar room when they'd arrived.

Milo and Horatio were discussing possibilities for the festivities programme when the Prince joined them. "So, what thoughts do you have on the music you will play for us?" the Prince asked.

"Well, Sire… " Milo began.

The Prince waved him to silence. "Not 'sire'. 'Sir' or 'my lord' is sufficient. I am not a King." Emma standing nearby overheard the remark and caught a look pass between Serra Olivia and Horatio.

Milo cleared his throat and said: "We can perform four-part harmony unaccompanied, both medieval plainsong and modern twentieth century works, and if we were granted access to some of the Castle's instruments, I'm sure we can accomplish something worthwhile in instrumental accompaniment."

The Prince turned to Horatio. "Is he always as pompous-sounding?"

"No." Horatio replied. "In fact Milo's normally very out-spoken. You have over-awed him, my lord."

"Rubbish!" Milo retorted.

"See?" Horatio said with a grin.

"Well," said the Prince, "tomorrow morning you shall see the music room and what we have to offer you. Will that do?"

"Sure."

"That's better."

Olivia turned to Emma and took her empty glass. "I'll get some more wine for you." Emma turned round, looking for Maggie or Jeff. Then she felt a hand below her elbow, turning her round towards him. Inevitably.

"Horatio," she murmured.

"You sound surprised. Surely you realised that we would have to talk."

"Do we?"

"Come, will you walk with me?"

As Horatio drew her under the balcony towards a window at the far side, Emma cast around for her friends and caught Maggie's eye. Her eyebrows went up a little, and then she raised a thumb in the traditional gesture. Her hand was held firmly in Horatio's as they left the throng for the relative quiet under the balcony. The windows were leaded, and overlooked the same quadrangle as their rooms. Horatio pointed out to her a window roughly half-way along on the adjacent wall, the north wall. Her room. The rooms that used to be the Prince's apartments. *Before what?* She wondered what Olivia had broken off from saying.

"Where are your apartments?" The question was out before she could stop it. Emma could feel his smile but would not look at him.

"One floor down from your rooms and two windows beyond to the right. And across on the opposite side of the quad – the south wall – that's where the King has his apartments. The Prince has the rooms adjacent to the Library…" He waved his hand to take in the whole of the side of the quadrangle in which they now stood, "here in the eastern wall of the quad." They stood in silence for a moment, and Emma decided to take the initiative.

"What you said out there in the corridor, about me calling to you. What did you mean, exactly?"

Horatio smiled. His eyes in the dimness looked very dark,

almost black. "Exactly? I meant just what I said. You called me to you. You were the centre of the energy I used in the contact." He paused, watching her frown gather. "Sorry, I'm not explaining this very well." He took in a long breath, gathering his thoughts. "First of all, you have to believe me when I tell you that all of this is new to me."

"What is?"

"All of this. Oh, not the travelling, the seeing other worlds, but what I feel for you and everything that's happening. That is all new to me."

"Horatio I'm lost. What are you talking about?"

He turned away, running his hands through his hair. "When I was asked – told – to organise the entertainment for the Coronation celebration, and to bring over someone from your world I was as, you Scots say, 'fair pissed' but I had no option but to comply."

"Okay, go on."

"One of the ways I can get an initial contact is through something like the Ouija board you were using. There are other ways, cards sometimes work, and so on, but it is normally quite hit or miss trying to find the initial contact. Sometimes it can take hours or even days to get a fix, but that day you came through very strong. The contact was easy because you'd already been calling to me."

"But it was Mhari who was doing the Ouija board. Not me. I was only there because I'd been having strange dreams and wanted to know about them. I had a real shock when I saw you appear out of nowhere! It was you who was in the dreams, yes, but I was not calling to you, Horatio. I couldn't have been. I don't know how." She turned away but he took her arm and turned her back.

"You called me, Emma. You were in my dreams too."

"You mean we each dreamed of the other? What happens when you dream?"

"I am out riding with you across the grasslands."

"The same as me."

Silence. Uncertainty. Then Horatio spoke. "I was really taken aback when I recovered from the crossing and discovered that Mhari was presiding over the board. It was not Mhari I had heard. It was you. And you were sitting in a huddle on the floor frightened out of your wits. I was confused. I had to do something."

"So you put a spell on me."

"I've explained that."

"Yes, and no I haven't had any after effects. Everything is just as you told the others after the spell took effect. But that's not what's worrying me. If I wasn't calling to you, and you weren't calling to me, what's going on?"

"To tell you the truth, I don't know. The mind is a very strange and complex organ. Especially where the higher powers are concerned. Who knows what the mind is capable of? I think it's probable that we were, somehow, calling across the void to one another."

"What? Without even knowing of one another's existence? That's crazy."

"Emma, the power of the mind continually surprises me, and remember, it's what I do. I'm a mage. You might say mind power is my job. And I sense power within you, a latent power."

"Whoa, stop this now, Horatio. This is getting to be too much for me to handle. It intrigues me, I admit, but at the same time this whole magic thing scares me like hell. And you're not doing much to ease that."

"You'll have to trust me."

"So you said in Kelvingrove Park. And I did. I came with you."

He said nothing, but moved his head in agreement. "I'm glad you did."

They stood in silence, each lost in thought. Emma watched a door open in the far corner of the quad where the south tower met the west, and a figure crossed to a small building in the centre of the quad. She was about to point it out to Horatio when he spoke again, throwing her completely off kilter.

"Will you miss Martin?"

She turned and looked at him.

"Martin is a very good friend, but that's all. The old cliché, but true in this case."

"Martin doesn't think so. He warned me off."

"When?"

"Almost as soon as I arrived in Glasgow. He could sense how I felt about you from the moment I arrived and saw you."

Emma turned to the window, looked out again. Her heart was thumping wildly against her ribs. Was this really happening? She'd only met Horatio a few days ago and rarely had any conversation with him worth talking about until today. Was it possible that there actually were relationships that were *meant to happen*? Fate? Already she had thrown Martin over for him. He was standing behind her now, silent, contemplative. Comfortable with silence.

Without thinking about it, she stretched out her hand to him. He caught it, held it. Then his hand moved round her neck to push her hair aside. His lips on her shoulder lit her like fire. She turned into his arms and they kissed.

Some time later as Horatio led her back to the Prince's library both were still smiling, but Horatio's vanished when he looked towards the library door where the Prince was speaking with a young man in his early twenties.

He turned to Emma. "Please join your friends, Emma. I have something to attend to." Then he turned abruptly and hurried across the room.

Maggie was standing by the buffet table holding two plates, her eyes on the Prince's back. Emma took one of the plates from her. "Hi Em," she said distractedly, her brow furrowing. "Would you credit it? There I was conversing, no less, with Prince Hamnet when he suddenly thrust this plate at me and without a further word turned and strode off to speak with that man who's just arrived. Rude, don't you think?"

"He's a Prince. I suppose manners might be a little different for them. Where are the others?"

"Around. Milo's somewhere over there talking to Serra Olivia. But never mind them – what about you and Horatio?"

Emma looked at her friend and smiled.

"Ah yes, I knew it!" Maggie exclaimed. "You have to tell me all about it!"

"Not now, Maggs," Emma replied. "Later in our room. Here come Serra Olivia and Milo. But where's Jeff?"

Maggie looked round, her eyes suddenly troubled. "I don't know. He's disappeared off somewhere. Heaven knows where. I don't think this is his scene, somehow."

"No, I don't think so, either. Did you notice his reaction when he was faced with the Prince? He seemed very conscious of his burn scars. I've never seen him react in that way before."

Maggie didn't answer her. They looked around the room, hoping to spot Jeff's lanky form, but still his tall figure was nowhere to be seen. Many more people had turned up since they themselves had arrived, and now the room was thronging with people dressed in any number of hues. Turning back to Maggie, she noticed her watching the group at the doorway where Horatio had now joined the Prince and the rather handsome but bemused-looking stranger. The newcomer was dressed in the same manner as most of the other men, in frilled shirt, doublet and leather breeches. His hair hung in long unkempt tresses. *Don't they have barbers here?* Emma wondered. Hung over his shoulder was an overstuffed leather satchel, and in his hand was a sheaf of papers, which he was showing to the Prince. She turned back to her friends as Olivia and Milo stopped beside them.

"Come and meet a countryman of yours," Olivia said to them, and taking Milo's hand began to lead them to where the Prince stood with the stranger.

Horatio broke off his conversation and moved swiftly to intercept them. "Will you come this way please, all three of you." He guided them to the opposite side of the room.

"Who is that, Horatio? Olivia said he was a countryman of ours."

Horatio looked as if he was about to refuse to answer, but in the end capitulated. "He is an Englishman who crossed the Ether with me a few months ago. His name is Master Will Shaksper."

"You are joking, Horatio, aren't you? Will Shaksper of Stratford?" Maggie asked with a laugh. The others stared at her, wondering if she had gone mad.

"Indeed, Maggie," Horatio replied turning to face her. "How did you know that he lives in Stratford?" All three heads turned and looked at him and then as one turned to the figure standing by the doorway speaking to Prince Hamnet. Horatio's eyes narrowed. "What's going on?"

"Tell us about this man," Maggie demanded.

"I visited England - your England – in the year of 1589. He and I spent some time together, and then he returned with me to Elsynvaal."

"1589? Is he a poet?"

"Yes. A very good one, in fact. He also has written the odd play or two for travelling performers."

"Good grief! It's William Shakespeare!" exclaimed Maggie.

They turned and looked towards the poet, still in conversation with the Prince. "He doesn't look much like his portraits," Milo commented.

"The only surviving ones were done when he was much older," Maggie replied. "In 1589 he hadn't even reached London."

"So this is where he spent his hidden years," Emma put in. "All that speculation about what countries he'd visited when he was travelling…"

Horatio's frown deepened. "Are you saying that you know of Master Will four hundred years after his time?"

"Don't you know who he is, Horatio?" Emma was smiling. "A certain William Shakespeare, born in Stratford, England in the mid-sixteenth century went on to become the greatest poet and playwright in the English language. You even saw one of them in Glasgow. The Royal Shakespeare Company's production of *'Othello'* at the Playhouse Theatre."

Horatio looked over at the playwright still speaking with Prince Hamnet. "It never dawned on me that it could be the same person."

Watching his gaze, Maggie said, "Has he ever mentioned his family? He has a son called Hamnet, you know."

"A son?"

"Oh yes. When he was still very young, only a teenager, he got married. Soon after, his wife, Anne Hathaway, had a daughter, and then twins a year or so later. A boy and a girl. The boy Hamnet died when he was eleven years old, while Shakespeare was in London writing and performing in plays."

Horatio turned back to them. His voice was low and deadly serious. "You know too much about him. It is imperative that you do not interact with him at all. There's no telling what you might change or cause to be changed by interacting with him."

Maggie and Emma were still watching the poet. The Prince had finished his conversation with him and had moved off. William Shakespeare still stood by the doorway, parchment in hand, nodding to someone who had just entered the room. With a shock, Emma realised that it was Jeff, who merely nodded in return and moved past him into the room towards them.

"Wouldn't it be possible to just talk to him just a little," Maggie said, "without telling him who we were?"

Horatio put his head to one side as if considering the request, but then shook his head. "No, I don't think so, Maggie. I'm sorry. But do you think it's remotely possible that you could hold a conversation with Will without him discovering that you were from his future? No, I didn't think so. He's a very astute man. For certain he would whittle from you details of his future fame as a playwright in London. It does a man no good to know his own future."

The Prince spoke abruptly from where he was standing behind them. In the hubbub of conversation, none had heard his approach. "I feel that sometimes it would be very useful to know one's own future – and how to change it!" His voice was hard. Then he waved a negligent hand in the direction of the Bard. When he spoke again the hardness was absent and his voice was lighter – with a note of humour. "But did I hear correctly?" he asked. "Is our Master Will really destined to become famous in your world?"

"Yes, my Lord Prince, it is apparently so."

The Prince's laugh was unforced and natural. In that laugh Maggie could perhaps see a little of what he was when not putting on a show or scowling.

"You didn't know who it was that you brought across, did you, Horatio? What a faux pas! You should pay more attention to your cards!"

Across the room, Master Will Shaksper turned to leave the reception. As he did so, he glanced across the room towards the Prince. A moment later Maggie hissed in Emma's ear. "He just eyeballed me."

"Who? What are you talking about?"

"Shakespeare. Just as he was leaving, he looked over and looked straight at me. Honest he did! He has very penetrating eyes."

Emma smiled. Maggie looked quite star-struck.

***

Emma watched from the carved window seat as Maggie gave a little twirl in her sleeping shift, showing off the intricate needlework. Elsynvaal was not an industrialised country – Horatio told them that in Glasgow, and now she was here Emma was beginning to think of it as a strange combination of fairy tale and medieval life. Magic. Princes. Lords and ladies, or rather Sers and Serras. She smiled and watched Maggie as she did a little pirouette in the middle of the room.

A pale shadow passing across the window caught her attention. She scrambled deeper into the recessed window seat and pulled up her feet under her gown. She turned more fully to the leaded window and looked out. Outside was darkness lit only by the candlelight spilling from the lighted windows of the wing opposite, and weak moonlight from a small, very distant moon. She peered out at the snow-covered square area below, and wondered what it was like outside the walls of the Castle. I'll ask Horatio to take us out into the town, she thought. She pulled her knees up, tucked the elaborate sleeping gown around her feet, and rested her chin on her knees. A shadow fell on the snow below – a white bird with a three foot wingspan. It wheeled around the quadrangle barely skimming the ground, then rose in height until it was at the level of the window from which Emma was watching. It flapped past the window and as it did, the head swung round as if to look in. then it wheeled away again and rose into the darkness above, to disappear. Just then, there was a knock on the connecting door.

"The guys are back," Maggie said. She ran to the door and opened it.

Jeff stood beyond the doorway; looked at her in her robe-like night-gown. "Oops, sorry. We thought you'd still be up. Stupid."

In answer, she pulled the door further open. "No problem. We've been waiting for you to come back. What have you been doing?" She stepped back into the room, allowing Jeff and Milo to follow her.

Milo looked around, taking in the room's lavish furnishings. "This is nice. Even better than ours, eh Jeff?"

Jeff merely nodded and wandered over to sit by the fireside. Milo swaggered over to the window where Emma still sat, and struck a pose.

"*They seek him here; they seek him there; Those Frenchies seek him everywhere...*" he intoned in a drawling false accent.

"Dream on, Milo," Emma riposted in like tone. "You cut a fine figure, I trou', but a Sir Percy Blakeley - I do declare - you're not!" Turning away from him, she gestured out of the window towards the darkness of the courtyard below.

"Do you see that room opposite with the candle on the window-ledge?" she asked him. "That's part of the King's apartments. Look at the shadows. There's something going on, don't you think?"

"Nope." A typical Milo non-answer. But then when does Milo *ever* think? She uncoiled herself from the window-seat and crossed to the large open hearth fireplace where Maggie was talking quietly to Jeff.

"Right," Maggie said as Emma dropped onto a rug in front of the fire. "Tell all. Word for word; blow by blow. What happened after we left?"

Emma smiled. She knew how much it rankled with Maggie that they'd had to leave so early. She'd wanted to stay and get in on the conversation.

"Not really all that much," Jeff began. "The old boy – Lord Polon, the King's Chancellor – came back again soon after you left."

"And the atmosphere changed immediately!" Milo was at pains to put in. "He didn't stay for long, though. I feel quite sorry for Loren, you know. His father is so – pompous – so heavy… Ser Loren didn't really come alive until his father had left again."

Emma nodded. "Yes, I know what you mean. He seems to have the same effect on Serra Olivia too. She's like a little starling with all her chatter."

"She's just a child," Jeff commented.

"She's sixteen. Old enough to be married, she told us. I think she has her heart set on the Prince." Emma's voice was wistful. "Poor child."

"I don't think he's of the same mind," Maggie added. "After that little spiel at the beginning he hardly spoke to her all evening. He's a bit strange, isn't he? Always on the move, never still. And dressed all in black."

"He's in mourning for his father," Emma said. "Horatio worries about him." She put a finger to her mouth, as she did when deep in thought. "You know something? This all seems a bit peculiar, as if I've seen it all before. A bit like a *déjà vue.* It's unsettling."

Milo gave a hoot of laughter. "Horatio would probably say it was your *sensitivity.*"

"Where is he, anyway?" Emma was glad when Maggie asked the question. She'd tried to ignore her disappointment when she'd opened the connecting door and Horatio had not been standing there with the others. *But why should he?* she counter-argued with herself. *He is a Mage, for God's sake, and the Prince's Companion. He has a position to keep, and more important things to do than sit and chat with me, us.* She pulled her attention back to the conversation.

"We were in the middle of a game of cards when one of Horatio's men came and called him away," Milo was saying. "I had to throw in a winning hand!"

"Was this before or after the Prince left?"

"Some time afterwards. Why?" Jeff seemed to have finally found his voice.

"I don't know," Emma murmured. "It's just a feeling." She wandered over to the window and looked out, resisting the impulse to throw open the window and lean out searching for a lighted candle in the room *one floor below and two to the right…*

It was snowing again. Clouds covered the tiny moon and silvery-white snowflakes were falling from the inky blackness. Then her eye was caught by a movement on the parapet above the Prince's apartments in the central wing. Not a large white bird this time, she realised. A guard moved along the parapet, standing watch. Unaccountably, she shivered.

Chapter 8

From his shelter near the West Wall, Horatio watched the guard glance towards the guttering watch-fire and saw the fleeting hope of imminent relief briefly flare and then die in the young man's face. Midnight had struck and his watch was almost over. From unseen clouds high above the towers of Elasyn Castle icy wet snow continued to fall. As the cold wind swirled the snowflakes around the young guard, he looked around, and wretchedly tugged his woollen cloak more tightly around his body. Eventually, the guard stamped his numb feet, clutched his musket in one frozen fist, and turned to begin another circuit of the battlements. As he approached the south-west turret, he suddenly stopped, his musket raised.

"Halt!" he cried out. "Who's there?"

From behind his shield of invisibility, Horatio stretched out a minor probe to the guard. *Yes, Rolan truly believes in this story of a spectre. His heart was beating very rapidly, probably in fear of finding truth in the stories he had been told by other guards.* Then suddenly he went rigid, staring into the shadows near the south wing. Horatio could almost hear his thoughts. Holding his musket firm, the guard moved forward, one small halting step at a time. "Answer me! Make yourself known!"

"Long live the King!" a voice called. The guard stopped and sighed with relief when the figure materialised out of the gloom.

"Berren! What the Hell are you playing at, creeping up like that? And you're late too!"

"Sorry, Rolan. But I'm here now, and Gaston's on his way. You can get off to bed. I'll take over the watch now."

"Good luck. It is freezing cold and I am tired and fearful."

Horatio stepped forward out of his invisibility. "Fearful? Has it not been quiet then?"

Rolan drew himself up and saluted the Prince's Companion. "Very quiet, my Lord. Not a mouse stirring."

"Well goodnight then Rolan. Sleep well. I will remain here with Berren until Gaston comes."

"Thank you, sir. Goodnight." Rolan turned, heading back towards the watch-fire. "I see someone… Yes, here is Gaston now. But he is not alone. My Lord, he has Master Will with him." He stopped, waiting for the men to approach.

Berren called the challenge, and heard Gaston's calm voice. "'Tis I, Gaston, liegeman to the Prince."

"Come," Berren lowered his musket as the two came closer.

Horatio looked from the poet to the guard. "May I ask why Master Will is here?" he demanded.

Master Will Shaksper moved forward. Horatio noticed that the poet had acquired a fur-lined cloak from somewhere, and was wearing stout boots. "I was unaware that I would be unwelcome here, my Lord. I thought to share the guards' vigil this night. I too have heard the tales. Will you not give me leave to stay?"

Horatio regarded him silently. What exactly he had heard? He shrugged. What harm could he do?

"Very well, Will. You may remain if you wish." He turned to the guards. "Now tell me, you have heard the tales. Has the spectre already shown itself?"

Rolan stood to attention. "It's all been very quiet, my Lord Horatio. I have seen nothing."

Horatio drew his cloak around himself, and looked about, peering through the thickening whirling snow into the darkness. Behind the clouds the minor moon, Diminu, was hidden. The larger moon, Principa, would not rise for another hour or so. "And nor will you, I wager," he said. "There will be no spectre." He swivelled on his heel to face Gaston. "It was but a fantasy that you saw last night, I believe."

Affronted, Gaston drew himself up to his full height, his cloak swirling around his leather-bound legs. "Sir, I repeat to you only what I saw two nights ago and again last night. A spectre walked the battlements over there, by the south turret. A spirit in the form of the old King Hamnet. Twice I've seen it, and I tell no lies. I have no doubt that it will return!"

"Then we will wait," Horatio replied, "and speak with it!"

Rolan left and headed for the guards' barracks. Horatio and Will settled themselves by the fire, while the two guards began their first perimeter of the Castle Walls. After some time, Berren reappeared and stood by them at the guard-fire. Their talk was low-pitched, centred on the mysterious sightings of the Ghost.

Then there was a cry and Gaston materialised out of the gloom, his face pale and frightened.

They followed the direction of the soldier's outstretched arm, only to widen in fear and horror as shadows began to thicken, solidify and form into the form of a tall man, fully armoured with a closed helm. In its upraised hand it held a sword.

"It is like the dead King!" the fear in Gaston's voice was clear.

Then Berren's voice. "Speak to it my lord. You are a mage. It will listen to you."

"It looks so like the King. Look at it, my lord," Gaston repeated.

Horatio moved forward. Within him, fear warred with curiosity. "It *does* have a very good likeness to the old king, Gaston. I agree. So much so that it chills my blood, but I will talk to it." Horatio drew closer to the ghostly figure. "My Liege Lord," his voice was a mere whisper. "My Lord, why are you here? Have you come to warn us of something?"

The spectre lifted its hand and raised the helm. Now the face could be clearly seen as the empty gaze turned towards him. A dead voice spoke two words before the ghostly figure began to dissolve into shadows that quickly faded amidst the snowflakes. "Stay!" Horatio cried out, stepping forward and thrusting out a hand and writing a hurried sigil in the air. To no avail. "I charge you, Spirit! Stay and speak!" But it was futile. The spectre had gone.

Horatio turned back to the two guards. Their faces were ashen; no doubt his own was the same. He closed his eyes in an attempt to self-heal; to force his sluggish blood through his veins and counteract his feelings of shock, confusion and fear. He had been unable command the spectre. He had failed to retain it. His coercion had bounced off it, as if of no account.

Horatio staggered as he crossed the slippery flagstones to where the three men stood, white-faced and fearful. His heart pounded, as if making up for lost time. The spectre had recognised him as the life-long companion to his son – of this Horatio was certain.

"It spoke the Prince's name." He paused, gathering his wits and his tattered dignity and addressed the guards again. His voice grew stronger. "It was the spirit of the late King Hamnet! It wants to speak with the Prince. This does not bode well, my friends." He looked swiftly around. "Berren and Gaston – remain on watch. But keep quiet about what you have seen and heard here tonight."

With a subdued "Yes, my Lord Horatio," the two guards saluted and turned away to begin a perimeter patrol, peering over their shoulders as they went. Watching them leave, Horatio cast a small magic to reinforce the guards' resolve, and then turned to the poet.

"Master Will, come with me. I must convince Prince Hamnet that the spectre is real." Turning swiftly, the mage strode along the battlements to the stairwell leading down to the Prince's apartments, his cloak billowing behind him. As they clattered down the stone steps, Horatio heard Will's voice from behind him.

"Why not go to the King? Surely, my Lord, if the ghost wishes to impart something of importance, then it is the king who should be told?"

"It was Prince Hamnet's name it spoke, Will. The message in the first instance is for his ears."

He was not in his rooms. Where then? The main hall, perhaps? It was difficult to tell where the Prince might be. Horatio told Will to go to bed, and to keep quiet about what he'd seen. But the poet did not move. His face was still very pale. "Go to bed, Will," Horatio said as he laid a hand on the other's shoulder. "This charm will help you to sleep."

As the poet turned away, Horatio scryed the Castle in an attempt to find the Prince. Elasyn Castle was a warren of corridors and staircases, built up over several centuries. The mage stood still, letting his inner eye rove through the Castle. Eventually he found the personality signature he was searching for – Hamnet was in the King's anti-chamber. Horatio hurried downstairs.

As he stood outside the King's Apartments, Horatio could hear raised voices coming from within. One voice was raised in anger; another quiet, cold and clear; the third a quavering female voice. The King, the Prince and the frightened voice of the Queen. Horatio had heard these same arguments on other evenings, and was unwilling to listen again. There was nothing he could do to ease the pain Hamnet was suffering. The mage, suddenly aware of the implications of the news he had to impart to the Prince, walked slowly back to the Prince's apartments to wait for him there.

It was not a long wait. Less than ten minutes later, the door was thrust open, causing Horatio to leap up, sword in hand. The small book of poetry he had been idly flicking through fell with a dull thud on to the wooden floor. The candle flame at his elbow flickered, and then steadied once more. He looked at the figure standing before him dressed, as always, in black. Even down to the lace on the shirt under his velvet doublet. Hamnet's obvious mourning for his father was only one of the things that irked the new King.

As he came into the room, Hamnet, Prince of the Realm, smiled.

But it was a cold smile totally unlike the open and warm smile of his youth. Two long months had passed since the days when his eyes shone with humour and mischief. Now he wore a thin, humourless smile, and his eyes were cold. He was no longer a callow youth. Horatio, despite his four year seniority, sometimes felt that it was he who was the younger man.

"Horatio!" the Prince exclaimed as he moved forward. His walk was graceful, like a dancer. The two young men gripped arms, and then the Prince turned away to splash some wine into two cut-glass goblets. Returning to his friend's side, he handed him a goblet and dropped into a hearth-side chair. Horatio judged it best to let him speak first. He would then perhaps be in a better frame of mind for the news of the appearance of his dead father's spirit.

"Who won the card game? Was there a good wager? And our visitors – are they well? Where are they?"

"In bed and asleep, I assume. It is late."

"Late indeed, my friend. You missed a fair discussion tonight. Everyone was there. My kingly uncle, and my mother. Even the Lord Chancellor. Half of the Court, it seemed…"

"I'm sure it was one I will ever regret not hearing," Horatio replied in a dry voice.

"*Ever* or *never*, my good Horatio?" Hamnet gave a short bark of humourless laughter then became silent, turning the goblet in his hand as he swirled the dark liquid within it.

When he spoke again the venom in his voice was clear. "The *King* thinks I should put away my grief, Horatio. And my mother, my father's widow, agrees! But I cannot forget, Horatio, nor forgive. My father was in good health. He was not old, nor ill. Why did he die?" He slammed his goblet down hard on the table and the wine splashed like blood across the cloth. Horatio watched as his friend, face contorted with despair, stood up and moved to stand by the fireplace. His voice was quiet but full of emotion as he continued.

"I have to leave Elasyn, Horatio. I cannot stay here. Every time I look at him, sitting in my father's chair, wearing my father's crown… fawning…" his voice threatened to crack "…over my mother…" He spun round suddenly. "You of all people must see that I cannot stay longer. He stands there, for all the world looking and acting as a King, while below his charming demeanour he means to take from me even more than he already has." He paused and drew a finger through the spilled red wine. "He means me serious harm."

"You cannot truly believe that, Hamnet. You must be mistaken. You are his heir."

The Prince's eyes were like ice as he glared across the room at his old friend. It was as if Horatio was just another who hated him. "I was *my Father's heir*." His voice, though quiet, held tremendous pain.

Horatio knew there was never going to be a good time to tell him of the Ghost. Best to do it now. "I saw him tonight, Hamnet."

"Whom? The King? Well so did I."

"No, my friend. Tonight I saw your father."

"My father? Horatio, you have taken leave of your senses. Or is it that you have forgotten *my father is dead*? How could *you* see my father?" He snatched up the goblet and threw the remains of the wine down his throat.

"Tonight, on the battlements, and for the last two nights it seems, a ghostly apparition has been seen. Your father, the late King Hamnet."

"What? If this is a jest it is in the poorest of tastes!"

"I do not jest, Hamnet. I knew the late king and this ghostly figure was as like your father as my own reflection in a mirror is to me. Believe me, friend, it was your father's ghost!"

"Did you speak with him?"

"I tried. The only word it spoke before it faded away was your name."

Hamnet began a slow steady pacing, as in the past he had been apt to do when deep in thought. The other waited, a gentle hope kindling in his heart. This was more like the Prince of the past than he had seen for a long time. Calm pacing. None of the manic continuous movement; none of the brooding moodiness. For that Horatio was glad. But he feared what would happen when Hamnet met with the Spectre. That he would meet with it was certain. After some thought filled pacing, the Prince came back to his friend's side, asking for every detail.

Chapter 9

The morning after their arrival, Maggie woke vaguely aware of strange surroundings. As her memories returned, she turned to wake Emma, only to discover that she was alone in the big canopied bed. Snatching up a wrap that had been thoughtfully left by the bedside, she scrambled down from the big bed. The curtains were pulled back from the windows, revealing snow-laden window ledges and rooftops. Emma was nowhere to be found. Casting about for a clue as to where she'd gone, her eye fell on a sheet of vellum, not paper, lying on the small table near the door to the boys' room.

Good morning sleepyhead, the note read. *You were snoring, sorry, sleeping, so peacefully we didn't have the heart to wake you. We're having breakfast in the boys' room. Join us when you're human.* It was signed *'Emma'*

She opened the door and peered into the room beyond. Three heads turned in her direction. "Morning," she called out as she walked into the room tying her wrap more securely around her. "Why did you not wake me?" she asked. All of them were fully dressed and looked as if they'd finished breakfast some time ago. "What time is it?"

"Ten-thirty or eleven," Milo replied, "Something like that I suppose. We've been up and around for ages. This is a seriously cool Castle – and I do *not* mean the temperature." Emma stood up and came to her side, her long skirts rustling. She was wearing a full-skirted gown with a tightly fitting waistcoat thing over it.

"Ignore him Maggie. He's all fired up and ultra-enthusiastic about the place, and Horatio's been filling us in a bit more about what's happening. And to think *he,"* she pointed over her shoulder towards Milo, "was the one who thought the whole idea was crap!"

"I heard that," came the rejoinder. "But don't forget you were the one who freaked out – remember?"

The two girls linked arms and went through the connecting door to begin the dressing process. They'd discovered the previous evening that the privy was not as primitive as it could have been, but water for washing still had to be carried to their rooms. Between that and figuring out how to get the shift, gown and overskirt organised as a complete whole, the girls would be absent for some time.

Left alone with Milo, Jeff put his wine goblet down with a grimace. "Imagine drinking wine at this time in the morning! I don't think I've done that since someone suggested it as a hangover cure." He limped across the room to the windows, looked out. "What do you think about the set-up here, Milo?" he said over his shoulder. "Seems to me that it's not just a straight-forward accession situation. Horatio let something slip this morning while he was showing us around. Did you know that Prince Hamnet was the son of the old King? Surely he should've become king?"

"Maybe the King is elected, and not hereditary."

"True, maybe it is. But there's real animosity in the Prince's attitude to the King."

"Maybe he feels he's been overlooked."

"Something else. The old king and the new were brothers."

"So?"

Jeff turned round and glared at Milo. "Good God, man. How come you're so obtuse? Does it come naturally to you or are you deliberately trying to wind me up?" He paused, getting himself under control once more. "Think, man. Horatio's said nothing about any elections – only that after the old king died he was succeeded, not by his son, but by his brother. Usurpation, in other words. The new king has since married the widow of the old King – the Prince's mother, one assumes."

"Keeping it in the family?" Milo quipped.

"There's something that stinks to high Heaven here. Politically, it's a time bomb and we're in danger of being counted in with the supporters of the Prince."

"What you're saying, in your round-about manner is that this place could be a serious health hazard for us? You're getting paranoid in your old age, Jeffrey old boy. Anyway even if there was a schism, do you think the Prince could do anything? He's just a kid."

"Think about it Milo. His father has suddenly died. His uncle married his mother and took his throne. Would you not feel a bit pissed off?"

"All that about the King grabbing his throne – you don't *know* that."

"I'm telling you. This whole thing could just blow up like that! I think Emma's right. It all seems familiar somehow."

"Oh lighten up, Jeff. I'm getting seriously pissed off with all this garbage. Anyway, we're only here for a couple of days."

"That might be a couple of days too long."

"Let me remind you that you were the first to decide to come. What has happened to your high intentions of singing for royalty? You going to pack up and leave letting everyone down because something's given you the willies? I honestly thought you had more gumption than that, Jeff."

"It's a gut feeling."

"Oh yes, you're pulling out the 'sensitive' bit now. God, you make me laugh. Well, whether you decide to leave or not, I'm staying. I'm not letting these people down. And right now I'm going to the music room get some practice for the big do tomorrow." With that, Milo turned away and headed for the door.

Jeff turned back to the window, angry with himself as much as with Milo. Was he right? Was he seeing dangers that weren't there? He leaned his hands on the broad window sill, and looked out. Across the courtyard a movement caught his eye. Jeff's window on the second floor of this, the north wing of the Castle, looked out over a square courtyard. At each corner of the courtyard there were circular towers which housed the staircases. In the courtyard a single-storey building stood off-centre, slightly to the right as Jeff looked down. Snow coated the roof and was still falling. The movement that had attracted Jeff's attention was a cloaked figure which had just left the doorway of the south-eastern tower. It was making its way across the snow-covered courtyard to the building, but stopping and looking around in a very furtive manner. Jeff instinctively drew back from the window as the glance swept up in the direction of his window and when he looked back again, the figure had gone. He'd only caught a glimpse of the face beneath the cowl hood but it was not someone he recognised. He was about to leave the window when he realised what it was that he'd subconsciously recognised as peculiar.

The figure had left no footprints in the snow.

***

Jeff took no time to think about what he was about to do. He lurched across the room, wrenched open the door and turned right along the corridor to the spiral stone staircase leading down to the courtyard. There was a distinct chill emanating from the stone walls as he neared the foot of the stairwell, and Jeff momentarily considered returning for a cloak. Shaking his head, he continued down. The wooden door at the bottom opened easily, swinging outwards onto the tiny porch at the base of the north-east tower. Beyond the porch the white snow-covered courtyard lay pristine, pure. Surely *someone* must have used the courtyard this morning. He stepped out, shivering as the air's cold blast hit him. His velvet doublet, linen shirt and fine woollen trousers, warm enough for indoors, were totally inadequate in the near zero conditions outside. He soon bitterly regretted not going back for a warm cloak.

Hugging the stone walls of the courtyard, he moved as quickly as he could to the south-eastern tower entrance, wondering at the same time just why he was doing this. His left leg dragged through the snow, leaving a deep furrow. Reaching the tower's porch, he noted that the snow that had been blown onto the porch had been swept back by the door when it had been opened outwards. So someone had come through the door very recently. He looked again beyond the porch. Apart from his own ploughed progress alongside the wall there were no signs at all of footprints in the four-inch deep snow. He shivered, and thought about going across to the stone building in the centre of the courtyard, but thought the better of it.

What was he doing down here anyway? Probably it was one of the mages who didn't want his feet wet in the snow! But something was still bothering him. He pulled the edges of his woollen waistcoat more tightly around him and stepped out onto the snow, heading for the central building. As he came closer, he saw there were footprints in the snow leading from the entrance round the side of the building that led to the door to the north-west wing.

Thinking the better of what he was doing, he was on the point of turning back and retracing his steps when he discerned voices coming from the building's interior. He walked forward up the three stone steps and laid his hand on the iron ring door handle.

One of the voices he recognised as belonging to the Chancellor, Lord Polon. The one Milo had begun calling 'Pompus-Prat'. As it was not the Chancellor that Jeff had spotted making his way across the courtyard his must be the footprints Jeff had noticed. The other voice was totally unfamiliar, but as there were probably upwards of a hundred people in the Castle that did not mean very much. Jeff's curiosity was rekindled, and he edged forward to listen making sure his bad leg did not give him away.

"Of course my daughter is obedient!" Polon's voice was strident, angry. "She will do whatever it is that I command. But this suggestion of yours – it is against everything I have in mind for her. To refuse the Lord Hamnet's advances completely? You may regard me a romantic old fool if you wish sir but there can be no doubt that the Prince loves my daughter, and she him."

"So. You see yourself as father to the future Queen." The second voice was old and very cold. It reminded Jeff of the ancient emperor in the old *Star Wars* films. He shivered but he was not certain whether it was from cold or the mere sound of that voice.

"I look to her happiness."

"And *I* look to the Kingdom's future. To that end your daughter must refuse the Prince. You know that he has always been unstable and thus should be declared unfit to rule as King. His very natural grief for his dead father has unlocked the instability inherent in his psyche. Unfortunate perhaps, but true. He is liable to go quite mad in the future, maybe even in the near future. Is that what you want for Elsynvaal? Do you want a mad husband for your daughter? And what of her children? No. It would be best for your daughter to look elsewhere for her marriage bed."

"Yours?"

A cruel laugh sounded out. "Was that a jest, Chancellor? Rather unworthy of you, and this is neither the place nor the time for such. Instead let us turn to the other matter. I trust the crossing has succeeded?"

"It has, Lord. The plan has worked. Horatio returned with the four, including the one you require, without mishap."

"Good. You are sure he is completely ignorant of my plan?"

"Horatio knows nothing Lord. It is a pity we had to bring all four."

"I will find some use for the others."

My God! Jeff thought, aghast. *They're talking about us!!* As the cruel laugh sounded once more, realisation hit and Jeff decided it was time to leave, but his feet refused to respond to the commands his panicked brain was sending. He'd only managed to reach the bottom step when the door was suddenly wrenched open. Jeff spun round, in order to make it look that he was approaching the building, instead of leaving. The Lord Chancellor stood in the doorway, his small piggy eyes fixed on him. Jeff stood stock-still for several seconds before he realised that though the Chancellor was looking straight at him, his eyes were unfocused. He coughed discreetly. The Chancellor blinked, focused, and smiled his thin smile.

"Ah, young man. One of our visitors from across the void. Now, which one are you, may I ask?"

"Zimlinsky, sir. Jeff Zimlinsky."

"Come inside, then, Jeff Zimlinsky, do not hang around there in the cold. Perhaps you have a death wish to walk abroad in such thin attire. We must look after you! " Jeff found himself ushered back up the steps and into the building. Every word the chancellor said now took on a new meaning. *Which one of us is the 'one you required'? Is it me?*

He took a deep breath to try and combat the fear flowering within him of coming face to face with *Dead Voice*. Inside the room, he cautiously looked around. He was in a guard room. It was empty except for a few tables and benches, and several racks lining one wall held swords, pistols and other weapons. The room was completely empty of people except for himself and the Chancellor. No mage. No sign of *Dead Voice*. Jeff swiftly looked around the room for other exits. There were none; at least none that he could see. But when does a mage need doors?

***

By the time Jeff made it back up the stone staircase and reached his room, the others had returned. In the music-room Milo had found a beautiful lute inlaid with ivory and his delicate playing greeted Jeff as he crashed in to the apartment ready to start packing but Emma waved to him excitedly.

"Guess who Maggie just met in the corridor?"

Jeff said nothing. Instead he went to the fireplace and stood with his back to them.

Emma ignored his silence. "William Shakespeare. Remember? We saw him last night? We told you about it. You walked past him as you came back into the library."

Jeff still said nothing.

"Well, what do you think of it?" Maggie pushed for a response. "I was passing along the corridor near to the Prince's apartments when he came out of a room and walked straight towards me."

"And what do you think she did?" Emma added, "She dropped a book she was carrying and he lifted it up for her!"

"Oldest trick in the book!" Milo scoffed. "Some coincidence, Maggie. How long had you been walking the corridor before he appeared, eh?"

Emma walked over and shook Jeff's shoulder. "Are you listening, Jeff? Will Shakespeare – *the* William Shakespeare, the Bard, is here in Elsynvaal. Horatio crossed him over about six weeks ago."

Jeff shrugged Emma's hand off and turned his back on the fireplace. "I don't care who the hell he is. We need to talk." His voice was harsh. But the others were too wrapped up in their news to notice. But after a while, her words penetrated his mind. "William Shakespeare? Here?"

"It's true," Maggie said. "I spoke to him when he gave me the book back. Would you believe he was flirting with me?"

"Flirting?" There was a laugh in Milo's voice.

"Why are you so surprised, Master Milo? Shakespeare wrote the most beautiful love sonnets – well one day he will anyway!"

"So, what did he say to you, this *William Shakespeare*? Apart from love sonnets, that is."

Maggie gave a small smile. "Wouldn't you want to know, sweetie?"

"You didn't tell him who you were, did you?" Emma asked.

Maggie bridled a little. "No, of course not. Horatio warned us not to, didn't he?"

"If he is *the* Shakespeare, then I think that Horatio the Mage has made a big boo-boo." Jeff sat down on the wooden bench by the hearth and began easing his wet shoes off. "He should have kept him well away from us. In a place as big as this it should have been possible. If this is the authentic Bard, then goodness knows what damage even a short exchange of information could have. Maybe even serious repercussions, colouring his whole attitude towards his plays. We could get back to Glasgow and discover that half of the plays don't exist, or are different."

"The time travel paradox?" Maggie interjected.

"Well," Jeff went on, dumping his wet socks into the fireplace. "Just one more thing that convinces me we have to leave. A.S.A.P. We are in danger here."

From the window seat they heard Milo groaned loudly. "Still going on about that?"

Maggie ignored him. She was gazing at his bare feet, now white with cold. "What have you been up to, Jeff? Your feet are freezing and those socks and shoes are saturated." She wrinkled up her nose in disgust. Lifting the hearth fire-stick she pushed the offending objects as far away as possible.

"I went out to the guard room down in the courtyard. There's something really funny going on. I heard voices inside. Someone was ordering Lord Polon to force Olivia to turn down the attentions of the Prince, maintaining that he was mentally unstable."

"Rubbish!" Milo called out, striding over to them, lute in hand.

"You must have been mistaken," Maggie said.

"Wait a minute." Emma's voice was quiet. "Polon's going to order Olivia to break up with the Prince? Oh, oh. I'm having a severe feeling of *déjà-vue.* Remember what we were talking about this morning? About the Prince and his Uncle? Let's look at this."

She started counting off on her fingers. "We have the Bard, Master Will Shaksper. We have a newly deceased King, whose brother has taken over his nephew's rightful throne. We have a young and very unhappy Prince, who is just about to be ditched by the girl he loves on her father's command. All we need is the ghost and we have the first Act of Shakespeare's "*Hamlet*". Good God! Even the names are the same or similar."

"You're right, Emma." Maggie took up the litany. "Hamnet becomes Hamlet. Olivia becomes Ophelia. Okay, not so similar, I agree. But look at the others. Polon becomes Polonius; Loren becomes Laertes; Horatio stays Horatio; the King, Claude, becomes Claudius. It all fits."

"No ghost." Milo put in.

"Not yet." Maggie riposted.

"There's more." Jeff stated. "I heard them talking about us."

"What?"

"Ridiculous!"

"I'm serious," Jeff said. "One of us was brought here for a reason that has absolutely nothing to do with any state performance. And Polon is in on it. It's a part of some kind of a plan he and another mage have concocted."

"Horatio?" Emma's voice was quiet.

"Apparently not. Polon said that Horatio knows nothing about it, whatever it is. Some wizard. So much for his vow of protection!"

"Which one of us is it?" Maggie asked.

"I don't know. *'Four, including the one you require'* That's all they said."

"They said 'require'? What does that mean?"

"It means we have to get out of here. We have to find Horatio," Jeff stated. No-one argued with him this time. Quite apart from this latest piece of news, there were too many coincidences here to be ignored. They left their rooms and each took a separate route through the Castle, searching for the Mage.

Chapter 10

Emma found him standing alone on the northern battlements and staring out across the plain that stretched away north from the base of the Castle's escarpment. He was so wrapped up in his thoughts that even when she leaned against the parapet beside him, the mage failed to feel her presence. Gently she laid a hand on his arm and spoke his name. He spun round, saw her and smiled.

"Emma." Horatio gave a bow, glanced around for the others. No-one was within sight. "It's chilly out here." he went on. "Are you warm enough?"

"I'm fine Horatio. See, Olivia has given me a cloak." She ran her hand over the warm fur trim on the soft leather cloak she had slung around her shoulders. "I came looking for you."

"Oh yes? Well, here I am, lady. Found just as I was about to come back indoors. I think perhaps I have left the Prince alone too long. He is in a rather disturbed state."

"So it seemed last night. But will you not stay here for a while? I need to talk with you." He inclined his head and smiled. "You looked very thoughtful when I came over," she said. "Worried even. Is there any way I can help?"

Horatio turned fully towards her and took her hands in his. *It is a nice feeling,* he thought. *A welcome change from the brooding and depressing thoughts of ghostly haunting.* He tried to keep the heaviness out of his voice, but failed miserably. Emma frowned, an anxious look crossed her stunning face.

Instead, he smiled in an attempt to ease her anxiety. "I confess I am worried, but unfortunately it is not my tale to tell. But thank you for your concern. Now, was there a reason behind your search for me, or was it just a desire for my company?"

She laughed quietly, but there was a wistful look in her eyes. *Something has happened,* he realised. *But what?*

"The latter of course, my lord," she replied, giving a tiny curtsy. Obviously she was reluctant to add to his burden.

"Then I am all yours, my lady." Simultaneously they turned to lean against the battlements. The wind played with the girl's long hair, pulling and teasing it around her head. Horatio's hair shifted gently and flicked into his eyes. He brushed it away. Emma caught up her hair in one hand and began to pull it into a loose plait.

"Will you not leave it free?" His voice came out husky and he cleared his throat. Smiling, she turned her back to him and allowed him to loosen it again. As his fingers lingered on the nape of her neck, he heard her breath catch in her throat, and his own breathing quickened. He touched her neck lightly, caressingly, but after a moment, dropped his hand once more and turned to lean on the parapet once more. *I must not let this get in the way!* he thought as he turned his gaze away to the far north once more.

"Tell me about yourself, Horatio, and about Elsynvaal." She was leaning on the parapet, her cloak-covered elbow inches from his.

"Where shall I begin, lady? What do you want to know?"

"Were you born in Elasyn? Are your family here?"

The mage turned to her and placing his hand gently beneath her chin, eased her face up so that their eyes met. "No, lady. I am not Elsynese by birth. I am Saralese. I was born on the fair Island Princedom of Saravaal, which lies to the south of Elsynvaal, across the southern sea."

"Well then, good sir. Tell me of fair Saravaal."

"Ha. That is the kind of story to tell over a flagon or two of good red wine with a bright fire burning in the hearth. But I shall tell you a little." He paused for a moment, as memories flooded into his mind. Selecting a few to give her was difficult. He turned round to face the south, gazing in the direction in which Saravaal lay.

"Saravaal is indeed a fair land. For one thing, the climate is much kinder. We have very little snow, ever!" He kicked sluggishly at the damp slushy snow around their feet and grimaced.

"Is Saravaal very far to the south?"

"No, not at all. With good wind behind you it's only a day's sail from Avendon on the south coast."

"But for the climate to be so different... "

"Ah. That's because Saravaal is a volcanic island – the largest of a chain of islands curving south away from Elsynvaal." His hand rose and swept in a curve, and an illusionary picture formed in the air in front of them. It was an island the shape an elongated tear-drop.

"Saravaal."

She laughed and reached up to touch the picture. Her hand passed through it without disturbing the image. He smiled and ran his finger down the ridge of mountains that split the island in two.

"That ridge is a actually a series of ancient volcanoes. None has erupted in centuries, but the magma is still there just below the

102

surface. The warmth seeps up through the rock and warms the soil. Add in the ancient volcanic soil, and you have a very fertile island. There are also several hot springs and an occasional geyser. And in the larger towns, we harness the heat for warmth in the winter."

"Central heating?"

"Of a sort."

"But don't you worry about your family living in the shadow of a volcano?"

Horatio laughed. "No more than is usual."

"Do you monitor the volcanoes?"

"The Prince employs volcano-watchers who monitor any volcanic activity. Of course every so often there are scare-mongers who forecast a massive eruption, but in the main we Saralese are happy enough to revel in our mild climate. You would like it, Emma. Perhaps I will take you there one day?"

Emma looked up at him. Her eyes were sad. But before he could say anything, she spoke. "Go on," she said. "Tell me more of Saravaal."

He gazed off into the distance, a smile on his lips. "On the talMerios Estate, we grow grapes. Acres of vineyards stretching as far as you can see, with the most succulent grapes you've ever tasted. Most of which are not destined for eating, but for the wine presses. We make vintage Saralese Brandy. The finest brandy in the world. So, as a child my playgrounds were the vineyards and the barns and the wine presses in the autumn and the dim cellars where the brandy matured."

"So you were brought up in the country?"

"Only partly. My father is often called to Court in Saraton. My brother and I often went with him. He wanted us to learn the ways of the Court."

"What did you do at Court?"

"We learned sword-play and archery and the use of pistols, and watched from the side-lines as the swords-master fenced with Prince-Elect Torven. The Prince-Elect is an excellent swordsman and sparred daily. My friends and I used to watch them, peering over the balcony down into the courtyard. Cymon, my brother, was pretty good with a sword. Gave Torven a run for his money, too, even though he was several years younger!"

He paused for a moment, lost in memory.

"What's your brother doing now?"

"He died. An accident when he was sixteen. I was thirteen, and already in training as a mage." Horatio looked off into the distance. "It was a long time ago." Then with a flick of his wrist, the island illusion faded and disappeared. He ran a hand over his face and rubbed his chin. "I need a shave," he said inconsequentially.

She lifted her hand and drew it gently across the stubble. "Yes, I think you do. But later. Go on. Tell me how you become a mage."

He took her hand once more and leaned back against the stone parapet. "By the time I was nine years old it was clear that I was mage-born. But magery was at that time outlawed on Saravaal."

"Why is that?"

"It's all to do with a powerful mage called Gheron talEbol, who went off the rails. It's a long story, and one best forgotten. But the Prince expelled him from his land, and banned the use of magic. So when I was twelve and decided that I would follow my ambition and become a mage, I left Saravaal and came to Elsynvaal. I was apprenticed to the Master-Mage Deveron di'Caledon."

"So you're not able to practice magic when you are at home?"

He shrugged. "I can now. Torven repealed the Anti-Mage law a few years ago. I don't know why. After my father dies, I will take over the running of the Estate."

"Tell me about your training."

"Part of my time I spent here in Elasyn as Prince Hamnet's companion and the rest of my time was spent in Deveron's Tower." He gave a small laugh. "Deveron is the most crazy old man you'll ever meet. He lived in a tower that is built of stone and mortar, but houses a thousand and one illusions." Horatio paused, momentarily lost in memory. A smile curved his lips upwards and his eyes crinkled up.

"My room looked out across the plain and I could watch the grasses change colour as the seasons changed. Picture it, Emma. From a distance, the Tower is stark and forbidding. It stands alone on a broad plain, a finger pointing to the heavens. Some say that the god himself raised it, but the feeling among the apprentices is that Deveron built it as a gesture of defiance at the god's interference in the world. It certainly looks like he's *giving the finger,* to use a phrase of Milo's."

Emma laughed. "The things you've picked up from Milo!"

The mage grinned back. "His 'cesspit of a mind' you called it the other day!"

"You think a lot of Deveron."

Horatio sobered up, but his eyes were still bright. "Indeed I do.

He was my mentor, my teacher, and my friend for many of my formative years. Last year he took up the staff of the Antriantara, and became leader of the Wizards' Council. I don't think he likes the position much. There are too many people in Rowlan Gayts, where the Council sits."

"When did you leave the Tower?"

"Four years ago, when I was twenty. I spent my last two years in Rowlan Gayts, as an apprentice in Mage Hall. Finally I took my vows as a Mage of Elsynvaal before the full Council of Wizards."

"So it's like getting a degree in my world," Emma mused.

"Yes, but I still have much to learn. Learning magic is one of those situations where knowledge gained is inversely proportional to the knowledge not yet acquired, if you catch my meaning. Sometimes I think I should not have beaten Deveron in that final game of *Mozzaea* and stayed on with him longer!"

"So it's a case of '*The more you know, the less you know*'?"

He laughed again. "Indeed, lady."

"I like it when you call me that." Horatio's arms snaked round her, drawing her round to stand in front of him. The back of her head rested against his chest, while he rested his chin on the top of her head breathing in the sweet smell of her hair. They stood together, content and quiet for a few moments looking out over the town, until Emma heaved a sigh, and Horatio knew that she was ready to tell him the real reason for searching him out.

"I'm glad I came to Elsynvaal, Horatio."

"But?"

A smile flickered, died. "But there's something that is worrying us."

Us? he thought.

"What's that?" His voice was muffled for his lips lay lightly on her hair.

She said, "After you return Master Will to his own time in Elizabethan England he will write a play entitled '*Hamlet*'."

"Hamnet?"

"No. Ham-*let*. But good, you see the similarity."

"What are you talking about, Emma?"

She twisted round and looked up into his face. "We think that the play will be based on events happening here and now in Elsynvaal. I've read 'Hamlet', and seen it performed, Horatio. It begins with the death of King Hamlet of Denmark, and the return of his son from university. Only the Prince discovers that his uncle has married his mother and become king in his stead."

Horatio gripped her arms and looked down at her, his eyes narrowing. "This is too poor a jest, Emma."

"No jest, Horatio. All of the play's names are very similar to real people here – Hamlet the Prince, Claudius his uncle, Polonius is the Chancellor, Ophelia and Laertes are Polonius's son and daughter. There even is a Horatio, the Prince's friend from university. Even the name *Elsynvaal* is similar to Shakespeare's *Elsinore.* Don't you see the similarities?"

Horatio dropped his hands. "Okay, that's fine. So Master Will uses Hamnet's disinheritance as the basis of a play. What's wrong in that? He changes the names. No doubt many writers use real events as the basis of plays and novels."

"Horatio, you don't understand. In the play Hamlet is visited by the ghost of his dead father and…"

"What?"

"His father's ghost appears and tells Hamlet that he was murdered by his brother. What's wrong, Horatio? Are you all right? You're very pale."

He turned away from her. His heart thumped against his breastbone. An intense feeling of foreboding flooded through him.

"The apparition," he murmured. "It appeared last night."

"Last night. Oh my God. This is worse than we thought. Tell me what happened."

"I was called away from the card game by one of the guards on watch. After speaking with them I came up here and saw the King's Spirit myself. Over there," he turned back and pointed towards the south turret. "I tried my utmost to bind it, but it faded and disappeared."

"It wants to speak with its son." Emma's voice was flat.

"Yes. Prince Hamnet means to speak with it tonight."

"Oh!"

Emma glanced round. The soldier on guard had now come round to their side of the castle battlements, but was still too far away to overhear them. "Horatio, you must do something to stop this train of events. Otherwise there will be tragic consequences."

But Horatio did not hear her. His thoughts were travelling along another line.

"So you think that because Will's play character king was murdered, that King Hamnet was? No, I cannot go along with that. The King died of natural causes. I am sorry Emma, but I cannot put that much belief in your theory. So let us just wait and see what happens tonight, okay?"

He gathered her hair in one hand and used it to ease her towards him. "Don't be so downhearted, Emma. It may be that nothing will happen. The Prince will speak to the ghost, perhaps, if it appears, but nothing else. Do not fear."

Emma pushed his hand away and began to plait her hair. "Please listen to me Horatio. Don't brush it away as a silly notion. If Will wrote from real events, then this castle is destined only for bereavement and sorrow. For in William Shakespeare's play, by the end of the last Act, *all the main characters are dead* – characters based on the Prince, Lord Polon, the King, the Queen, Lady Olivia and her brother. All of them – *dead. Only Horatio survives."*

Horatio could not stop himself. He laughed. "Well, I always knew I was a survivor. But, think about it, Emma. The whole of the Royal Family wiped out in one fell swoop? It's ridiculous."

She stood in front of him, hands on hips and glared at him. "Do not mock me. Once you described me as a 'sensitive'. Surely because of that *sensitivity* you should at least *listen*!"

"The kitten has claws, I see. Well what if I should take Will back now? If he leaves now, then what he writes *has to be based on invention*. He can kill off as many people as he pleases. You could even give him the plot and send him home to write it!"

"I wish you would take this seriously."

"Believe me, I am. But there's nothing we can do about it. Either Will uses his imagination or real events. At this stage of the game, we cannot tell. If I send Will back too early, things could be changed. In your history, how long was he away?"

Emma frowned in thought. "I don't know," she eventually said. "Maggie is the Shakespeare scholar. She'll know."

"Okay. When was the play written?"

"I think '*Hamlet'* was first performed around 1601."

"And in Will's world it is presently 1589, or maybe 1590 by now. So Will does not write the play until nearly twelve years have passed. Which is about…" He stopped and mumbled as he did time conversions in his head. "About 8 years here. And that's if I keep to the continuum."

Emma grabbed his hands to catch his attention. "There is some evidence that he was working on a version of '*Hamlet'* in 1594 or even earlier."

Horatio lapsed into a dark silence, but remained very aware of

Emma's continued scrutiny. She had not finished yet.

Then she came close to him and folded his arms around her as if looking for reassurance. "There's more," she said.

Horatio felt uneasy. He bolstered himself with a light *heal*.

"I'm afraid of what it means. I came looking for you because Jeff overheard Lord Polon and someone else talking." She paused, suddenly reluctant.

"What is it?"

She looked up at him. "Polon used you to bring us over for reasons other than the Coronation celebration."

"What?"

She told him of Jeff's discovery. Horatio frowned, puzzled.

"Was he sure the other was a mage?" he asked.

"Yes."

Polon and he were the only mages in Elasyn Castle at the moment. An icy wave flooded over him as he remembered Deveron's warning. *Be vigilant. Watch for a disguised aura.*

He tore his thoughts back to Emma. She was still speaking. "…not only Jeff who wants to leave. So does Maggie. I'm not sure about Milo – but if they go he will go too. They want you to send us back now."

"What about you? Do you want to return too?"

She moved away a little so their bodies were no longer touching. "I don't know," she murmured. He had to strain to make out her words. "On my way up here, I began to wonder if it is me they are after. If it is then I ought to go. After all, if it wasn't for me none of us would be here? Would we? And now… being here with you… I don't want to leave, Horatio."

He took her small hands in his and looked into her deep dark eyes. "If you are in danger here then you *must* leave. You cannot stay here with me, not even for a short time. Just remember the tie between us. Remember, Emma. Without pre-knowledge we called to one another. And we will do it again. If what Jeff heard is true, you have to go home as soon as I can set it up. When it is safe I will come for you – if you want me to."

"You promise?"

He bent over and kissed each of her palms in turn. They were icy cold. "I promise."

He looked around and noted the guard walking in their direction. "Let us go back inside now and get warmed up. I want to talk to Jeff."

Hand in hand, and oblivious to the guard's eyes watching, they crossed the wet flagstones to the tower casement. As they started down the steps, a large white hawk squawked loudly and took flight northwards.

Chapter 11

They went to the suite turned over to the other-worlders. Empty. Horatio stood in the centre of the room, closed his eyes and sent a mental probe through the Castle, searching for the auras of the missing three. "Maggie is in the Hall. Jeff is in the Prince's library and Milo is... outside in the stables? I will send for them. We'll go to my rooms and await them there."

Both were silent as they walked downstairs. Horatio's rooms had a similar outlook to Emma's own, but the decor was much more austere. While he instructed a manservant on where to locate the others, Emma wandered round the main room. One wall was lined from floor to ceiling with books of all kinds. A desk sat at an angle to the window and on it lay writing implements and several picture frames.

Horatio watched her as she Emma strolled over and looked at them. "Photographs?" she asked. "No, not photos," she went on, in effect answering herself. "They're drawings or artwork, aren't they? Very similar to photos, but the backgrounds are vague – barely hinted at." She lifted each of the frames in turn. Horatio came round the desk to stand beside her and she looked up at him.

"They're pictographs."

"How do you do them? They're very good, almost like photographs. You don't have photography here, do you?"

"No. We use these instead. Thought pictographs can only be drawn by a mage. Some mages make quite a living out of them. I am not a particularly good artist, so the results are short on fine detail. These portraits are the nearest to real creativity I think I will ever reach." He picked up the pictograph of the stone-built manor house. "This is the talMerios' home on Saravaal. And these," his hand swept over the other portraits, "my family. My mother, my father, my sister... and my brother Cymon as I remember him."

Emma picked up the last picture and looked carefully at it. "It's not as clear as the others."

"It was done from memory several years after he died. Hence its haziness."

"And this one? The girl on the horse?"

"I drew that from my dreams before I came to your world."

"Oh," she said. She studied the drawing. Horatio reflected that it was not a good likeness, not now that the real Emma was here in front of him. It did her no justice. He told her so. She smiled and laid the picture frame down, colour rising in her cheeks.

There was a knock and the door opened with a thud as a man servant showed Milo in. The manservant bowed to them. "The lady and the other gentleman will be here shortly, my lord," he reported.

"Very good, Silas. Please have some food sent up for us. We will eat here."

The man sketched a bow and turned to leave. Emma turned round to find Milo doing what could only be called a recce of the room. "Making out an inventory?" she called to him as he stopped beside a rack of foils and swords. He ignored her gentle jibe. Instead, he reached out a hand and ran a finger over the hilt of a duelling rapier.

"May I?" he asked his host.

"By all means, Milo," the other said. "That is a favourite of mine. It is very well balanced." He watched as Milo carefully unsheathed the blade, swung and feinted through a few moves. Smiling, the mage lifted a second blade and took up a stance. "Ho!" he cried, whipping the thin blade around in a tight arc.

"En garde!" Milo responded, and the two blades met with a metallic clink. They circled one another, smiling as they took one another's measure. Then Horatio moved. Milo parried and returned with a fine thrust, which was turned easily. Both grinning, they circled and feinted and thrust and riposted.

Then Milo lunged low, aiming for his opponent's unprotected left side. A parry caught the point and carried the blade out of range, but not far enough for Horatio to be out of danger. Milo's sword continued on its swing round the outside of his blade, leaving him dangerously vulnerable for a second, before curving round to stop, perfectly motionless, at the mage's throat. Horatio dropped his sword in surrender.

"I salute you, Milo Diaz. You are at home with a sword, I see. What other talents are hidden beneath that imperturbable exterior, I wonder?"

"It was a lucky stroke, Horatio. I took you by surprise. That's all. No doubt you'll give me a good thrashing the next time!"

"We will have to make sure there is a next time, then! Where did you learn?"

"At school initially, then at fifteen I moved on to an amateur club. My swords-master once told me I could reach national or even international level, but I let it slip when I started at University. Now I only fence as a workout and occasionally for pleasure."

They sheathed the rapiers and sat down beside Emma who was looking strangely at Milo. "You're a dark horse, Diaz!" she said. "You've never let on you were that good!"

Milo shrugged, and turned towards the door as Jeff and Maggie came in, followed by Silas and a second servant carrying a tray piled high with food. Silence fell as the food was laid out in an impromptu buffet and wine was poured. Finally the two servants gave a small bow and left the room.

"Come, all of you, eat. Then we will talk."

Minutes later they were sitting down, full plates in front of them, and Horatio listened carefully as Jeff described his run-in with the Lord Polon – both concerning Serra Olivia and the '*One that was required*'. Hearing the description of the cold voiced mage, Horatio's mind winged back once more to Deveron's warning. But how does one search for a mage with no signature? Jeff was the only one who had seen this mage or heard his cold voice. No signature. Horatio's unease grew.

He closed his eyes and sent a mental probe through the castle, searching for a Mage signature or aura. Nothing. Despite Deveron's warning, Horatio had remained sceptical, unwilling to believe that a mage could negate his or her aura and signature. After all, mage accountability was one of the base tenets of wizardry. But now...

The only logical explanation was that the mage had left the vicinity and was outside the reach of the probe. He extended his search further afield, through the town and the partially snow-covered grasslands to the north. He sought out the scrubland and mountains that formed the border with Elsynvaal's neighbour, Cheam. He searched the hills to the west. Nothing. Pulling on more reserves, he scanned both the interior wastelands and the cultivated land to the south of Elasyn. The only auras he found were those winding their way to Elasyn for the celebrations, Deveron's aura bright among them. Nothing more.

He opened his eyes. Four pairs of eyes watched him intently, some anxious, some curious. He smiled ruefully as he read the expressions on their faces. "Sorry, friends. I should have told you what I was doing."

"What were you doing?" Emma asked in a small voice.

"Mind travelling. Searching for the mage who spoke with Polon.

Unfortunately I can find no trace of him. Polon is with the King, but his is the only magical aura I can find."

"What does that mean?" Jeff asked.

"It means that if this mysterious mage is still in the vicinity we are all in deep trouble, and you must all go back home as soon as I can send you."

Horatio rose abruptly and went to his desk. Snatching up a writing implement and a sheet of parchment, he began calculations on the time differential between Elasyn and Earth. Emma watched closely as the paper was swiftly covered with mathematical equations and differentials. Then he dropped the pencil and asked what Mhari was likely to be doing at three a.m. on a Friday morning. "Sleeping!" Maggie replied.

"She's not likely to be receptive right now then."

"Can't you get into her dreams?" Milo asked.

"No. I cannot."

"So it only works with Emma, does it?"

Horatio glanced at Emma, then back to Milo, his normal equanimity suddenly shaken. He did not like the thought that had just come to mind. "It would seem so," he told him. "What would be the best time to try to contact Mhari?"

"Evening time, I suppose," replied Maggie.

"Then we will have to wait until early evening, Earth time, which will be about two hours after midnight Elasyn time." He paused, suddenly thinking of a problem. "You should know that I would not be able to cross with you. You will have to do it alone. If Polon is up to something with this mysterious mage, he cannot be trusted to act as anchor. In fact he might even prevent a link."

"What do we do till then?"

"You stay together. Go nowhere on your own. No, not even to the privy."

"We could go to the music room and practice," Emma suggested.

"What's the use of that? We're not going to be here for the performance," retorted Jeff.

"We could ride!" Milo smiled his pleasure. "I know that all of us can ride and there are some gorgeous horses in the stables champing at the bit for a gallop – or at least a canter."

Niggling thoughts held Horatio back: *Should I allow this? But if I did, should I go with them? I can't risk letting them go alone. But what of the Prince and my duties here?*

Emma's voice broke into his thoughts, and he remembered the dreams. "You will take us riding, won't you, Horatio?" she said and the decision was made. After all, this could be the only chance he and Emma would have of fulfilling their shared dream of riding out across the grasslands.

Horatio smiled, then stood up and went to the window. The temperature must have risen slightly, for the snowfall had turned to rain. "We'll wait till the rain stops," he told them.

Emma's eyes shone as they met the mage's. Both smiled. This was what they had dreamed of, indeed.

Over the top of Emma's head Horatio caught Jeff's frown, and realised that he had caught the look of complicity passing between the mage and his best friend's girl. The next instant however, Jeff's frown had disappeared and he smiled his crooked grin. "I'll need some help getting on a horse," he said, "but I'll be fine after that."

Horatio looked at him closely, and gently asked him what had caused his injury.

"Car crash," Jeff's voice was flat, shorn of any passion. "The car burst into flames. My face and right side was burned and my left leg crushed. They tried grafts and rehabilitation, but..." His voice faded away to nothing.

Horatio said quietly, "I may be able to help with some of the damage. If you would like me to try, that is. It might be possible at least to ease some of the pain and discomfort from the knee and hip."

Jeff sat very still. The Elsynese Mage and the engineering student watched one another, each weighing up the other. Then hope suddenly flared in Jeff's eyes – hope of a normal life, and Horatio knew why Jeff had been so keen on crossing to Elsynvaal, to a land ruled by magic. He was looking for a cure, but was too proud to ask outright for help. Now he sat there, immobile but with blazing eyes, as the offer of help was made. Slowly, his eyes never leaving the mage's face, he nodded.

***

Milo led the girls downstairs to the north courtyard where the stables stood, while back in the room, Horatio listened as Jeff bared his soul and his injuries.

"It happened during the winter seven and a half years ago. The roads were dodgy with ice. My brother's birthday treat was to meet up with some friends and I had a football game to play in. I persuaded Mum and Dad to drop me off at the football ground on the way because of the weather. I usually walked to the ground, you see. It was only a slight detour so they agreed. Mum started worrying about how I'd get home if the match was cancelled, and Dad and I were tying to convince her I'd be fine. Then the car hit black ice and went into a spin. It was like the whole thing was happening in slow motion. The car spun hopelessly as Dad tried to regain control. Then there was a dreadful scrunching sound and I remember nothing more until I woke up in a hospital bed, with bandages covering half of my body... I had been unconscious for over two weeks. My parents and brother had already been buried. The doctors had thought I was going to join them too. But I pulled through. No-one knows what it was that caused the fire."

"How did you escape?"

"It seems that someone pulled me out, but my mother's front seat had been driven hard back against my leg and that's when my hip got damaged."

"Let me see what I can do for you," the mage suggested.

"I'm game."

Chapter 12

The rain had melted much of the previous night's snow, and green grasslands lay stretched out before them as they rode. At first Emma, looking dubiously at the uneven ground, had wanted to take the ride at a steady trot. But Horatio assured her that the ground was fine for letting the horses have their heads. He watched her as she leaned over her horse's head and whispered in his ear. Then she shouted aloud and urged the willing horse into a canter and then a full gallop.

Soon Horatio and his black-haired beauty were far away in front, exhilaration and adrenaline coursing through his veins. It was just like his dreams, yet different. She was actually here, with him, galloping flat out across the open grasslands, free and untrammelled, her hair now blown and weaving in the wind.

"My hair's going to be a tangled mess of knots when we return," she shouted across to him. "But what the hell?" She smiled across the distance between them and he grinned back.

Then she reined in slightly and pointed towards the north-west horizon where the grasslands gave way to the Northern Forest.

"What's that building over there?" she called, pointing to old Jarek's cabin, standing alone and desolate against the backdrop of ancient trees.

"A broken-down hut by now, I would guess," he responded, slowing his horse to keep pace with hers. "Hamnet and I used to escape from the Castle sometimes and come here. It belonged to an old Castle retainer, who took his pension and came here to live. He snared rabbits and so on for food. He died some years ago and the place has been empty since. It's years since I've been here – probably it's falling down by now."

"Can we go and see it?"

He shrugged. "If you want to. There's a well round to the side that had good water. We could slake our thirst there."

"Won't it be frozen over?"

He laughed. "If it is, then I'll melt it!" They slowed the hard breathing horses to a walk, and turned round in their saddles to wait for the others to catch up.

Far to the south they could see the towers of Elasyn Castle, a clump of darkness on the horizon. Over to the west the horizon was a pale shadow stretching to the Western Sea, while to the east the dark and forbidding outline of mountains rose from the plain.

"That's the border with Cheam," he told her when she asked, "a land whose rulers have in the past coveted Elsynvaal's fertile plains. Luckily we are at peace for the moment." Emma frowned but Horatio did not allow her to ask any questions and swept on in his description. No politics, he thought.

Emma turned back to look at the hut. "What lies beyond the trees?"

"Beyond the Northern Forest? Not much. The land changes to tundra and then in the far north the ice fields begin. I've never been through the Forest. It's not something that's encouraged." At Emma's silent query, Horatio's eyes narrowed as he gazed northwards. "The Forest belongs to the Northern Sylvan."

"Who are they?"

"A people whose ancestors came to Elsynvaal many hundreds of years ago. They too have magic, but it is different from Elsynese magic, so most people fear them. But as they rarely mix with us, the question rarely comes up. You do get the occasional Sylvan who leaves the Forest and lives among humans, but they're very much the exception."

"Do they look like us – I mean normal?"

"Oh yes. A bit smaller in stature, and their eyes are not a constant colour."

"You mean they change colour?"

"Yes. The colour is tied in with their emotional level. One of the Sylvan is performing at the Coronation festivities. Alain tirNorest is a Sylvan bard. He's a very interesting fellow."

"I'm sorry I won't be able to meet him. It might have been interesting," she said, but he could hear the doubt in her voice. She turned her horse away and looked south again. "The others are coming."

Horatio turned and looked. The others had slowed down, walking their horses and taking their time. He lapsed into silence, gently stroking his mount's silky mane. He felt her watching him.

"What's up?" she asked.

"Emma, is this how you dreamed it?"

"In some ways, yes. In my dreams it was summer, and the grasses were laced with colourful wild flowers. And there was a warm wind – not this icy blast." She gave a shiver and glanced at him. "Why do you ask, Horatio?"

"I've been thinking about something that's puzzled me since Milo's comment about trying to contact Mhari through her dreams. How is it that we achieved our dream-connection? It must have been done *totally unconsciously*. But how?"

"What are you saying, Horatio?"

"We did not know of the other's existence, so how could either of us have sent the dreams to the other? How could you visualise Elsynese locations when you've never been here before and send them to me?"

He stopped, frowning as something new occurred to him. "It is very puzzling," he said, his voice slow and reflective. "It is almost as if the dreams were sent as bait for us to find one another."

"Now hang on. Are you saying that someone invaded our sleeping minds and planted dream sequences? Can that be done?"

"Probably. All I know is that I found you because of the dreams, and…" He stopped, remembering Jeff's words.

She remembered too. "Someone *required one of us…* to come here. It's *me*, isn't it? It's me they want. Why?"

"I don't know. But this makes it all the more important that you cross back home tonight."

"If this is true, then what of those things you said earlier up on the battlements, about being able to contact one another if I went home?"

"Emma. This does not change anything about how I feel for you. Do you remember the instant recognition in Mhari's attic after my crossing? That would have happened, dreams or no dreams. What I feel for you is real - and will endure. I know it! This is all speculation. Even if it's true - if someone else sent the dreams… we *will* be able to contact one another. Maybe not in our dreams, but I know that I can reach you now. I will find you no matter which world you are on."

"But how can we be sure that what we feel is true and not induced, like the dreams?"

"*I* know, Emma. I am aware of magic in the air. It has a tang, a vibrancy - as if the very air is tingling and singing. I know when it is working around or in me. That's why I have been so slow in picking up on the dreams – I could *detect no magic.*" His voice slowed as he said the words, and a chill shivered through him. With horror he recalled his train of thought in the Castle only a few hours ago, while he searched and failed to find a mage's aura.

"What's wrong?" Emma had moved her horse close to Horatio's and was leaning over, scrutinising his face. "You've thought of something."

"Look at me, Emma. Even without being able to read my mind, you should be able to see that what I feel for you is real. Your perception and sensitivity should tell you it's true. But, do you feel the same?"

She looked away, gazing off into the far distance. One of the others was waving. She raised her hand and waved back. Her voice was very quiet when she replied, causing a small lump of ice to begin to grow within Horatio's chest.

"I do feel very attracted to you, Horatio, but I hardly know you," she began, "or who you really are. I don't know what you like doing, what you do to relax, or what you're like when you're upset or angry. A week ago we had not even met. After today I'll no longer even be in your world. And now it appears that the dreams – the bond I thought existed between us is not of our making, after all." She paused and turned back to him. "I think I believed in the dreams, Horatio."

"More than you believe in me?"

She spun back to face him. "What future can we have? Tell me that. I have to go back to my world because it's too dangerous for me here."

"I'll come for you later when all of this is over."

"Look at it realistically. We come from different worlds. Literally. Even time runs differently. A year here is what… twenty months in my time? How can we have a relationship on those terms?"

"Time is not linear," he said.

"I don't know what you mean by that."

He glanced towards Jeff, Maggie and Milo. They were much closer now. *This is the wrong time for such a conversation,* he thought.

"I believe in what we *might* have had," she went on, and each word ripped into him. "I admit that I'm attracted to you. I feel more for you than I've ever felt for anyone, even Martin. These few days have been wonderful and I dread to think what life will be like back home without you. Will it all seem like just another dream? Would anyone even believe me if I tried to talk to them about you – a mage from another world? Probably not." She gathered up her reins. Milo, slightly ahead of the other two, was almost upon them.

"Emma – I... "

But the others were now in earshot. Horatio bit off what he was about to say as the girl of his dreams wheeled her horse, joined her friend and rode away from him towards old Jarek's cabin on the edge of the forest. The mage turned his horse, following. Then to his surprise, Jeff walked his horse up alongside him.

"How is the leg bearing up?" *Safe question. Parry Jeff's own.*

"Not too bad," Jeff answered. "I want to ask you, Horatio – do you really think you or some of the other wizards could fix me up properly?"

"As I said back at the castle, there's a strong possibility we could do something. But you are all going back tonight..."

"If I stayed... what would be possible?"

"What of the danger?"

"I do not think somehow that I am the one that was 'required'. Do you?"

"We don't know who it is that they need, or why. It might be any of you. But you were the first to decide to come to Elsynvaal, if what Emma told me is true. And I'm inclined to believe too that you persuaded Milo to come, and Maggie. But you were also the one who first advocated leaving as soon as possible."

"That's as maybe. But now I want to stay."

Suddenly the tension that had been building up in Horatio all day exploded. "What is it that is getting you?" he rounded on the unsuspecting Jeff. "Is it that you just can't stick with it? You persuaded the others to come to Elsynvaal on the small chance that your damaged body might be healed. Do you feel hard-done-by because of the accident? Do you think that getting your body back whole will make you the man you feel you should have been?"

He stopped, shocked at the things he'd said. Miraculously, the three riders ahead had heard nothing of the outburst. They were out of earshot. Slowly Horatio turned his head to look at Jeff.

"Look Jeff. I'm sorry for saying all that. I should not have."

"It's what you think – so why not say it? It's probably all true, anyway. But you – who can probably heal yourself of every cut or bruise or broken limb you have ever had – how can you know what it has been like to be me? I'm not full of pity for myself – the accident happened and nothing can turn back the clock. But what's wrong with me trying to improve my life? You say I can't stick with it. Well I suppose that's how it looks to you."

"So you want to stay here when the others cross over tonight? Won't they object?"

"Probably. I'll have to come clean but I don't think they'll be all that surprised, after our clinical get-together earlier."

"True."

They rode on in silence, urging the horses into a gentle canter to close the gap between them and the trio in front.

***

The cabin was not the ruin Horatio had been expecting. As they drew closer, he could see signs of recent habitation, though it seemed deserted at the moment. They dismounted and tied their horses' reins to a nearby bush, and wandered around the cabin. As Horatio walked round to the rear of the cabin in search of water, he found a small pile of stones fused together into a single mound. The edges of the stones were smooth and glassy, tell-tale magical residue. Powerful magic, at that. He bent down and lifted a stone that had slipped to the side while the magic was flowing, and turned to run back to the others, shouting a warning.

His warning reached them a second too late. Maggie reached out to open the door and her scream rang out across the plain as a bolt of energy coursed up, tossing her away from the door to land on the ground like a broken doll.

"Don't touch her!" Horatio yelled. Laying the charred stone down, he knelt down on the ground beside her and closed his eyes. He gathered the power within him and formed it into a healing and plunged his mind into her unconscious body. Re-start the heart. Gently, now. Yes, done it. Now, lungs – inflate. Deflate. Inflate. Is she breathing yet? Yes, good. Brainwaves. No damage that he could see. He came out, breathed in deeply several times and looked at their anxious faces.

"She's okay. She'll wake up soon, but before she does, I'll see to her hand."

Maggie's right hand was red raw, as if the skin had been flayed from it. Horatio took the damaged hand in his and began a healing spell, a temporary salve to cover the damage and allow the skin to repair and re-grow. There was little more he could do at the moment. Jeff sat down beside her, stroking her hair absently.

Shortly after, Maggie's eyelids fluttered open. Emma dropped down beside her, weeping with relief. "I thought you'd died, Maggie," she sobbed over and over.

Seeing Maggie wince as she moved the fingers into a fist, Horatio explained what he'd done. "I've replaced the burned skin with a thin membrane for the moment. Don't try to use it too much while your own body completes the process of healing. The burn only damaged the top layers. You were lucky."

"I was lucky that you were here, Horatio," she said quietly. "Thank you. What caused it?"

"It was a fairly simple but potentially lethal spell to prevent would-be snoopers."

"A booby-trap," she murmured. She lapsed into silence, aghast.

Horatio picked up the discarded stone. "This is what I was bringing back to show you. See how the edges of the stone are smooth and glassy?"

"It's as if it has been melted," mused Milo.

"Yes, that is what I was thinking. Powerful magic has been used around here very recently. And there is a defensive shield around the cabin that renders its magic invisible to any casually scrying mage. Very interesting," he ended on a thoughtful note, a frown creasing his forehead. More disguised magic. Horatio came out of his trance-like state and looked towards the early winter sun. "We have to get out of here."

Following Horatio's eyes, Milo said, "Because it will get dark soon?"

"No," Horatio replied. "Because whoever put these spells in place could return any time."

"Oh, yes."

Horatio held out a hand to help Emma to her feet. "Are you all right?"

She nodded, gave his hand a squeeze for a moment before turning away to mount her horse.

Horatio smiled.

Chapter 13

"Think you all's well with the Prince?" Master Will Shaksper's voice was uncertain. He stood in a huddle with the guards Berren, Rolan and Gaston, fighting a losing battle with the demons Cold and Fear. Although no snow was falling tonight, icy winds from the North once more whipped across the moors to the north of the Castle. The bleak wintry landscape offered little resistance to the fierce winds that blew up over the parapets and across the battlements, dragging the temperature down even further. Ice had formed in the tiny puddles lying in the cracks between the flagstones making walking treacherous. Seeing their miserable plight, Horatio called up a *banish* charm which dried their cloaks and warmed hands and feet. He could – no, would – do nothing for the fear, which was a healthy one.

"Yes, Will, he is in no danger," the mage replied looking in the direction in which Hamnet had disappeared, following the apparition of his dead father. "I do not believe the ghost will harm him. Though a denizen of the otherworld, it comes here for a purpose other than hurt. More likely it comes to finish something left undone at his death."

"Have you foreseen this, Lord Horatio?" The awe-struck tone of Rolan's words reminded the mage of the guard's extreme youth. He suddenly himself felt far older than his twenty four years. He shook his head wearily and began pacing again, his boot-heels clicking, not slipping, on the treacherous ice-covered flagstones. The ice melted where his footsteps trod.

But Horatio's thoughts were far from mundane things such as warmth. He longed to follow his Prince and be at his side in this trial, but Hamnet had forbidden it. Forbidden him even to create a protective charm. Despite his assurances to Will and the others, he was desperately afraid for his Prince's safety.

Finally he saw a familiar shape materialise out of the dark shadows. Hamnet moved slowly, hesitatingly, despair drawn in every line of his body. "The Prince has returned," he called to the three silent watchers. "Wait here."

Swiftly he covered the ground between them. Up close Hamnet's face was bloodless, and his lips tinged with blue. Hearing Horatio's voice, his head slowly came up and he staggered forward using his sword as a crutch, only to collapse into his friend's waiting arms.

"Are you injured?" Horatio asked, running healing hands over the chilled body. The Prince shook his head.

"Only my spirit," he replied. "He was murdered, Horatio. My uncle murdered him. And it is I, weak and mindless fool that I am, who is charged to revenge his unlawful killing." He raised his eyes to meet those of his Companion, and read the horror that Horatio could not conceal. "Aye, Horatio," he said, "this is an evil night."

They made their way back to the place where Will and the guards waited. The Prince gathered his dignity around him in the same manner as donning a cloak and faced his companions.

"Good gentlemen, I charge you now to swear an oath on this, my father's sword, that you will say nothing of the events here tonight to another soul."

"But my Lord… Was it really the late King?" Gaston could not keep silent.

Hamnet's eyes closed for a second, and Horatio stepped towards him. The Prince waved him away. "This is a sad time for the House of Elasyn, but I can say no more. *Swear on my sword that you will say nothing!*"

"But my Lord Prince…" began Gaston.

"SWEAR!" The Prince's eyes shone with a new mad light. Glancing from one to the other, each in turn – Master Will, the guards Gaston, Rolan, Berren and finally Horatio – laid his hand on the hilt of the sword and swore the oath.

"Now, Gaston, continue your watch. Gentlemen, I bid you goodnight." The Prince turned away with Horatio close behind, leaving the still badly frightened men on the battlements with only the icy wind for company.

Some time later, downstairs in the Prince's apartments, Horatio poured out some wine into two goblets and went to stand by the Prince's side as he stood at the window, looking out over the quadrangle. Horatio followed his gaze to the King's apartments below in the South wing. A light still burned, despite the late hour. While the Prince stood watching the vague shadows, Horatio's eyes were drawn to the opposite wall and the rooms where Emma and her friends were. No lights shone and in his imagination he was there in the room, watching her as she slept. He resisted the temptation that suddenly flared within him to eavesdrop on her slumber. Mage he was – but a voyeur he was not. There was time enough yet before he had to wake them for the crossing back to Earth.

The Prince abruptly turned away from the window and swallowed the remains of his wine. His eyes were shining with unshed tears. Tears for his father's premature death at the hand of a brother, yes, but even more they were tears of pity for himself. A pampered and protected Princeling who had smiled and laughed his way through life, and had now been violently thrust into reality.

"Tell me what to do Horatio, for I am lost. It is an evil thing that a dead King must nightly return to his earthly home until his death be avenged." His voice was strained.

"These are evil times, my lord. We must do what we can to combat them."

"But how? By what means can I do this? Should I go down there," he jabbed an angry finger in the direction of the King's lighted window, "and put a sword through him? Or do I go to the Wizards' Council pleading for understanding of my plight? I have no proof of Claude's guilt, merely the tormented anguish of a father's murdered spirit."

He walked unsteadily to the table and poured more wine. The crystal flagon now empty, he threw it into the fireplace where it shattered into a hundred pieces that glittered and sparkled in the firelight. "Hell and Damnation be upon the murderer! And upon me if I cannot do the deed. But, listen good Horatio. What if the ghost is a malevolent sending? What then? You are a mage. How can I tell if the apparition was in its true shape and not a demon sent to plague my soul?"

"As certain as I could be, it seemed to be truly the spirit of your late father, my lord. I could discern no magical spells tonight. Nor demons." But even as he spoke, Deveron's warning came yet again to mind. Could the ghost be connected with the dream sendings, or is it mere coincidence?

"Horatio, friend and Companion, tell me – what should I do?"

The mage lifted his wine glass and peered at it, tossing alternatives in his head. Finally he took a mouthful and turned to the Prince. "Perhaps the best you can do is to watch the King for evidence that will point one way or the other. Once you have proof then that is the time to go to the Council and present the facts."

"Yes, perhaps that is the wisest course of action. I will watch my uncle until he trips up in his own wiles and then I will gut and skewer him on his own dagger." He fell heavily into a chair and closed his eyes. "Leave me now, good Horatio. I have much to think about."

"Do you wish your attendants to ready your bed?"

"No. I will call them." Horatio, looking down at him, sighed. The Prince had drunk too much since returning from the cold battlements. But who could lay any blame on him for such a weakness? He would be asleep before long.

"Goodnight, sweet Prince. May the god guard you as you sleep." On his way out of the door, he told the Prince's gentlemen to be ready to attend him when he called.

Horatio left the Prince's rooms and headed down the curved staircase towards his own apartments, but so deep in thought that he was standing in front of Emma's room before he even realised where he was.

Giving into temptation, he sent a small probe into the room, to determine whether any were awake. He found only the deep smooth aura waves of sleep. He stood alone in the corridor and sent his mind's eye into the room and across to the bed where Emma slept. Silently he watched as the woman he loved turned over onto her side, freeing one arm from beneath the blankets to lie on top of the satin bedspread. The delicate lawn of the night-dress she wore had slipped off one pale shoulder... Sudden desire flared through his body and imminent loss speared his soul. Abruptly he withdrew his mage-sight from the room and stood leaning against the wall while his heart raced and his breathing faltered. The chill of the stone helped, but it took much longer than a few deep breaths before he was calm and composed enough to turn away and go to his own rooms.

***

The cellar room smelled dank. The torches smoked. And each of the bewildered group saw it slightly differently.

Maggie's eyes rarely left Jeff as he followed Horatio's terse instructions setting out the void circle. Only half understanding his motives for staying, she ceaselessly shook her head, convinced that she would never see him again. All at once he seemed the most important person in the world to her. Occasionally her eyes would flicker around the room, taking in the coldness and the shadows and alight on Emma – silent rigid Emma – who had found her love and was about to lose him again. Then her eyes would flick back again to Jeff, who was not coming with them. She ran a hand through her hair, vainly wishing there was some way she could persuade him not to do this, while knowing that he had to make his own decision. "At the festivities I'll do a solo dedicated to you all," he had said, only slightly mockingly.

Emma watched Horatio while inside her head her thoughts trembled and churned. Once the young mage looked up from the circle and caught her eye. His lips stretched in a smile, but his eyes were dead. She thought back to her words that afternoon. It was true when she said that she and the young mage did not really know one another, but there was *something* there. *There was something.* The tragedy was that now they'd never find out if it was a lasting something. *Will you come to me in my dreams?* she beseeched him silently. *For whoever said that parting was sweet sorrow was very very wrong. There is no sweetness – only the foreknowledge of approaching pain.*

At last the circle was complete and Horatio sitting cross-legged in the centre began the mental search for Mhari among the myriad of auras that comprised their combined Universes. No-one spoke. Time passed. Then one of the four torches in the wall brackets around the room began smoking and flickering. Emma felt her eyes drawn to the torch as the tension mounted. Still no-one spoke. Horatio sat still and pale, the only indication of life the slow movement of the laces in his velvet jerkin as his chest rose and fell. More time passed.

Then the first torch guttered and died. Shadows began to cluster in the corner now devoid of light. Moments later a second torch began flickering, guttered and went out. Almost immediately a third suddenly extinguished itself as a wind rose from nowhere. Horatio's eyes flew open and stared around the room, his back ramrod-straight, watching something that none of the others could see. He lifted up his hands and called out in a commanding voice. A cold laugh echoed jeering around the room and Horatio clutched his head and screamed in agony before collapsing onto the floor. For several seconds the wind and the laughter continued, then suddenly both ceased. In the sudden silence the sole remaining torch steadied once more. With a cry, Emma rushed to Horatio's side, screaming his name. As she cradled his head his eyelids flickered and he pulled in a great breath. Failure was written in every line of his body and etched on his face.

"Something is blocking the way. I cannot open a way across." The words were exhaled on a wave of sheer exhaustion. Emma sat with him in the middle of a chalked wizard's circle, oblivious to the chill of the stone seeping through her thin garments. After a while, his hand rose, pushed the hair back from her tear-streaked face and touched her lips gently.

"You'll have to stay here in the meantime," he murmured and their arms once more enfolded one another, consoling and comforting, each quietly relieved at a painful parting postponed.

It was a very subdued party that made its way back upstairs to the Scots' rooms. Once behind the closed doors, they sat silent while Horatio marshalled his remaining strength and called up a protective veil for the room.

"So you cannot get us home." Milo's voice came out flat.

Horatio looked up and met his eyes without flinching. "At this moment in time, no."

Jeff, looking pointedly at their joined hands, took up the attack. "How hard did you try, I wonder?"

Emma whirled round on him. "How dare you, Jeff? You saw what happened to him. He collapsed!"

"No, Emma" Horatio said. "Don't blame Jeff for his suspicions. Under the circumstances it is a perfectly reasonable assumption. He knows I don't want you to leave. But the fact is that you are wrong, Jeff. I did my best and I failed. There is a force here that I have not encountered before, a force powerful enough to block my entry into the void. The voice was that of this force. The wind was an illusion, a minor addition for effect. But no mage that I know of is powerful enough to accomplish such a feat." His eyes were bleak, worried.

"Would Polon be able to do it?"

"No. It was not Polon. He's not strong enough. Nor has he the training."

"Who then?" Maggie struggled to keep a tremor out of her voice.

He turned to her. A faint smile curved his lips but his voice was sombre. "It would need a more powerful mage than I. Perhaps the Antriantara Deveron, or one or two of the mages at Rowlan Gayts, could break through, or a *mindmeld* of several wizards. I will have to speak with Deveron. Soon. After the festivities I will organise for you all to leave the Castle and go somewhere safe."

"Where?"

"I don't know. Some place where you will be safe. Rowlan Gates, perhaps. In the meantime I need to sleep. I will remain here tonight. We should stay together as much as possible. I will lay a spell to warn me."

"Warn you of what?"

Horatio shrugged. "Anything we need to be warned of, I suppose." He could feel what little energy still remained within him ooze out of his pores. He was very near to collapsing with exhaustion, and very aware of it. He desperately needed restorative sleep. With the last vestiges of his power he wove the sigils of the early warning spell and collapsed into a chair.

"Put him in the bed," Emma commanded. "I will sit by him. The rest of you, well just try to get some sleep. It's no use discussing it all *ad finitum*. In the morning we can decide what to do."

Jeff stepped towards her, his hand reaching out. "Emma, don't do this. Remember Martin." She looked at him and shook her head.

No-one else argued. Maggie helped get the mage's outer clothing off, left Emma sitting by the bed, and moved into the men's bedroom, where the boys hastily made up a third bed on the floor.

***

Dreams are fickle creatures of the night. For a final time Horatio dreamed of riding out across the familiar grasslands with Emma beside him. *Laughter and smiles. Wind and sunshine. Grass and meadow flowers. All is well. Then... Emma's face changes - flows into something hideous - an evil parody of her matchless beauty. Aghast, he reins in his horse, but the heinous Emma slows too, reaches out with arms suddenly rubbery stretching across the space between them to grip him in a slimy and suffocating embrace...*

He awoke, sweat pouring from him, to Emma's soft voice murmuring in his ear and her warm *human* arms round his shuddering body. His eyes opened. Emma's face was inches away. Saying nothing, she kissed him lightly and pulling back the satin sheets and woollen blankets, slipped into the bed beside him. Desire coursed once more through Horatio's body to be answered in equal measure by Emma's. Their slow outpouring and receiving of physical and emotional love healed Horatio's tired and over-burdened spirit much more effectively than any wizard's spell.

Dawn on the King's Coronation Day arrived grey and dismal, throwing light on the sleeping form of Horatio talMerios, companion-mage to the Prince of Elsynvaal, and curled up beside him, her head on his shoulder, lay Emasiyo Campbell, the other-worlder.

Chapter 14

The view from the balcony would be more interesting, Ser Loren decided. So, armed with a half-flagon of wine, he left the chaos of the Main Hall and escaped to one of several half-hidden alcoves on the north wall of the Gallery. During the coming Coronation procession, he'd have enough smiling and waving and bowing to last him for quite some time. It's not as if the people who would line the route this afternoon would even be aware who he was. To them he would be just one of the Prince's entourage.

But no. Father had to insist in *all* of his family attending the King in the Coronation procession. Olivia would enjoy it, he knew. All the pomp and the ceremony. But then, she had her heart set on winning Hamnet's hand in marriage and one day becoming Queen. So the practice would be good for her.

But he, Loren, had had enough. As soon as was possible he was leaving. The day he was finished with his studies, he would leave Elsynvaal and never return. He would travel to other countries, perhaps Cheam in the East, or sail across the Western Sea to places where he was not known as the normal, i.e., non-magician, son of the King's Chancellor-Mage. Maybe one day he would even learn the secret of travelling between worlds. That was his aim in life, an aim kept secret from his father, whose plans for his only son's future studies were immeasurably different.

So, petulant and sullen, young Ser Loren, son of the King's Chancellor, hid himself from the chaos of the festivities shaping up below, refusing to take part. But as he settled himself on a comfortable chair in one of the alcoves along the north balcony, he noticed a movement outside the Prince's apartments off to his right. Ready to slide backwards into the shadows, he paused when he realised who it was. Master Will, writer of plays and poetry, as he styled himself, had exited the Prince's rooms and was hurrying along this way carrying a piece of parchment. The young Lord then remembered that the Prince had charged the writer to produce a short playlet for the actors to perform this afternoon. He leaned back, the better to remain hidden from the poet.

"How now, young Ser. What do you here, half-hidden? You should be down in the Hall, or preparing for the procession."

"Yes, sir. I will go down soon, I promise. I wish to watch from here for a while. In the meantime, please say nothing to my father about seeing me here."

"Thou art a child yet, Ser, to hide away thus. Does not your father need your aid? There is much to do."

"Master Will, I am fifteen years old, and no longer a child."

"I tell you this young Ser, you will be a child until you learn how to be a man facing his responsibilities. Now, I must leave you for I must away to the Prince. I have here a script which the Prince Hamnet did bid me write, though I swear it is not one I would have deemed suitable for such a day as this!" He waved the parchment he held in his ink-stained hands at the young man.

"What is it about?"

"A murder by stealth."

"Is there much blood and gore?"

"No, Ser Loren, there would never be enough to satisfy your desire for such. Now, if you will excuse me, I am required to attend the Prince below. See, the actors are arrived, and I have great need to speak with the Prince." He turned away and disappeared behind the curtains towards the staircase.

At the bottom of the stairwell, Horatio could hear someone clattering down the narrow staircase, and waited until Master Will appeared.

"Good morrow, Lord Horatio," the poet said as he reached the bottom. "Another who wishes to escape the festivities?"

Horatio laughed. "No, Master Will. I will return soon enough. But who else is escaping?"

"Young Ser Loren resides yonder in the gallery tending a flagon of wine."

"Ah. You think I should speak with him?"

"Methinks his father will be searching for him soon."

Horatio nodded and gripped the other briefly on the shoulder and continued on his way.

When the curtains parted beside him, Loren looked up to see Horatio leaning casually against a pillar, his hand lying lightly on the hilt of his sword, and his cloak thrown back, displaying an embroidered doublet over a fine lawn shirt.

"Ho, Loren."

"Ho, Horatio."

"May I join you?"

The other shrugged. "If you wish."

Horatio dropped into an upholstered chair beside the young man and leaned forward on the balcony wall to look down upon the scene below. Servants were scurrying to and fro, carrying tables, benches, linens, cushions, crockery, wine and a hundred other items needed for the festivities soon to begin. The staging should have been completed by now, but still carpenters were hammering and banging as they re-arranged one section of it. Hamnet obviously had something extra in mind to demand changes to be made at this late stage.

He searched for Emma and her friends and spotted Milo plucking on the ivory lute in a corner by the raised dais where the King and Queen would later sit. Jeff, Emma and Maggie were standing together, heads bent over a piece of parchment, checking details. As his glance rested on Emma, she raised her head and looked around. He waited, still watching. Finally, she looked upwards, scanning the gallery, and saw him. He could see her slow smile and her hand rise in greeting. Jeff turned his head just in time to see the wave.

Horatio saw a deep frown suddenly cross Jeff's face. He knew then that despite his offer of a healing attempt it would be some time before Jeff's animosity towards himself completely faded. Despite being aware of the development of the relationship between Emma and himself, Horatio knew Jeff still wanted to protect what he saw as Martin's relationship with Emma. Perhaps he thought that once they were back home things would revert to how they had been. Who knows?

Emma had seen Horatio's glance shift and turned to Jeff, who said something. She nodded and smiled once more up at the balcony. Seeing that smile, Horatio felt his burdens lessen, and his heart leaped.

Emma turned back to Maggie and Jeff and the matter in hand, and Horatio recommenced scanning the Great Hall. Polon was busy as always, ordering people hither and thither and inadvertently creating yet more chaos. He should be pensioned off, the mage thought. Master Will crossed the hall with his playlet in his hand towards the Prince who stood with some of the newly-arrived touring troupes of entertainers. Horatio, recognising some of them, smiled to himself. It would be good to renew their acquaintance.

He turned to the silent and brooding Loren beside him. "Do you remember when this same troupe performed on their last visit in the

132

summer?"

He was rewarded with a grunt of affirmation. "Ah, yes. The Sylvan Bard and his troupe. They were passable, I believe."

"Aye, he's Alain tirNorest, a Sylvan of the Northern Forest. I'll wager that they have a goodly entertainment lined up for today. I am glad to see that they have arrived safely."

"Master Will has written a playlet for them to perform. A murder, he said. Most diverting."

Horatio frowned and his spirits drooped. Hamnet had said nothing about using a murder as the centre of his playlet. What was the Prince planning?

And where was Deveron? He scanned the crowd of people below but could not see the Antriantara's robes anywhere. In the light of what Loren had just said, he urgently needed to speak with him to seek his opinion on the ghostly apparition. Not to mention the problem of the mage without a signature. He continued to search for his old mentor and finally located him, standing with two others in the shadows almost below his own position. One he recognised as Alain, the Sylvan Bard who had just arrived. He sent a mental hail to Deveron, aware that his voice would be lost in the tumult. The Master-Mage stepped forward out of the shadows and raised his eyes to the gallery. He signalled that he would come up, and spoke to his companions. The Sylvan too glanced up and waved, before moving off with the other man.

Horatio became aware that Loren was watching him. "You used a mental hail, didn't you? A form of di'speak, is it not? A useful skill," he observed. He paused, turning to look down into the Great Hall before demanding, "Why is it that I have not been able to use di'speak since that day, Horatio?"

"I can only think that the stress you were under at the time made the link possible."

"So you agree that I have the aptitude be a mage?"

"You may have the potential, but usually magical aptitude is noticeable at a younger age, often before the age of ten. You are almost fifteen, Loren."

"But I contacted you by means of di'speak. You maintain that speaking over distances is a very difficult practice to master. But I, without training in the arts, succeeded! Surely that means that I should begin my training. What I would be able to do then! When will you begin tutoring me in the magical arts, my lord?"

"When your father permits it, and once you have learned to

leave sulks and moodiness behind you. Magic is a dangerous weapon in hands of those too immature to wield it. It can destroy the user." His voice softened. "Loren, you are a good lad, but you let your feelings against what you perceive to be your father's too severe strictures rule you. No matter that you feel his treatment of both you and your sister to be unfair, unjust and suffocating. He is your father. Be thankful that you still have one. Don't waste your life in seeking revenge on him for doing what he feels is right for you. He loves both you and your sister."

"Would that my mother had lived!"

"There can be no doubt that the Lord Polon would echo that thought. He loved your mother dearly."

Loren looked away, his face clouding-over.

"Think about it, Loren. I will speak to your father, if I can. I've got to leave now though, as the Antriantara Deveron is on his way up here and I have things to discuss with him."

"Very well, Horatio. I'll think about what you said. Before you go though, tell me - was your father like mine, really hard on you?"

"Of course he was. Fathers want their sons to grow up tough, so they are hard on them. I too had to fight for my rights. He means well, so try to be less judgemental of him. But I have to go now. Later, Loren."

Loren smiled a little. "Later, Horatio."

He let the curtain drop behind him just as Deveron reached the top of the stairwell. As he looked at his old teacher, Horatio frowned. He knew about the controversy surrounding Deveron's accession to the post of Antriantara of the Wizards Council, but was not really prepared for the change in Deveron's whole demeanour. The Clerical Mage obviously had a lot on his mind.

"Come, follow me, Deveron," he said. "We will sit over here." He led the way along the north wall away from the alcove where Loren still sat hidden. As he passed, he twitched open the curtains on each of the other alcoves.

***

Horatio had struggled long with his conscience before making the decision to tell Deveron of the Ghost's appearance. If Hamnet learned of his broken oath, he might be unable to forgive him. That was a risk he had to take. He, Horatio, could not tackle this alone. So he broke his solemn oath and Deveron's gaze roamed over the clamour below as he was told of the events over the last few days –

134

the appearance of the Ghost and the charge that had been laid upon the Prince to avenge his father's murder.

Deveron sat silent, his face a mask. When he spoke, he sounded weary. "What do you think the Prince will do?"

"He's had a playlet written about a murder. It may be based on what the Ghost told him of the circumstances of the King's death."

"To what effect?"

"To test the conscience of the King his Uncle *and* that of the Queen his mother, I fear."

"Why say you that?"

"You know that since the marriage, he has been cold and distant with the Queen. He feels that she is debasing his father's memory. Her obvious joy in her new-married state rankles with him."

"Indeed this is a difficult state of affairs. I will speak with the Prince, try to ensure that he does nothing rash. Don't worry, Horatio, I will be subtle. He will not hear from me of your broken oath. If the King is guilty of murder, then…" He stopped, shook his head. "One thing puzzles me. The natural emanation from such a deed would be immense, but none of us on the Council had any indication of such a dreadful development. I gather that you felt nothing either? No, I thought not. It is as if *something has been cloaking the outflow of emanations*. I will have to think about all of this, and di'speak with the other Watchers. What of the other matter?"

"The mage without a signature exists."

"You are sure of this?"

Horatio shrugged. "How can one be sure of an impossibility?" But as he related the events of the previous day, Deveron seemed to fold up within himself, as if Horatio's words had confirmed a horrifying suspicion.

"There is something else, Deveron." There was no time for a long explanation. "Last night I tried, and failed, to send the other-worlders back to their world through the Ether. Something or someone was blocking entry to the Ether."

"Ah, Horatio. How many other things are going to happen? Do you have inside information? Do you have a channel to the god? For mine I fear is closed…"

Horatio, thinking of the dream last night looked away, down into the Great Hall below. "We will prevail," he said.

"We must, Horatio, my friend. We must! But for now, let us join the others down below. It appears that the Coronation procession is beginning to assemble."

***

A scarce two hours later, the procession was over and the massive doors leading from the courtyard were opened to the courtiers to take up their places for the evening's entertainment. Ser Loren, thankful for his release from public view, sauntered into the Hall. He looked around narrowing his eyes. There was something going on, he knew it, he *felt* it. Something to do with Horatio and the Antriantara and Hamnet. Though if challenged on how he was so certain he would not have been able to answer. But whatever it was, he was determined to figure it out.

He dropped into a vacant space in the row of seating behind his sister Olivia and Prince Hamnet, who was dressed as always in black. From this position there was a clear view of the Royal Dais and well as the central performance area.

He glanced around and saw Horatio and the Antriantara take their places opposite to Loren's position. Loren was convinced that they were talking mind to mind, thick as thieves, because Horatio frequently shifted in his seat and looked around, his eyes often lighting on the Prince.

Curious.

Prince Hamnet sat in the row in front of him, with Olivia next to him. Occasionally Hamnet would lean across to Olivia and whisper something to her. As time went on she began to edge away from Hamnet, as if uncomfortable.

Once all were seated, the newly-crowned King entered the Great Hall and mounted the Royal Dais. Splendid in his Coronation robes, his new wife beside him, the King took his seat in his plush upholstered throne-like chair – the signal for the entertainment to begin.

Loren closed his ears as his father, Polon, the Lord Chancellor, introduced the performers with long rambling orations and watched as the Prince leaned across and once more spoke to Olivia. Her head jerked up, as if startled. Loren frowned. What had the Prince said to his sister? Olivia looked down again, her hands clasped on her lap. Hamnet nonchalantly crossed one leg over the other, seemingly completely relaxed. Loren glanced in Horatio's direction and caught his eye. The Mage nodded and gave him a smile before

136

resuming his restless watch over the festivities.

Then – finally – the festivities began.

Loren looked up as a beautiful ethereal tune began weaving through the Hall, and the Sylvan Bard appeared from the rear of the seating playing a set of pipes. He walked gracefully through the audience to the staging, his flowing pale hair glinting in the torchlight. He stepped up onto the stage and sat on a stool near the edge. Only then did a lithe dancer, dressed in the robes of a mythical muse, dance in from the wings. She was followed by a second, in similar dress, twirling and twisting in the dance of the twin goddesses.

The man sitting on Loren's left leaned towards him. "Is the Bard Sylvan?" he asked. "Seems like, to me."

"Aye, he is. Alain tirNorest, his name is."

"You know much of them then? I've always been a bit wary of Sylvan, myself. With their strange colour-changing eyes and elusive ways. Never much to say for themselves, I always think."

"I believe Master Alain belongs to one of the Northern Forest Clans. He's been travelling as a Bard with this troupe for some time now. They visited the Castle last year. Were you not here then?"

"No. I have been abroad with the King. Came back with him from Cheam in the spring."

"Really? It must have been exciting out in the field!"

"No, Ser Loren. Not exciting. Cold and uncomfortable? Yes. Exciting? No. You don't get anything like this in the field!" he asserted over the tumult of the applause. "A hard act to follow, wouldn't you agree? But the next should be interesting. The Mage," he pointed in Horatio's direction, "has brought them from another world. The wonders of modern wizardry."

The four young people from another world stepped onto the staging. Loren watched as they set their instruments up and prepared to begin. When he'd first seen them on their arrival two days before, they'd been cold and confused. Here as they set up their instruments on the stage, they were assured and confident. He glanced at Horatio. For once he was unmoving – sitting forward in his chair, elbows on knees, his eyes fixed on the four on the stage. *He brought them from another world.* Loren raised his eyes to the stage.

The slighter of the young men, Milo, introduced each member of the troupe and then each song with a little chat. Their first song, he told his audience, was an unaccompanied ballad, based on an old folk song of their country. The arrangement, apparently their own, suited the four voices perfectly. Layers of sound interwove and lifted the hearts of all who listened. Truly otherworldly, speaking of potent love and searing loss, it transfixed the audience. Loren nodded to himself. Yes, they were good.

Their next song was accompanied on the lute, played by the narrator, Milo Diaz. Once again the voices brought to the song a vibrancy Loren for one had not heard before. This was followed by a slow ballad sung by the two girls alone. The quartet finished their programme with a lively dance tune accompanied on pipe, lute and a drum beaten with a double-headed drumstick. Someone in the audience began clapping in time, and soon the whole audience joined in. When the song ended, the clapping continued. Ser Loren glanced across at Horatio astounded to see the mage on his feet, enthusiastically clapping. His face no longer wore the worried look and as he turned and caught Loren's eye, he laughed aloud.

The Antriantara Deveron touched his arm, leaned over towards him. Horatio sat down and the glow on his face faded. He began his restless searching of the Hall once more, repeatedly glancing at Prince Hamnet.

What's going on? Loren asked himself.

There was a pause as scene shifters moved furniture, then his ancient sire, the Lord Chancellor, took centre stage once more to introduce the acting troupe's two playlets. While the old man droned on, Loren watched Horatio whose eyes never left the Prince. A feeling of trepidation slithered across Loren's innards.

The first playlet was a section from an old epic. As the Sylvan Bard's pipe music took flight, Loren became aware of a change in Prince Hamnet's stance. He was sitting very close to Olivia now, running his hand across the silk of her gown and whispering. Olivia's back was rigid, but with what emotion, Loren could not say. He could not see her face. But Horatio could. Horatio was watching with narrowed eyes everything the Prince was doing. *What's going on?* Loren asked himself once more.

The second playlet began, and soon it became apparent to Loren that this was no light-hearted amusement. Throughout the play, Horatio avidly watched the Prince, who in his turn seemed to have his eyes fixed firmly on King Claude sitting happily on his dais, his hand resting lightly on the Queen's arm. However, as the playlet developed, and the play-murderer poured a phial of liquid into a goblet and handed it to the play-king, King Claude began to shift in his chair, glancing around. Once he glanced with narrowed eyes

138

towards Hamnet, who returned his stare. Then suddenly the playlet was over. The play-king lay dead on the ground, and his shining diadem now graced the evil one's brow. Loren's head whipped round towards the dais. The King sat rigid in his chair.

For a moment there was perfect silence, before someone tentatively began clapping. Ragged applause followed, which swiftly ended when the King abruptly stood. "Enough! Enough!" he shouted. Then turning on his heel he left the Hall, followed quickly by the flustered Queen and their attendants. The Prince slumped back in his chair, his eyes closed. The angle of his head allowed Loren to see the grim smile that played around the edges of his thin pale lips.

After the abrupt departure of the King, a cacophony of sound broke out. The Chancellor approached the Prince, asking him if he wished the entertainment to continue. The Prince waved him away dismissively, and then rose to leave signalling to Horatio to follow him. Serra Olivia was left alone, ignored.

Loren leaned forward towards his sister and laid his hand on her shoulder. She jumped, but turned to him, a startled look on her face.

"Are you all right?" he asked. Her eyes were bright and blotches of red marred her pale cheeks.

"Yes, Loren, I am well. But I am afraid that the Lord Hamnet may not be. He has been acting very strangely today." She paused and turned to look around her, then continued in a whisper. "The playlet we have just seen performed was written at his command."

Loren frowned. Was this the reason for his own unease? But surely the Prince was not trying to accuse the King of complicity in his brother's death! Though it certainly looked like that. He looked across at Deveron, but the Antriantara was staring off into the distance, his eyes curiously glazed. Olivia touched his arm. "Will you sit with me, little brother?" Loren smiled at her and slipped quietly into the seat vacated by the Prince.

The Lord Chancellor despondently watched the Prince and his mage leave, then stood dithering over whether to dismiss the entertainers or let the performances continue. Eventually he stood centre-stage and announced that the programme would continue until such time as the King recovered from his malady and he and the Queen could rejoin the festivities. Then he signalled to the actors and players to continue.

Alain tirNorest, the Sylvan Bard, took to the stage again, this time as story-teller, and soon the hubbub in the audience was silenced as he wove his tale of mystery, suspense and heroic deeds – very different from that which had so disturbed the King. Loren ached to leave and find out what was going on, but Olivia was still shaken, and he dared not leave her.

Act after act moved through their paces on the stage. There were songs and tales, dances, recitations, music played on a variety of instruments, even jugglers, but the enthusiasm so obvious earlier in the evening had gone.

***

In a small side room Horatio sat by a fireside, a worried frown on his face as he watched Hamnet pace up and down. The euphoria the Prince had shown following his uncle's abrupt departure from the Hall had dissipated somewhat, but he still seemed very agitated. Each comment of Horatio's was met with a tirade of words.

Everything had to be planned carefully, the Prince said.

Claude's reaction was proof of his guilt, he said.

Contact the Wizards' Council? That crowd of degenerates? The prince was scathing. They'd *agreed to the change in the succession!* Why should they back him up now?

Horatio had seen moods like this before - but in the last few days he had seemed even more manic than before. He'd seen Olivia's reaction to him and wondered what he'd said to her to upset her so much.

Horatio's attention was caught by a movement behind the Prince as the door quietly opened to allow a figure to enter. Horatio waved Master Will into the room. Hamnet, in full flow, did not even notice the bard's entry. He continued to vent his feelings for some time. Sometimes it seemed to Horatio that the Prince was bordering on a nervous breakdown. His pampered upbringing had not prepared him to cope with recent events.

"I am charged by my dead father's spirit," he raved, "to avenge his foul murder. My uncle's reaction to the playlet proves it. I must do something. I must *act!*"

As his voice gradually rose in volume, Horatio glanced towards the door at the far side of the room that led to a minor audience room. It was lying slightly ajar. He moved quickly across the room to close it while the Prince continued to rant and pace up and down.

"Yet I cannot act. How can I avenge him, my murdered father? Am I meant to do murder also? Do two wrongs balance one another out? And so it seems all *I* can do is talk! Words! Words! Words!

They say that words can be as swords, they can wound – aye, but can they *kill*? No. Words alone will not avenge my father's ghost! So it seems that I must do something. *Do you not see, Horatio, that I must do something? I must act*! But how? Is there sufficient hate within me to wield a sword or a dagger? Therein lies the central question." He suddenly stopped, and looking around for the first time noticed Master Will standing in the shadows.

"My Lord," the poet said, "I fear that my words will be unwelcome."

"Say, man, what ails you?"

"I come from the Queen your mother," he replied. "She is distressed, my Lord, at your actions and would speak with you."

Hamnet's voice rang with laughter. "Hear you this, Horatio? My mother is *distressed* and would lay the cause of it on me! I fear… I must … away."

"My Lord Hamnet…" Horatio began, but the Prince cut in.

"Fear not, good Horatio. I will *speak* daggers to her, yes, but I will use none." He pulled the jewelled dagger from its customary sheath at his belt, looked at it then slid it back. He laid a hand of farewell on Horatio's shoulder before turning to leave. "I will go to my Lady mother," the Prince said. He turned on his heel and left the room swiftly.

Horatio took Master Will's arm. "Stay near by him, Will, and see he comes to no harm. I fear for him." As the door closed behind the poet, Horatio slumped down on a nearby chair, cradling his head in his hands. He thought of mind-following the Prince, but could not bring himself to spy on his friend and liege Lord.

***

Emma and Maggie stood near the rear of the hall watching as the audience broke up into small groups talking about the performances they'd just watched. Maggie nudged Emma and pointed to the seats near the front where Serra Olivia was still sitting. Milo had just sat down in the chair Olivia's brother had vacated.

As they smiled at one another, a number of richly-clothed personages approached them, congratulating them on their performance. The conversation soon turned to their own world, and Maggie found that some of them had some strange notions of Earth. She laughed as she tried to correct them. Emma looked around for Horatio, and through a gap in the throng saw Jeff in earnest conversation with the Sylvan Bard, Alain.

She gripped Maggie's arm. "I'm going to join Jeff," she whispered to her and began to move off in Jeff's direction. She would like to talk with the Sylvan herself. Her curiosity had been thoroughly aroused by Horatio's description of the Bard's people while they were out riding. But as she reached Jeff and the Bard, she felt a hand on her arm. Turning she saw a servant carrying a silver platter. Bowing his head towards Emma, he offered the platter to her.

"Mistress Emma, a message for you."

Surprised, Emma took the slip of parchment and read it. Horatio was asking her to meet him in the Music Room. She laid her hand on Jeff's arm and told him where she was going. "Should you?" he asked. "Horatio wants us all to remain together. Why would he ask you to meet him away from the Hall?"

"I don't know, Jeff. But I'll be fine. Don't start worrying. Look – Alain's starting to get restless. Go on back to your conversation! I'll see you later upstairs."

Jeff smiled and nodded to her, and then turned back to Alain. Emma turned back to the servant, meaning to ask him to direct her to Horatio, but he had gone. She closed her eyes to help visualise which direction the Music Room lay and then once more felt a hand on her arm.

"Are you all right?" Jeff asked.

"Yes, I'm just trying to remember where the music room is, that's all." He laughed and told her.

As she left the Hall following Jeff's instructions, Emma smiled at the change in his demeanour over the last couple of days. At the reception, he had been diffident and reclusive. But now, with the possibility of a cure, he had blossomed and become much more confident. She smiled as she walked along the torch-lit corridors towards the music room, not really aware that the further she left the Hall behind, the fewer people she passed in the corridors.

The room was in darkness when Emma opened the door. Leaving it open, she turned back and lifted a torch down from its bracket. Pushing the door to the music room wide, she stepped in holding the torch in front of her. "Horatio?" she called. "Where are you?"

The torch flickered, causing the shadows to jump around her. Holding the torch high, she went to a wall bracket to light the torch there, and discovered it empty. Strange. Why should Horatio arrange to meet her here in a dark deserted room, on the other side of the Castle from everyone else? She had already turned to leave when the door suddenly slammed shut and the torch blew out. Emma stood paralyzed as the dark engulfed her.

Then she saw a glimmer of light over in the far corner, near the shuttered window, and watched, fascinated as it began to glow. Slowly at first, the point of light grew clearer and larger until it filled the room with its pulsing changing colours. At the same time she became aware of a strange cloying scent hanging in the air. She backed towards the door and found the handle. She tried to turn it. It was stuck. She pulled at the handle, but the door refused to budge. Frightened now, she turned back into the room, and immediately regretted it.

The walls of the room had begun to change shape and form. She watched, mesmerised and frightened. First the room became longer, as if stretching away from her to an elongated point. Then, suddenly it collapsed back in upon itself, rushing towards her until it was a minute space, so small that it threatened to squeeze the very air from her lungs. Then it changed again, and began alternately expanding and contracting, repeating the sequence again and again while at the same time the light began pulsing faster, its psychedelic colours swirling around her, faster, faster and the scented drug heightened her senses until she was screaming with fear. She shut her eyes and put her hands over her ears in an attempt to shut out the sight of the ever changing walls and the nightmare sound of the swirling light's throbbing and pulsating beat. Defeated and overcome by sensory overload, she staggered backwards and cowered shaking against the door.

"Horatio!" she cried out weakly, just before darkness overtook her. As she slid down the door to lie crumpled up on the floor, the psychedelic lights faded to a dull glow.

Chapter 15

"You know – in some ways I'm glad Horatio didn't manage to send us back last night."

Jeff looked back over his shoulder at Maggie as they climbed the circular stairway. "Really? I thought I was the only one thinking that."

"No way, Jeff old boy," Milo called up from behind Maggie. "That was an exhibition not to be missed in a million years. I thought the King was going to blow a gasket!"

"Ssshhh," Maggie hissed. "Don't go saying things like that out in the open! At least wait until we're in our rooms."

Milo stifled a snigger. He knew he'd had too much to drink, but decided nevertheless to take heed of her warning, and he said nothing more as they walked along the dimly-lit corridor and into the girls' room. The room was in darkness, the only illumination the banked-up fire.

Jeff took the poker and stabbed at the embers. "Maggie, will you pass me some of that kindling?" A few licks of flame flickered and caught as he added the small pieces of wood. Maggie lit the candelabra and the wall torches while Milo headed for the wine decanter.

When the room was bathed in a gentle light and the fire crackling merrily, Milo, a goblet of wine in his hand dropped heavily into one of the fireside settles. Kicking off his boots he waved his toes in front of the fire. "Mmm. That's nice."

Maggie sat down opposite him. "I wonder where Emma is," she said. "It's been ages since she went off to meet Horatio."

"I wouldn't worry, Maggie, they're probably downstairs in his rooms." He glanced at Jeff. Yes. He was staring at him – silently defending his pal.

"Oh give over Jeff, old boy," he said. "You're not Martin's keeper. Emma has made her decision, and you can do absolutely nowt about any of it. Martin will have to accept it, that's all. Pity he couldn't have been here though, all the same. He would have enjoyed hearing some of those other pieces."

"True, he would have," Maggie mused, "but on the whole I'm glad he's not. One less to be caught up in this nightmare."

Milo sat up. "Nightmare? That performance downstairs was

classic. Someone should write it down!"

Jeff came and leaned over Milo. "I think you're forgetting something, Milo, *old boy*. Namely that someone *is* writing it down, or he will do!"

"Oh, yes," Milo tapped his head. "I'd momentarily forgotten about Master Will."

"Yes, well we have yet another part of the plot now. The *play-within-the-play* and the murder of the old King."

Milo stood up and walked across to the window. "Well, I think you're all over-reacting to this…*Hamlet* rubbish."

"I don't think so." Milo could feel Jeff's glare from across the room, and Maggie predictably stepped in as referee.

"Shut up, both of you. Maybe, Milo, you should just stop drinking and get some sleep. Horatio will be trying for an opening in the Ether tomorrow, and you don't want to be facing that with a hangover, do you?"

Milo didn't reply, but turned away and looked down on the icy courtyard. It was as still as it had been five minutes ago when he'd last peered down. Lights were still showing in the King's apartments.

What was he looking for anyway, he asked himself. Any reason to get away from here. He knew how the conversation was going to go from here – a continuous rehash of events from Jeff, interspersed with Maggie's pathetic *I wish I'd not come here*. He thought of where Em and Horatio might be. He's nothing if not a quick mover, he thought. It's less than a week since they met and already… A holiday romance with a difference, he supposed. What about poor Martin though? He shrugged. Nothing to do with him.

He turned back to Jeff and Maggie. "I'm going for a walk," he told them. "I can't stand all of this."

"You will not!" Maggie retorted. "You will stay here with us, or go and lie down. Horatio told us to stay together."

"Yeah. And a couple of hours later he sends a messenger for Emma. I'm leaving."

"No, you are not, Milo. This situation is getting out of hand and if any of us leaves this room then Emma will not know where we are."

"She's with Horatio," Milo retorted. "He can do one of his mental scan-things and find out where we are. Anyway, I think you're both taking everything far too literally."

"But maybe it's just that you are not taking things seriously enough," Jeff said. "We are in the middle of the plot of Shakespeare's *Hamlet, Prince of Denmark*…"

"Oh here we go again! You're repeating yourself, again."

"…and we have now reached Act 3 Scene 2 where Hamlet writes a play to test his uncle's conscience. '*The play's the thing wherein I'll catch the conscience of the King.*' Remember it? Or did you not do Shakespeare at school?" He finished on a scathing note.

"Some of them, but not *Hamlet*. So, scholar, enlighten us. What happens next?"

Jeff refused to rise to the bait of his sarcasm. "Hamlet goes to speak with his mother and Polonius is killed." Jeff and Maggie looked at one another as realisation dawned.

"If the next scene is not merely Master Will's imagination," Maggie gasped, "then Lord Polon is in great danger. We've got to do something to help him. Do you know where the Queen's apartments are?"

Jeff frowned a little. "The King's are in the opposite wing from here across the quadrangle," he said. "The Queen's are likely nearby."

Milo gave a short laugh. "So you're willing to go chasing around the castle now, are you?"

Jeff turned on him, his face twisted with anger. "This is different Milo, and well you know it!"

"And what will you say when you burst into the Queen's apartments – assuming you even find them? *Pardon me, Ma'am, but your son the Prince is about to murder the Chancellor?*"

"No, but we'll think of something," Jeff said. Then he turned and left, Maggie on his heels.

"I'll stay here then," Milo shouted at the closing door. "Damn!" he said through closed teeth. He went back to the window and thumped the sill. What the hell was going on? So what if they were stuck here for ever? It's not such a bad place to be. He could easily think of several that would be much worse. A fleeting memory of his ex-girlfriend came to mind. He shuddered. That had been a close escape.

A tentative knock on the door somehow penetrated his despondent mood. A frown on his face, he went to the door. As he laid his hand on the door handle, he paused, thinking of Horatio's warning about not being alone.

"Who is it?" he called.

"Serra Olivia," came the answer. Astonished, he opened the door and stood aside to let the girl enter. She looked around the room and back to him. "You are alone?" she asked. Sudden irrational fear clutched at his insides before he had a chance to tell himself that surely this girl could be no danger to him. But before he could stammer any reply, she continued speaking. "I had hoped Lord Horatio would be here. He is not in his apartments."

"You find me alone, my lady. Is there any way in which I can help you?"

"You are kind, Master Milo, but you would not understand because you do not know the background."

"Try me." He took her tiny hand and led her to one of the fireside seats. "Is it about Prince Hamnet?" She nodded. "And the fact that he has been acting strange towards you." She nodded again, her eyes beginning to fill with tears. He pulled out a handkerchief and handed it to her while a little voice in the back of his mind scoffed at the gallantry. "You don't know where you stand with him." Another nod. She dabbed at her eyes. *She even cries beautifully*, he found himself thinking. A little voice in the back of his mind hooted with laughter.

"Tell me," he said.

"We are to be wed. But since his father's death he has been so distant and filled with grief. But it was understandable, I suppose. However since his mother the Queen remarried he has been very cruel to me. This afternoon during the festivities he told me that…" she paused and looked down at the handkerchief she was twisting in her hand. "He said better that I should become the wife of a beggar of the street than marry him. He despises me, Master Milo."

"But *you* love *him*." Her whispered *Yes* pierced him like a knife. "It's hard to love and be rejected. I've been there."

"You? But who would reject you?"

"Hard though it may be for you to believe, a girl named Joanna. But I am getting over it, finally. I had to meet someone who would outshine her."

"And this other - you have met her?"

"Oh yes," he mused. "I do believe I have now met her."

She looked up at him, read something in his eyes and smiled. "Tell me about your world," she commanded.

Thankful that he had managed to relieve her sadness at least a little, he began a rambling and amusing account of life in Glasgow's student-land.

He was in the middle of a tale about a rag-week raid on another College when the door burst open. Jeff and Maggie staggered in supporting Master Will.

"Get him something to drink!" Jeff yelled to Milo. "He could go into shock."

"Then wine is the last thing he should be given. Sit him down. What happened?"

Jeff looked past Milo and saw Olivia standing by the window. By his stance and the look in his eyes when he turned in his direction Milo knew that his friends had been right and he had been horribly wrong.

"We were too late," Jeff's voice was quiet, and dull with shock. "Will was already there. We could do nothing. He's dead." His eyes were irresistibly drawn back to the girl.

"Who is dead? Is it the Prince?" Olivia's eyes were huge, deep blue, Milo noticed once more as he stood helpless, watching her wring his handkerchief.

Maggie cleared her throat and spoke. "It is not the Prince who has died, Lady, but your father."

"Oh!" She blindly put out a hand. Milo rushed to help her sit down, keeping her hand enclosed in his. She did not seem to notice. "I must go to see my father, Milo. Will you take me?"

"It would be better, Lady, if you went to your rooms and lay down with your maid to attend you. I will take you there myself."

As the door closed quietly on them, Will gave a shudder. When he spoke his voice was quiet and monotonous – very different from his strident actor's voice. "After the play," he muttered, "the Queen sent for her son, and Lord Horatio bid me follow him. He paused outside the chapel and talked to himself. He drew his dagger, but after a few moments put it away again with a curse. Then he continued walking. As I passed the doorway I glanced in. The King was there – inside the chapel.

"I followed the Prince as he wandered along this and that corridor. He mumbled to himself continuously. Eventually he reached the Queen's apartments. I waited outside, hiding in an alcove after the Prince entered his mother's rooms. Soon voices were raised, and I heard shouting. Sometime later the door opened and Hamnet came out, dragging the Lord Chancellor's dead body behind him. He passed by not two paces distant, and I could hear him mumbling. The Prince's own jewelled-hilt dagger protruded from Polon's chest. I pray Serra Olivia never discovers the author of her father's death. I fear it would drive her to madness."

"Oh my God!" Maggie gasped. "This is a nightmare, Jeff. What do we do? What *can* we do?"

"What we can do is get you all somewhere safe!" All three spun round at Horatio's voice as he stood in the open doorway. "It is far too dangerous for you here now. Where are the others? You must leave for Rowlan Gayts now – before it is too late. Both moons are up – we can use the ley-lines."

"Milo is taking Serra Olivia to her apartments. But we thought that Emma was with you."

Horatio shook his head. "I have not seen Emma since the disruption at the performance."

"You sent a message saying you wanted to see her!"

"I did not send for her. When was she last seen? Tell me!"

"An hour ago?"

Horatio's face froze in horror. "Emma was the one *required*," he said.

And now she was missing.

Horatio opened his eyes, breathed out slowly. "She's not in the Castle," he said with a voice devoid of expression. He felt sick. "I cannot find any trace of her aura anywhere in the vicinity." He stood up abruptly, ran fingers through his unruly hair. "Stay here. Do not leave this room. You too, Will. I have to find Polon to get you back home."

Maggie gasped. "But Polon is… We thought you knew about him, Horatio. Lord Polon is dead. Hamnet killed him. *Just as Hamlet did in the play.* Just like everything else in the play. They're all going to die! And now Emma's missing."

Jeff reached out and took Maggie in his arms as she broke down, painful sobs wracking her body.

Horatio became aware that he was staggering, and felt himself caught and eased into a chair. He summoned a self-heal and gradually feeling returned to his legs and the blood returned to his face starting low down in his neck gradually clawing up suffusing his jaw, cheeks, forehead in turn with his natural olive colouring. He opened his eyes. Jeff was watching him with undisguised awe.

"A self-healing spell?" he asked. Horatio nodded. Jeff gestured towards Maggie. "Is there anything you can do for her?"

Horatio gave himself a mental shake, and his eyes focused. "For Maggie? Yes, I can help *her*." He lay one now firm and calm hand on her head and wove a sigil above her head. Gradually her sobs lessened, and together they carried her to a couch.

"What now?" Jeff asked the mage.

Horatio paused, listening. "Milo will be back in a moment or so. He's coming up the stairwell now. Now just give me a moment, Jeff. I need space to sort some things."

He closed his eyes and sent a di-speak hail.

<Ho Deveron>

<Horatio. So you know about Polon?>

<Yes. I have just been informed>

<Did you not feel it as his aura erased?>

<No. I did not. But that is not why I contacted you. Emma has disappeared. She was the required one.>

<Meet me in the Main Hall ante-room. Bring the other-worlders.>

<Master Will?>

<No>

<Five minutes>

When Horatio opened his eyes, Jeff was sitting with Maggie while Master Will and Milo sat by the fireside cradling wine goblets.

"I have asked some others to meet with us. We will want you to tell us what you know. Everything. Leave no detail out – your hunches, suspicions, anything that could have any implication on what has happened. Master Will, you should not be there. Some of this information may impinge on things you will do in the future. You should not run the risk of foreknowledge."

"But I could gain so much if I knew what was to happen to me in my future, my Lord."

"It does no man any use to know what may be in his future. Time is not linear."

"But look at what's been happening here – Regicide, mysterious disappearances, murders… What a play this would make!"

"Exactly my point," Horatio's voice had taken on a wry tone. "Jeff, will you waken Maggie? She should be fine now. But you, Master Will, remain in your quarters, if you will."

Chapter 16

The Court is in session.

Maggie chuckled to herself as the thought tripped into her mind and Jeff looked at her with concerned eyes. She made a valiant attempt at keeping hysteria in check and paying attention as Horatio introduced his companion, but failed miserably. She could not concentrate – an after-effect of the sleep spell, she supposed.

They were in a room she'd never seen before. It looked like some kind of minor dining room, which made her wonder why she was so hungry. It wasn't all that long since she'd last eaten. Resignedly she shrugged off thoughts of the food-laden trays in the banqueting hall for the Coronation nosh-up. Nothing had prevented that. Not even the King being held up to all and sundry as one of the primary movers in the death of his brother! And now – the Chancellor was dead, and the Prince declared a murderer. But, she mused – it was not only the *Prince* who was going mad – the whole place was insanity personified!

And that was only for starters. Her mind doggedly shied away from the other reason for their being here, Emma's disappearance, and flicked back to the scene upstairs when Jeff had wakened her from Horatio's sleep spell. She'd felt as if she'd slept for a week, but had in fact only been out for minutes. Potent stuff, she realised. And that was only a 'minor sleep spell'! Watching Horatio now as he stood quietly speaking with an older man, she wondered for the first time what it really meant to be a mage.

She looked across at the stranger. He was quite elderly, his shock of white hair reminding her of a picture of Einstein. His eyes were a pale blue, and crinkled at the edges with laughter lines. But he wasn't laughing now. Nor even smiling. Instead, his face was a mass of worried lines and tiredness.

She tried to remember his name, but it eluded her. Jeff and Milo sat beside her, one either side. She pulled them both towards her and said, "Who is he?"

Milo snorted, but had the answer out pat before Jeff could respond. "He is the Antriantara Deveron, Leader of the Wizard's Council. He was one of Horatio's tutors."

The Antriantara nodded towards them as he and Horatio sat down opposite them.

"Are you all right, Maggie?" Horatio asked.

"I'm okay. I feel a bit light-headed. That's all."

"Let me," Deveron said, leaning over to lay his thin hand on her head. A flood of warmth flowed through her, clearing her head and heightening her senses. She smiled. "Thanks, sir."

"Not *sir*," he replied. "To you my dear, just plain Deveron. Well, Horatio, will you lead off?"

Horatio cleared his throat. "The Prince is still to come."

The Antriantara inclined his head. "Of course. The Prince. Delaying his arrival intentionally, no doubt. I would have thought that you would have had him under surveillance, Horatio! In the circumstances."

"He is, Deveron. A guard is with him."

Just then, the door opened once more and Maggie found herself rising to her feet as a guard opened the door and ushered the Prince into the room. With a murmur and an off-hand gesture, he signalled everyone to sit and took the remaining seat on Jeff's left. Jeff leaned forward, thereby allowing his hair to partially cover his facial scars. Maggie frowned and laid her hand on his.

"We find ourselves in a situation here that no one person can solve," Horatio began. "There are many strands being woven and I hope that by meeting together we can resolve some of our fears and decide on the steps to be taken.

"There are several points we have to discuss: the late King Hamnet's spectre..." Prince Hamnet's head jerked up and his eyes swivelled to meet Horatio's but he said nothing. "...Master Will's play; Emma's disappearance; Chancellor Polon's death and finally, the emergence of a signature-less mage. Deveron and I are convinced that there are links between at least some of these events, and possibly them all. Each of us here has played a part in one of these affairs or has some information to bear."

He stopped and looked at the Prince, whose face had paled even more than usual. "Prince Hamnet, will you tell us of the apparition?"

The Prince lurched to his feet, his hand clenched in fists by his side. "Need I tell ought, Oath-breaker?" he snarled at Horatio. "For it appears that you have already told of it. These people, these *other-worlders*, are not ignorant of the appearance of the spectre. Do you see shock in their faces? Disbelief? Incredulity? No. None of these. Rather you should say to me *'What have you to add to what I have already* broken a solemn oath *to divulge to others?'* "

Deveron rose slowly to his feet and raised his hand. As he did so, he seemed to grow massively in stature as the mage power within him blazed. "Matters such as these on hand are weightier than a Prince's vanity or pride. Horatio broke his oath, aye, but to the greater good. The matters in which we are embroiled concern the whole of Elsynvaal, and very likely the rest of our world also! Take your seat, Prince, and tell your tale as you have been asked!"

The Prince stared at Deveron, shock etched on his face. At first it seemed he would defy the Wizards' Council leader, but after a moment he sat down again.

"Very well." He cleared his throat and sat for a moment or two collecting his thoughts. Then he began again. " Horatio came to me with the information that an apparition very like to my father had been seen on the battlements. The very next night I accompanied the watch and saw for myself the truth of the matter. I followed the spectre and there discovered that my father had not died a natural death but one most unnatural – murder by the one who now wears his crown and beds his queen. *My* crown! *My* mother!" The Prince paused, slowly unclenched his fists and drew in a long breath. His face was pale above the black lace of his doublet and undershirt.

Deveron leaned towards Horatio. "This was a true spectre?"

Horatio nodded numbly. "As certain as I ever can be, Deveron."

The Antriantara turned back to the Prince. "You believe that Claude your uncle murdered your father?"

"Yes, because thus my father's ghost states. But initially it was hard to believe such a deed of the uncle I remember from the days when I was a child."

"Why is that?"

"He was kind to me then…"

"Horatio, do you concur with this? Is the Claude who returned from abroad eight months ago the one of your memories?" Deveron's eyes were sharp as he turned to his former pupil. "Think carefully before you answer."

Horatio frowned as he cast back his mind. "When I arrived at Elasyn to become Companion to Hamnet, Prince Claude was preparing for war. He was following up his successful defence of Elsynvaal after the army of Cheam attempted an invasion. For my part I remember him as a kindly man just as Hamnet does but I only knew him slightly, for our paths did not cross often. He rarely came to Court."

"You did not experience his mage signature?"

"His signature? Claude is no mage, Deveron."

The Antriantara's eyebrows reached great heights. "Perhaps not then, but he is now. The question is – where, and how, did he gain those powers?"

"Deveron – King Claude has no signature! I would have felt it."

The Antriantara of the Council of Wizards smiled. "Of course you would."

Hamnet leaned forward demanding an explanation.

Deveron's smile was thin and cold. "It is my theory that Claude is no longer the uncle you knew as a child, Prince. It is my belief that the man who sat out there on the king's dais, wearing the robes and crown of Elsynvaal is not Claude of the House of Elasyn."

"Then who is he?" Hamnet's knuckles were white as he gripped the arms of his chair. "Who is he who has stolen my birthright?"

"I believe he is Gheron talEbol."

"TalEbol the Renegade?" Horatio's incredulity showed in his voice. "But he was stripped of his powers and expelled from Elsynvaal years ago."

"He was. In fact he was expelled not only from Elsynvaal, but from this world, sent through the Ether to a world where magic has no sway. I was one of those who officiated over the sending. But I have recently been wondering if he has returned once more, somehow."

"A mage so powerful he can work magic without leaving a signature?" Horatio seemed to be talking to himself.

"You are telling us that King Claude is really a renegade mage?" Jeff spoke for the first time.

The Antriantara nodded. "If I am correct, then Claude and Gheron talEbol are one and the same person. I dread to think of the extent of his powers if it is true."

Silence followed his words. Deveron's narrowed eyes gazed upwards at the heights of the rafters above their heads, as if to find answers there. Horatio held his head in his hands. Hamnet leaped from his chair and began a furious pacing. To and fro, to and fro, his boot-heels clicked angrily on the wooden floor. Milo leaned back in his chair, looking sceptical. Maggie's face had gone so pale that Jeff was sure she was about to pass out. He gently squeezed her hand. She did not seem to notice.

"Maggie, are you all right?"

She looked up with stricken eyes towards Horatio. "Horatio, please tell us. Does this have any bearing on Emma? You said at the beginning that there might be a connection." Horatio's sudden pain-filled and anguished eyes silently answered her. She slumped back in her chair, eyes closed against the tears that welled up beneath her eyelids. From a long distance she heard Deveron further question the Prince on Claude's recent actions.

After a time, Horatio spoke with a voice rough with emotion. "Enough. We will move on. There is still much we have to discuss."

Deveron leaned forward, gesturing to the Prince to re-seat himself. "You have heard Prince Hamnet tell of the apparition of the late King. The little charade we watched this evening was intended to elicit a guilty reaction from King Claude. If I read this right, Prince Hamnet, now convinced that the spirit was truthful, intends to kill his uncle. Am I correct, my Lord Prince?"

"All the more so now, if it is true that he is the talEbol."

"My Lord Prince!" Horatio exclaimed. "Surely you see that if Deveron is correct, then it would be suicidal for you to go up against him!"

"Perhaps, but I will not stand by and watch a renegade mage take the throne!"

Deveron's voice was quiet, but his eyes drilled into the Prince. "If you insist on this course of action, than for your own safety you must leave the Castle until solid proof can be found and presented to the Council."

"I refuse. You cannot command me, sir. I am the rightful King of Elsynvaal."

"True, but I am Antriantara of the Wizards' Council. In matters of magic, *I* have seniority. You will depart Elasyn until this is resolved. You already have Polon's death on your hands."

"Ah yes. Poor Polon." The Prince slumped back down into his chair. "The poor man was just in the wrong place at the wrong time."

"You *did* kill him."

"It was my dagger that killed him. An accident. He was eavesdropping on my conversation with my mother. I believed him to be a spy. It was but a single thrust. He should be only lying wounded. Not dead!"

"What did you do with the body?"

"I took him to his apartments and left him there." Hamnet paused, the petulance in his stance fading gradually as reason reasserted itself. "Very well. I will do what you ask. I will leave Elasyn."

"Where should he go?" Horatio asked. "Rowlan Gayts?"

Deveron smiled. "No. There is too much activity there at the seat of the Council. I think the Tower of Illusion in the east would be more suitable. I think you will find that place interesting, my Lord Prince," he said. "Horatio no doubt has spoken of his years there."

"Ah yes, the Tower of Illusion... Deveron's Tower."

"Just so. Then it is settled. Let us turn to other matters."

Jeff leaned forward. "There is one thing that puzzles me. If this Gheron talEbol is in fact the King, then who was it I saw talking with Lord Polon yesterday?"

"What exactly did you see, Jeff?"

"A cloaked figure crossed the courtyard leaving no marks in the snow."

"I'm afraid that a mage capable of taking over a body and identity could easily change his appearance at will," Deveron said. "What else did you see?"

"I heard his voice. It was a very deep bass and cold enough to make me shiver. The King's voice is more of a baritone. They were talking about us – the four of us brought through the Ether. One of us was 'required' they said. Emma." He gave Maggie's hand another squeeze as she shuddered, but she pulled it away, rounding on him.

"We don't know that, Jeff. The King, renegade mage, or whatever, is still in the Castle, isn't he? Surely that means if he has anything to do with Emma's disappearance, she must still be here too!"

Deveron looked at her. "Well noted, my dear. We must consider all angles. But it would appear that if Polon was involved, perhaps others are too."

Milo heaved a sigh. "I don't believe what I'm hearing. Not only is the king not a king but a renegade wizard in disguise, but he has a team of accomplices?" He theatrically laid his hand on his brow and slid down in his chair, his eyes closed. Maggie glared at him.

"Where is Claude now?" Jeff asked Deveron.

"He is in the King's apartments, despite the fact that neither Horatio nor I can get a hint of a magical aura from him. We can only assume, if we are right, that this is another result of his new increased power. I also think that he used a highly disguised spell to adjust the emotions of the people around the Castle and the surrounding countryside to be more accepting of Claude as king."

"I wondered about that too, Deveron."

The older mage nodded.

"Where is your proof, Antriantara? All I have heard so far is theory. Have you any proof at all?" Hamnet demanded.

The Antriantara shook his head and chuckled. "None. None whatsoever. Not a single shred of evidence. I fear it all comes down to gut feeling and intuition."

"What else do you know about this renegade?" Maggie asked. "Can you tell us anything about him?" She glanced around at the others, fearfully. "I mean if he's really responsible for Emma's disappearance…"

Deveron leaned over and took her hand. Maggie felt a warm surge of reassurance flow over her. "I am sorry to have to tell you this, my dear, but Gheron talEbol is the most powerful Mage this world has ever birthed. Since records began no wizard, except Rowlan the Spell-Maker, has possessed the power it appears he can draw upon. But TalEbol is as evil as he is ambitious. He wanted absolute control of the world."

"Oh give over!" Milo interposed. "Isn't this original! A wizard with a penchant for World Domination! I'm starting to feel as if I have been lifted up and dropped in the middle of a third rate fantasy novel!"

Horatio's voice was quiet but full of emotion. "You might feel that you *have been lifted up and dropped*, as you put it, and for that I apologise, but this world is real, *Master* Milo. It's not a book, not a play, but reality. And we are facing real danger. If you want to remain alive and in good health, I suggest that you take it seriously and do your part."

"Which is…?"

"I don't know yet."

"Ah…"

Deveron waited a moment then took up the tale once more. "Gheron talEbol was eventually brought before the Council for his crimes against humanity and sentenced to exile."

"Exiled where?"

Deveron looked directly at Maggie. His eyes softened. "TalEbol was exiled to your world. Earth."

"Oh my God!" Jeff burst out. "You sent a wizard to our world to get him out of your way? Now that is irresponsible. When did you do this?"

"Eighty or ninety Earth years ago." Horatio looked to Deveron for confirmation. Silence settled over the table as the three visitors mulled over this new information. Maggie looked shocked, while Jeff's impotent rage was clear on his face as he glared at Horatio.

Then Milo spoke: "Eighty years. Why did you not just kill him and be done?"

The Antriantara stared at him and Milo, with obvious bad grace, backed down. "We do not take life easily. The Council's decision was perceived as just – at the time."

"Funny thing…" Milo mused. "Years ago I read a fantasy novel about this very thing."

"Oh Milo, shut up! This is serious." Over the top of Maggie's head, Jeff glared at Milo.

"Okay, okay." Milo slid down in his chair with his arms folded across his chest like a chastised adolescent. "Go on, Deveron. How did the wizard get away from the planet you sent him to?"

"We are not sure, but certain things have occurred in the last few years that convince me that he has indeed returned and recent events indicate, as I have said, that he has in fact taken the part of Claude."

Milo's bark of laughter echoed to the rafters. Jeff ignored him. "What now?" he asked.

"We find a way to neutralise him…"

Silence fell once more, and Horatio let it lie for a minute or so before speaking again. "Jeff, it's your turn now," he said quietly. "Will you tell Deveron why you came here?"

Five pairs of eyes turned to Jeff who once more let a lock of hair fall half across his face. Maggie stretched out a hand and squeezed his arm. He turned his head, smiled briefly and began to speak.

"Emma had been having recurrent dreams that were affecting her work so we thought of using a Ouija board to find out what was causing them. Instead, we found Horatio." His blue eyes held Horatio's for a moment then Horatio cleared his voice and spoke.

"This is significant because I too have had dreams. Just as Emma dreamed of me, I dreamed of her, even before we knew of each other's existence. When I crossed over and saw her, there was instant and mutual recognition."

Once more Horatio and Jeff's eyes met and finally a tacit understanding was reached. Jeff looked down momentarily as he collected his thoughts, then he continued with the story.

He explained about Master Will – who he was and what he would become in their world – and spoke of similarities in names and parallels between events in Elasyn and the scenes of William

Shakespeare's play *'Hamlet'*. Finally he touched on the cloaked figure in the courtyard and the conversation he had overheard.

"Someone wanted Emma brought to Elsynvaal," he repeated.

After a pause, Horatio took up the tale.

"When we met, Emma and I believed that we had been unconsciously calling to one another. But just recently I have come to realise that Emma and I had no part in creating the connection, even though I am a trained mage and Emma an Intuitive."

"She's a what?" Jeff asked.

"Intuitive. If Emma was Elsynese, she would by now have completed training as a mage."

"Oh…"

"There *is* an outside force involved," Horatio went on, "someone who wanted Emma in Elsynvaal, and manipulated our dreams to forge a contact between us. I was used to entice her from her own world to Elsynvaal."

He paused and ran a hand through his unruly hair before continuing. "It is significant," he said, "that it was Lord Polon who originally suggested that I bring performers though the Ether. Also, it was a messenger sent by Lord Polon who told Emma that I was waiting for her in the music room. She went, thinking nothing amiss. Thus the plan succeeded and we were duped. She was taken and no-one saw anything."

"But I don't understand!" Maggie burst out. "If Polon and talEbol are responsible for Emma's disappearance where is she now? Polon's dead and talEbol's in the King's quarters."

"That is what we must discover," the Antriantara said. "I think that Horatio is right. Both threads are entwined but also we must remain open to the possibility that others may be involved."

During the talk, Milo had begun once more shifting uneasily in his seat. Finally he burst out: "Okay, Mage. You can't have it every way. But let's just go along with your theories. The Renegade, or his accomplice, has got Emma. So what are we going to do about it? Sit here and talk? Or do we go and find her?"

"I will find her. I promise you!" Horatio declared.

"What about us?" Jeff asked. "Can we help search for Emma?"

"There's not much you can do," Deveron said.

"I can handle a sword," Milo offered.

"Can you indeed?" the Prince queried, one eyebrow slightly raised.

159

Horatio, unable to help himself, smiled fleetingly, before soberly addressing the three students once more.

"I will find Emma," he said in a tight humourless voice, which informed all of them that he could conceive of no alternative. "But I am responsible for bringing you here to Elsynvaal, and thus responsible for your safety. So – this is what I suggest. You should travel to the safety of the Tower of Illusion with Prince Hamnet and his escort when they leave. It should be reasonable to set out at dawn tomorrow. Once you have reached the Tower, you should ask one of the mages to contact us via di'speak."

Jeff, Maggie and Milo exchanged glances. "But…"

Horatio looked towards his old mentor, who nodded in affirmation.

"Yes," Deveron said. "This is the correct course of action. You must be kept safe."

"Indeed." Horatio's face was set in grim lines.

Chapter 17

After the meeting, Milo accompanied Horatio to his rooms. "Thanks for the offer of your lute, Horatio. I don't think I could sleep if I turned in now." He wandered around the room looking for the instrument while Horatio poured wine into two silver goblets.

"It is over in the corner, behind the screen. It is likely to need tuning. I have not played it for a while."

"No problem." Milo disappeared behind the screen just as the mage's door was unceremoniously thrust open.

Prince Hamnet stood in the doorway. Below the blond hair, his pale face was suffused with anger.

"Traitorous Horatio!" he cried as he entered the room. "Oath-breaker!" He kicked the door closed with a crash. "False friend! Only last night you swore a solemn oath to keep knowledge of my father's apparition secret. But you wilfully broke that oath, and not only once! Does the whole Castle now know of my father's torment? Why not shout it from the battlements or put it in a proclamation? But I took your insult well today, don't you agree? I did not call you to duel for your betrayal. I called you friend, Horatio, but no longer!" And with that he whipped out a rapier and swung at Horatio. Unprepared, the mage leaped backwards and tripped on a footstool. There was no time to conjure a spell to aid himself – he fell heavily backwards and hit the edge of the stone fireplace with a crash.

Hamnet walked to the fireside and stood over him, balanced on the balls of his feet in case the mage was faking. But blood was beginning to seep from a wound in the back of his head and he was unconscious. The Prince kicked him. "Wake up, weakling mage! I have not finished with you!"

A voice from behind made him whirl round to face Milo. "Oh yes you have, *Your Highness.* And now you can continue with me!" Milo stepped calmly from behind the screen and whipped a rapier from the nearby sword-stand.

The Prince laughed. "Who do we have here? Master Milo Diaz! Yes, I remember now. You are the one who can use a sword. So you think to cross swords with me? Desist, sir. My argument is with Horatio – not with you. Put up your weapon and leave now. Or stay and take the consequences."

Milo struck a pose, his finger-tip brushing his lower lip. "Let me think. A hard choice, but I think I'll go for the second alternative. En garde, sir!" He lifted the sword circling it tantalisingly in the Prince's face. Out of the corner of his eye, he saw Horatio move slightly. *Thank God he's alive!* he thought, before turning his full attention to the fight he'd stupidly got himself into. *Well this is one way to find out if I really am any good!*

He thrust forward and the prince parried easily, before lunging in return. The two swords came together with their distinct clang as Milo parried and feinted to the left before twisting his wrist to bring the sword round for another lunge. Again the Prince parried easily. Each took a step backwards, breaking contact, and began to circle one another. Then suddenly Milo went on the attack again, swinging and lunging and only just managing to remain out of trouble as the Prince, trained in sword-play almost from the cradle, parried and dodged every lunge and thrust. Before many minutes had passed, Milo realised that he was hopelessly out-classed. Recreational sword-play, even at National level, could never attain the heights that these men, born with swords in their hands, could reach. His breathing was becoming ragged, and his arm heavier with each stroke.

Seeing his advantage, the Prince began to press him more. Rips appeared in Milo's sleeve, in his waistcoat, his left trouser leg. *He's playing with me, like a cat with a half-dead bird,* he thought, frantically parrying yet another lunge. Then his foot caught on a rug and he fell heavily onto the stone floor. Immediately the Prince was there with the point of his sword at Milo's throat.

"Stop, my Lord Prince. He is defeated. Surely that is sufficient?" Horatio's voice was weak, but Hamnet, turning towards him, saw that he had managed to drag himself to his feet. Blood still trickled from the scalp wound, staining his white linen shirt and blue doublet. "After all, your argument was with me."

But the Prince's anger has been diluted by the physical battle with the musician. When he turned to his erstwhile friend there was sadness, rather than ire, in his eyes. Milo took the opportunity to get up and move away from them both.

"Why did you do it Horatio?"

"This is more than you and I can deal with, Hamnet. Sometimes you cannot think rationally – no, think about it and let me finish, please. I knew that on my own I could not really help you. Also, many other strange things have been occurring, things of which I have only recently become aware. Surely you realise that from the meeting?"

Hamnet's sword was hanging limply from his hand. He looked at it now, a puzzled frown marring his fine-chiselled features. "You believe all the Antriantara said about Claude being in fact the rogue mage? If this is so, why would my father's spectre not tell me of it?"

"I cannot answer that, Hamnet."

"*Cannot* or *will not*, Horatio?"

"I cannot, because I do not know."

Prince Hamnet stood up once more and began his restless pacing. Milo stepped forward into his path.

"What about Polon?"

The Prince stopped. Milo moved further forward until his face was inches from Hamnet's. "What will you say to the Lady Olivia, my lord Prince?" he murmured, his voice icy cold. "Do you think that she'll marry you now, the murderer of her father?"

Horatio stepped between them and put his hands on Milo's shoulders. "I thank you for your timely help, Milo. But I think that the time has come for the Prince and I to discuss this alone. Also I think I will need Deveron's help with this." He put a hand to the back of his head where the blood was still flowing.

Stung, despite the gentle tone, by Horatio's dismissal, Milo dropped the sword and turned towards the door. "Will you be safe?" He threw a glance at the Prince standing several paces away from Horatio. The mage's nod was followed by a wince. "Will I fetch Deveron to you?"

Horatio knew that he had sufficient energy to call mentally for him, but realised that Milo was in need of some objective. His self-esteem had been badly hit by his defeat at the Prince's hands. He nodded again, this time less enthusiastically. "Yes, if you would. His rooms are in the East Wing, near the stables. Goodnight, Milo."

"Horatio, *Your Highness,* goodnight to you both." He gave a stiff bow and turned to the door.

After he left, a silence descended upon the room that lasted some minutes as Horatio felt his way to a fireside chair through the tumbled furniture and scattered books.

"I apologise, Horatio," the Prince said from the middle of the room. "It is true that I have on occasion not been acting coherently. But to lower myself to the level of believing you to be a traitor, I ask your forgiveness."

163

"Granted." Horatio's voice was muted and indistinct.

"What do we do now?"

The mage took a deep breath and wondered how long it would take Deveron to come. "Your stay in Deveron's Tower of Illusion will help you get things into perspective. It is not far – as you know," he told the Prince. "Only a day's ride from here. Elsynvaal will need you, my lord, in the days and months ahead."

"My Uncle will be glad to see me go. Olivia too, no doubt," he added, maliciously. Horatio declined to reply, busy trying to quell his head pain sufficiently to call to Deveron, just in case.

***

It took Milo some time to find the Antriantara. The East wing, apart from the floor given over to the Lord Chancellor's family, was unfamiliar to him. In the end, he met the Antriantara in the ground floor corridor, already on his way to Horatio's aid. "What happened?" he demanded. "All I can receive from Horatio is an impression of spilled blood and chaos in his apartments." He looked at the musician's ripped and bloodied clothing. "Is it yours?"

"Some of it. The rest is Horatio's. Prince Hamnet attacked him." He gave a twisted smile and a short bark of mirthless laughter. "I, for my part, tried to defend him."

"And now?"

"The Prince has calmed down and has worked out the anger that made him go for Horatio. They're both still up there. But you'll have to go quickly. Horatio has a head wound, but he's conscious and rational."

Deveron turned to pass him, but then called over his shoulder, pointing to an adjacent door. "Alain's in there. You remember meeting him earlier today? He has healing powers. He'll fix up your cuts, if you want him to. I must go to Horatio."

Do I want Alain the Sylvan to fix me up? Milo stood alone in the chilly corridor trying to decide what to do. He thought of going to Jeff and Maggie *and* of the questions they would ask. Then he remembered the Sylvan Bard's quiet dignity at the performance earlier today. His shoulders slumped with weariness and a cut in his shoulder made him wince. He could not face questions he could not answer. For all the ferocity of his own attack, Milo knew that Hamnet had been merely toying with him. But two of the cuts were still bleeding, one that had laid open the skin of his right forearm,

164

and one on his left thigh. He limped to the door that Deveron had indicated and knocked.

The door opened almost immediately. Alain tirNorest took one look at him and opened the door wide, wordlessly inviting him inside. Milo looked around taking in the other occupants of the suite of rooms. The two dancers who performed with the Sylvan were there, plus several others.

"Deveron sent me. But perhaps this is not a good time," Milo whispered looking round. "I shouldn't have come." But Alain just took his arm and guided him through a connecting door to a bedroom where he indicated a chair. Milo sat down while Alain went to a small travelling chest lying on a table in the corner of the room.

"There is no need for worry, Master Milo," he said. "No-one will say anything of your visit if you do not wish it." Milo watched the Sylvan as he removed herbs and a soft moss from the chest and held them in his hands, closing his eyes. He was small and slightly built. When standing beside him, the top of his head reached no higher than Milo's chin, but his movements were sure, controlled and efficient. After a moment, Alain opened his eyes again and looked directly at Milo with his clear yellow un-human eyes. A smile touched his lips as he noticed Milo's reaction, but he said nothing. Carrying the moss in one hand, he placed a stool beside Milo's chair and sat on it.

"Give me your arm," he said. "Yes, the cuts are not deep. They will heal easily." He spread the mossy paste on the gaping skin and gently pressed it on the wound. Closing his eyes, he began to murmur. Milo felt nothing more than a minor tingling, and was astounded when Alain took away the moss and all he could see was a red mark that sliced across the skin where before the skin gaped open. Now Alain turned his attention to the leg wound. This time, Milo watched carefully, but could see nothing as the Sylvan healed the wound there. Back home, these gashes would have needed stitches.

When he had finished, Alain stood up. "Your leg may feel a little stiff in the morning, for the cut there sliced into the muscle, but the other is fairly superficial and should cause you little pain."

"That's amazing," Milo said, flexing his arm.

The Sylvan smiled. "It is a useful skill. One that comes to me from Mother Nature herself. The moss is the healer. I merely supply the strength for it to work. Now, you must go back to your friends now, they will be anxious about you."

Milo rose from his seat. With muttered thanks and an unsteady bow, he left Alain and his friends to make what they would of his appearance.

Rather than go back to his rooms and face Maggie and Jeff, he climbed the three flights of cold stone steps to the battlements. Once there, he stood in the chill wind letting the wet snowflakes chill him.

If you had no friends... if you had no family... who would you be then?... Cold... freezing...

He shook his head to chase away the song fragments. One of the windows down there was Olivia's. He tried to work out which one, but his brain synapses would not fire. He was too cold, he realised.

He heard a footstep behind him, but did nothing until a figure leaned on the battlement parapet beside him. "You will catch pneumonia if you do not take care." The Sylvan voice was quiet and calm. "And that is much more difficult to cure."

Against his will, Milo felt his lips curve in a smile. "True," he acknowledged. Then he felt a warm fur cloak being placed around his shoulders. "Thanks, Alain. You know when to talk and when to shut up, don't you?"

"Many Sylvan possess that trait. I am not special."

"I wish I knew when to keep quiet. Sometimes I'll say something and immediately realise I should have kept my big mouth shut. But by then it's too late. I can't take the words back. I can only cover up by making more and more comments until people just stop taking me seriously at all. 'Oh, it's only Milo fooling around again' they say."

"So what did you say tonight?"

"I challenged a very angry Prince to a sword-fight, which I lost in a very grand manner."

The Sylvan was silent, gazing out over the courtyard below. In one of the rooms on the second floor, a candle's flame flickered behind a leaded window. A female hand pushed the casement window open and leaned for a moment on the window-sill before withdrawing again and closing the window. *"Olivia."* Milo murmured.

Alain's eyebrows rose, but Milo did not notice.

***

Jeff was waiting up for him when he eventually returned to their room. "Good God!" he exclaimed when he saw his ripped clothes. "What the hell happened to you?"

"Sword-fight. Which I obviously lost."

"With whom?"

"Prince Hamnet."

Jeff rolled up his eyes. Milo merely shrugged. "I think I need proper sword-fencing lessons. Earth rules do not apply here."

"The Prince cheats?"

"No. He's just better than me. My type of fencing is too stylised. Swords are a way of life here in Elsynvaal, I realise now. The moves are much more fluid."

"There's probably someone here in the Castle who can give you some pointers. The Prince probably had a swords-master. He's still here, I would wager."

"Picking up the lingo, are we?"

"Think of the advantage you'd have when we go back home."

"Surely that's 'IF', Jeff."

"No, Milo. It's 'WHEN'. We will get home. You'll see."

Milo went to the chest, took out a clean shirt and began to change. He winced as he pulled the ripped shirt off. The cuts were closed, but the skin was still very tender. "Why the hell am I doing this? I should just go to bed." He threw the clean shirt back into the chest. Over his shoulder he called to Jeff. "Horatio told me that you spoke to Deveron about the possibility of working on you. Any more news?"

Jeff looked away, but after a moment replied. "It will have to wait for a bit, obviously with all this going on, but Deveron suggested travelling south to Rowlan Gayts. Apparently it's a town on the south-west coast, on the far side of the Western Forest, where there is a plethora of wizards."

"The Wizards' Council. Yes. That would be good. You should do that." Jeff looked up at the tone in Milo's voice. Milo smiled. He could almost hear Jeff's thought: *What? No Milo quip? Did he get hit on the head during the fight?*

"Jeff," he went on, still in that quiet voice. "Don't tell Maggie what happened to me tonight – the fight and everything. She's wound up enough already." Glancing at the connecting door, he noticed light still showed at floor level. "She's still awake."

As if in response to his words, there came a knock on the connecting door, followed a moment later by the door opening tentatively. "I heard your voices, guys. I can't sleep in there alone. I'd like to sleep in here tonight, if that's okay?"

Jeff smiled and called to Maggie to come in. He waved his hand towards the mattress still lying on the floor. It was where Maggie had slept the night before, after leaving Emma alone with the sleeping and exhausted Horatio.

Milo sat on the edge of his bed. Was that really only last night? he asked himself. So very much had happened since then. And now the fight with the Prince. *I can't believe I actually did that!* he thought. *And all for what?* A girl!... *Olivia...*

Maggie slipped into the makeshift bed and looked at Jeff, her eyes filling with tears. "What are we going to do, Jeff?"

Jeff sat down on the mattress beside her and put his arms around her, pulling her close to him ignoring Milo perched on the edge of his bed. Jeff ducked his head and dropped a tiny kiss on Maggie's head. She moved away slightly at the touch of his lips, and looked up at him. Then she smiled, just a little, and laid her head back in the curve of his shoulder. Milo stood up. Throwing a towel around his bare shoulders, he left the room in the direction of the privy.

When Milo returned, Maggie was tucked up but still very much awake in her makeshift bed, which she insisted was perfectly comfortable. Jeff was behind a carved wooden screen, stripping off. He glanced at each in turn trying to determine what, if anything, had happened in his absence, but could sense nothing. Behind his quips and nonsense he was very fond of both Maggie and Jeff. They would make a good couple, he realised, if they gave themselves a chance.

"I'm not happy about leaving the Castle tomorrow," he announced as he dropped his towel on top of the clothes chest and began stripping off his ripped breeches. "I'd prefer to remain here."

"I agree." Jeff modestly clad in a loose sleeping tunic, stepped out from behind the screen. "After all, Horatio and Deveron will be here to give us the protection we might need."

"Horatio feels responsible."

"Well so he should. He *is* responsible!"

"I think you're being a bit too hard on him, Jeff. He didn't intend all this to happen."

"Of course not. Therefore, the Lord preserve us from well-intentioned mages! Why could he not have foreseen this happening?"

"He cannot see the future. I asked him about it once. He can only predict events and occurrences that do not intrude on his own future. His life and ours, at this point in time, touch. That's why he could not *see* anything to do with us."

"He can see *nothing* that impinges on his own life?"

"It seems so. So all this with Emma – her dreams, and his, and the kidnapping – he had no inkling of any of it because he is involved. Even the old King's death and Prince Hamnet's peculiar behaviour touched his life."

"He can't make us go with the Prince's keepers." By this time, Jeff's face had set with a grim determination. The clear skin of the left side of his face was paler than normal, while the scarred tissue on the right seemed to have flared up angrily, as if in response to his emotions. The two young men lapsed into silence as they climbed into their respective beds.

Milo leaned over, blew out the candle flame and lay back, his hands beneath his head, thinking.

Maggie's voice in the darkness was wistful. "Emma cannot be too far away from the castle…can she? I wonder what she is doing now. Or even if she's safe…"

Neither Jeff nor Milo had an answer.

Chapter 18

The guttering candle finally died, leaving only one still burning. Horatio sat by the still glowing embers of the fire, fingering the healed but still tender area of his scalp, too lethargic to move. An empty glass goblet and wine flagon lay on a table close by. Deveron had left long ago, after they had finally given upon the search for Emma's aura. They would begin the search once more tomorrow. For now there was nothing left for him to do. He had spent hours poring over a scrying bowl or sitting with eyes closed, travelling and searching with his mind. He was tired out, both physically and mentally, but sleep was an unattainable prize.

He stretched out a hand and lifted the wine flagon. Empty. He pushed himself to his feet and lurched unsteadily to the door. A short laugh escaped his lips as he opened the door. Too drunk to walk but not drunk enough to pass out. Another failure to add to his total sum. Out in the night-deserted corridor, he staggered to the steps leading down to the kitchens. Sensibility told him that he should stop drinking, but he was studiously ignoring sensibility tonight.

The bobbing ball of light that he pushed along in front of him as he went swayed erratically in time with his own staccato movements. As he approached the turn in the steps leading to the kitchens, he let out a low curse. There was a torch burning. He took a deep breath and walked as steadily as he could down the remainder of the steps. Unfortunately for him, his heel caught on the last step and he lurched forward into the kitchen, arms flailing as he tried desperately to regain his balance.

A strong hand caught his arm, allowing him to get his feet under him. A chair was placed behind him and he was gently pushed back into it. Horatio of Saravaal and Elsynvaal, Prince's Mage, peered up into the face leaning over him. "Alain?" he queried.

The Sylvan bard bowed, unsuccessfully hiding a smile. "At your service, my lord mage."

"I came for some wine," Horatio managed to say. "I seem to have run out of wine."

"It might be sensible if you drank no more, my lord."

"I am ignoring sensibility tonight," came the slurred reply. "With sensibility comes pain and loss and a knowledge of one's limitations and incompetence." A part of his mind applauded him for the use of such long words while in his drunken condition. He smirked.

"We all have limitations. And as for incompetence, I'm sure you and Deveron working together will find where the girl is." The Sylvan pulled a chair up beside the mage and sat down. "She's one of the musicians from the other world, is she not?" Not waiting for Horatio to answer, he went on. "Their music was most astonishing, I felt. Very varied. Theirs must be an unusual world."

"Indeed it is, my good Man of the Woods. I spent time with them there while they were deciding whether or not to come to Elsynvaal. Now they know they chose badly."

"She means something to you, this missing girl." Horatio squinted up at the Sylvan. Was his comment just a shot in the dark? Did Alain know something? Or was the remark merely an attempt to find out why he was so spectacularly drunk? Alain knew him well enough to recognize that it would be very uncharacteristic for Horatio to so drastically seek the oblivion of the wine flagon.

He decided that there was no malice in the Sylvan's remark.

"She's my world," he replied simply, his voice less slurred now. "When we met the attraction was instantaneous. We thought it was because of our dreams – do you know about that? Well, it was not our dreams. Somebody else sent those dreams. Gheron talEbol. Cursed be his name. But it does not matter that they were not our dreams. The spark was, and still is, there. You do not know what it is like to love and suddenly have her snatched away."

"No, probably not," Alain murmured softly. Horatio looked up, his eyes narrowing as he forced himself to focus on the Sylvan's dark features. "I have never been in love. Not seriously anyway. But they do say that things have a way of working out."

"What are you saying?"

"Merely that no matter how bleak things look at present, how useless and incompetent you might think you are, something good can come out of it. You will find her."

The two sat in silence, each wrapped in his thoughts. Eventually Horatio gave his head a shake, attempting to clear his brain of the wine fumes.

Alain noticed the gesture. "How about trying a healing spell to clear the alcohol from your system instead of topping up with more wine?"

"It will not work. I cannot focus."

"Shall I help you?"

After a second, the mage nodded resignedly. Sensibility had, after all, won out.

The Sylvan took a blue stone from his belt-pouch and holding it against Horatio's forehead, closed his amber coloured eyes and began summoning up his healing strength from the depths of his being. Gradually the intoxicating effects of the wine began to fade from Horatio's brain. After a time, Alain dropped his hands, pocketed the gem and sat back and waited.

Horatio lifted his head and looked out of clear eyes at the Sylvan. "Good work, Alain. I could not have done better myself. You have my thanks for both the cure and your counsel."

"The day may come when I may need your help, Horatio. But now I think you are in need of some sleep. I will accompany you to your room, if you wish."

Horatio gave him a grin. "I think that is unnecessary, Alain. I am fine now." To prove it, he stood up steady and walked to the staircase. "Till morning then, my friend. Goodnight."

"Goodnight, my lord Horatio."

Horatio turned and climbed up the stairs. Behind him, Alain the Sylvan Bard left alone once more, sat down at the table to continue his own musings. Sleep was far from him.

***

At some time or another during his apprentice years Horatio had experimented with many spells and potions. Some had resulted in unexpected or frightening dreams, visions, and fantasies. He experienced them all. But this dream was different from all of these. Barely an hour after he had parted from Alain, Horatio woke up drenched with sweat and mind ablaze with certainty. *I know where she is!* The vision was so clear, so compelling.

He threw back the blankets, dressed hurriedly in warm woollen clothing and leather jerkin. His fur-lined cloak riding boots and sword-belt completed his attire. Uncaring of noise, he strode along the corridor and down to the stables. He saw no-one. *Where were the guards? No matter – I cannot wait to find out.* He opened the stable door and lit a mage light to see his way. His bay gelding, Starfleet, eyed him with curiosity as he whipped the warm night blanket off and replaced it with a riding blanket.

"Yes, my lad," he whispered, "I know it is still night. But you and I have an errand to go on."

"And what would that be?" The voice came from behind him.

Horatio whirled round, throwing his cloak back over his shoulder to free his sword hand. His sword appeared in his hand as if by magic.

"Hold! Horatio. I do not wish to be skewered! It was but a simple question."

"Alain. You again! Do you never sleep? Or have you been detailed to keep track of my doings?"

"Nay, my lord. We Sylvan need less sleep than Humans. This is but chance – or perhaps foresight."

"You knew I'd come here?"

"Not with certainty. Foresight is rarely conclusive. Surely you know that. But I had a feeling you would do something. I see I was right. Whither are you bound, my lord?"

"An early morning ride."

"It is hours yet till morning and it's snowing. Try again, my Lord."

Mage and Sylvan regarded one another. The Sylvan wore an open look, inviting confidence, and his clear amber eyes were calm. Horatio realised that here was one man whom he could trust, yes, and confide in. He let his breath out. "I had a dream, Alain. I know where Emma is."

"Then it is all the more important that you do not go alone without informing Deveron. And I would wager that you have told no-one. Have you?"

"No, I must confess that I haven't. I felt compelled to leave immediately."

"And was it a compulsion spell?"

"Possibly… I don't know, Alain! All I know is that Emma needs me, and I have to go to her! It is what you too would do, is it not?" Without waiting for an answer, he turned away towards the horse stalls. After a moment, Alain's voice followed him.

"What of the others? Emma was not the only one you brought to this world."

"Deveron will keep them safe. They're due to leave Elasyn for the Tower of Illusion in the morning anyway."

"Then I will come with you. Promise me you will not leave without me." Horatio looked towards the stable doorway where Alain stood. "*Promise!*"

Reluctantly, Horatio nodded. "I will wait for you."

173

"Saddle a horse for me. One not too tall." Then he turned on his heel and moved swiftly and silently across the stable yard to the main building.

Horatio was leading Starfleet and his stable mate Guildera, a roan with a white flash on her forehead, out of the stables when a shadow broke away from the wall across the yard. *Creepy how he does that,* he thought, watching as Alain slid through the shadows towards him. It was no wonder that some people feared the Sylvan. Their peculiar changing eyes and their uncanny abilities of movement were so strange and alien to most people that many, unable to cope with their own inadequacies, took refuge in prejudice and racism.

Alain nodded to the mage as he took the reins, but instead of mounting, he turned and reached over to grasp hold of Starfleet's reins. Horatio swung round as he felt a presence behind him. A cloaked figure stood between him and the castle gates. Glancing back at the Sylvan, he saw Alain meet his angry stare with equilibrium. "I trusted you, Sylvan, and you betrayed me!"

"No, Horatio, you are wrong." The Antriantara's voice issued quietly from the darkness of his hood. "Alain has not *betrayed* you, as you so melodramatically put it."

"Have you come to stop me?" he asked.

Deveron merely shook his head. "I only wish to verify a few things and ask something of you."

"Such as?"

"Are you sure you know where the girl is being kept?"

"Yes. I saw it in a dream. It is a cabin on the edge of the Northern Forest. An old castle retainer Jarek lived there. We rode up there yesterday – or the day before. It's spelled."

"Signature?"

"I didn't register it. I should have, but I didn't." *Another error*, he berated himself.

"This dream," Deveron asked. "Was it normal?"

"What are you saying, Deveron?"

"It could be a trap."

"That may be true, but I still have to go."

Deveron paused, thoughtfully. "Yes, perhaps you do. Very well. Where exactly is this Jarek's cabin?"

"It lies north-west of here, on the fringes of the Northern Forest. Normally a ride of less than an hour."

"Draw it for me, here." He leaned forward and tapped his forehead. As Horatio sent the information from his mind to that of the older mage, Alain stood nearby, watching.

"And what of your plans when you get there?" Deveron said. "Bearing in mind the various traps you discovered when you were last there."

"I had not thought that far ahead. I cannot take on the Renegade alone…"

"At least you appreciate that!"

"…so I'll have to watch and wait until I can find a way of getting her out. I'll think of something."

"Which brings me to my request. It is essential that you keep in touch with me. Regularly. We need all the information on talEbol that you can uncover. But do not in any circumstances allow yourself to get into a power battle with him. A rescue cannot be accomplished if the hero is dead!"

"Thank you, Deveron, for understanding."

"Do not think that I am being altruistic, Horatio. I doubt if any of us could counter the Renegade at this stage. It may even require a mindmeld. Any information you discover could be crucial." With that, he stood back and nodded to Alain, who dropped his hand from Starfleet's reins and swung neatly up onto the back of his own horse. The roan snorted and lifted her head, eager to be gone.

Horatio took one last look at Deveron di'Calidon, Antriantara of the Wizards' Council, wondering when he would see him again. Then he swung up onto Starfleet's snowy back. Silently the mage and the Sylvan moved the horses forward. Calling to the guards as they passed the gate-house, they walked the horses out of the Castle and headed north through the snow flurries, easing into a canter.

It was still dark.

***

"Horatio's gone!" Milo slammed the door behind him and strode across the room to throw open the window drapes. It was barely dawn.

Jeff threw his blankets off and swung out of bed. "What do you mean?"

"During the night. He left on horseback with the Sylvan Bard, Alain tirNorest."

"What?"

175

"For God's sake, Jeff! Don't parrot me! Just get some clothes on. We have to find the Wizard Lord. He's the only one who will know anything. Maggie, are you coming?"

***

Deveron, with narrowed eyes looked Milo over. "Not bad," he murmured. "You allowed Alain to fix you up then?"

Milo cast a glance at Maggie, but she was not really paying attention. "As you see, Deveron. But that is not why we have come to see you. Do you know where Horatio is?"

"He has left Elasyn, on a quest to find his Lady. Oh, several hours ago."

"He knows where Emma is?" Jeff burst out.

"He thinks he knows, so we must hope that he is successful."

"Thank God!" Maggie exclaimed.

"Why didn't he tell us?" Jeff asked.

"It could be very dangerous. He will cope better if you are not there." The Antriantara stood up and gestured towards a tray holding a teapot and several cups. "Tea anyone?"

"How the hell can you just stand there so calm?" Milo burst out. "We could have helped him!"

"How? With your sword, Master Milo?"

"Oh! I don't know. Somehow."

Jeff waved a hand at Milo. "Deveron, is it true that the Sylvan went too?"

Deveron turned back towards them, tea-cup in hand. "I wonder how you came by that piece of information? But yes, it is true. Alain is with Horatio. They are headed for a cabin on the edge of the Northern Forest, which is Alain's homeland. If talEbol has a lair in that area, the Clan tirNorest may know something of it."

Maggie tipped her head quizzically. "Who exactly are the Sylvan?"

Deveron sat back in his chair and took a sip of tea, and told them of how many ages ago, the Sylvan had arrived in Elsynvaal. "They came in boats from lands far across the Western Sea. The lands of the Dying Sun. Some say that they escaped persecution; others feudal war, but all that is certain is that by the time they reached Elsynvaal's shores, they had divided into two groups. One group settled in the great forests of the North and became the tirNorest of the Northern Forest. The other group settled in the West and became the tirAldae of the Western Forest. Most of the Sylvan," Deveron

176

continued, "remain within the borders of their Forests, but just occasionally one, like Alain, leaves his Clan to travel."

"What about their healing powers?"

Deveron smiled thinly, remembering Milo's combat with Hamnet the previous evening. "Some of the Sylvan, the Magicands, have powers that could be likened to Mage power, but any Sylvan I have met is remarkably reticent about the acquisition of such power. Humans are not welcome in their Forests. The things people fear so much of Sylvan are the manner of their colour-changing eyes, and their silent movement. They can move as if under a *Sileans* spell – a spell that renders one's movements totally silent and unnoticed. Alain, by the way is very tall for a Sylvan. Most are much slighter in stature. Do not worry. Horatio is in good hands. But now, since you will not have any tea, I suggest that you return to your rooms to prepare for your journey. Prince Hamnet's entourage will be leaving shortly."

"We're not going. We refuse to leave if there is any chance that Emma will be back here soon." Jeff glanced at the others, saw them both nod in agreement.

"As you wish. You will remain here then and await Horatio's return."

As the door closed behind them, Deveron was smiling.

***

It was after dawn, but the watery sun in the western sky hardly seemed to have sufficient strength to climb the heavens. Three figures stood on the battlements facing the moat and the lowered drawbridge. Wrapped in warm clothing, they huddled together using the roof of the Great Hall behind them as shelter from an icy north wind and the snow flurries that rode on its wings.

Down below in the square the troupe of entertainers, with Prince Hamnet among them, walked their horses and pack mules out of the gates and down the cobbled street towards the river. The gateway was still in deep shadow, making recognition of the party's members difficult. It was not until the troupe had crossed the moat and had started down the street that there was sufficient light for the Scots leaning over the parapets to make out one shrouded figure wrapped up in a heavy dark cloak. The Prince.

They watched with mixed feelings while the figures grew smaller and finally disappeared amidst the huddled houses of the town. Milo turned to the others. "Let's go back inside." His nose was red with cold. Maggie hadn't even noticed that she'd been shivering. Jeff stamped his feet as he turned to limp after the others.

Chapter 19

Mhari McLeod sat in her attic room in the West End of Glasgow and watched Martin pace. The autumnal evening had passed now, and it was now fully dark. He looked over to the table where Mhari sat. "They're late" he said. "Horatio said he'd bring them back today!"

"Remember the time differential he told us about. The contact could come any time from seven tonight until dawn. It's not yet nine o'clock. He told us that it was very difficult to determine relative time factors."

"I have a bad feeling, Mhari."

"You've been having bad feelings all weekend! Do you have any idea what a bloody pain in the neck you've been? All we can do is hold the path between the worlds open, the way Horatio taught me."

"Can you feel anything?" She did not answer. "There's nothing, is there?"

"There's nothing at this precise moment, but that's only because the Ether has not yet been opened. When Horatio tries to make contact, I'll be ready."

She watched Martin lift a book he was meant to be reading for a tutorial tomorrow, but laid it down again, obviously unable to concentrate. He stood up and wandered over to the narrow dormer window and looked down to the street. "Duncan's just coming in," he called over his shoulder.

"How about you going down to find out if he'll make some coffee? I could do with a cup, and you could do with something to do."

With a shrug, he walked to the door. "I'll leave the door open, just in case."

Mhari heaved a sigh of exasperation as he disappeared down the stairs. Sure she could understand his anxiety. His girlfriend, not content with ditching him, had left without a backward glance for another world with a new rival. Poor Martin. He was probably only the latest in a long line of ardent admirers and would-be lovers. The inevitable result of the combination of her exotic and enigmatic looks and an innate magnetism, she supposed. Beauty and charisma, ye cannae beat it.

Smiling a little ruefully at the turn her thoughts had taken, she laid her hand on the spinner on the table and sent her mind swinging away, searching through the windy darkness, as the mage had taught her, for an answering mind. Nothing. No response. Three hours they'd been here in the attic room, trying to make contact. No wonder Martin was getting impatient.

Footsteps on the stairs warned her that the young composer was on his way back. She pushed back her chair and pulled the door fully open. Martin was not alone.

"Hi, Dunc," she called to her brother as he followed Martin into the room.

"Hi, sis. Martin said you were up here. I thought I'd come up and find out what mischief you're brewing up now."

"Nothing that you'd be interested in, brother."

"Sounds intriguing from what Martin has said."

Mhari narrowed her eyes at Martin as he handed her a mug of frothy coffee. He shrugged, feigning nonchalance. "Okay, brother. What has he told you?"

Duncan ducked his head to dodge a rafter and sat down on a vacant chair. He took a sip of coffee before looking across at her. "This and that," he said.

She leaned over and playfully landed a punch on the arm. "Don't come the innocent with me!" she retorted. "What has blabbermouth here said to you?"

"That you're waiting for Emma and some of the others coming back. I would have thought that the front door would be a more convenient place to wait. So, where are they? Don't tell me – this one of your little forays into the mystic realms! Anyway, I'm curious."

"So you said before."

"What harm is there in telling him, Mhari?"

She shrugged her shoulders and leaning over she put down her coffee and laid her hand on the spinner, ready to search for the opening once more. "Tell him then, if you think you can make him believe you!" And with that, she closed her eyes and sent her mind away.

She came back to hear Duncan's concerned voice, but kept her eyes shut, listening. "Mhari? What's wrong with her?"

"She's mind-travelling," Martin explained. "She's looking for an opening to another world. She'll be back soon." At Duncan's astonished gasp, Mhari opened her eyes and listened as Martin tried to explain the inexplicable. "Through a Ouija board we contacted someone from a parallel world, who can cross between his world and ours."

"You ran a Ouija board? If Mum finds out about that, she'll kill you, Mhari! You know what she thinks of that hocus-pocus."

"Wait, Duncan," Mhari said, "let me finish. Last Monday he crossed over here and on Wednesday evening he went back, accompanied by Emma, Jeff, Milo and Maggie. Your sister was taught how to open the Ether – the space between the worlds – and what we're doing tonight is to open the Ether again to let them return."

"You're telling me that some of your friends have been escorted to another world by little green men? How? In a space-ship? Didn't notice any UFOs in the sky last week, I don't think."

"It wasn't like that," Mhari said. "This is serious, Duncan. No little green men; no UFOs. Horatio's as human as any of us, or so it would seem."

Duncan's eyebrows shot up. Martin leaned forward, towards him. "I know it's difficult to credit it, and I probably would have difficulty in believing it, but I saw it with my own eyes. Horatio appeared here from nowhere, and I watched them disappear two days later. All five of them, just like that!" He clicked his fingers with a loud snap. Mhari could see that Duncan was still sceptical, but he was also curious.

"So when does the intergalactic train arrive?"

"That's the problem," Martin murmured, taking a long drink of coffee. "We're not sure, exactly. Time runs differently over there, so…" Duncan looked bemused. With a sigh, Martin glanced at Mhari.

She tried to explain. "There's a time difference between the two worlds, which means that we're not exactly sure when the link between the worlds will open. I send my mind out and search for the opening Horatio will create in his world. The nearest I can get to it is this – use a method Horatio taught me to sort of *think* into a different dimension."

"Are you saying that there really is an 11th dimension?"

"11th? What are you talking about?"

"For years now there has been a raging row in physics circles about whether alternative universes might exist. The most recent findings seem to indicate that there *are* other universes touching and

181

maybe overlapping our own, where different physical laws apply. You're telling me that these alternative universes *do* exist – and that Jeff and the others have gone there? That you can contact this other dimension?"

Mhari smiled as Duncan looked at her, a deep frown on his face. "No, you're having me on. A big joke. One bit you've got wrong though, the both of you. This is October, not April Fools Day!" Yet Mhari knew that her big brother was intrigued. The curiosity remained.

"I'm going to try again," she said and closed her eyes.

***

Blinking in the sudden light, Mhari looked first at Duncan and then at Martin, shaking her head at his unspoken question. No response yet. She got up to stretch her legs and wandered over to the window to look down on the street. From behind her he could hear the murmurs of the men as, she supposed, Duncan quizzed and Martin answered as well as he could.

Outside, an old banger of a car came rattling up the street, drowning out even the sound of their voices. The door of one of the houses opposite opened and a man and a woman came down the steps to the street. Linking arms, they turned down the street in the same direction as the bone-shaker. Down to the pub for a Sunday night's dram, she supposed.

"So you're going to sit here patiently all night, waiting for something to happen?" she heard Big Dunc ask.

"That's about right," Martin murmured. "To tell you the truth, I'll wait forever if need be. Not patiently, granted, but I will wait. Yes, for her I will wait."

Duncan looked at Martin for a moment and then turned to look at his sister with new eyes. Then he raised his now empty coffee mug in a salute. "Go for it, Mhari!"

***

The hours dragged by. Midnight came and went. Mhari suggested that Martin go home and try to sleep. Then she suggested that he kip down on the floor. Duncan went downstairs and brought back some sleeping bags. Then she tried to teach them how to reach out with their minds and search, but either she wasn't explaining it properly or neither of them had the innate ability that she had.

About four in the morning Duncan asked what they were going

to do if there was no response by the daylight, pointing out that they had four missing persons on their hands. "Someone is going to start asking questions. They will be missing lectures and tutorials – what are you going to tell people?"

"Nothing. They'll be back. It's just the timing that's out. Horatio will get them back."

"Are you sure? Aren't you just a little bit worried that this Horatio chap isn't who or what he said? Of course you both are. You just won't admit that you've been playing around with something you do not understand and have no means of controlling. Face it. You have no real reason to believe they'll ever come back, do you?"

"They'll be back." Martin's voice was still calm and sure, but underneath the quiet tones Mhari could hear uncertainty in it.

"You can't go to the police – what would you tell them? It would be recorded as another missing persons file and you would be taking regular trips to a psychiatrist." Duncan kept up voicing his misgivings.

"For God's sake, Duncan, shut up." Martin yelled. "You're as bad as Milo."

Mhari laid her hand on Martin's arm. "Horatio is someone we can trust. He will not let them down. If it is at all possible, Horatio will open the void and bring them through."

Martin looked up, his eyes suddenly bleak. "If it is at all possible…" Mhari looked away and closed her eyes, ready to try searching again. Martin's voice broke into her concentration. "Are you sure he taught you properly?" He stopped, realising what he'd inferred. "I'm sorry, Mhari. I know you're trying your best. I just feel so useless."

***

Dawn broke on a cloudy sunless sky. Fine drizzle fell weeping from clouds so low that they seemed to scrape the chimney pots and TV aerials on the grey roofs. Drips gathered on the satellite dish on the house across the street. Duncan rubbed the glass in the window to clear away the condensation and peered out. "Another fine day in sunny Glasgow. Such a distinguished type of rain we get here isn't it?"

"Shut up, Duncan," Mhari retorted. "Go and see if you can get some breakfast for us. What time is it anyway? I have a lecture at eleven."

183

"Just after eight thirty. You mean you're going to leave all this and go to a lecture?"

"I can't keep this up continuously. I'll come back again after the lecture and try again. What about you, Martin? Don't you have a tutorial this morning? I thought you mentioned something about one yesterday."

Martin turned and listlessly picked up the book he'd tried to read yesterday evening. He shrugged and ran his fingers through his unkempt hair. "Is there somewhere I can have a wash?"

As the door closed behind him, Mhari looked at her tall rugby-playing brother. "He's in a bad way." Duncan did not disagree. Mhari sighed and sat at the table again. "I'll just have one more try before we leave." She stretched out her hand to the spinner and closing her eyes, she sent her mind away. After a few moments she tensed up, her hand tightening over the spinner.

"Sis?"

"Hush, Duncan, I think I can feel something... Horatio, are you there? ... Please help me hold the contact – it is difficult... Ah! Thanks. That's much better now... Wait – you're not Horatio!... Who are you?"

Chapter 20

The mid-day meal came and went and still the three Scots exiles remained closeted in their rooms. Restlessness gnawed at Milo; it was impossible to sit still. Every few moments he stood up and went to stand by the window, watching the snow twist and curl in the wind as it fell. Then, as the chill crept back into him and made him shiver, he retreated to the fireplace where several thick logs burned, crackling and sparking. Eventually when Maggie yelled at him to be still and stop, he decided enough was enough, and with a sketchy goodbye, left the room. Maggie's entreaties about staying together followed him, echoing eerily as he strode purposefully along the castle's myriad maze of corridors.

Finally, he ended up on the gallery outside the Prince's Library, and heard a familiar sound from behind the half-open door. Pushing it gently, Milo looked inside. Master Will was walking back and forth, speaking or reciting verse from a sheet of parchment in his hand. A high-backed chair hid the identity of the person to whom he was addressing himself. Milo pushed the door wider and silently entered into the room. Master Will looked across to the doorway at his movement and nodded before continuing his verse.

". . . Yet eyes this cunning, want to grace their art,
They draw but what they see, know not the heart."

The end of the verse was greeted with applause. "That was lovely, Master Will," Lady Olivia's voice was clear and calm. "You should have recited it at the King's celebration."

Milo joined in clapping as he walked further into the room. Olivia craned her youthful and supple neck round to discover who was approaching and stretched out a slim and welcoming hand.

"Master Milo! How lovely to see you. Will was trying to take my mind off things by reading me some poetry he has composed."

Milo moved to her side and surprised himself by taking the girl's hand and raising it to his lips. Her eyebrows rose slightly as she raised her eyes to meet his. Then she smiled and let her hand fall back into her lap. Turning back to the poet, she demanded another of his verses.

Will paced up and down, theatrically rubbing his smooth chin, while Milo took a seat near Olivia, very aware of his quickening pulse rate. Forget that, he told himself. Think about it later. He turned towards Will, who was pulling another piece of parchment from the bundle in his satchel.

"Shall I compare thee to a summer's day ..."

"I know that one!" Milo broke in, before continuing with the next line.

"Thou art more lovely and more temperate
Rough winds do shake the darling buds of May
And summer's... "

He broke off, fumbling, trying to remember the next line. Will continued, somewhat bemusedly.

"...Summer's lease hath too short a date."

"Ah, yes, that's it!" Milo exclaimed. "It's a long time since I studied that sonnet."

Olivia frowned in puzzlement. "I pray you, Master Milo, tell me of what you speak. Master Will has but recently penned this verse. How is it that you know what he would say?"

"Aye, Master Milo. Tell."

"I'm sorry, Master Will. It just slipped out. I was not thinking. Forget I said it."

"No, Master Milo. I will not. This is not the first time you or one of your friends has mentioned something of my work that has left me vexed and somewhat puzzled."

Milo looked away, mentally kicking himself for shooting off his big mouth yet again, but the poet would not give up. "Pray tell, Master Milo!"

"All right, all right. It's just that Horatio warned us against telling you anything referring to your future, and that sonnet would come under that heading."

"Well, now you have told me this much, you may as well tell me the rest." Milo glanced at Serra Olivia, whose eyes were much less troubled than he had expected. Under the circumstances, he would have expected her to have remained in her rooms all day, wanting only solitude to grieve her father's death and the departure of her betrothed.

"All right Master Will, I'll tell you a little. But you must promise that you will not tell Horatio I've told you anything." At the poet's nod of agreement, he continued. "I come from your world. You know that. Yes?"

The poet inclined his head. "The Lord Horatio brought you over as he did me."

"The difference being that I come from your future world."

"Ah. Now I begin to see your earlier remarks in a different context. And you know and can recite my sonnet? How is this? Does it sell so well? Will I be paid much for it?"

"Oh, Master Shakespeare, there is so much more. You will become famous for your plays and your poetry."

Will was bemused. Milo knew he should say no more and leave, but Olivia was looking at him with wide-open beautiful eyes...

"That sonnet," he said, "is one of the most famous of the sonnets you will write. By the time I was studying English Literature they, along with your plays, had become the backbone of the English texts studied for exams."

"You *study* my plays? Why should you do this? How is it possible? You must visit the theatre very often."

"No, it's not like that. Yes, if we are lucky we will see a play on stage, but usually if we see it at all it is a film adaptation – moving pictures. Film is a twentieth century invention. Mostly though, we read the texts of the plays in written form."

At Will's confusion, he blundered on. "Your plays will make you immortal. They are performed and watched and read and studied all over the world. The language you use is looked upon as classical poetry, and your themes are such that people have been able to relate to them though all the ages." Milo knew he had no real aptitude for drama or poetry, not like Maggie – but he *had* studied two or three of the plays for the Standard Grade exams.

"So your people read and study my plays as literature in your schools? Astounding." He stood up and struck a classic actor's pose. Milo was reminded of Laurence Olivier in 'Henry V'.

Will was still expounding. No other word for it, Milo thought. He sneaked a look at Olivia. She was smiling and clapping her tiny hands like a child at a party.

"Then I must make sure that they are worth your study! I will write beautiful verse and successful plays." He paused thoughtfully for a moment. "I will be successful, will I not?"

"Yes, Will. You will write for the Queen!"

Master Will sat down, almost missing the chair in his distraction. Serra Olivia stood and laid her hand on his shoulder.

"I have ever told you that your work was of the highest order. So now you know what your capabilities are. You will be famous. Even my father thinks so... no, not think, but thought... He is gone, Master Milo. Did you know? Ah yes you were there when I discovered it so…"

Milo and Will exchanged glances, but before either could do anything, the Serra rose and shook out her skirts. "I think I will leave now," she said. "You have been very kind in giving me so much of your time, Master Will. You have amused me and made me laugh when my heart should be breaking. But, soft," she broke off and her gaze shifted to the window and the falling snow beyond the window glass, "perhaps it is broke already."

She dipped to the floor in a graceful curtsy. "I will leave now and go to my father. Farewell, kind sirs, farewell."

Milo hurried to her side to open the door. "Master Milo, would you walk with me?"

Without looking back, she passed with a soft rustle of petticoats and moved out into the balcony overlooking the Great Hall. The carpenters were once again at work, dismantling the staging. The performance seemed weeks away, yet it was only yesterday. Twenty-four hours ago.

And now Milo walked with Serra Olivia as she moved serenely along the balcony and at the apex point of the unusual triangular Hall turned into the East wing. She began to speak, but it was an expressionless monologue, addressed to no-one but herself. She seemed to have forgotten Milo's presence, unaware that he was still beside her. "I will go to my father's room. It is where a good daughter should be. I am a good daughter. My father bade me dissuade Hamnet from marriage with me. I fear I have succeeded too well. I am a good daughter. My father's wishes will be honoured. My father lies in his bed chamber. There will I go hence. I am a good daughter, I will renounce Hamnet. I will forsake my love."

They reached the door to her father's bed chamber, and as she opened the door, she seemed to come out of her daze and notice his presence. "Master Milo, I thank you for your kindness. If you wish, you may wait in the ante-chamber, if you will." After the inner door closed, Milo looked around the small room. This was obviously the room Polon had used for people waiting to see him – chairs were uprights rather than comfortably upholstered, and the table by the window held several decanters of wine. The windows here overlooked the cobbled square at the front of the Castle, with its portcullis, drawbridge and stables. He stood and looked down for a while, watching the activity, then over in the corner Milo spotted a small lute. He lifted it and checked the tuning, then began to play.

Perhaps his music could help her.

***

On the floor above the room where Serra Olivia kept vigil at the side of her Father's mortal remains, Deveron was mind travelling. He was half lying, half sitting on a couch, but his mind was winging far away, flying over the now blizzard-lashed northern grasslands searching for two life-forms. It was always much more difficult locating an aura in adverse weather conditions, and the snow blizzard, heralded for several days by frequent snow flurries, had finally arrived. His mind swung far to the north until he saw in his mind's eye the stunted trees and the frozen grasses of the tundra. He'd missed them somehow and gone too far. He shifted his attention more to the south-west and moved slowly over the white landscape. Nothing… nothing… nothing. Then… a glimmer, an aura, but neither Horatio nor Alain. Nor anyone he knew… Whose? An unknown source struggling to keep the contact…help him… yes it was clearer now. Who was asking for Horatio?

As he struggled to strengthen the contact, Deveron tried to stem the sudden panic that had overtaken the owner of the unknown aura. *<I am not Horatio>* he sent across the Ether, *<but a friend of his. My name is Deveron. Who are you?>*

Mhari's response was slow and uncertain. *<I am Mhari, a friend of the four people who crossed to Elsynvaal with Horatio. They have not returned. We are worried. When will they return? Where is Horatio?>*

Deveron thought fast. He remembered that Horatio had tried to return them the night before the Coronation and had failed because of a blockage in the Ether. Now for some reason it had reopened. He should return the Earth people now, while the crossing was viable. Also there was a possibility that this person might know something of Emma that could explain why she had been kidnapped by Gheron talEbol.

<They are well, and will return soon> he answered. *<How did you learn to do this>?*

<Horatio taught me>

Deveron's eyebrows rose. If that was the case then Horatio's teaching talents, it would seem, are great indeed.

<He has done well. Do you think you can keep the contact open while I reach your friends?>

<I think so. It's becoming easier.>

189

<Tell me, what do you know of the girl Emma?>
<Not much. Why? Has something happened to her?>
<She is well. Can you tell me anything about her background?>
<At this point in time I'm telling you nothing. Either you send them back through to me or you bring me through the Ether to you. Choose. I'm telling you nothing unless you can convince me that my friends are well and that they are coming back.>

Deveron sat upright on the couch and began extending the scope of his range.

<Very well, if you insist. Hold open the contact and I will go to their room>

He opened his eyes and while carefully holding open the tenuous connection, he stood and walked to the door. On his way to the north-western wing where they were lodged, Deveron was thankful that he met no-one to whom he had to speak.

Only Jeff and Maggie were in the rooms. Deveron frowned, but said nothing. Retaining the contact with Mhari was more important at this point in time. Still silent, he sat on a comfortable chair by the fireside, and motioned them to sit near him. Then he closed his eyes.

Pulling up reserves, Deveron struggled to maintain the connection with Mhari while speaking to Jeff and Maggie. It felt like his mind was splitting in two. His speech even to his own ears was almost intelligible. He tried again.

"Av contac marrry."

"He's contacted Mhari!" Maggie's voice sounded incredulous. "We can go home!"

"Sshhh! Listen."

Then Deveron did something he had never allowed himself to do before. He slowed his breathing and his heart rate to an almost dangerous level and then surrendered his mind completely. He became a *de facto* conduit between the young people on both worlds, allowing them to speak to one another directly through his own mouth.

"Mhari," said Deveron's voice, "speak to your friends. But be quick, I cannot hold this connection for long."

"Guys? Are you there?" Mhari's voice issued from Deveron's mouth. Jeff and Maggie looked at one another.

"Mhari?"

"Yeah! Yeah! I'm here. What's happening? When are you coming home?"

"Wait a minute, Maggie," Jeff whispered. "How do we know

this isn't another trap or trick?"

"Course it's not!"

"Guys," Mhari's voice came from the Antriantara's mouth. "Are you there?"

"Mhari, what is Martin's last composition called?"

"What?"

"We need to know you are really Mhari. So, what is Martin's last composition called?"

There was a pause. Deveron felt a cold sweat break out on his face.

"Lucky Martin is here. He says: '*Friends, an introduction and rondo for unaccompanied voices*'. Right? Okay, are you ready to cross over and come back home? Deveron says he can do it for you."

"No," Jeff said. "We're going to stay here for a bit. There's something we have to do."

"What?" came Mhari's voice.

"Emma is off somewhere. We're not all together," Jeff said.

"What do you mean?"

"She's missing!" Maggie cried out. "Emma's been kidnapped!"

"We'll get her back," Jeff said. "Horatio's gone for her now."

Deveron struggled to maintain the contact, but it was slipping. "Twenty-four hours, Mhari. Open a contact in twenty-four hours," he said then the darkness took him, his last memory hitting the floor after tipping off his chair.

***

He was lying on a soft bed. He groaned and felt a soft hand on his forehead. "He's coming round," Maggie said. Deveron opened his eyes and looked at her.

"We were so scared, Deveron. We didn't know who to go to."

"How long was I unconscious?"

"Five minutes or so," Jeff was standing behind Maggie, his arm around her shoulders.

"Help me up."

They arranged the pillows behind him and eased him to a sitting position. "I will be better soon. Get me some wine," he said.

He closed his eyes and began an exploratory of his body, checking for damage. Not a good idea to try that again, he thought. But interesting that I could even do it. He chuckled, and then opened his eyes to the concerned looks of the two young people.

191

"I'll be fine," he said, and took the proffered goblet. His hand was steady. "No harm done."

He drank from the goblet and handed it back to Maggie. His strength was rapidly returning. Good. There's life in the old dog yet.

"Mhari will re-open the contact in twenty-four hours time, that is, in thirty-eight point four hours Earth time. Hopefully Emma will be restored to us by then and you can all go home."

Jeff said: "No!"

Maggie said: "Yes!" then she looked at Jeff.

"I have to stay, Maggie. It could be my only chance for a normal life."

"Then I'll stay too until we can all go home together."

"You can discuss this later, yes?" Deveron continued, "but now, we have to find out why talEbol wants Emma. Please tell me as much as you can about her. In particular anything you know about her background."

"Emma's childhood and background?" Jeff mused over it. "She doesn't talk much about that, does she? Her father is Scottish, and her mother was Japanese. She died when Emma was very little. Her father brought her home with him and later he remarried."

"I don't think her mother did die. It was more like she disappeared," Maggie put in. "I remember her telling me about it, how that one day her mother just disappeared and was never seen or heard of again. Apparently all sorts of searches were made but it was as if she'd disappeared into thin air."

"Yes, that's right," Jeff said. "One night Emma arrived at our flat in tears. She'd been to visit her Dad, but he'd laid into her for something, saying things about bad blood and the like. She was really scared. I just got out of the way as soon as I could and left Martin to comfort her."

"Yes, I remember that night," Maggie added. "She was really scared. Why are you asking, Deveron? "

"It was not chance that brought her here."

"It was the dreams. We keep coming back to those dreams. But why should a renegade Elsynese Mage want Emma?" she asked.

"That is where I had hoped you could enlighten us."

Maggie shook her head. "I don't know how we can help you in that. Apart from her parentage, Emma had a fairly normal upbringing. She always felt a little out of it because she was the only Anglo-Japanese around, but I can't think of anything else."

"She's a very private person," Jeff added. "Difficult to get close

192

to. At least that's what Martin found."

"Would Milo have any more to add?"

"I doubt it, we have only known him since he joined the choral group. We don't meet up socially except after rehearsals."

"Where is he, by the by? You were to remain together, if I recall correctly."

"He is with Serra Olivia, I believe. He has taken quite a shine to the Prince's betrothed and prefers her company to ours." Jeff's voice held more than a little contempt. "Well it's his life and he can do with it just what he wants."

Deveron sighed, remembering Horatio's warning concerning the continuous bickering between the two young men. They seemed to have little in common beyond a love of music. He knew he should leave and go back to his own rooms, but the wine had encouraged lethargy. He sent a self-heal though his body once more and shifted his legs round to the edge of the bed.

"I'm leaving now. But in twenty-four hours time," he told them, eying each in turn, "I would have all three of you come to my quarters in the west wing, on the ground floor. Do you understand?"

He stood up. Steady. Good. "We will have Emma back soon," he said. "Horatio is a powerful mage and Alain has powers of his own. Never fear. They will all return soon."

But each of them knew that it was far from certain. Deveron, despite the fruitful contact with Mhari, still feared what may still lie ahead of them all. He sighed and turned to the door. As his hand turned the doorknob, he froze, rigid and alert as a dreadful shudder sheered through the Ether.

"What is it?" one of them asked from behind him.

"It seems there is something I have to attend to. Please excuse me. I suggest that you remain here in the meantime. I will return… later." And without anything further, he left the room and hurried downstairs, taking readings as he went of the dimensions of the disturbance.

The last time he had felt this… he pushed the thought away harshly as he swiftly travelled the corridors to the north wing.

Silence fell inside the room. Outside, the wind had risen and was hurling huge snowflakes at the windows as an alternative to howling around the quadrangle of the courtyard. Across in the Queen's apartments lights were lit, despite the early hour. Darkness would come early today.

Mhari was shaking by the time she broke contact with Deveron. She took deep breaths and forced her shaking hands to be still.

In the dim attic of an ex-Council house in Glasgow, she told Martin Patterson and her brother Duncan that she'd contacted with Deveron, Horatio's old mentor.

"And?"

"Jeff and Maggie and Milo are fine, but they're not returning yet, for one reason or another. Emma…"

Martin stood in front of her, his face rapidly losing colour. "What's happened?"

"She's been kidnapped," she said, looking down at her hands to avoid Martin's aghast and unbelieving look. "I don't know any more, but they're doing all they can..."

"Like Hell!" Martin shouted.

Duncan stepped over, laid a hand on Martin's arm. "Cool it," he said. "Leave her alone."

Martin wrenched his arm from Duncan's grasp and rounded on his sister once more. "Why did you not send me over?" he demanded. "You could have done it."

"What could you have done Martin? Be realistic. It would not do any good for either of us to have crossed over just now."

"How can you say that? Emma has been kidnapped, Mhari! She's in a parallel world and no-one has the faintest idea where she is!"

"That's not true, Martin. Deveron said that Horatio was on his way to get her back."

At Horatio's name, Martin's face tightened.

"We'll just have to wait until the next contact."

"Which is. . .?"

"In twenty-four hours, their time. Thirty-eight point four hours in our time. "

"Shite!" Martin swore and stomped to the dusty attic window to take up his accustomed position, looking down on the street below. The silence grew. Duncan dropped into a chair beside his sister. Eventually Martin spoke again. "So there's nothing we can do until you re-open the contact in – what was it? – oh yes. Thirty-eight point four hours time. I *knew* there was something wrong when they didn't contact on Sunday night. I *knew* it!"

"That is not helping." Duncan said.

Mhari shot a glance of warning at her brother before addressing Martin's rigid back. "I feel just the same, Martin. I don't know them as well as you, apart from Jeff, but they're my friends too, Martin. I hate the idea of being so helpless. Don't think I didn't want to just throw myself into the void and let Deveron pull me across! I almost did."

"So what do we do for the next day and a half? Tell me that!"

"You could go to class…" Duncan said.

Martin lifted the empty coffee mug from the window-sill and hurled it across the room. It smashed to pieces against the wall.

"Damn the lectures!" He strode to the door and yanked it open. "I'll be back tomorrow." His footsteps clattered down the uncarpeted stairs.

The silence left behind him was eloquent.

"Can't take pressure, can he?" Duncan remarked.

"He's worried. He'll be full of apologies tomorrow." Mhari stood up and turned towards the door. "I think I'll go and get some fresh air." Duncan stood up, stretched and they left together.

"He really loves her, doesn't he?" Duncan pondered as they went downstairs.

"Yes, I think he does, but he knows as well as the rest of us that something has sprung up between Emma and Horatio."

"Jealous?"

"And very uncertain of her, which just makes him even more possessive."

"Not a happy situation."

"But one Martin will have to accept if Emma decides on Horatio."

"You don't think she'd stay in that other world?"

Mhari shrugged. "Who knows? It sounded quite cool."

"Until people started getting kidnapped!"

They reached the bottom of the stairs just after the doorbell rang. Martin stood on the doorstep. Mhari stood in the hallway, half hidden by the heavy door, and they regarded one another. Then Martin held out a conciliatory hand. "I apologise. I was seriously out of order there. My behaviour was inexcusable."

Mhari moved forward and took his proffered hand. "No problem, Martin. We understand, don't we, Duncan?"

The big rugby-player nodded. "Sure."

"I'll pay for the smashed mug." He turned and walked down the steps leading to the street.

"Toldya' " Mhari said, a little smugly.

"You said it would be tomorrow."

"Okay. But I was right, wasn't I?" She stepped through the doorway and watched Martin as he walked towards his car. "If only we could be that sure about Em and the others…"

Part Two

Snow, Spectres and Sorrow

Chapter 1

Alain tirNorest reined in his horse, leaned over and caught Horatio's bridle. Spitting out snow and sleet, he yelled into the howling wind.

"We cannot go on in this! The temperature is still dropping. We need shelter! We have almost reached the Forest. I can feel it close by. It's this way."

He turned his horse side on to the fierce northern wind and urged the beast on. Horatio, frustrated and impotent, followed wordlessly behind. He knew it was senseless to continue to battle on in such conditions. Even by extending his senses to the limit he could not determine the location of the cabin.

Heads low, the two dejected horses ploughed their way through the knee-high drifts of snow. In a gap through the driving snow, Horatio glimpsed the shadowy trees of the Northern Forest. Closer they came until they reached the dim shelter of the Forest. Alain climbed down from his mount and proceeded on foot a little way. There, he knelt down and bent forward until his forehead was touching the thin snow covering the woodland detritus. Horatio dismounted and watched in silence for a moment. A Sylvan rite, he surmised. The blizzard had remarkably little effect here under the ancient trees. He reached out with his senses and found the power protecting the trees from blizzard damage. Not human wizardry, but Sylvan.

Alain returned and took hold of his horse's reins. "We will be safe enough here. We should try to sleep. This storm is set in for some time. Several hours, at least. In the meantime, tell me this – how do you plan to rescue Emma?"

Horatio gave a short laugh. "I don't know. Have you any ideas?"

The Sylvan inclined his head. "Perhaps. But I would be of more use to you if we could communicate mind to mind. We could then perhaps create a diversion and free her when the Renegade's attention is elsewhere."

"You want me to teach you di'speak?" Horatio's voice was wary. He turned the idea over in his mind. There were no precedents for this – Sylvans and Humans were wary of one other, and he had never heard of a Sylvan and a Human communicating by di'speak. Would he be penalised by the Council if he did it? But without doubt, it would help to be mind-to-mind with Alain. He made the snap decision. I'll face the Council later, if necessary, he thought, and his misgivings melted like the occasional snowflake landing on the toe of his boot.

Alain smiled.

He proved a willing and able pupil. The Sylvan had an instinctive feel for the use of mental and internal physiological energies. Soon the two were talking to one another using only thought while the blizzard still raged beyond the shelter of the Trees.

Alain rose to his feet and looked down at him. "If what you tell me of this talEbol is true, then we cannot rescue your lady alone, Horatio," he said. "I will go to the Clan and ask for aid."

"Will they give it?"

"Perhaps they will, but perhaps not. You should remain here, however. Not all of the Clan elders would welcome a Human into their midst. Rest here and try to sleep. If you do not move in any further into the Forest you'll be well. I will return as soon as possible."

The Sylvan turned to go then paused. "Horatio, use no magic here. The Forest has its own power."

The mage nodded. "Yes," he replied. "I feel it."

Time went on and still the blizzard raged. Horatio's head began to feel heavy, and finally he sank into a doze.

***

In his richly-decorated rooms in Elasyn Castle, the newly-crowned King Claude opened his eyes. They were sticky with mucus. He shifted cramped muscles, rubbed his rough chin with his hand, and then sat up with a jolt.

I have my mind back! He threw his blankets back and sat up, revelling in freedom. *The Demon is gone! My body, my mind are my own once more.* He stood up. His legs felt weak, as if he had been lying abed for a month, but he could walk. Still dressed in his sleeping robe, he staggered to the doorway and into the dressing room beyond. A courtier standing outside attempted to help him, but he brushed him off, accepting only a heavy velvet covering robe. He left his rooms distracted and wandered the corridors in a daze, ignoring all around him, soldiers, courtiers and servants alike.

Eventually he reached the North wing, and stood once more in the Chapel, the place the Demon had brought him the previous night. He half-staggered, half-fell onto one of the wooden benches as memories began to assail his mind. Things he had done in the past four months. *But I was not responsible. I was an unwilling victim! The Demon made me do these things. I am innocent.*

And now poor Polon was dead. *It might have been me hiding behind the arras when Hamnet burst in! And if I had...*Claude shuddered at the thought. But the Demon would not allow his host body to be killed. Would he? Poor Polon. He did not deserve to die. But neither had his brother.

Was Hamnet's act yet another orchestrated by the Demon? He ran his hands over his arms, revelling in possession of his own body. *I must stay free of the Demon. But how?*

"Demon!" the King suddenly yelled out, thrusting his hands up in the air in front of the altar of the one god. "What are you doing to me?" His words reverberated round the small dark and enclosed place slowly dying away to silence.

A low husky voice whispered into the silence.

"Who's there?" Claude called. "Is it you, Demon, come to take possession again? I will fight this time! I will fight!"

"Why do you seek a demon in a holy place?" The husky voice sounded once more, tantalisingly half familiar, this time coming from behind him. Claude swung round in the direction of the sound. From the dark recesses of the far corner of the chapel a man's ghostly form was watching him.

"Why do you call on a Demon, brother?"

"Brother?" Claude gasped. Falling back, he crashed into a bench and fell sprawling on the floor. "Have you come here to haunt me? No! This is but another manifestation of my madness, my possession!"

The spectre moved from the shadowed recess towards him. Claude scrambled backwards, mumbling incoherently. The spectre moved forward menacingly. "Answer! Why do you seek demons here? You already carry your Demon within you. You wear a bloody crown, and you will never be free of your sins, brother. Did I treat you unfairly, to warrant my premature death? Claude, my brother. Why did you do it? Why, brother?"

King Claude cowered in the corner of the small chapel, blubbering incoherently. The ghastly semblance of his brother's voice rose in volume and venom as it gave vent to its grievances. Then, all at once, the apparition began to lose substance and grew fainter. At last, it was gone. But still it seemed the voice remained, repeating over and over again the same words.

Why did you do it, brother? Why?

Claude, shaking on the cold stone, knew these words would follow him to his grave. He pulled himself to his feet and stumbled to the chapel door. Wresting the door open he leaned out and yelled out: "Help me! Bring me a priest!"

***

After Deveron's abrupt departure, Jeff and Maggie stared blankly at the closed door. Then Jeff stood up and crossing to the table by the window poured some wine. Maggie took the goblet from his hand still puzzled and frightened.

"Something's terribly wrong, Jeff. Did you see the way his face changed? Do you think it could be connected with Emma's disappearance?"

"I don't think so. At least not directly. But there's so much else going on here. That meeting yesterday was a real eye-opener. Milo's not the only one who feels dropped in the middle of it! For once I find myself agreeing with him."

"I never thought I'd ever hear you say that about Milo, but of course, he's not here so it doesn't really count does it? So – what about the Antriantara bolting like that?"

"I think he got some bad vibes from somewhere. No doubt we'll find out about it if he wants us to know."

"I wish Horatio was here."

"Yup. He'd tell us, I reckon. But, hey you never know, he might be in the midst of a valiant rescue even as we speak!"

"Don't scoff, Jeff. Deveron was right to make us stay here. This is not our world and we don't belong here. We would just make any rescue attempt Horatio and Alain try less likely to succeed."

"You mean he's more of a knight in shining armour than us? I suppose there's no real call for heroes in our world."

Maggie took a long drink of wine before replying. "I would not say that. You're a bit of one yourself." Then she rushed on, hoping that Jeff would not comment on that slipped-out observation. "I wonder how Martin's feeling."

"If he's running true to form, he'll be swinging between anger, frustration and worry. I don't envy Mhari having to deal with him."

"It will be good to be able to go back home."

"I'm not going back yet, Maggie."

"I know."

"I can't leave just yet. Just think of what it will mean for me, Maggie. No more lingering looks from strangers who are obviously thinking 'What happened to you, mate?' No more embarrassed averted eyes. Tell me, how long did it take you to get used to my blotched and scarred face, Maggie?" Goading her into answering, he threw his long hair away from his face leaving the scarred and puckered skin in full view.

Maggie did not answer at first, looking at him closely, trying to see him as would a stranger. She looked at his deep brown eyes and saw there a fear he was showing her for the first time. She'd always known he had immense courage, but with this gesture he was baring his soul to her scrutiny. "I don't know, Jeff. I think I just accepted it, as you yourself seemed to do. That's what I meant when I said you were heroic yourself."

Jeff smiled wryly. "So that's what you think. Well, it's not heroism, Maggie, whatever you might think. It's only survival."

"It takes courage to go through life refusing to just accept its knocks and kicking back instead. That's what you're doing now. Taking Horatio up on his offer of a cure is kicking back. I'm proud of you, Jeff."

"Thanks, Maggie. You're a good friend."

"Is that all?"

Jeff looked at her and Maggie panicked, wondering if he'd just throw it back at her, but just then door was thrust open and Milo stood on the threshold ushering Serra Olivia into the room.

"Oh shit!" Jeff mumbled under his breath, but from Maggie's look he knew she'd heard it. She threw him a grin, and turned round to the others as Jeff let his hair fall forward around his face once more. As she turned, Jeff gripped her arm and turned her back to face him. "To answer your question," he said quietly, "the answer's 'no'. You're much, much more." Maggie placed her own hand lightly on top of his and smiled. Enough said.

"Hi, guys!" Milo said. "How's it going?"

"Better." Jeff replied. "You've just missed a visit from Deveron. He's managed a contact through the Ether and spoken with Mhari."

"Good God! Does that mean that we're going home?"

"She's been told to contact him tomorrow. Deveron hopes that Emma will be back by then, assuming Horatio and Alain are successful."

"Did he say anything of their chances?"

"No, nothing. I don't even think he's been in touch with them since they left."

"I do hope your friend Emma is all right." Serra Olivia put in. "She's a lovely girl. But if Master Horatio has gone to find her, she is in good hands. Sometimes poor weather conditions can affect communications between mages. I often hear my father speak of such…" She stopped, remembering.

Milo moved to her side immediately, attempting to distract her with the offer of some wine.

"Where's Will?" Maggie asked.

"Writing," Milo replied as he sat the Serra down in the chair Deveron had lately vacated. "He's being very mysterious," he went on, "scribbling away in corners and refusing to show anyone anything. Would it not be brilliant to be able to take back an original piece of work by William Shakespeare?!"

"Even if we could, it would no doubt be rejected as fake. Wrong kind of paper, ink, the lot." Jeff commented.

"There is that, I suppose. Oh well, another Diaz money-making scheme down the drain." He turned to Olivia. "Are you all right?"

She smiled. "I am well," she replied. "But it is so recent that sometimes I forget that my father is no longer with us. And when I do later remember, it is as if it is fresh news. My father lies abed, and nothing is yet settled on his burial. Think you that the King will give him a proper burial?"

"I'm sure he will, my lady." Milo's voice was soothing.

"My brother Loren is at a loss on how to proceed, as I am. If only my Lord Hamnet were here."

"And if he was here? What do you think he would do? I don't think he even knows what day of the week it is."

"He would… see that things were done properly. He is the Prince, master Milo, and you should not speak of him in such terms."

"Why is he not here, then, Lady? Do you know where he is, or why he has fled?"

Maggie laid a hand on Milo's arm. "*Don't*, Milo," she pleaded, but Milo shrugged her off.

"Prince Hamnet has run away because he fears justice. He is responsible for your present agony, Olivia. It was *his hand* on the dagger that killed your father. Do not waste your tears on him."

As Milo's words sank in, the blood drained from Olivia's face. For a long moment she sat immobile, a marble statue. Then she looked up into Milo's eyes and asked, "Why should you say such a thing?"

Maggie had buried her head in her hands, so it was Jeff who answered. "It is true, my lady. But it was done in error, and not maliciously."

Olivia's gaze turned slowly to Jeff's face. "And why should you lie?" She looked at the handkerchief in her hands and wrung it once more. "So. My father lies dead at the hand of my lover. Oh this is too great a burden to bear. I must away. My father awaits my vigil at his side." And as they watched, the light in her eyes went out.

Jeff insisted that he should be the one to take her back to her rooms, and Milo, realising that he'd shot his mouth off once too often, agreed. As the door closed behind them, Maggie turned on Milo.

"What on Earth were you thinking of, Milo? Why did you have to tell her like that? She's got enough to be going on with without that knowledge!"

"She'd have to find out sometime, Maggie."

"Aye, *sometime*, but not yet. The girl is in shock already over her father. She's an orphan now with, as far as I can gather, no relatives except her brother, who is even younger than she is. She's been pampered all her life and now, thanks to you, she has to deal with the odious idea of Prince Hamnet as a murderer."

"I'll be here for her."

"You? What dreams and fancies with which you delude yourself, Milo! You may have fallen for the beautiful Lady Olivia, but *she loves the Prince*. That is very clear. You've no chance. Look, will you, you thick-skulled idiot, she called Hamnet her *Lover*! Or did that small piece of information slip your notice? Or the fact that in a short time you will be going home to Glasgow?!"

Milo for once stood silent, abruptly aware of the immense wrong he had done Olivia. *I will make it up to her. Somehow, I will,* he thought. He wandered off to the window. Snowflakes had begun to fall once more. Silence fell, each waiting for something to happen.

Eventually Jeff burst in.

"You bloody idiot!" he yelled. "That girl is out of her mind with grief! Well I hope you're happy. When ever will you learn to keep your mouth shut? As for me – I'm washing my hands of you. I'm sick of your comments and remarks and your lack of consideration for other people. Love? You don't know the meaning of the word!"

Milo knew there was nothing he could say to stem the tide of Jeff's hard words. Instead he let them wash over him, each syllable hardening his resolve to rectify his error.

***

"A Priest!" Claude gasped out as he gripped Deveron's robes. "I need a priest – not a mage! I wish to make a confession." He slid down onto the stone floor heedless of its chill.

Deveron's hand wove a sigil in the air, but the modicum of calm did little to break Claude's panic.

"I am possessed," he screamed. "I need an exorcism! I have done wrong, sir, a great wrong. A Demon has possessed me and forced my hand to do murder. Fratricide. By my hand my brother died, and now his spirit has come back to haunt me."

Deveron nodded, realising the source of the disruption he had felt. He swiftly scanned the chapel for traces of protoplasm or energy residue, and caught a hint in one of the corners of the room. Storing the information for later examination, he turned his full attention to the quivering man on his knees before him.

"Tell me."

"It is true that I was jealous of him. The people called him *Good King Hamnet*. But he was *not* a good king. He was content to hide himself away in his library and let the country go to ruin. It was I – I, Prince Claude – I who held back and finally defeated the invading armies of Cheam.

"There are only two things in this life that I have truly craved and *he* had possession of both. The crown, and the woman I loved. The crown he had because he was first-born, but Greta was meant to be mine. She is the only woman I have ever loved and she loved me in return. But she was wed to my brother! Is it any wonder I was consumed with jealousy?

"I did the only thing I could. I left Court and led Elsynvaal's armies against the invaders from Cheam. *I* achieved peace. Not my brother, *Good King Hamnet*. And, even then, once peace was secured, I stayed away from Elsynvaal. Why? Because of the feelings between the Queen and myself.

"I travelled. All over the world. But then a year ago I met a wizard who was in touch with events in Elsynvaal. The portents, he told me, were good for my return to Elasyn. When I arrived, I was greeted with open arms. Then walking one day in the rose gardens, I came upon the Queen weeping. We realised that our feelings for one another had not changed.

"We did what we should not have done." He paused, calmer now as memories flooded through him.

"A few days later the wizard I had met on my travels arrived at Elasyn. He showed me a way to gain my brother's throne and at the same time free Greta from her loveless marriage. I refused. So the demon wizard invaded my body, discarding his own. Since that day to this I have been unable to prevent anything that has happened. With my body the Demon also took my mind, my will, my identity. He cast spells to cause my brother Hamnet to change his will and disinherit his son, and altered the sensibilities of the general populace towards me, increasing my popularity. The way to the throne was almost open. Only Hamnet my brother stood in the Demon's way. All I had to do was… *murder my brother.* Fratricide… he forced me to the deed. I was impotent. My hand poured the poison into his cup, even as I screamed within against it." Claude's voice faded as he uttered the words.

"And now?" Deveron gently asked. "Where is the Demon now?"

"When I awoke a short time ago, I was free of the Demon. I know not why…"

"What happened here tonight? Was it the Demon?" Deveron asked.

"No, not the Demon. The spirit of my dead brother appeared, berating me for my sins. I fear his haunting, Mage, but it is the Demon that I fear the more. It is my puppeteer, and I *must* do its will. Beware of me, Mage. It will return! I know it."

Chapter 2

When Horatio awoke he was alone and surrounded by silence. The blizzard had ended. The light had almost gone from the sky and the first stars were shining fitfully amidst broken clouds.

He stood up, brushing twigs and loam from his breeches, and called Alain's name. The words came back to him, echoing from the massive tree trunks surrounding him. He closed his eyes and gave Alain a mental hail, as they had practised only a few short hours ago, but felt no contact. How long had he slept? He looked around for the horses. Nothing. They had disappeared, their hoof-prints obliterated by the snowfall.

He strained his senses outwards, searching first for Alain, then more desperately for the cabin. Searching, his mind flew north and then south along the edge of the forest. On an indrawn breath, he found it. Not so far. But south-west. In the blizzard they'd travelled too far north. He walked to the edge of the forest and peered into the growing dark. Then with a single backward glance, he gathered his cloak around him and headed out into the snow in the direction of the cabin. Emma was there, waiting for him. He could feel her calling.

***

"Are you missing him?" the hag asks. *"Your Romeo? How romantic to be able to communicate between worlds. I have never been back, you know. All these years and I never went back. And now you're grown. Emasiyo, my little girl. He will come, your Romeo. We have sent for him. He has dreamed a dream and even now he is coming. He is coming."*

Emma wonders if the voice belonged to a real person. Or is it just another part of the nightmare she has been living since she opened the door to the Music Room? *The room swimming before her eyes as it changed shape and form as she watched mesmerised and becoming increasingly frightened. Lights flashing in psychedelic swirling colours, swirling around her faster... faster... faster... then darkness.*

And later – but how much later? – there is cold stone beneath her bare flesh. Hands are pressing down on her abdomen. There's pain, then darkness.

Later again – the voice. An old hag of a woman leans over her, all rotting teeth and stinking breath. *"Are you missing him?"* the hag asks. *"Your Romeo?"*

Emma's eyes flew open. She was lying on a large comfortable bed in a small white-washed room. A fire burned in the open hearth, and a curtain of thick red fabric covered part of the far wall. A woman sitting by her bed – not a hag with rotting teeth after all – smiled and leaned over towards her and offered a bowl of thick soup and soft fresh bread. What was happening? Where was she? She looked at the woman, and was shocked to discover that she seemed familiar – but who was she?

"Emasiyo, my dearest daughter!" the woman exclaimed. "You are awake!"

***

Rising painfully through the sleep fog clouding his mind, Horatio felt Alain's feather-light touch inside his head but the contact was broken before he was able to strengthen it. He collapsed again, aware that his clothing was soaked through from lying in the snow. He had to move, or die of hypothermia, but he could not find the energy to force his eyes open and haul himself to his feet. His eyes closed. He slipped back into unconsciousness, and he dreamed.

The warmth of a fire registered before the fact that he was sitting down with something lying in his lap. He opened his eyes. The fire burned brightly in the hearth, casting flickering shadows on the walls of a white-washed room. He looked down at his lap. At his slight movement Emma lifted her head from his lap turned and turned her face up to his.

"Are you all right?" Emma asked, twisting round onto her knees and flinging her arms around his neck.

"What's going on?" Horatio whispered, breaking off the kiss and lifting her onto his lap. "How did I get here?" He looked round.

"I was so frightened at first," she whispered, "but now I know about her and it's okay. You're here, just as she said you would be."

Horatio's defences crumbled. His fears faded to nothing. He let himself be guided across the tiny room to a curtained alcove. Stumbling, laughing, they tumbled onto the bed that lay beyond. And fell...

Horatio came slowly back to consciousness, desperately holding on to the dream. She was close. He could feel it. He pushed the snow off and struggled to his feet. His head ached and an unaccustomed weariness permeated his whole body. He tried a self-heal, but he was so near to hypothermia that there was little he could accomplish. Squinting, he peered at the small building not fifty feet away from him. A sound behind him made him twist round, his hand reaching for his sword and finding only an empty sheath. He staggered and his vision swam. He forced himself to remain upright.

An old woman was standing four paces away from him, her wicker basket held up in front of her as if ready to throw it at him. It was half-filled with twigs and small branches.

"Are you ill?" she asked, hesitatingly moving forward. Her voice was unclear to his befuddled ears. "Come with me, young sir. I will help you." Without another word, she took his arm and with small steps tottered towards the shabby building. Smoke rising from the chimney hung low in the heavy sky, a promise of further snow. His head spinning, he allowed himself to be led forward, aware that he was not thinking clearly. But as he approached the door, his stomach knotted and nausea rose in his gullet. His step slowed. But the old woman turned and gently led him on. Her voice penetrated his thoughts, garrulously telling him how, many years before, she had lost her husband and only child and after many years travelling she had come upon this cabin where she now lived.

Inside, the cabin was warm and spotlessly clean. Still chattering, she watched him as he wandered around the room. It was sparsely furnished, two comfortable fireside chairs, and a small table, over on one wall a kitchen area with a long table and a sink. Beside the fireplace, and looking out of place in such a rural setting stood a set of shelves crammed with books with unusual bindings. He touched one, a thick tome in pale leather-like binding, very smooth and delicate to the touch. On the spine, the title was written in an unfamiliar script. He frowned, running his hand over the smooth binding. Not ordinary leather, he thought. As he reached for another, he felt a hand on his arm, gently drawing him towards the fireplace where it was warm.

The old woman pulled at his wet and sodden cloak, peeled it from his shoulders. How long had he lain in the snow to become so wet? What about Alain? But his thoughts faded to insignificance as he felt the warmth from the fire penetrate the damp jerkin and shirt he'd pulled on in haste before leaving the Castle. He felt gentle fingers on his arm and a soft voice behind him. "Take these wet garments off, my lord. They will dry well soon enough." Gentle fingers loosened the ties on the jerkin, eased it down his arms, and began on the lacing of his loose shirt. Somewhere in the back of his mind he knew this was unnecessary – a simple dry spell would suffice – but he could not remember the words or signs. Stupid. Such an easy spell, too.

The old woman stood up. As she did, her image wavered. The lines in her face faded, her skin became softer and younger, her hair darkened. Her eyes changed shape, becoming more oval. Like Emma's, he realised. As the changes solidified, he watched uncomprehending. *She looks like a slightly older version of Emma!* he thought, aghast. *Who is she, this shape-shifter?*

"What in the name of the god is going on here?" He stepped forward, threateningly.

She danced away. "No, my dear Horatio. I am saying nothing. You must find out for yourself." She gave a little giggle, which came out more like a cackle.

"How do you know my name?" he asked through his teeth as he stepped back a pace in disgust. He tried to conjure a spell – any spell – but once again the words would not come. Neither could he gather any power from his inner spirit. He was powerless. There must be a *Nulato,* a power-negation, in force, and in his befuddled and weak state he had been unable to sense it.

"We have long known of your existence, Horatio. We even sent for you. We created your dream last night, and other nights also." The high-pitched laugh sounded again. "Your magic is useless here. This place has been secured by the greatest Mage in this or any other world. Of course, I have my own power, as you will find out in good time.

"But for now, I know why you have come here to my cabin in the woods. It is my daughter Emasiyo that you seek. She is there, beyond the curtain. Go to her. Enjoy her."

211

He edged away from the woman, confused, bewildered. *My daughter, Emasiyo*, she had said. Memories of the dream flashed into his mind, and he remembered Emma once saying that her full name was Emasiyo. But what was it she had told him of her mother that one time in Kelvingrove Park in Glasgow before they crossed to Elsynvaal? But his mind was foggy with the pressures of the *Nulato* spell. Keeping his eyes on the woman, and clutching his cloak around him, he slid along the walls till he reached the curtain covering the back wall. He pulled back the curtain. Beyond was a small room, dominated by a full-size bed. At the swishing sound of the curtain, the small figure in the bed raised her head.

"Horatio?"

He crossed the room in three paces and gathered her in his arms. Behind them, the curtain closed once more and they were left alone.

***

Long afterwards, he turned to her, smoothing her hair back from her face while Emma told him all that had happened.

"When I came to," she said, "I was here in this room," she gestured around, "and she was sitting beside me, holding a bowl of soup. My mother didn't die twenty years ago, Horatio. She's been here in Elsynvaal all this time! It was she who sent the dreams to us. She knew we were meant for each other and arranged for us to meet. A cross-world blind date!" Her laugh rang out, and Horatio hearing it realised it was the first time he'd heard such unforced laughter from Emma. He wanted to share in her laughter too, but there were too many questions.

"How did she come to Elsynvaal?"

"Oh Horatio, you're never going to believe this. Her father, my grandfather, brought her through the Ether, the same way as you did with us! He's here in Elsynvaal! So you were right when you said I was a sensitive! My grandfather is a Mage of Elsynvaal."

Horatio felt a shiver of premonition run down his spine. "Who is he?"

"She said his name is Gheron talEbol."

Horatio's heart thudded against his breastbone. *TalEbol! The Renegade!* He felt the blood drain from his face. Automatically, he tried a self-heal, but the *Nulato* prevented the spell forming. Horatio rolled off the bed and straightening his clothing and grabbed Emma's hand. "Come!" he whispered. "We have to get out of here. Now!"

"But why? Surely…"

"This is Jarek's cabin. Remember Maggie and the booby-trap spell? The woman who says she is your mother is the mage who did that. She may not even your mother. Shape-changing is not impossible for an accomplished mage. And going by the quality of the *Nulato*, she is proficient enough to have the ability. We have to leave!"

He tugged on her hand.

"Listen, Emma. I don't know why she's worked to get us here together – all I know is that we *have* to leave. Come with me now. There's more – *much more* – to this than she's told you. Once we are back in Elasyn we can find out the truth."

"But Horatio…"

Horatio took both of Emma's hands in his and drew her to him. "Please listen to me, Emma," he said his voice low and intense. "Gheron TalEbol is a renegade mage who refuses to abide by the Council Laws," he stated flatly. "He was expelled from Elsynvaal many years ago for crimes against the people."

"He's a renegade?"

"Yes! Now, come on!" He strode across the room to the curtain, drawing her behind him. They dashed across the room beyond, making for the door. Horatio reached for the door knob but jerked his hand back as a tremendous shock shot through him. He staggered back, gasping and clutching his swiftly blistering fingers. Emma snatched up a jug of water lying nearby and thrust Horatio's hand into the liquid.

"Stupid! Stupid!" he berated himself. "I should have tested it first. God save us!"

He bound his hand up with a cloth lying nearby, and looked around. "We cannot get out that way, and I cannot use magic to get us out. A *Nulato,* a spell-negation, permeates the whole building." There were no windows in the room; the only entrance was the curtained doorway leading to the bedroom.

Horatio's breath caught in his throat as coldness spread through him. Under his breath, he cursed his utter foolishness in rushing into this situation. Instead of rescuing Emma, he had merely given the Renegade an extra prisoner. "TalEbol… We *have to get out* somehow. But without magic…" His voice trailed off, uncertain, thoughtful. "They enticed me here because they want both of us, Emma. Why I do not know, yet. They were responsible for all of our dreams because they wanted you here in Elsynvaal." He paused. "If she really is your mother."

"If she is, then why did she abandon me?" Emma's joy at finding her long-lost mother was finally fading, trampled into the bare earth of the cabin floor by reality. Her mood swung from elation to despair.

Horatio reached for her, pulled her into his arms. "Perhaps we do not know why she has done any of this, but remember that without her interference, we might never have met."

She pulled away. "Oh, so I've to be thankful that my *mage mother* who abandoned me as a baby has now decided to make amends by throwing me at you?"

"You belittle us both, Emma. You weren't thrown at me. We have to think clearly now."

"Good God, Horatio. Think clearly? How would you feel in my shoes? Your family and home life were happy and stable. I didn't have that stability. When I was one year old my mother disappeared, never to be seen again. I was brought up by a grieving father and at five years old I left my native land for a cold wet country where I looked and felt different from everyone else. That's how I grew up, Horatio. A sad and lonely little girl, especially after my father remarried. And now… Now I find my mother alive and well after all! And more – she's a mage in a parallel world. It's too much."

Horatio took her hands and pulled her towards him. Slowly they made their way back to the curtained room. Once back in the room, he eased her head on to his shoulder and murmured to her. Slowly the tension began to ease from her knotted muscles. Then he saw the curtain move.

"Come in!" he called. "Perhaps you will deign to answer our queries."

The curtain was thrown back, and the woman stood in the opening. She was in the form she'd changed to as Horatio had left her – a small Japanese woman seemingly in her late thirties. Walking slowly towards the two lovers, she smiled, but not with her eyes.

"I will answer some of your questions," she said in a voice now totally unlike Emma's, deeper with clipped overtones that suggested that her English was a learned language. "Firstly, this is my true form. Secondly, Emasiyo, I am indeed your mother. On Earth I was known as Midori Campbell. Yes, I was happy married to Julian, your father, but when my own father came to Takamatsu for me, I could not refuse him. I came with him to Elsynvaal. My only regret is that I missed your growing-up."

"And what of *my* father? You left him too. He had no means of knowing you were not dead! He was even arrested on suspicion of your murder!"

"Poor Julian. He is a good man. I did love him, Emasiyo, but it was fifteen long years ago."

"Twenty-one years."

"Twenty-one Earth years. Fifteen Elsynvaal years." She shrugged and the slightly wistful edge in her voice disappeared. "You come of fine wizard stock, Emasiyo," she continued. "Your child will have a fine inheritance."

"My child?" Emma stammered. "I have no child."

The woman had now reached the edge of the bed and leaned across the short distance to lay a hand on her stomach. "Maybe not yet," she replied, "But soon you will."

Emma shifted away from this strange woman as fear clouded her eyes. Horatio's arms snaked round her shoulders, and she moved back tight against him, twisting round to look up into his face and seeking comfort in his nearness. Her mind whirled. She had carried a mental picture of her mother for such a long time that her mind refused to accept this woman's words. Yet in this form, she looked uncannily like the photographs her father had shown her as she was growing up.

The woman had moved back towards the curtain. "Horatio, come with me. Daughter, stay here and rest a while." She waved a hand and mumbled something. As Emma's eyes grew heavy she became aware that Horatio was moving away from her. She fought the sleeping spell and feebly clutched at his hands. "Don't leave me, Horatio!"

But he was unresponsive. Unable to prevent him leaving, she watched as he swung his legs over the edge of the bed and walked zombie-like out of the room without a single backward glance. "Horatio!" she tried to shout, but there was no response as the curtain flapped closed behind him. Emma's eyes closed and she fell into a dreamless sleep as the mage once known as Midori Campbell gleefully turned to follow her other captive. What amusement was in store for her with him! She licked her lips and pulled back the curtain to follow him.

***

When Emma awoke, she was hungry. From that she supposed that some time had passed since Horatio had left. She still could not cope with the thought that the mage might be her parent. She sat up and looked around. Everything seemed the same, except that SHE was sitting on a chair nearby, watching with a speculative eye.

At her movement, the woman rose and leaned over Emma in the bed. She pulled the blanket down and reached over to lay her hands on Emma's belly. "No!" the girl shouted. "Don't touch me!"

"This will not hurt. I merely wish to check if all has gone well."

"Get away from me!"

"If you will not agree, then I can make you obey me."

Eye to eye, the two women remained immobile. Then Emma lowered her eyes. Better than being hit with a spell again. A tiny smile curved the woman's thin lips. Her hands sneaked out and came to rest on Emma's bare skin. Eyes closed, she listened for a moment through her hands to the tiny life just beginning within Emma's womb.

"Success," she murmured. "My dear daughter, you are about to become a mother. It is essential that you remain calm and quiet to ensure your child's survival and wellbeing. After all, its father is your beloved Horatio."

Emma sat still as the colour in her face drained away. She felt light-headed and the room was beginning to sway. A hand on her shoulder eased her back onto the pillows. The blanket was pulled up over her. "Dear Emasiyo. How often I have wished I could have tucked you up in bed like this when you were little," Midori's voice sounded very close to her ear. She gripped Emma's hands and a faraway sound came into her voice. Emma tried to pull her hands away, but they were held in a steely grip.

"What a heritage you have, my dear Emasiyo, for your Grandfather is Gheron talEbol, the greatest mage ever to grace this, or any other world! His power is limitless, his largess bountiful and I, his daughter, am blessed. For I too have a vast array of power, far more than I had ever imagined would be mine. And now you are there. The third generation. You too will come into your power. I can feel it, there inside you, untapped, unplumbed. Waiting to be released. You too will learn the ways of power, as will your child." She pulled out a small book from her pocket and laid it beside her. "Read this, my daughter," she said. "It will explain everything."

Emma's dizziness had passed and she ignored both book and sentiment. "Where is Horatio?" she demanded.

216

"Your lover is downstairs, in his own prepared chamber, and will remain there for the rest of the day. You have to rest and stay calm. Is there anything you wish me to convey to him?"

Emma opened her mouth and closed it again. Instead she turned away from the woman's unsettling and watchful eyes. Midori dalEbol Campbell compressed her already thin lips and turned away.

Chapter 3

It was well after dark when Alain returned to the place he'd left Horatio. It had been difficult persuading the Elders to help. A number of them had been very much against giving aid to a Human, but as Alain pointed out, it was mainly those who had never gone out amongst them. Rian ruefully shook his head at Alain at that point, knowing that it only gave them the opportunity to re-assert their opinion that Alain had 'been out there too long', and that he was becoming contaminated by the Human ways. Indeed it looked as if the Elders would refuse to give their help until Rian himself stood up and added his weight to Alain's arguments. He reminded them that it boded the Forest no good that a Human wizard had taken up residence so near to them.

"Why do you think we have been watching this woman since she arrived at the cabin a month ago? Now we discover that she has taken a friend of Alain as a hostage. This is not a situation we can afford to ignore. We have been watching her comings and goings, our unease growing. Sooner or later she is going to come into the Forest proper, and we already know she has no respect for the Trees. Have they not told us so themselves?"

Ferund stood up. "But if we antagonise her, she will come for us."

Rian turned, his eyes darkening with sadness. "Even if we don't do anything, at some point she'll come for us."

The arguments began again. And so it went on, while Alain chaffed at the delay. Twice he tried to contact Horatio by di-speak, but was unable to raise him. Eventually a vote was taken, which Alain won by a larger majority than they had hoped for, and Alain and Rian headed back to the place he'd left Horatio. On the way, they found the horses, which had wandered further into the Forest looking for fodder. On reaching the place where Horatio had been lying down, they found only a discarded blanket and a scuffed trail that led away from the clearing out onto the snow covered plain.

Mounting up, the two Sylvan followed Horatio's erratic trail, noting several places where Horatio had fallen. Anxiety mounted as the trail wound across the snow-bound plain, heading roughly south-west along the edge of the Forest. Eventually they came within sight of a cabin.

"That must be it," Alain said. He waved Rian back to the shelter of the trees while they discussed what to do.

"I'll try again to contact him mind-to-mind." He concentrated, thinking the shape of Horatio's signature, but could feel nothing.

"Now I will try," Rian said. "Let me concentrate." The old Sylvan pushed away the snow at his feet. He sat down cross-legged and pushed his hands deep into the forest loam. Then he closed his eyes. Alain stood silent, his eyes trained on the cabin through gaps in the concealing tree and sapling branches. He knew what Rian was trying to do. After some time, the old Sylvan looked up at Alain. "There are three people in the building, but that's all I can say. There is some tension, but no real fear."

"Good," Alain said. He glanced again through the trees, and then dived down as a shaft of light was emitted from the cabin as the door opened. "Get down!"

From the forest floor, the two watched as a woman left the cabin and walked round to the rear of the building. "What's she doing?" The answer came soon enough when she returned with an armful of logs.

"If she's as powerful as you say she is, Rian, why is she carrying logs?"

"How should I know?" the old Sylvan said. "But my theory is that there is some kind of impediment on the cabin, blocking the use of magic. It is not as easy as it was a few days ago for me to read activity within. The reason for doing something like that, though, I couldn't possibly say."

"But you could hazard a guess?"

"Perhaps. Your friend is a mage, is he not?" At Alain's nod, Rian went on. "So. If as you say this woman has indeed enticed him here, then a block on the use of magic may be a logical step."

"Will we still be able to tunnel?"

Rian turned to look at Alain. "You and Phin are the tunnelling experts. Well Phin is, and you used to be, before you began consorting with Humans. You tell me!" He gave a snort and turned back to watching the cabin.

"I suppose it depends on how deep the block goes."

They lay on the ground, watching and waiting. Then Rian hauled himself up. "We should return to the village, and as some say, ready the troops. And we will return in the morning, when the sun has risen."

Alain looked one last time at the cabin. Much could happen in the hours before they returned. But they would need the sun's help to tunnel. He only hoped that Horatio would be all right till then.

***

Emma waited a few moments before climbing down from the big bed and dressing. The small leather-bound book lay where Midori had left it. Frowning, she fingered it lightly and flicked through it. It was filled with small concise writing, and laid out like a diary. Frowning, she closed it and pushed it into a pocket. Then, on tiptoe, she crossed to the doorway and opened a chink in the curtain.

The room beyond seemed to be empty. She crept out into the main room, and looked around for some access to the 'room downstairs' but the place seemed completely devoid of a staircase. A trapdoor then? But none was visible. She stamped down hard on the earth floor, trying to find a hollow sound that would give away the location of a trapdoor. She sat down, trying to make her brain work. *If what she said was true,* she thought, *I am the daughter of a mage – a witch's daughter! Does that mean I possess magical power? Horatio said that power was inherited. Is it possible?* She sat quietly and composed herself, then began to search the room for openings that might have been missed before. As her gaze alighted on the doorway, she thought she could see a slight shimmer of coloured light around the door. A magical screen perhaps? She continued her perusal of the room's walls and floor. Nothing. *Horatio!* A small moan left her lips. *Where are you?*

She moved quietly over to the door, but knew that she would not be able to open it. Memories of what happened when Maggie and then Horatio himself had touched the door knob rose up before her and she slowly backed away. Looking around the room once more, she noticed the stacks of books on the shelves of one wall. She peered at some of the titles. None was familiar, but their bindings were similar to the book in her pocket. A few titles were in English, but there were none in Japanese script. Then she noticed a framed picture tucked away in a corner near the large fire-hearth. It was of the same type as the thought-pictures in Horatio's room in Elasyn Castle, but this one was of a year-old baby girl. Her heart gave a lurch when she realised that it was similar to a photo in the family album back home in Glasgow – a photo of herself as a baby with her mother and father. She staggered away from the fireplace and back to the curtained room, her heart thumping.

Lying curled up on the bed, she tried to figure out a way of finding Horatio and getting out of here, but once again sleep overtook her. This time, though, her sleep was peppered with psychedelic dreams of flashing lights and voices screaming. There was no way of telling what time it was when she woke up exhausted and drenched with sweat.

She swung her legs over the edge of the bed and stood up. Her head swam. Looking around, she noticed a tray of cold food on the small table. Seeing it, she realised how hungry she was. She sat on the bed with the tray on her lap and began to eat. Afterwards, she stretched out again on the bed and took out the book, but just as she was opening it, she sat bolt upright, thinking she'd heard a scream. Memories of her dream flooded her head. She sat tense, listening.

Yes, there it was again! A man's scream! Horatio! *Oh my God! What's happening?* She rolled off the bed and ran from the room, redoubling her efforts to find the entrance to the underground chamber she was now certain existed. The screams penetrating the hard-packed dirt floor became louder, more frequent, and did not seem to come from any one area of floor, but from all over. Frantic now, Emma grabbed a broom-handle and began scraping at the ground. Then suddenly the cries ceased.

As the minutes grew and the silence continued, Emma stood motionless in the middle of the room, waiting. Her heart pounded painfully in her chest. The minutes seemed endless, but eventually a scraping sound came from the region of the fireplace. She twisted round in time to see a section of the side wall of the hearth swing across the now low-burning flames of the fire. A figure emerged from the hidden chamber and stopped in front of the fireplace.

"Daughter. I see you are up and about." Glancing at the small indentation in the floor that was all Emma's efforts had produced, Emma's witch-mother gave a low chuckle. "And busy, I see."

Emma's eyes lingered on red splashes all over the woman's gown. "That's blood!"

The other looked down at her clothes. "Oh dear," she sighed. "Butchery is such a messy business. I thought I'd managed to stay clean, too."

"What have you been doing?"

"A little butchery, my dear. He screams so well, don't you think?"

"What have you done? Is Horatio down there?"

"You want to see him? Well then, I hope you have a strong stomach!" With that, she laughed, a high guffaw that held more than a little insanity. The hideous sound tied Emma's stomach in knots.

Emma felt the blood pounding in her ears, and forced herself not to faint. *Breathe!* she told herself. *Breathe! You can't help him if you pass out.* She forced herself to take one step forward and then another until she was face to face with the mad mage. "Let me pass."

With another high laugh, the woman stepped aside and watched the girl pass and climb into the stairway to the underground chamber. "You will need light!" she called out as Emma disappeared into the cavity. "Here!" She snatched up and threw at Emma a burning piece of wood from the fire. Emma caught the firebrand, scorching her hand as she did. Lifting the hem of her gown, she wrapped the fabric around the unburned end of the wood, hoping that it would not catch fire. The burning wood masked to some extent the sickly vile stench that wafted up from the cellar below.

The steps, only a dozen or so, were rough hewn from the earth itself, and holding the makeshift torch in front of her as she descended Emma could make out a stone slab near the far wall and the figure stretched out on it. Dark liquid dripped from the slab and trickled down the side of the stone to the filthy straw-covered floor. Blood?

Emma lifted the firebrand higher and a wave of yellow light reached the stone slab. Her heart thudded and vomit rushed to her throat. She clapped her hand over her mouth and stared in horror and unbelief. Horatio's naked body lay on the stone slab like a carcass in a butcher's shop. From throat to foot it glistened wetly in the flickering light.

This time she was unable to stop the tunnel of darkness from enveloping her. She pitched forward down the final remaining few steps to lie still among the filthy blood-covered straw only a few feet away from Horatio's bloody body.

Chapter 4

Alain tried to sleep, knowing what he would be required to do at sun-up. But after an hour, he gave up. As he was dressing, his brother Phinnemon came to his room.

"I did not think you'd be able to sleep much," he said, "and I see I was right. So, we will go together to talk with Rian."

When Alain and his brother entered the old Sylvan's home, the Clan Elder was sitting in his usual comfortable chair, his head held in his hands. On hearing them, Rian raised his eyes to Alain's. His amber eyes had changed to a deep purple. Alain knew the news was not good.

"Tell us," he said.

"Pain," the old one muttered. "Massive waves of physical pain, emanating from someone in the cabin. But I cannot tell which."

Alain felt his blood chill and knew his eyes were darkening. "How long?"

"So far, about an hour or so."

"Can you feel it now?"

"It starts and stops, probably because the person lapses into unconsciousness. I have to break the contact. It weakens me."

"Will they last until sun-up?"

Phin stepped forward. "We must hope so. We cannot attempt the tunnel until then."

Rian raised his pain-filled purple eyes. "We must pray to the earth mother."

There was little cover from shrubbery around the cabin and the snow layer was likely to betray their position, so the Sylvans had laid their plans accordingly. Alain and his brother Phinnemon lay crouched in hiding within the shielding cover of the trees, waiting. Nearby lay the small band of hunters and most accomplished of the magicands of the Sylvan Clan of the Northern Forest. Their plan was simple, but for it to work the captives had to be alone and the wizard woman unsuspecting of a rescue attempt.

Now as he sat within the cover of the friendly trees, waiting with the small team of liberators, he thought on Rian's experience again, wondering whose pain he had felt, and wondering if the old Clan Elder's words this morning as they set out were true. "*We have to face the fact that we might be rescuing a corpse."*

Alain shuddered.

Their watch continued as the sun slowly climbed into the sky. A chilly wind blew up, creating mini snow-funnels and shallow drifts. Eventually a movement at the cabin indicated that their time had come. Forewarned, the team ducked down, out of sight. The cold wind Rian and his fellow magicands had gradually built up caused the woman leaving the cabin to hunch up her shoulders and pull her cloak more tightly around her. Over one arm she held a basket, just as Rian had predicted. Alain knew enough of Rian's skills not to ask questions.

As the tiny woman entered the forest, Alain could see trees shift and change position. So much depended on the trees doing their part – so very much. Alain touched the soil at his knees and sent a silent prayer to the goddess of the earth. Then Alain and his brother Phinnemon rose to lead the hunters across the snowy open ground.

They stopped and Phin raised his hands into the air and moved them around lightly, feeling for the magic field surrounding the cabin. He walked round the perimeter, marking the extent of the screen with his boot-marks in the snow. Behind him, the wind had risen further, enough to cover the sound of his magic, but not enough to cause the wizard woman, by now hopefully lost in the forest, cause for concern.

Rian had the remaining magicands spread out to keep watch on the wizard woman in the forest, while Phin and Alain took measurements at the front of the cabin and readied themselves for the tunnelling. Once the angle had been agreed, the two brothers nodded and Phin began his quiet chant to the Mother. Then, his feet braced well apart, he gently eased the wooden staff he always carried into the ground at his feet. The winter-hard earth gave way like butter under a warm knife and a fissure opened. Moving the staff this way and that, Phin laboriously began to dig out a sloping tunnel.

Alain stood with Rian watching anxiously as the tunnel grew, casting fearful glances over their shoulders towards the section of the forest holding the wizard woman. Then as Phin began to tire, Alain took over, leaving Rian to keep watch on the forest.

Beginning outside the perimeter of the spell-shield, Phin's tunnel angled sharply downwards and then levelled off in the direction of the shield. After a while, Phin took over again from Alain, who followed in his wake and compared the quality of his own tunnelling to that of his brother. No contest. Phin's work was masterly. Alain ran his hand across the surface filled with admiration. The soil had been compacted as if blasted with great pressure creating the solid pipe-like tunnel. The sections he, Alain, had done were much rougher.

After a time the tunnel sloped upwards again, angling to come up underneath the cabin. Phin paused. Murmuring an incantation, he stopped the formation of the tunnel. Then over his shoulder he spoke in a whisper to Alain.

"There must be some kind of underground store-room here. We have not come high enough yet to have reached ground level. Be alert. If there is something on the other side, it will have the initiative."

The last section of raw earth collapsed and they gasped as the stench in the putrid air hit their lungs and made them gag. After a moment's recovery they took in the scene in front of them. A flickering torch in an ancient wall bracket showed a short flight of steps leading up into darkness with a stone slab against the wall opposite the steps. But it was not this that drew the two men's eyes. For lying on the floor beside the slab among a heap of dirty straw was a mangled mass of bloody flesh and bones. Fighting to keep the nausea down, Alain tirNorest approached the body that had been Horatio, mage to a King-in-Waiting.

"Sprites and dryads preserve us!" Phin's oath came as through a fog to Alain's ears. He knelt down in the midst of the blood and gore beside him, astounded and shocked at the extent of the mutilation. The man had been skinned, and skilfully too. His head was untouched, his eyes closed, but hardly an inch of his chest, legs and arms had any skin left on it. Alain could only guess at the extreme pain Horatio must have endured before he died. "I have to take him back," he said looking up at Phin. His voice shook, but neither noticed. Then he turned back to lift the bloody mess. Some parts were still oozing watery blood. Wincing, he began to slide his arms under the body and discovered that Horatio's back had been skinned in the same way as the rest of him. It was then that the miracle happened. A low moan emanated from Horatio's ruined throat, and the eyes flew open, staring, and unseeing. A whisper issued from the bruised and bitten lips. "No more… Please, god, no more."

"He's alive!" Alain gasped. "In the name of all that is good – he's alive!" He swiftly drew upon his healing strength within him to give his friend a measure of relief while they moved him, only to remember that there was a block on magic. *"He could not protect himself,"* he thought. He turned to Phin. "Magic is inoperative in here, Phin. I cannot sedate him. We will have to be careful when moving him."

"What about the girl?" Phin asked. "She's probably upstairs in the cabin proper."

"Yes. We have to find her. Take Horatio out, Phin, and I will find Emma."

Phin waved a hand to Dirk, the leader of the hunt, who slipped his cloak off and began to make a makeshift sling in which to carry Horatio's bloody body. Alain turned away and headed up the steps which ended in a blank wall. Feeling round the edges, he found a hinge, which opened with a loud click. Easing the stone slab outwards a few inches, he peered through the gap. In front he could see part of a room, simply furnished. The stone door to the cellar seemed to be on one side of the fireplace. The ashes of a dead fire lay in the hearth behind the slab-door. Pushing the gap wider, Alain slipped through the narrow space and into the room. Two chairs, table, sink, cooking pots by the hearth. Against the wall at the side of the fireplace, incongruous in its setting, was a considerable array of leather-bound books. On one wall a long curtain half open indicated that there was a second room to the cabin.

Alain crossed silently to the curtain and peered through the gap in the fabric. Gripping the curtain with one hand, he threw it aside with a sharp movement and with his other hand knocked away the metal water jug that was rapidly descending upon his head.

"Hold, Lady!" he cried out. "I am here to help you!"

The jug dropped with a clatter and Emma stood before him, face bloodless and tear-stained. Her eyes stared out at him afraid of what she saw.

"Alain the Bard? Is it really you – or are you another trick of that murdering hag?"

"No trick, lady. I am Alain as you see…"

"Jesus Christ!" she swore, "I almost brained you!"

"Come now and follow me. We have a way out through the cellar."

"The cellar?" She looked at him, her face strained and white with shock. "Horatio… she took him to the cellar… I couldn't find a way back in after she left…"

"We found him. He's alive, Emma. He's alive."

But she would not hear him. Inside her head she could hear his screams and could see his bloody body and smell the blood. The blood! So much of it! Deep red glistening blood all over his body. How can he still be alive? How could he have survived what had been done to him? A stinging blow to her face broke her internal horror and she looked with wide eyes at the Sylvan in front of her.

"That's better, lady. Now, come with me now, before the wizard woman returns." Half dragging and half carrying her, Alain made it back to the fireplace and to the stone door. There she balked, hysteria rising once more.

"I can't go in there! I can't!"

"You have to. It is the only way out of here." Alain spoke soothingly but firmly, enunciating his words carefully. "Horatio is alive. He is safe. He has already been taken out. Listen," he said in a quiet voice, gripping her shoulders with both hands, "there is a tunnel from the cellar that leads outside. You must come with me now – before it is too late."

Gradually, her shaking faded and she nodded.

"Good," he replied and smiled at her. Hand in hand they made their way down the steps into the blood-stench that still hung in the air of the cellar. He could feel the tension in the desperate clutch of her hand.

"Pinch your nose and breath through your mouth," Alain cautioned her. "We are leading for the tunnel. Over there. Do you see it? Look at the tunnel. Only at the tunnel. Almost there. Well done. Now into the tunnel and soon we will be out of here." Keeping up a flow of calming words, he led the traumatised girl through the torture room and into the tunnel. Despite Alain's words, though, Emma found her eyes irresistibly drawn to the blood-drenched stone slab. Superimposed on her inner eye was the tortured body of the man she loved. Eventually they stumbled to the tunnel mouth to breath what should have been the clean crisp air of a winter's morning.

Instead, the smell of burning wood assailed their nostrils. Looking round quickly as he eased his head out of the relative safety of the tunnel, Alain took in the aftermath of a battle. Three of the Sylvan hunting party were fighting a losing battle against flames that were rapidly consuming several of the trees at the forest edge. One of the magicands was sitting on the ground, nursing a burned arm. Rian was leaning over the blood-soaked cloak covering Horatio's mutilated body. Of the wizard woman, there was no sign.

Helping Emma out of the tunnel, they walked towards the old Clan elder, who looked up at their approach.

"Ah, the damsel in distress. I am pleased that you are well. Better than your friend here, I fear."

Emma knelt down beside the makeshift stretcher, and gently touched his so very pale face. Tears flowed down her cheeks. "Horatio," she murmured.

"He cannot hear you. No, he is not dead – yet," he went on rapidly, "he is merely unconscious. I have heavily sedated him so we can transport him back to the village. But I will not tell you that there is much hope for him. He has suffered much in the way of both physical and mental pain. He will be severely traumatised even if he survives. I am sorry, lady." He stood up, shaking out his cloak into meticulous folds around his ankles. "Come, we have a long way to go."

As they approached the fire fighters, Alain noted that one of them was a soot-covered Phin.

"We cannot get the flames out!" he called to them above the roar of the fire. "We will have to ask them to come down." Rian, with a sigh, nodded acquiescence.

Phin signalled to the other fire-fighters, and the three stepped back. Tears glinted in their eyes as the voices of all of the Sylvans joined in a beautiful haunting melody – the death chant for three old tree-friends. Emma stood open-mouthed as one by one the trees uprooted themselves and tipped forward, quenching the fire consuming them in the wet snow. A pall of smoke lingered over the blackened stumps as Rian laid a caressing hand on each in turn. Three trees had died to prevent fire spreading to their fellows.

As they made their way through the forest, Alain felt the shiver in the trees as they passed the news from one to the other. A light touch on his arm broke his reverie. Phin had come alongside. "What happened back there?" Alain asked his brother.

"What in particular?"

"The fire – and Forin burned. What caused it?"

"The wizard woman discovered the trees' ploy and returned. She is very powerful. She flamed the trees, knowing that we would attempt to save them. Then she tried to torch Rian. That was when Forin was burned. We ringed her, attempting to work together to increase our power, but she just laughed and disappeared. She turned herself into a hawk and flew south."

"So we do not know where she is now."

"Right."

"You sound very cheerful, I might say," Alain commented.

"You'd be right," Phin replied. "Why not? We have accomplished what we set out to do. With casualties, granted, but Forin's burn is only a surface one. Rian or one of the others will have it healed within a day or so. Your friend Horatio is a different matter," his voice had momentarily sobered, "but we will do what we can. At least we got him out alive! And the lady too." He glanced at Emma in front of them, walking beside Horatio's stretcher. She trudged on, one foot after the other, silent, seeming unable to take her eyes from the blood drenched figure on the stretcher.

Chapter 5

Alain was glad to see that the whispering trees had made an easy path for them to the village. It ran straight and clear all the way, though he could hear the trees shifting back into their usual places after their passage through. In the central clearing, within the benevolent ring of Guardian Trees, thirty to forty of his clan brethren were gathered to watch as the magicands carried the blood-covered stretcher forward. Alain wondered what Emma was thinking of all of this as others appeared from behind curtains made from twigs and small branches near the base of the trees. Few Humans had seen the village of the Second Clan tirNorest. A murmur grew as the magicands carried Horatio towards Rian's tree. Rian's grandson leaned forward and twitched back the twig curtain concealing the tunnel behind.

Alain glanced at Emma. She had stopped, fear written on her features. He took her arm, coaxing her on, much as he had through the cellar. Probably the tunnel was too similar to the one she'd just passed through on leaving the blood splattered cellar. But at Alain's quiet words her legs moved forward, carrying her into the smooth walled tunnel. With Alain guiding her, she followed Horatio's bearers down the slight slope and into the heart of Rian's home hollowed out from among the roots of the trees above.

Emma refused to leave Horatio, so Alain and Phin set up two pallets side by side in Rian's side room. There she lay, watching as Rian and two others created a floating device to keep the pressure off the raw muscle and exposed flesh and began to work on Horatio's body. After a while, Alain looked at Emma. Overcome by exhaustion and trauma, Emma had slipped off into sleep.

Now they could begin their repair work. Somehow Rian managed to stop the bleeding by pinching off vein endings, and had stabilised his breathing and pulse rate. So far so good. Alain helped Rian as far as he could. But his occasional work in the land of the Humans had hardly prepared him for such a gross undertaking.

Well into the afternoon and early evening they leaned over the floating bed, working on Horatio's pus-ridden and festering flesh. They had to prevent infection setting in, and to cover the exposed flesh with a protective membrane.

The main problem was that membrane had to be grown from existing skin on the body, and there was little left of Horatio's skin.

"The skin," Rian explained as Alain listened with mounting horror, "has been systematically removed in long wide swathes, leaving skin only in places where it was difficult to peel off or was damaged in some way. Thus we have a section of thigh where he has an old puckered scar. I wonder why he never healed that properly? His head and part of the neck are clear, and his feet, and awkward areas like under the arms and pubic and rectal areas. It is from these small parts that we have to work. Come, my boy. Let me see your handiwork!"

Watching and working with the skilled healer, Alain learned several alternative methods of skin repair. He found that only if he thought of Horatio's ruined body as a thing to be repaired rather than a living breathing entity, could he do his grisly work. He had grown up knowing this wise old man, but watching and helping him now, he realised how seriously he had underestimated Rian's skill as a healer.

Towards sunset, their work for the moment complete, Alain fell into a sleep born of exhaustion. It was his first real rest since the day he played his pipe at a King's Coronation.

When he awoke, Rian was holding court. The remains of a substantial meal lay on the table. Phin sat nearby listening as Rian spoke. Alain got up and joined them. Phin was sober and calm – there was no dancing devilment in his eyes now. Rian sat thoughtful and very worried.

"We have him covered in a thin membrane," he was saying as Alain sat down and began raking through the debris for scraps. "But he will need a long time to recuperate. We must watch for infection. I am astounded that putrefaction had not already set in certain sections."

"Perhaps she used wizardry to keep infection at bay until she was finished with him," Alain suggested.

Phin scowled. "She is evil – that woman. But who is she?"

"She had her identity closely covered during our little foray outside the cabin," Rian said. "I could not reach her mind. But there was madness there, and an incredible depth of magical ability. Indeed such as I have not heard of since…"

"…talEbol?" Alain enquired.

"I hesitate to mention the name, but yes. Gheron talEbol."

"In that case I must contact Deveron immediately!" He glanced at these two, a trusted old friend and a beloved brother, and hurried on in explanation. "The Antriantara of the Council of Wizards, Deveron, is at present in Elasyn Castle. If there is a possibility that this wizard woman is Gheron talEbol in a different guise, then he must be told about it! But how can I reach him quickly? Horatio has begun teaching me the mage-skill of Distance-Speaking, but I think my power will be too weak to reach him."

"If you were stronger, had more power, could you do this thing – this Distance-Speaking?"

"It is possible, I would say."

"Then link your mind to mine and I will give you my strength." Alain almost laughed with relief. He thought that his only alternative was to leave Horatio and Emma here and ride through the deep snowdrifts on the plain to reach Deveron. He leaned back and closed his eyes. Soon he felt the Rian's fine mind-threads slip into his brain, tying and knotting synapses. It was not a pleasant sensation, but thankfully it stopped short of pain. Once the tying was completed, he heard Rian's voice within his head in the same way as he had heard Horatio's during their training sessions.

"I am with you, Alain. Call to the mage."

Alain called. Throwing the linked mind up and away from their bodies, the Rian/Alain mind travelled the miles across the forest canopy beneath the myriad stars, seeing for the first time how the forest looked from above. It was an intoxicating feeling, to be flying free across the skies swifter than the most powerful of all the birds. Far they travelled across the snow covered plains and scrub-land to the very walls of Elasyn Castle, where the flag hung limp in the cold frosty air. Up over the walls they travelled, to the inner eastern courtyard and to Deveron's room.

Despite the late hour, he was not alone. Two of Emma's friends were there, the girl and the boy with the scarred face. Maggie and Jeff.

<Deveron!> Alain tirNorest called with trepidation. *Would he hear?*

Deveron raised his hand silencing the boy who was talking. The girl leaned forward, asked something. Deveron made a short reply and then leaned back, eyes closed.

<Who calls to Deveron, Antriantara of the Wizards' Council?>
<It is I, Deveron. Alain tirNorest.>

232

<The god be thanked. Where are you? Where is Horatio? How did you learn to do this?>

<Horatio taught me.>

<Ah, he did? I wonder why? Now, Alain, your voice is clear, but your image is blurred. I will try to clear it... There that is better. I can see you now. Who is with you? Speak now.>

<I have news, Deveron. Mixed good and evil. I am with my Clan in the Northern Forest. The two you see are Clan Elder Rian tirNorest and Phinnemon my brother. Rian is a very accomplished magicand, in power equivalent of a human mage. He has joined our minds temporarily to increase my di'speak abilities.>

He could see Deveron's eyes widen in surprise, but he said nothing, and merely nodded his head.

<We found Emma and Horatio. They were indeed in the cabin of Horatio's dream. Emma is well, but Horatio...>

<Go on.>

<Horatio was tortured. Brutally mutilated and his skin sliced from his living body. Even now he is barely alive. He is lying unconscious in a healing floater of Rian's devising.>

<The god save him. This is bad news indeed. What are his chances of survival? Will he make it?>

<Perhaps. We cannot be sure. He is still unconscious. But Deveron, there is more. We think that Gheron talEbol is involved.>

<TalEbol? Surely... What makes you think this?>

<Rian is familiar with magic, and tells me that the magic of the wizard woman who tortured Horatio is on a par with talEbol.>

Deveron started and took a long-indrawn breath. *<Was there a signature?>*

<Rian is unfamiliar with wizard signatures. But powerful charms guarded the cabin, including a spell that inhibited the use of magic.>

<A Nulato? Mmmm. Very interesting. That would explain how it was possible to so abuse Horatio. Tell me... Do you know when Horatio was tortured? When this mutilation took place?>

There was a pause as Alain consulted with Rian. Then at Alain's instigation, Rian took over the dialogue.

<Rian, Elder of Second Clan tirNorest is pleased to make your acquaintance.>

<And I, you, Rian of the Forest. Pray, tell me what you know.>

<The mutilation took place over the last twelve to fourteen hours, as far as I can tell. Normal decay seems to have been held at bay magically.>

<Have you any indication of the identity the wizard woman took?>

<I think I caught the word 'Midori' or 'Midora' but I am unsure whether it was a name or a Human's spell chant. There was a spell exchange after we freed Horatio and she transformed into a white hunting bird. Amidst the smoke and fumes, she flew away.>

Rian watched as Deveron deep in thought rubbed his chin. *<What of Horatio? Will he live?>*

<If we can keep infection at bay; if the membrane sets; if we can get some food into him; there is a chance of recovery. His mental state is another matter completely.>

<What of Emma? Was she harmed?>

<Not physically, but she is in a state of mobile pseudo-catatonia. She moves around, eats when given food and even speaks occasionally and flatly refuses to leave Horatio's bedside. She is in deep shock and badly traumatised. Poor child – there is little chance that she did not hear Horatio's torture and his screams. She may even have been forced to witness it.>

<The god forbid it! How do you suggest we go forward?>

<The girl needs careful handling and counselling. Though it is possible she may recover spontaneously. Horatio? A long period of mage-healing, rest and recuperation, assuming we can keep infection and complications out. He is a mess.>

<Where are they?"

<In the adjacent room. We may be able to let you see them.>

Together, Alain and Rian guided Deveron's line of sight to the room where Horatio lay. Emma's eyes were still fixed on his body.

<Poor children> Deveron murmured. *<I will break contact now, Alain, Rian. Will you contact again in an hour's time? This will allow me to put some things in motion. We are going to need Horatio's magic soon, so he must be sent somewhere to recuperate quickly. I will see what I can do. Farewell. Peace be upon you and your Clan, and upon you, loyal Alain.>*

<May the Dryads' blessings be upon you, Deveron.>

The contact broke and the Rian-Alain mind flew swiftly back to the village of the Second Clan. Immediately Rian began the uncomfortable unravelling of their mind-threads. Eventually, they opened their eyes and looked at one another. Rian grinned. Alain's smile was rueful. Phin looked on, unconcealed curiosity writ large across his face.

"Well," Rian said, "I hope we do not have to repeat that particular exercise too often. Very tiring. But it worked. A very useful tool, I must say. I'll make some nice bark tea, shall I?" Ignoring Phin's sharp look, Rian pushed himself up from his chair, ambled away towards the tunnel entrance and disappeared through the curtain.

Phin leaned forward towards Alain, his face alight with curiosity. "Tell me Alain!" he commanded. "All I could see were gestures and facial expressions. What happened?"

Alain told him word for word as far as he could remember. Then he rose and went to stand by the doorway to gaze at Horatio's still form. Phin's puzzled voice reached him from the main room. "What did Deveron mean by saying that he had need of Horatio's power? And what in the Dryad's name are the Humans doing?"

"I wish I knew," Alain replied over his shoulder as he watched Emma sleep. A shuffling in the tunnel made him turn to greet Rian as he reappeared with fresh bark tea.

Chapter 6

"You must let us come with you, Deveron!" Jeff stood up and stared down at the top of the wizard's head.

But Deveron merely shook his head. "With that leg you'll never keep up. I will be riding fast and as hard as I can. The roads north of here are non-existent. Also, there is no ley-line to the north, so even though the moons are up, I cannot use their power. No, you two and Milo must remain here. I will return as soon as I possibly can."

"Are you sure Emma is all right?"

"She is in shock at what has been done to Horatio, but she will recover once she goes home."

"And what about us? When will we go home?"

The old mage looked up at Jeff, considering his question. "My suggestion would be this – stay here until we sort this out and then you can travel to Rowlan Gayts. Worry about going home when you are healed." He stood up, and headed for the door. "But I must leave you now, and prepare for my journey. While I'm away, you should think about the things we have been discussing, and keep watch over your friend Milo. I will return soon."

"Can we come to see you off?" Maggie spoke for the first time since the contact with the Sylvans.

Deveron smiled. "If you wish, my dear, if you wish. I will be leaving in about half an hour, from the front quadrangle."

They watched silently as the Antriantara crossed the ice-covered moat and turned his horse's head to the north, to clatter through the silent night-time cobbled streets of Elasyn town. His face was drawn when he'd leaned down from his horse to say goodbye to them. Drawn and desperately worried. Maggie, wrapped deep in furs, shivered.

***

Both moons shone down on him as Deveron urged his horse through the snow-covered plains north of Elasyn, tiny Diminu low on the horizon but rising, while Principa shone down half-full from the mid-heavens. But Deveron was oblivious to the beauty of the sparkling aftermath of the snow blizzard. Deep in thought, he was barely even conscious of his mount as it fought its way through the deep snow. No. His thoughts were elsewhere.

He pondered on the task in front of him, wondering if he was up to it. Sending an injured mage through the Ether was not an undertaking to be attempted lightly. It might be too dangerous. But if this girl Mhari was as raw a talent in Ether-handling as it seemed… It might just be possible. To be able to contact him across worlds, untrained as she was, was unheard-of. If this goes well, he decided, she must be encouraged to come to Elsynvaal and be given the chance to develop her skills.

It was slow going traversing the snow-fields, but Deveron was confident that the blizzard had blown itself out. Up above, Principa shone in an indigo sky dotted with pin-prick stars.

Eventually he saw the forest in the distance. The area he was heading for was south of Jarek's cabin. As he approached, two figures on horseback moved from the cover of the trees. Once Alain had introduced his brother, Deveron asked about Horatio.

"Much the same," Alain said. "Horatio is stable and there is no sign of infection, but he was still unconscious when we left and Emma is still refusing to leave his side."

Phin told him that the cabin had remained deserted, and suggested that if Deveron wished, they could visit it on their way to the village. Deveron agreed. Perhaps there would be some clue as to the identity of the mysterious wizard woman. There was no mage answering her description in Elsynvaal. Phin suggested that Emma might know who she was, but reluctantly agreed with Alain that at the moment she was in no state to be questioned.

They entered the cabin through the tunnel. Deveron gagged at the stench in the cellar. He tried to call up a wych light to test the strength of the *Nulato*. A tiny light sparked in his palm and died. "Strong."

Phin crossed to the wall bracket and pushed some straw into it before setting fire to it and handing it to the Mage. Crouching down, Deveron played the light over the blood-covered filthy straw.

"So much blood. How in the god's name did he survive it?" he asked, shaking his head. Neither Sylvan attempted an answer. In silence the trio made their way up the earthen steps to the upper room. Deveron wandered, seemingly at random, around the room. Alain and Phin watched in silence.

"I must admit that when I heard of your fears I was sceptical. But being here, seeing all of this," he threw his arm out encompassing the whole room, "I must agree with your view that talEbol could be involved. This magic is not his, but the signature is uncannily akin to his as I recall it." He turned to the two Sylvan then gestured towards an empty bookshelf. "Alain. You came in here to bring Emma out, am I right? Do you remember what was on these shelves?"

Alain stood still, seeming to go into a trance. Deveron waited, watching Sylvan magic for the first time in his long life. "Books. A shelf of books," Alain said. "Leather-bound, old-looking."

Deveron went back to the shelf. "Hmmm. I wonder if they were in fact bound in leather. Knowing what we know now, I have the horrible suspicion that the bindings did not come from any animal," he said but hurried on, ignoring their gasps of shock. "As the books are now gone, we must assume that she returned for them at some point. Also, there is no sign of the skin ripped from Horatio's body. Phinnemon," he asked over his shoulder, "you said that your clansmen have been watching the cabin."

"Yes. The woman did not return in human form."

"Did they by chance see a large predatory bird? A hawk or eagle perhaps?"

"I cannot say. We would have to ask them. But," he went on, "surely this shape shifter fiend is able to change her form at will – she could have taken the form of a rat or a soil worm, but I cannot explain how she could have taken the books away."

Deveron nodded and went across to the curtained-off sleeping room. There was little to show what had passed there during Emma's captivity. A rumpled bed, an empty goblet and crust of bread, and on the floor near the curtain, a metal water jug. He returned to the main room, and stood in the centre of the room. He closed his eyes and sought out the origins of the *Nulato*, only to be stunned by its power and complexity. Even he could not gather up power. No wonder Horatio was unable to fight it.

"I cannot remove the spell," he said. "It is too strong to be dealt with at this point in time. I will need time to pinpoint its origins and make-up. Also, I do not wish to drain myself any more than I have to. It will have to be cleansed later." He led the way back to the empty fireplace. "We will have to leave the way we entered."

As he went down the steps, Deveron staggered a little.

Once clear of the cabin, Alain looked up at Deveron's face. His eyes narrowed. "You drained yourself in there, didn't you? Trying to negate the spell?"

Deveron smiled and nodded. "I confess it was difficult."

"Shall I help you?" the Sylvan healer asked. At Deveron's

weary nod, Alain rummaged in his hip satchel for his healing stones. Deveron brushed the snow from a rock and sat down. Alain crouched beside him. When it was completed, Deveron looked at Alain closely.

"You have grown in power, my friend. That was well done."

"Yesterday I learned much from Rian, who is a powerful healer." His eyes changed slightly, growing darker. "Had he not been, Horatio would be dead. I could have done nothing to save him, had I been alone."

"Then I look forward to meeting this paragon, and thanking him." He stood up. "Are we far from the village? We should go there quickly to set up Horatio's transfer."

***

They were ready. Standing in a circle around Horatio's still form floating in his liquid bath, they waited for Mhari's second contact with Deveron since his arrival at the Sylvan village.

Arguments had been settled, objections over-ruled and finally plans were agreed. All they needed now was the contact. Deveron sat with eyes closed, his mind flowing free in search of the girl Mhari. As Alain watched him, he thought over what the Mage had told him about the girl.

During their Ether contact, Deveron had described to Mhari the tricky operation they were about to attempt and had warned her that to complete it successfully, it would need all of his own skill and all Mhari had to offer as well, hoping that it would be sufficient. He was impressed with her plucky words when he described what it could be like if it went wrong. *Jeff's friends are mine too. I will do whatever I can to help them.*

Alain had said his farewells, drawing Rian aside one last time. "Are you sure about this, Rian?" he asked. "It will be a very perilous journey crossing through the void."

Rian waved his hand negligently. "I have listened to the Antriantara's descriptions. I think I know what to expect."

"But will your heart stand up to the strain?"

"Ah, I see now. You think I'm too old. Well, I'll tell you this, Alain – my heart is every bit as strong as yours! And at the risk of repeating myself yet again, I tell you this: only I, at this moment in time, possess the skills to create the fluid bath in which Horatio floats, and we cannot take this one with us." He patted Alain's hand. "Do not worry about me, Alain my son. And my healing skills will immensely increase your friend's chances of survival."

Alain backed down.

"Besides," the ancient Elder said with a chuckle, "I have always wanted to travel!"

Emma stood by the fluid bath, her eyes still fixed on Horatio. No-one could tell what went on inside her head. Her waxen face showed no emotion at all. But she seemed somehow, at some level of consciousness, to be aware of what was about to happen, and the part she had to play. Then, just as Deveron prepared to begin the crossover, Emma moved forward, pulling something from her pocket, a small leather-bound book. She held it out towards Deveron.

"She... my mother... gave me this. She... she said it would explain everything. Take it, sir mage. Read it."

Deveron's breath caught. "Thank you, my dear girl. I will."

Emma turned back to her place beside Horatio.

They were ready.

***

When contact came, everything happened at once. Deveron held the opening in the Ether open, forging a strong link with the girl Mhari. Rian took hold of one of Horatio's hands and one of Emma's. Emma's other hand grasped Horatio's right hand in a firm grip. Alain allowed himself a small smile. She *did* understand. That was good. That was *very* good.

They stood as in a tableau as Deveron made final adjustments with Mhari. "*If* this works," he told her, "it will prove that you have great mage potential. *If* this works you should seriously consider training as a mage in Elsynvaal. If it does *not*," he added ruefully, "all of this will be moot. Are you ready?"

An instant later they were gone. As they disappeared, Alain thought he saw a flicker of fear cross Emma's features. Deveron stood alert, focused, concentration written deep on his sharp features as he held the opening, giving them time to make the crossing safely. Time crept by, each second like an hour to the anxious waiting watchers. Finally the mage let his breath out in a long sigh and opened his eyes. Phin voiced the question on everyone's lips.

Deveron's head shifted tiredly. "Yes," he said, "They made it."

Minutes later, the first screams were heard and a boy rushed in from the tunnel. "The Guardian Trees are aflame! They are burning!"

Chapter 7

Alain and Phin dashed out of Rian's cave together, with the Human mage close behind. Six of the Guardians were aflame, their screams echoing in Alain's mind. People were fruitlessly beating at the flames with wet blankets or attempting to douse the flames with buckets of water from the well. As he stood there stunned, a seventh caught light.

Deveron strode forward. "Get them away from the well and into the centre of the clearing!" he yelled. Phin ran to the well crying out commands to his clan brothers and sisters. Alain saw Deveron's fingers twist in the air, drawing an intricate magical sigil that blazed for an instant before his eyes before fading away.

He's going to use Human magic, Alain realised. He ran towards his brother yelling, "Away from the Trees! We have help! Away from the Trees! Gather in the centre!" Still yelling, as he pushed and tugged at them, trying to force them away from the burning trees and towards the safety of centre of the clearing. Then, over the roar of the fire, he heard a whoosh and turned back to where Deveron stood. The old Wizard's whole body was rigid, his face taut with effort.

Alain watched as Deveron worked. From the well there emerged a thin ribbon of water. Up into the air it rose as Deveron's fingers wove the molecules of water into a spiralling water-spout. Swiftly it grew then until it rose fifty feet into the air. Carefully Deveron guided this wall of water towards the raging fire engulfing the moaning trees. The water fell upon the first of the burning trees and smoke billowed outwards. Coughing and wiping fruitlessly at stinging eyes, everyone huddled together.

But the first of the fires was out. The wall of water moved on to the next Tree. More steam and smoke enveloped them as they watched, but the ring of fire was broken.

"Into the Forest!" Alain yelled. Phin began leading their Clan towards the break in the firewall, and through into the forest. Alain remained, fascinated, as Deveron broke the water-spout into two then four, and sent each to a single tree. Gradually the crimson glow faded as tree after tree was smothered in water, and the fires extinguished.

Eventually Deveron slumped down onto the ground, as the ash from the stricken trees floated down to coat everything in a dark residue. He sighed and brushed a hand across his face. It came away filthy with soot and damp with sweat. Alain began to walk forward, to aid him.

But then a large white hawk flew in from above the tops of the trees and landed ten feet away from Deveron. Alain froze.

A shimmer of air and a petite woman stood in the clearing, dressed in a colourful robe of figured satin, tied with a broad white band. Her hair hung straight down her back, a cascade of black. Alain gasped. The resemblance to Emma was extraordinary. Alain began to slide round the perimeter edging towards the old mage, keeping his eyes on both Humans.

"Where is my daughter?" the bird-woman asked Deveron.

"Somewhere you cannot find her," he replied.

"I doubt that!" Her eyes narrowed and the perfect image slipped a little. "Nowhere on the three worlds is there a place you can hide her from me!" Her arm lifted and a bolt of pure energy shot from it to scorch the patch of ground revealed by Deveron's instinctive roll.

"Missed," he commented.

She shrugged. "Tell the Sylvans that this," she gestured around at the burned and dying trees, "is a warning. Sylvan should not aid Human! They have stolen my daughter, and taken away my toy. I, Midori dalEbol, tell you this." With that, her form shimmered once more and the white hawk with a snap of feathers shot up into the air. Over the treetops she flew – south-east, in the direction of the cabin.

Deveron dropped down to sit on the sodden grass and wearily put his head in his hands. Alain crouched down beside him.

***

In silence and darkness the uniformly dark-eyed Clan drifted back to the clearing, to begin the death-keen beside the devastated Trees. When dawn broke Alain and Phin came and stood before Deveron. "It would be best if you left now," Alain said. "We have work to do here. Four of the Guardians have died, despite your heroic efforts, and we must see to their dispersal."

Phin stepped forward. "On behalf of the Clan Elders, I thank you, Antriantara Deveron. Without your quick actions, the whole Clan could have perished, in addition to our Guardian Trees."

With a courteous bow, Phin turned back to his people and left Alain to wordlessly lead Deveron back to the edge of the now silent

243

Forest. There, they found Deveron's horse, tethered where he had left it.

"I will return to Elasyn, Deveron. One day," Alain said. He raised his hand in farewell. "When you contact Rian, please tell him of the disaster, but urge him to remain where he is until his work is done. The elders who remain will speak the Trees' Farewell."

Alain watched Deveron mount his horse and move off into the snow. He looked up. The stars had faded, and dawn was beginning to lighten the skies. Alain was glad that Deveron would have good weather for his slow journey back to Elasyn Castle.

**

Clattering across the drawbridge, Deveron threw the reins of his horse to a stable-boy and headed towards his rooms in the east wing, hoping to reach them without meeting anyone. He was so very tired… Perhaps he could get some sleep before being confronted with whatever had happened in the eighteen hours he'd been away. Then he would speak to Alain's companion troubadours and reassure them he was safe. Emma's friends would also need to know what had happened. As he climbed the steps, he wondered about using levitation, but decided that it would take more energy than he had to spare. All during the ride through the snow, he had been bolstering up his energy levels with healing spells, but his exhaustion had taken its toll. *I'm not getting any younger*, he realised more than ever. *It's time I began grooming a successor. Would that I had never left my tower!* What he needed now was quiet healing sleep. He laid his hand on the handle of his door and paused, hearing voices coming from inside the room.

He heaved a sigh and opened the door. Three expectant faces turned towards him.

"Deveron!" Maggie cried out. "You're back! Are Horatio and Emma safe now?"

Chapter 8

Once again Milo stood with Jeff and Maggie on the battlements of Elasyn Castle looking down on the square below as Polon's funeral procession gathered. It was a good place to watch from, Milo reflected, despite the biting wind. It seemed that everyone was leaving Elasyn except them. First, Horatio had left on his abortive rescue. Then the next day, they watched Prince Hamnet leave, bound for the Tower of Illusion, whatever that was. Then the Antriantara Deveron left on his mission to rescue the rescuer.

And now Deveron was back and Horatio and Emma were in Glasgow. How ironic. Milo wondered what else Deveron could tell them, but the Leader of Wizards had kept a very low profile since he returned yesterday morning.

Maggie was obviously thinking along the same lines as him.

"I wonder if we'll see the Prince again," she said.

"It's unlikely," Jeff said. "If all goes well, in a day or so we three will go to Rowlan Gates where I will get sorted out, then we will go home."

"What about the play?" Maggie asked him. "In Shakespeare's *Hamlet*, the Prince is sent away, accompanied by Rosencrantz and Guildenstern. But he tricks them and comes back early, and disaster follows."

"Hamnet told Deveron that he would remain with the mages in the Tower until sent for," Jeff said. "He's a Prince. And a Prince would not break an oath."

"Bullshit!" Milo commented. "I'd put nothing past that piece of… "

"Milo!" Maggie broke in, casting a hasty glance around for the guards. "Shut up!"

Milo spread his hands in a placating movement, before clutching his fur-lined cloak about him, moving away slightly for a better view of the scene below.

Milo had an unusual feeling of foreboding as they stood watching the procession forming below in the castle yard. He tied to brush off the sensation of impending disaster but for some reason found it difficult. So he stood in the cold wind and waited as Mage-Chancellor Polon was made ready to process to his last resting place. Drums beat a monotonous dirge as the funeral procession finished forming up and moved to the gateway and under the raised portcullis. The moat under the drawbridge was still covered in ice. Milo shivered as a cold blast of wind hit him.

From his perch high in the battlements, Milo could see right across the town's rooftops, even as far as the outer wall. Eventually, Maggie and Jeff left to go back to the warmth indoors, but Milo remained where he was, tracing the route of the funeral cortege as it began its laborious journey through Elasyn town to the graveyard east of the town. He saw the crowds that lined the streets; the news of the unexpected death must have spread quickly. But it was not the watching crowds that his eyes were fixed on, but the slight figure walking slowly behind the bier. Only when the procession moved out of sight at the far edge of the town did he shift from his stance. With a heavy sigh, he turned towards the stair well.

***

Loren and his sister, the only remaining members of their family, led the procession, walking as custom decreed directly behind the bier. Behind him Loren could hear the snuffling of the Queen as she walked at the side of King Claude. As they moved slowly through the town, even Loren was aware of the murmurs and whispers flying through the gathered watchers. *Where is Prince Hamlet? Why is he not here?*

Beside him, Olivia walked as in a daze. She had shed no tears, and all of his clumsy attempts at comfort were ignored. Loren walked in silence, thoughts churning in his head, his emotions tangled and confused. One single thought kept emerging from the turbulent brew inside his head – that he was now free of his father's torments and ridicule. He would now be free to follow his desire to become a mage, if any of the masters would accept him as apprentice. But then his gaze fell on the wooden coffin in front of him and shame coursed through him. But as quickly as he suppressed the thought, up it rose again. *To yourself be true*, he murmured to himself, keeping his head lowered. *I cannot truthfully regret my father's death. I am mage-born, and my abilities are good enough to deserve development. My di-speak to Horatio proved it.* He looked up when a small bunch of herbs, thrown in respect onto the coffin, slipped and hit him on the head.

***

Milo was in no mood for company or light conversation. As he passed along the balcony overlooking the Great Hall he paused to watch the long tables being set out for the funereal banquet. Unwilling to go back to his rooms, he dropped into one of the upholstered chairs, drew the curtain closed behind him, and brooded.

The candles were already being lit – banks of them were standing everywhere. The Great Hall, the shape of an isosceles triangle, was heavily adorned with richly-worked tapestries, which glinted gold and silver in the candlelight. The heavy fabrics masked the cold stone of the walls, and gave the Hall a semblance of warmth and majesty. At the far end of the gallery, opposite the apex, half a dozen servants were manhandling a new tapestry into place over the existing one. It was a different design from the others, and peering at it, Milo wondered if it depicted the life of the dead Chancellor. Someone was quick off the mark if it was. Underneath the tapestry a table decked out like an altar was set out, smothered in candles set out in a pattern. Milo tried to read what was written, but the angle was wrong. He turned his gaze to the Hall itself.

A raised table, now being set for a handful of people, occupied the apex of the triangular Hall. Below this table, others were set out. Two long tables ran along the sides of the Hall creating a 'V' shape, while a third table bisected the space between the arms of the 'V' making a gigantic letter 'A'. Milo sat watching as gold and pewter plates and goblets were set out, and baskets and platters of cold meats, fruits, nuts and breads were brought from the kitchens. Milo watched, slouching in his chair until his eyes grew heavy and sleep overtook him.

***

He awoke with a start as the heavy main doors to the Hall were thrust open and a blast of trumpets rent the air. The funeral party had returned. He leaned forward, searching for one single forlorn figure. Serra Olivia.

The King led the procession into the Hall, moving with the Queen to the raised table at the apex of the Great Hall. Milo watched as Ser Loren entered and took his place on the left hand side of the King. Slowly the other courtiers entered the Hall and took their places. The volume of noise rose in proportion. On Ser Loren's left side the chair remained empty.

247

He scanned the faces below in the Hall. How could he have missed her? Why had she not taken her place at the King's table? He stood up and wandered along the balcony still scanning the crowd of people below as platter after platter of delicious-smelling food was brought into the Hall.

Then his eyes were drawn to the main doors, one of which was slowly opening. Milo watched as through the gap a solitary figure entered carrying a clutch of wild winter grasses. As she moved into the Hall and between the tables towards the King's table, the chatter and noise faded to silence. She was singing a low melody whose words carried clearly to Milo's ears.

"He is dead and gone lady, he is dead and gone.
His beard was white as snow lady, and flaxen was his poll
And will he come back here lady, will he come again?
Nay! He is dead and gone lady, he is dead and gone.
They bore him on a bier lady, in his grave his face to the sky
And ne'er again will we see him lady, for he is dead and gone."

Milo watched as Serra Olivia made her way along the tables distributing grasses to this person and that, her voice sad and melancholy. He could not make out her spoken words, but gradually a murmur arose from those by whom she stopped and to whom she spoke. Eventually Ser Loren stood up and squeezed between the tables to reach her side. He said something to her and she looked up at him, a strange smile on her features as she caressed his face with a grass frond. Her words were maddeningly indistinct, but the look of panic on Ser Loren's face as he turned towards the King was plain. In the silence, his words floated up to Milo.

"My sister, my dear sweet sister, has lost her mind with grief. Give me leave Sire to take her away from here to somewhere quiet, where she may recover her senses."

The King assented and the murmuring grew as Ser Loren led the laughing, grass-throwing girl from the Hall. Milo ran along the balcony trying to find a way of intercepting them.

First he headed for Olivia's rooms, but she was not there. Unsure of where Ser Loren had taken her, he wandered the corridors, searching for her. Deep within him a formless fear took root and grew. Eventually he found himself back at his starting point, shocked to find that the banquet was almost over and that Ser

Loren was back in his position beside the King. Olivia's seat was still empty. *Where was she?*

He wandered to the windows that looked out across the moat to the town. A movement caught his eye. He stood transfixed as Olivia's slight figure, clothed only in a thin bed-gown, eased a large boulder over the edge of the drawbridge so that it fell with a dull thud through the ice. *How did she manage to move a boulder that size? What is she doing?* The answer came to him in the instant before she leaned forward over the edge of the drawbridge and fell tumbling into the icy water through the jagged hole the rock had made in the ice.

Milo ran swifter than he ever had in his entire life. He ran along the corridor, skidded down two flights of stairs, sped across the courtyard to the open gates and stopped, panting, on the drawbridge. He screamed for help as he scanned the ice-covered moat below. *Where was everyone? Where were the soldiers and guards?* He paced the drawbridge, scanning the ice below. There was no sign of her. Then he saw her, under the ice near the far bank, her eyes wide and her hands pressed against the unyielding ice. She was not moving.

Milo grabbed up a piece of wood and scrambled down the bank and on to the ice, where he began frantically hammering with wood and feet. A sliver of ice spun up and cut his face, but Milo was beyond noticing his own injury. Eventually his pounding broke through the ice and he continued hammering until the hole was large enough to reach in and pull the girl out of the freezing water.

But Milo had underestimated the weight of the icy water in Olivia's clothing. As he reached forward to gain a better hold, he overbalanced and fell forward. The shock of the icy water made him lose his hold on Olivia's gown and she slipped away from him. He took a breath and ducked under the ice, not even half aware of the danger to which he was committing himself. He could see her. She had floated only a few feet away, her un-bound hair trailing and waving in the water. As Milo clutched with rapidly chilling fingers at her hair, he became obscurely aware of the translucency of the ice above his head. A sudden realisation of his plight made him gasp and the breath exploded from his lungs. Panic-stricken, his fingers still entwined in Olivia's hair, he lunged with his free hand for the edge of the ice hole, kicking his feet out frantically behind him. His fingers reached the sharp edges of the ice hole and thrusting his head up, he dragged into his lungs pure fresh cold air. Hands reached down and grabbed at him, and pulled him to safety.

"If it were only you, naked on the grass,
Who would you be then? This is what he asked.
And I said I wasn't really sure,
But I would probably be cold.
And now I'm freezing.
Freezing".

The words are so bloody apt, Milo thought as he stood on the bank of the moat. The song lyrics he had last heard just before he crossed to Elsynvaal ran through his head in a loop. Water dripped from his sodden and rapidly freezing clothes. People fussed over Olivia's cold form lying almost naked on the snow-covered grass.

As the song began another loop, he remembered the night he lay on his bed at home in Glasgow, listening to the singer's pure voice. Then, such a short time ago and yet so long, he was mourning the loss of a girl who had proved unworthy. Now he had to begin mourning a girl the likes of whom he would never find again.

And now I'm freezing... Freezing...

Chapter 9

It was not an easy thing to do. She knew the toll this was taking of her, for if she were being totally truthful Mhari would describe Ether-travelling as a beautiful psychedelic or hallucinatory drug. All her life she had dabbled in psychic phenomena, séances and Ouija boards, trying to find her way into the human psyche. But it was only through Horatio she had found the real thing – a gateway to travelling to a whole new world.

She smiled at her brother and Martin and then closed her eyes to begin her meditative routine. Wrapped in a blanket against the chill she knew she'd find once out in the Ether, Mhari relaxed her muscles one after another, slowing her breathing and ultimately her heartbeat. Then when she was ready, she ingathered her strength as Horatio had taught her, and hurled her consciousness out into the darkness of the Ether to search for Deveron's aura. Into the void, the nothing-place where Time has no jurisdiction. Back in the attic, mere minutes had passed, but where Mhari's mind was – inside the Ether, time was rootless. Endless.

Darkness, dankness, void, nothingness. Tiring. Must return soon. Then – a presence. Sightless, blind in the blackness, she felt a mind touching hers – the now familiar strands of Deveron's aura. She'd done it! Wordlessly the mage strengthened her flagging energies and forged a solid bridge between their two worlds.

<Are you ready?> he asked.

<As ready as I'll ever be> she replied.

<You are absolutely sure of this? Have you thought it through?>

<I'm ready> she said. But even as she said the words, a thought flashed through her mind, betraying the falseness of her words. She hadn't really thought about the risks Deveron had warned her about, mainly because there was no way she was not going to help her friends.

<Right, I will begin. Good luck, Mhari.>

Another period of endless time passed then suddenly there were other presences there in the void with them. Other minds to which she had to link. Tentatively she reached out and touched one. Emma! But subdued, almost inert. Catching hold was very difficult. Mhari grappled with her friend's mind-strands, caught and then it all slipped away. She'd lost her. She thrashed around frantically searching and touched instead a strange mind. An alien mind.

<*My name is Rian*> a soothing mind voice intruded on her consciousness. <*Gather your strength and we together will carry Horatio and Emma.*>

Mhari followed him. They gathered Horatio, and she received a second shock. His mind was in utter tatters. Rian gently gathered Horatio's consciousness from the Void, while Mhari helped as she could. It was so difficult. Mhari felt her strength waning. His mind strands were knotted and dishevelled, bunching together in a great clump, but somehow Rian gathered him together and handed him to Mhari. Then he began the search for Emma. Long endless minutes while Mhari held on to Horatio.

Tired. So tired. Then she felt Horatio slipping away. She reached inside herself and pulled up the last of her reserves, desperate to keep a hold on Horatio's frail and fast-fading consciousness. Then Rian was back. Emma too. Mhari turned and led the way.

Back. Back.

The wind was against her now and it was so hard to do. The hardest thing she had ever done.

She came to sluggishly, shivering. A cold sweat covered her body. Someone was leaning over her, tucking the blanket in around her. He was talking but it was difficult and too tiring to make out his words. She closed her eyes and tried to summon what energy she had left. Very little. Washed-out. Wrung out and hung up to dry. But sound returned. Noise of voices. Hands shaking, she covered her ears.

"You're all right, Sis. Welcome back. You did it. They're here. They arrived safely." Duncan helped her to sit up. Strange sights assaulted her senses. Something out of a Grimm's fairy-tale was standing by the old blow-up paddling pool. Something perhaps not even human. A goblin? A tiny wizened man who had more than a passing resemblance to the Arthur Rackham illustration of the fairy-tale creature, Rumplestiltskin. With a shock she realised that the wizened gnome must be Rian. His eyes were closed and his wide lips were moving.

He leaned over into the paddling pool and plunged his hands into the water. After a moment, steam began to rise from the pool. "It is a strange material, this *plastic*. It is not natural, so I have little control over its properties," she heard him say. "I dare not make the water any hotter than this. We do not want the plastic to deteriorate, which it could do, I think." He removed his hands and turned to Martin and Emma. Both were extremely pale. As Emma moved, Mhari caught sight of what Emma's body had shielded from her. They were gingerly holding the semi-conscious Horatio upright. Why had they not laid him down? Mhari wondered. Then as they shifted him forward she saw the state of his body. *Oh my God! Oh my God! What had happened to him*?

His skin was shiny and very pink, almost transparent. He seemed barely aware of what was happening, and struggling to hold his head up. There was a dreadfully blank look on his face. A dead look. That would certainly explain the tangled mind threads she'd encountered in the void. Shocked and unable to move, she watched as Rian took hold of Horatio's ankles and manoeuvred his feet forward one at a time over the edge of the pool. Horatio's face contorted with pain as the warm water touched the raw new skin grafts. Gently they lowered him into the water. After a word with Rian, Duncan turned and swiftly left the room. Rian began mumbling over the water in the tub again. Emma stood by, her eyes glued to Horatio's face. His eyes closed and gradually the rigidness left his body as he sank into unconsciousness.

After a while, Rian stood back, wiped his hands on a towel. Red smears marred the towel as he dropped it on a nearby chair. "It is best this way. In an unconscious state he will be able to cope better with the inevitable pain."

Emma lifted her eyes from the thing in the pool for a moment and looked over at Mhari. Her eyes had welled up with tears. She stood up slowly and walked round the side of the tub to where Mhari was sitting. Kneeling down on the rough wooden floor beside her armchair, she laid her head against Mhari's knees and let silent tears flow. Mhari leaned over and gently put her arms around Emma, stroking her hair. Gradually her crying grew in intensity until heart-rending sobs echoed around the attic. Mhari slid off the chair and the two of them knelt on the floor, arms around one another as Emma let the fear and shock flow from her. After a while, Mhari looked up. Martin stood nearby, watching Emma. His face was pale, no doubt all of them were, under the circumstances, but his eyes… his eyes looked as dead as Horatio's.

***

That first day Emma sat by the tub most of the time, watching over Horatio and seemingly oblivious to everyone else. Mhari covertly watched Martin. It was obvious to everyone where Emma's heart lay. Surely Martin could see that he hadn't a hope in Hell with her. Not now. He hung around silent and morose until Emma suddenly stood up and said she would like to have a shower. Mhari smiled with relief that she'd even moved, and headed for the door to show Emma the way to the bathroom. As they passed him, Martin caught at Emma's sleeve. He whispered something to Emma and at her nod, he turned and followed the two girls out of the attic.

When she returned, Mhari took up a position by the cheap children's paddling pool, watching over Horatio. The water was a sickening deep red colour, as if tinted by the mage's own blood. With revulsion she saw that even deeply coloured as it was, the water could not totally hide the wretched condition of the body floating in it.

What kind of a fiend could have done this? Rian had told her that all of his skin, except his head and hands and feet had been peeled off. His body was covered in what appeared to be skin grafts, but where had they come from? They were very smooth, without the ugly puckering of Jeff's scarring. A pity something like this tub had not been available for Jeff after his accident!

Emma was alone when she returned some time later. She unwrapped her towel from her head and began to dry her hair. She was looking much better now.

Martin had decided to go home, she told them, and Mhari wondered what had been said between them.

***

Things settled into a routine. The gnomish Rian seemed to be enjoying himself very much. In between sessions working with Horatio in the tank, he stood by the attic window, watching the street below, alternately describing his life in the Northern Forest and asking questions on every subject under the sun. He even persuaded Duncan to bring his TV up to the attic so he could see for himself what this marvellous thing was. They were watching the ten o'clock news on the BBC when they heard a commotion behind them. Emma called out frantically. Horatio was thrashing about in the pool. They dashed over to find Horatio conscious and trying to get a grip on the sides of the tub to pull himself up. Obeying Rian's frantic commands to touch none of the new and very fragile skin,

Duncan and Emma gripped his hands and eased him up a little. He looked up at the faces peering at him from around the bathtub. He stretched out a hand towards Emma, who took it in both of hers.

His voice was barely more than a rasping whisper. "Tell me what happened."

Emma hushed him. "Not now," she said. "Rest first, and we'll talk later."

"No. Tell me."

Emma looked at Rian, and Horatio's eyes followed her eye movement. Rian nodded, moving round into full view of his patient. He introduced himself, and told him the bare facts of Alain's rescue and how Deveron and Mhari engineered the crossover to Glasgow.

"I see. Thank you," was all the mage said before closing his eyes once more.

All night they watched over him, but his condition remained stable. Several times he awoke in pain, and Rian with a hand on his forehead gave him relief.

***

In the afternoon of the second day, Emma suddenly aroused herself from the daze she was in, and asked to borrow a jacket and some shoes. She wanted to go round to her flat and get some things, she said. She refused her friend's offer to go with her. "I need to be on my own for a bit," she said.

She was away for two hours. Mhari began to worry. Then she had a thought and dialled Martin's number. After ringing for a time it was answered. She had been there, Martin averred, but had left twenty minutes ago. Then he hung up.

Mhari pocketed her mobile and scribbled down its number on a piece of paper.

"Here, Rian. Call me if you need me, or if Emma returns. I'm going to try to find her."

Then she bolted for the door and outside headed for the direction of Martin's flat. No sign of Emma anywhere. Where could she have gone, what might she have done? She didn't really know Emma that well, despite the fact that she'd just risked her sanity to bring her through the Ether. After all, they'd only met a few times before the evening of the Ouija board.

Eventually, she reached the tenement building where Martin and Jeff lived, and toyed with the idea of going up to the flat. At that moment, her mobile phone rang. Snatching it from her pocket, she hit the *answer* button. "Hi!" Emma's voice sounded in her ear.

Mhari mumbled something incoherent.

"Look I'm sorry, Mhari," Emma replied. "I didn't mean for all of you to get worried. I'm back at your place now."

"You're okay?"

"Fine. I went to Martin's and we talked and I took the long way back, along the river… " Her voice trailed off.

"How's Horatio?"

"Much the same. Rian's working with him now."

"Okay. I'll come home now."

"Okay. See you." Then silence. Mhari broke the connection and pocketed the phone. Then looked up at Martin's window and wondered whether she should go up. Just to make sure he was all right.

He wasn't. In the intervening hour he had managed to get outside of three quarters of a bottle of whisky. Mhari fed him strong black coffee and tried to sober him up a bit, wishing again in vain that Jeff had come back. Why hadn't he? Surely he would have known how Martin would react? Why had he decided to remain in Elsynvaal? Damnation. But through it all, she could only pity Martin. Eventually, he began talking.

By the time she left, he was in bed sleeping it off. She left a phone number beside him, unsure of what else to do. She didn't know any of his friends apart from Jeff, and had no idea how to contact his family – or even if she should. If only she could speak with Jeff! She clomped down the tiled stairwell to the street door and headed home.

Shortly after Mhari returned, Emma for once left the pool-side, and moved over beside Mhari. Hunched over yet another mug of coffee, she started talking. It was as if a dam had broken. She talked about everything that had happened to them all in the fabulous land of Elsynvaal. How, without even trying, Emma managed to fire Mhari's imagination! She told her of Elasyn Castle and its ghost, and poor Prince Hamnet and Olivia who loved him. She described the Coronation and the celebrations afterwards. She described meeting William Shakespeare. But for Mhari, all this outpouring merely left her with a desperate longing to see that fabulous land for herself. Emma eventually fell silent, and looked down at her hands clasped tightly in her lap. As she watched her, Mhari realised that Emma had studiously avoided Horatio's torture and who had done it to him.

Mhari's eyes met those of Rian across the room. His sorrow-filled eyes changed colour as she watched, darkening from pale blue through deep blue, until they were almost violet. Most strange, Mhari thought.

The next afternoon, Mhari's mobile phone rang.

"Hello?"

"Hi, Mhari, it's Martin."

"Hi, just hang on a minute, will you?" She stood up and went out into the stairwell, away from the others.

"Okay Martin. How are you?"

"I'm fine, thanks. I was just ringing to let you know that I appreciated what you did for me last night."

"No problem. I couldn't just go off and leave you in that state."

"Did you tell anyone?"

"About how out of it you were? No."

"Thanks."

"Do you want to speak to Emma?"

There was a pause. Then: "I don't think that would be a very good idea, really. Have you heard anything about Jeff?"

"No, not yet."

"And him – Horatio – what about him?"

"Things seem to be going well. He's still alive."

"That's good. Listen, Mhari, if I give you my number, will you keep me in touch? You know…"

"'Course I will."

"Bye, Mhari, and thanks again."

"Bye, Martin." Mhari hit the 'end call' button. He really is a sweet guy, she thought.

That evening she tried to contact Deveron, but got nowhere. When she returned , Rian took her aside.

"Deveron wants you to think about going to Elsynvaal to train as a mage."

"Whoa, Rian. You don't believe in soft-pedalling, do you? Deveron thinks I have mage-potential?"

"Most definitely. I could not do what you have done."

Mhari was quite taken aback. Despite everything, she'd not really thought of that possibility. Study magery in Elsynvaal? Could she do it? *Should* she?

"This is not something I can decide at once."

"No," the little gnome said, "Nor should you try. Just think about it. In the meantime, I have thought of another way of getting round the problem of contacting Deveron. We could try co-joining our minds to pierce the void," he said.

Mhari waited for enlightenment.

"My fellow Sylvan Alain and I once achieved a mind-meld. We could try something of the same."

Mhari was sceptical. "We are of different species…"

Rian chuckled, looking even more like a wizened gnome than ever. "I never said it would be easy. It will be difficult, if not impossible, but we could try…"

Mhari soon discovered that connecting and forging with Rian was a very different sensation from her Ether contacts with Horatio and Deveron. It was Pain! Sharp, bewildering pain. It felt as if Rian was ripping her mind out. As if sections of brain were being manoeuvred around inside her skull, cut about and cauterised without even a local anaesthetic. Then the pain subsided, and miraculous – she heard Rian speak mind-to-mind. Telepathy! Almost overwhelmed, she caught a glimpse of the immense knowledge and vast wisdom contained in his truly wonderful mind. Then, in tandem, they sent their minds out to search for Deveron.

They travelled further than Mhari had dared to go before, deep into the dark dank nothingness that was the Ether. Searching for Deveron's elusive signature. Then, at last, they forged a contact.

It was with downcast hearts that Mhari and Rian heard about the raid on the Sylvan village and Serra Olivia's death.

For four days, Horatio talMerios lay floating in his blood-red recuperation pool. Initially, he was barely conscious and oblivious to Rian's efforts to keep his heart beating and his body and soul together. But gradually, as Horatio began to rally, his sub-conscious began its own self-healing and augmented the Sylvan's works of healing. Little by little Horatio remained conscious and lucid for longer periods as he floated in the ridiculous child's paddling pool, and as he lay at rest he investigated and probed at his inner powers. Something had changed within him.

At first he was unsure what the difference was, but gradually a certainty grew within him that his innate mage-born powers had grown to a magnitude that only a week ago he had thought impossible to acquire.

His thoughts were clearer and more focused, allowing complex magic to be accomplished with less effort. As he floated in his gruesome bath, he tried visualising spell configurations. He discovered that he had now attained almost perfect recall of every spell he had ever seen, written, or loosed. He smiled a little to himself. Such are the rewards of physical pain.

First of all, he concentrated on bringing his ruined body back to a functional state, working at ordering cells and building up skin layers to supplement Rian's emergency membrane. By the end of his fourth full day in the pool, he was ready to begin leaving the pool for short periods. The others supported Horatio the first time he stood up and stepped from the pool into a warm bath towel.

"It is important," Rian said, "that your skin should not dry out."

Horatio smiled. "I think you'll find that my skin is perfectly stable. Tender, yes, but I doubt that it's going to shrivel up and fall off."

"You are actively self-healing," Rian reproached his patient. "Horatio, beware. There is danger in doing such a thing. You could over-tax your energy reserves without realising it. You *must conserve* your energies, young man."

Emma declared it a miracle, but Horatio shook his head.

"It is a well-known fact in my world, that pain or extreme suffering can have a profound effect on the brain," he said. "It would seem, my friends, that the extreme circumstances and intense pain I experienced opened new channels of communication."

"What?"

Horatio laughed. "Today I am a much more powerful mage that I ever in my wildest dreams dared think it was possible for me to become, and the bird-woman is responsible. By the act of her inhumane torture, Midori dalEbol has inadvertently given us the weapon we need to defeat both her and talEbol...myself. I will go back to Elsynvaal tomorrow."

Amid the cacophony of voices, Rian's calm voice stood out. "So, you know who the witch-woman is? This Midori dalEbol?"

"Yes," Horatio replied, looking at Emma. "She is the daughter of the renegade mage, Gheron talEbol."

"She is also my mother." Emma's voice was very quiet as she spoke the damning words. It was as if only she and Horatio were there. "I'm sorry, Horatio," she said. "If there was only some way I could have prevented it all. What she did to you was my fault."

She looked round at these people who had in such a short time become her friends, and lifted up her chin. "It was my mother who... skinned... Horatio."

"What?" The listeners were dumbfounded. Emma's mother? It was unbelievable. Emma looked at them with unfathomable eyes.

"A year after she gave birth to Emma, Midori was kidnapped by her natural father, Gheron talEbol," Horatio said. "He crossed her to Elsynvaal and trained her in the Wizardly arts. But," he went on, "it would appear that she's mentally unable to cope with the disciplines. It's also probable that talEbol's malevolence played its part in her instability. Now she is far from sane. She decided that she wanted her lost daughter, Emasiyo, there with her in her exile, so she planted dreams in Emma's head and my own to induce Emma to come to Elsynvaal. Her plan worked better that she had dared to hope."

Mhari spoke for the first time since Emma's revelation. "And what do we do now?"

"Now we must find her." Emma's voice was almost unrecognisable. Hard, intense, with an undertone of hatred no-one had ever heard before from her.

"How do you know all of this, Horatio?" he asked.

"When she took me to the cellar," he replied, and an involuntary shudder passed through his body, "Midori made a point of telling me the whole story. She picked on me because of my genes. She wanted a mage-born grandchild with outstanding magical armament. And she is determined to get one." He paused and looked at Emma. Her eyes were downcast. "Even now Emma could be pregnant."

Mhari's mind whirled at this new turn of events. Emma was pregnant? Boy, was she glad Martin was not here!

Emma touched Horatio lightly on the arm. "She gave me a book, Horatio, a little leather-bound book, and told me that it would explain everything."

Horatio looked at her, a frown appearing on his smooth forehead. "A book? What happened to it?"

"I don't know. It was still in my pocket when we left the cabin. Things are a little hazy."

"She gave it to Deveron," Rian said, "just before we crossed."

"Good. There could be valuable information for us in it. I will speak to him about it as soon as I can engineer a contact."

It was only the fifth day after Alain's rescue, but Horatio's skin now was whole and almost unblemished, though it had yet to acquire its natural olive tint. He began to make preparations to return to Elsynvaal.

Chapter 10

Horatio's voice was cold with fury. "Serra Olivia is dead?" Mhari and Rian had decided to keep the news from him until he was fit, but wilting under his furious response Mhari began to regret the decision.

His heart heavy, Horatio winged out into the Ether to contact Deveron, and Mhari hooked in, eavesdropping. She had an immense raw talent, Horatio realised.

Deveron's obvious joy at his recovery was gratifying, but his mental voice saddened as he told Horatio of the circumstances of Olivia's death. He said that he would remain in Elasyn Castle in order to attend Olivia's funeral the following day.

<Do you think her suicide could be connected to talEbol?>

<Only indirectly, I would say. It was not he who told her the name of her father's killer.>

<Who did?>

A pause. *<Master Milo.>*

Milo? Mhari almost lost Horatio's strand, and he gripped her more tightly, urging her to return. She refused, wanting to know the whole story.

Deveron was still carrying on the dialogue, though aware of Mhari's pseudo-presence. *<He was angry at the Prince's off-hand treatment of Olivia, and blurted it out in a moment of rage.>*

<If only I had been able to return them on the Eve of the Coronation!>

<Milo is not to be blamed, Horatio. He is torturing himself with remorse and guilt. And remember that the Prince himself has a lot to answer for.>

<Does Hamnet know about Olivia?>

<No. He has disappeared from Deveron's Tower, and has not been in contact since. We do not know where he is. I have tried scrying for him, without success. He stole a cloaking device when he absconded. Try not to concern yourself with these happenings for now, Horatio. Concentrate on your recovery. We need you back as soon as you are able.>

<I am ready now to return.>

<What?>

The Antriantara was astounded as Horatio recounted to him the results of his time in Rian's miraculous pool.

<This is good news, Horatio. Just think of it – more power; more spells – together we might just have the power to overcome Gheron talEbol! Perhaps you should cross directly to the Mage Hall in Rowlan Gates instead of coming to Elasyn.>

<Deveron, think. The spell books of Mage Hall cannot help us here. I have a terrible foreboding that things are coming to a head in Elasyn. Speak to Maggie and Jeff about Master Will's play. We have little time left to us. We must strike at talEbol while he is still in or around Elasyn. He is still there?>

<Yes, but I know of two occasions when he has left Claude's body.>

<Where did he go?>

<He's untraceable.>

<Give me a day or so Deveron and I will be back with you in Elsynvaal.>

<Wait, Horatio. I have a book that might help. A small book bound in human skin. The one Emma left with me.> He paused. *<Could we use Midori's magic against them?>*

<There are spells in the book?>

<Indeed, my friend. Some are quite ingenious. Some are inhumane. I will search though them once more.>

<Contact me when you are ready to return. Till then, Horatio, my friend, stay well.>

<Stay well, Deveron.>

With contact broken, Horatio knew they would have to sit down and decide what to do. Who was going back to Elsynvaal, who was staying here as anchor? Decisions had to be made. Rian would want to return home, of course. Mhari's face fell whenever the subject of an anchor was brought up. The mage could see how desperate she was to cross over. But was this the time to bring her over? It was a dangerous time.

And what of Emma? Horatio could not bring himself to look at her. They'd had no time alone since his time in the pool and he was horrified to discover within him a distinct element of fear of her. His mind whirled to last night when she'd slipped into his makeshift bed, her body warm against his. He kissed her, because it was expected of him, but he was shocked to discover that all desire for her had vanished, as if it had never existed. He'd pleaded weakness and she had lain still, murmuring about time and it being too soon… But he knew that was not the reason for his incapacity. Even now, he could not forget who she was. The daughter of his torturer, Midori the mad, and the grand-daughter of the Renegade talEbol. What unknown and untapped powers did Emma – Emasiyo – have? With such antecedents?

While Mhari relayed to them Horatio's conversation with Deveron, Horatio himself sat and watched the play of emotion on their faces. Once more Mhari's brother Duncan was there, but Martin was not. Horatio wondered about Martin. Horatio had not seen him since he'd had regained consciousness. Martin had gone, he realised, leaving the way open for him… and now… As if hearing his thoughts, Emasiyo looked over at him.

He stood up. *It's time,* he thought. "I thought I'd go for a walk."

Rian threw a thought beam at his erstwhile patient. Horatio soothed his fears. "Not far. It is just to test my stamina. Will you come with me, Emma?"

It was raining. Horatio was tempted to raise a field, but thought the better of it, so they huddled under an umbrella and made their way down the empty wet streets, heading for a pub that Emma said would be relatively quiet tonight, despite it being Saturday night. They walked in the rain in silence. There was too much to say; too much to ask; too many questions and not enough answers. And – god's blood – the baby. He still hadn't asked her if she thought it was true. Horatio stopped walking. She continued on for a few steps and turned round, watching him as the rain fell on him and soaked his hair and jacket. Eventually Horatio cleared his throat and said: "About last night… "

"Don't worry about that, Horatio. A near death experience is likely to have all sorts of repercussions, if that was what you were meaning."

"Well, perhaps, I suppose."

"You think it might be more permanent?"

He shrugged. "Who knows?"

"Ah! I see." She turned away and walked on.

A few long strides and they were level once more. He gripped her arm. "Is it true what Midori said?" he asked. He could not say *your mother.*

"Is what true?" Her voice was cool.

"Are you with child?" Horatio glanced around. There was no-one nearby.

"With child? What a quaint way of saying it."

"Are you?"

"You don't know much do you, Horatio? It only happened a week ago. I won't know for weeks yet."

"If you let me touch you, I might be able to tell."

"The way *she* did?" She moved away, her eyes flashing.

Horatio ran after her and after a quick glance around, did a quick spell on his hair and jacket. It was good to be warm and dry again. They walked on in silence until they reached the pub. Horatio's stamina was holding up fine.

The table they found was in a corner. They sat toying with their drinks as the silence grew, each of them unsure of what they wanted to say.

Eventually she leaned across the table and said in a low voice, "If I am pregnant, then I'm sure I'll be able to manage. You don't have to stick around. You have your work to do in Elsynvaal – you have a world to save, for God's sake! I have friends here, family. Being a single mum is not the bogey it has been in the past. I'll be fine. Take a year out and go back to take my final year later. It's been done before. Anyway, if I am in the club it could even be Martin's."

Horatio's eyes narrowed. "Could it?"

Her head drooped as if in shame. "No. Horatio, I'm sorry for saying that. It can't be Martin's. Martin and I... we didn't... not since. . . weeks ago. The dreams..."

"Oh." He did not know what to say. "You would not contemplate abortion, would you?"

Her head shot up, her eyes blazing. "Is that what all this is about?" she hissed. "You want me to kill it – if it exists! You don't want a great-grandchild of your renegade wizard wandering the universe."

He caught hold of her hands as she began to stand. "No, Emma, you've got it all wrong. Totally wrong. Sit down. We have to talk this through, whether there is a baby now or not." He lifted her chin and made her look at him. "That you are Midori Campbell's daughter is something I have to come to terms with, just as you have. But if you are pregnant then it is my child too and I would never, ever, ask you to terminate a child's life. Life is the most precious gift any of us has to give. Also there is the fact that any child we had would be very likely to be mage-born, and inherit from us considerable potential as a mage."

"You want me to cross back to Elsynvaal with you."

"Yes."

"Because of the potential baby."

"Yes. No!"

"Which?"

"Both."

"I'm out of here." She stood up, putting on her jacket as she strode towards the doors.

"Emma! Wait!" Horatio dashed through the doors and looked up and down the street, but could not see her. He stood in the pouring rain and did not notice as it trickled down his neck. Where had she gone? He ran hands through wet dripping hair.

Then a voice came from behind him. "You look ridiculous standing there like that, Horatio." He swung round. There she was, leaning against the wall around the side of the pub. She moved towards him. "But it's much better than seeing you lying unconscious in Mhari's paddling pool." Then they were standing close together while the rain continued its unending downpour. She looked at him, but there was no smile, no encouragement in the look.

"Rian tried to tell me what it was like for you after Alain brought us out. He said you refused to leave me for a moment. Is that true?"

She nodded, her eyes finally dropping from his. "I don't think I could go through that again."

"I'd not be very keen on it either."

She turned away. "Be serious, Horatio."

"I am," he replied as he gripped her shoulders and turned her back towards him. "I do not mean to be caught unprepared like that again. I underestimated the danger. It's something I will not repeat, if I can possibly avoid it. No more rushing in, guns blazing. Next time I have to go up against her, it will be after full preparation. But what of you, Emma? What are you going to do?"

She shook her head. "I don't know."

"I think you should return to Elsynvaal. Only there you will be able to confront your fears. Remain here and it will always be there with you – shadowy in the background wherever you are. You are who you are, Emma. You cannot change that. If you don't return to

Elsynvaal, you'll never have the answers you need. For the rest of your life you'll be watching over your shoulder, seeing the White Hawk in every overhead shadow. You will always wonder what your inheritance was and what it meant. I will be crossing back over tomorrow. You have to decide."

She nodded and they began to walk back along the street, oblivious to the rain. After a while, she spoke, her voice so quiet he had to strain to make out the words.

"You're right, Horatio. I would always wonder. I see now that I have to go back."

As they walked back to Mhari's attic Horatio once again brooded on his lack of physical reaction to her and wondered if her answer really was the outcome he had envisioned or hoped for when he asked her on this walk.

The next morning they readied themselves to make the crossing to Elasyn. Mhari held the Ether-strands while Horatio, still learning the bounds of his new powers, thrust himself out into the void, searching a contact with Deveron.

There was nothing there.

Chapter 11

Milo Diaz swallowed hard and forced his eyes closed to stop the tears forming. *She's dead. She's dead.* The words swung crazily around in his head, spilling over into mumbles as he walked. *And whose fault is it? That damned arrogant Prince. He spurned her, killed her father, and drove her over the edge of sanity. When he returns... Just as Will Shakespeare wrote in his play, so shall it be. Only I shall be the duellist. Not Olivia's simpering and ineffective little brother.*

At the appointed place a hole yawned in the earth, only a very short distance from a fresh grave filled only a few days ago. Thus was his lady Olivia to be laid next to her father. *Laid to rest.* Milo looked around, taking note of the number of mourners – Loren, the King, the Queen, Master Will, three of Serra Olivia's female companions, several soldiers and a number of courtiers. *So few to mourn the passing of one such as she!* Though, of course, Olivia took her own life. Of necessity the funeral party of a *suicide* must be significantly smaller than that of a King's Chancellor. He looked at the Antriantara, leading the tiny procession. *Thank you, Deveron.* He knew that it was only through Deveron's intercession that she was to be buried on Holy Ground and not taken in a boat to be unceremoniously dumped in the sea to be fish food. Still mumbling, Milo gagged at the thought.

Maggie was whispering in his ear, urging him to be still, to keep control, to quieten down. He threw off her support with a snarl, and saw the look exchanged between his friends: *We shouldn't have let him come!*

Yeah, well I'm here, ready or not!

Then suddenly the long walk was over and they stood around the yawning grave. The open bier lay propped on two wooden planks while Deveron conducted the funeral rites. The interminable rites. Milo heard nothing of it all. His eyes, hot with tears he refused to let fall, were fixed on his Lady's face soon to be covered with cold wet earth. A gossamer shroud covered her slim young body, her beautiful features that would never smile or laugh or frown again in this life. And for what reason? His foot moved forward of its own volition, and only Jeff and Maggie holding his arms kept him from stepping over to the grave's edge. Instead, as the bier was lifted on sturdy ropes and the wooden planks removed, Ser Loren stepped forward and begged the boon of seeing his beloved sister's face one last time. The four soldiers detailed to hold the ropes strained against their burden as Ser Loren stepped forward and lifted the veil.

"NO!" A voice screamed from behind.

Everyone turned in consternation towards the yell. From behind a tussock of scrubland, there rose the returning, and in some eyes, unwelcome Prince Hamnet of Elsynvaal. The soldiers holding the ropes of the casket lost their grip and the open bier slid to one side, hit the edge of the open pit and tumbled sideways into it. The Queen stepped forward, but the King held her back, gazing over his shoulder as the Prince Hamnet charged across the wet grass towards the tiny group. Such was his passion and fury that a path cleared for him.

He swept past, over the edge of the grave and down into the pit. Only then did his rage abate somewhat. Slowly, gently, he leaned over and eased his hands under Olivia's body to lift her from her unseemly resting place to the grass at the side of the grave. Then he leaned over and kissed her gently on the lips. His words, though whispered, carried to the ears of every man and woman standing there. "I loved you, Olivia. Ten thousand brothers could not love you half as well."

Then he turned to the crowd gaping at him. "What happened here? Who is to blame?"

His mother stepped forward. "She drowned herself, Hamnet. In despair."

Hamnet leaped out of the grave and rounded on the King. "Are you, whoever you are, are you to be blamed for this death also? You murdered your brother, my father! You set Polon to spy on me! And now you are here presiding at Olivia's burial. I loved her. I loved her! Why did she too have to die? Why not just be done with me? Is that not your final intention?"

The King backed away from his wrath, waving to the soldiers to step between them.

"Well, *Uncle*? Will you not answer?"

Milo Diaz threw off the hands restraining him and walked forward. "Whatever the King is guilty of," he said quietly, "Olivia's death cannot be counted among them. You and only you, my Lord Hamnet, are responsible for this tragedy!"

Hamnet narrowed his eyes. "You are… yes, I remember. The singing would-be swordsman. But what can you know? Take back that foul accusation."

"No, I refuse to back down! *Olivia loved you* and what did you do? You treated her like dirt! You ignored her! You tossed her love aside. You say you loved her – but did you ever tell her? Did you ever *in your whole life* do *anything* that was not selfish and self-centred? No! Instead you mocked her and sent her away. You murdered her father and then left without a single word to her."

Hamnet stood as if turned to stone. But Milo was not finished yet. "Well you were not the only one to have loved her. She was the most wonderful person I ever met, and I loved her, helplessly, hopelessly because *she loved you. YOU*!" He stepped forward until the two were face to face, inches away from one another. Then Milo deliberately placed his hand flat on the Prince's chest and pushed. The onlookers gasped.

Hamnet took a step backwards to regain his balance. "How dare you!"

"I challenge you to a duel!" Milo announced.

"NO!" Maggie screamed, dashing forward and pulling on Milo's sleeve. "No Milo. You're upset and grieving. Don't do this. *Please*!"

Milo shrugged her hand off, his eyes fixed on the Prince. "Shall I tell you something of my background, my Lord Prince? I am Maximilian Diaz, son of Tomas Diaz of Sicily. And we Sicilians have a tradition of payment of good for good and bad for bad. The Holy Bible says: "An eye for an eye; a tooth for a tooth." But I say a life for a life. Yours for *hers*!" A grand Latin gesture accompanied his last words.

Hamnet's eyes flashed. Maggie had never seen that actually happen, until now. His blue eyes blazed with cold ice. "As you wish, Sicilian! Two days hence, at noon in the Great Hall. As the one challenged, I choose the weapons. No foils this time, Master Milo. Have you a rapier? If not, I suggest you find one soon."

Deveron stepped forward. "This has gone far enough! Calm! Peace! Have you both forgotten why we are here?"

Silence. Shame as eyes were drawn back to the body lying forgotten by the open grave.

Hamnet and Milo stepped back from one another and Deveron bent down and lifted Olivia's body from the wet grass. Two of the soldiers leaped into the pit to retrieve the casket. Gently the mage

270

laid the girl's body back in the casket and the lowering ropes were slid once more beneath it. Slowly and carefully the casket was laid in the ground to the quiet tones of Deveron's chant. One by one the mourners threw a handful of Elsynvaal's soil into the grave.

It was over. In twos and threes the mourners began to make their way back to the Castle. Loren walked back with the King and Queen, followed by the courtiers. Deveron had vanished. Hamnet stood watching as the gravediggers stepped forward to shovel in the soil. As Milo turned away guided by Jeff and Maggie, he suddenly broke from their grasp once more and stepped up to the Prince.

"Is it worth another death?" the Prince asked without taking his eyes from the partially-filled grave.

"Don't you mean *'Is* she *worth another death'*? To that question I say, *yes*. I will meet you two days hence, at noon. Say your prayers, Prince."

Hamnet was still standing there by the pit when the grave-diggers had finished filling the grave. On a hill-top some distance away, there sat a large White Hawk.

Chapter 12

"What do you mean *There's nothing there?*" Mhari demanded. "There must be. It's the Ether! There must be something there!"

Horatio looked at her, his face unsmiling and troubled.

"Mhari, please believe me – there's nothing to get hold of out there. The way is blocked in the same way it was when I tried to send Emma and the others back here the night before the Coronation. It feels the same, but without the voice, this time. *I cannot get through.*"

"Does this mean that we cannot cross over? What are we going to do?" Emma's voice was quiet in the silence that followed.

"No, it doesn't have to mean that." He paused, looking down at his hands gripped together in his lap. When he raised his head, determination was writ in his face. "Up till now I've been merely toying with my new powers, but now the time has come to give them a real try-out. I have to find out just what I'm capable of doing. I'm going to go out again. Rian, Mhari, this time I want you both to anchor me, but don't try to come with me. I'm going to have to experiment out there and I need you as a lifeline in case it goes wrong."

Emma looked worried. "Are you sure, Horatio? Your powers are still so raw …"

Horatio gave her a grin that held more than a little bravado. "What is that phrase you have? *A man's gotta do...*"

"*...what a man's gotta do!*" Duncan finished for him.

Emma rounded on him. "That's bullshit, and you know it! You don't have to do this. Why not leave it for now and try the simple call again later? The block was removed the last time. It will probably fade this time too."

"No, Emma, we can't afford to wait. I don't know how the last block was caused or how it was removed, so there's no certainty that this block will fade. We haven't got any more time."

He prepared himself as well as he could for the effort ahead of him and leaning back in Mhari's comfortable armchair, he sent forth his consciousness into the void.

For many long minutes, those remaining watched with trepidation.

Horatio's breathing slowed until it seemed dangerously shallow. Rian held his wrist, his sensitive fingers resting gently on his pulse. Mhari sat on a chair beside Rian. Her hand rested lightly on Horatio's arm, knowing that physical contact strengthened the connection. Duncan paced to and fro near the window, watching the sun attempt to dry up the rain.

Emma sat on Horatio's right side, holding his hand, stroking it, wishing there was some way to help him. She began thinking of the descriptions Horatio had given them of how he channelled the power – built it up in the centre of his being. She was Midori Campbell's daughter... She concentrated. Midori Campbell's daughter should be able to do things.

Still holding her lover's hand, Emma began to experiment with the powers that were supposed to exist within her. She called upon the nexus of power as Horatio had told them and willed a pencil lying near her foot to move a few centimetres across the floor. Nothing. She tried again. Gather the power... *Ah!* That was it. She definitely felt something that time – a steady build-up of a force within her near the centre of her chest behind the ribs. *Up!* she commanded. *Pencil, you* will *move. You will move closer to my foot!* And suddenly, it did. Only a centimetre, and the movement was uneven, but it was there. She tried again. This time the pencil rolled over so she could see the maker's name stencilled on it. Again, and the pencil spun in a complete circle before coming to rest having hit her foot. *I did that!* She thought. She brought Horatio's hand to her lips.

It felt cold.

She looked at her friends' faces. Rian's eyes were fastened on Horatio's face as he whispered, "His pulse is racing. Something has happened out there! Can you bring him back, Mhari?"

"I don't know how, Rian. He's never gone this far before."

They felt the tense shudder run through Horatio's body before the shaking began. It began with a slight twitching of his hands and a slow shaking back and forth of his head. Then his arms went rigid and the muscles under the skin began twitching and trembling. His breathing quickened till he was gasping, gradually building up until his body was almost in convulsion. His eyes shot open, the pupils so enlarged that his hazel irises were but a thin rim encircling the blackness, and there was no intelligence behind them, no understanding, no awareness...

273

Blackness surrounded his spirit as soon as he left the confines of his body to range the Ether. The cold dampness felt subtly different. That of course could merely be a greater awareness of the components of the Ether occasioned by his heightened power. On the other hand... he ranged further out. Stretching thinner the invisible silvery thread that anchored him to his body and to Mhari, he stretched further away, his senses heightened and aware. The normal sensations of Ether-travelling were absent. He had no awareness of any other presence as he winged his way through the empty spaces. It was as if no-one anywhere in any of the worlds was asleep and dreaming. He remembered this absence from the last blackout, back in Elasyn Castle the night before the Coronation when he'd tried to send Emma and her friends back home. Range further. Gather the power. Loose out the thread tying him to his physicality.

But wait – a glimmer. He sent a thought beam towards the invisible gleam. The strand contacting him to Mhari and Rian grew dangerously thin. On one level of consciousness, he became aware of this, even as he stretched it even further. Where had it gone? Yes. There!

The intelligence within the glimmer was pre-occupied. Horatio began to catch stray incoherent thoughts. This consciousness had a confusing familiarity about it. Tantalising, it was almost but not quite recognisable.

He tried to build a shield around his aura, even as he tried it unaware whether such a thing was even marginally possible. He knew only of one wizard who would be powerful enough to create the disguised consciousness in front of him. As he contemplated what he must do, his body at the other end of the silvery thread reacted by physically chilling his blood, but Horatio's naked consciousness had no notion of the effect his efforts were having on his body back on Earth in Mhari's attic. Holding his improvised shield around him, he opened himself to the void, to attempt a psychic eavesdrop on the Renegade of Elsynvaal.

***

The shaking intensified. Emma screamed at Mhari. "Bring him back, can't you? Do something, Mhari. He's convulsing!"

Mhari's voice was shaking. "Get him down on to the floor, in the recovery position. I'll try and follow him, and bring him back."

"And how will you get back?" Enmma yelled. "Send me instead. Midori's power is within me, Mhari. Tell me what to do and let me try to find him."

Rian stood up from easing Horatio on to the floor. The convulsions had stopped. Mhari stooped and rolled him on to his side, drawing his knees up into the classic recovery position. His breathing was ragged, his skin somehow cold and clammy at the same time. His pulse was racing.

"If you feel you have to do this," Rian said to Emma, "I will anchor you, child. If anyone can find Horatio out there, you can. Search for him with your feelings, your love. Follow the silver strand that links the two of you throughout eternity."

Emma lay down on the floor beside Horatio and tucked herself in behind him, one arm curved round his body, her head resting against his back. Rian sat cross-legged beside her, his hand lying gently on her shoulder.

"You are kindred spirits, Emma. Pull the power from your core; follow the silver strand."

***

It was very unlike the two crossings of the Ether she'd already made. The first time across, Horatio had led the four of them – Maggie, Jeff, Milo and herself. His hand holding hers had communicated a security she'd not realised at the time she'd needed. The second crossing was a blur of incomprehension mixed with worry over Horatio's hideous injuries. This, her third, was likely to be her worst yet. She gathered the little ball of cold fire that existed behind her ribs and sent her consciousness out into the Ether. *I can do it!* she realised as all physical feeling fell away and the sensations of her body ceased to matter. She looked round, searching for Horatio's invisible silver strand. How thin it was, stretching far, far away. She ignored the blackness and the dank darkness, concentrating on the silver strand that was all that held him to his body. Nothing else existed. Onwards. Following, following. Up ahead what was that? A glimmer, shifting. No – there were two shifting and dodging. Go! Go! He can't do this alone. As the glimmers grew, she felt Horatio's soul-strand twitch and weave as the two glimmers shifted and danced in the distance. Panic, *How can a soul panic?* swept through her. Then the strand pulled tight and stretched beyond invisibility. *Horatio!* she cried out to him, *don't give up!*

275

She thrust forward ever harder, aware that her own soul-strand was wearing dangerously thin. Then one of the glimmers winked out, no longer there. Horatio's strand grew less taut, began weaving and swaying, as if blowing in a gentle breeze. The glimmer grew closer, closer, and she felt the panic rise again as she agonised over whom it was that existed within that bobbing glimmer. What if it was not Horatio? What if it was some creature of the void that would sever her silver strand and devour her soul? *I can't even hide!* she thought. *There's nowhere to go!* The glimmer grew ever closer and her panic grew proportionately, until with a wave of relief she recognised her lover's mental signature, the shape of a white rose-like flower. His thrown thought winged its way to her, and she patiently waited for him to find her and take her home.

Horatio opened his eyes, momentarily confused. The wooden floor beneath him was hard, and his left arm was crushed under him, numb. He lifted his head gingerly and looked towards his right shoulder to where Emma's head was lying. Her eyes were still closed, but she was smiling. He shifted slightly, easing his numb upper arm from under him. Emma's eyelids flickered and opened. Her smile widened. They sat up and soundlessly hugged one another then looked around, hands still clasped. Mhari was sitting on her chair, wiping tears from her face and grinning like the proverbial cat. Rian beamed down on them. Duncan was over in the corner doing his personal version of the New Zealand National Rugby team's rallying shout.

Their initial euphoria at Emma's success in locating Horatio faded rapidly when Horatio told them what he had found in the Ether void.

"I did not find Deveron," Horatio told them, sitting on one of the rickety wooden chairs at the table, and sipping at his hot coffee. "Instead I found talEbol himself. I formed a shield and crept closer in order to hear his thoughts. I found out quite a lot about him before he pierced my shield and turned on me. He attacked me and we thought-fought, something I'd previously have said was an impossibility, and then abruptly he turned tail and disappeared. I don't know where he went. Perhaps he found her."

"Who?"

"Midori, his daughter. He was searching for her when I came upon him."

"The bird-woman," Rian murmured.

"My mother," Emma whispered. "Go on Horatio. Tell it all."

"It would appear that talEbol is not overly pleased with Midori. She had apparently flouted orders he had given her, transformed herself into a White Hawk and flown away. For some reason he was convinced she'd fled to the Ether, perhaps trying to reach another world."

"A white hawk," Emma murmured thoughtfully. "I saw a white hawk once. But when was it?"

"That is how she escaped from us at the Cabin," Rian was saying when Emma clicked her fingers.

"I remember where it was I saw the White Hawk," she exclaimed. "It was the night I first dreamed of you, Horatio. I woke up and went to the window to draw the curtains because it was too early to get up. Outside the window there was a white bird perched on the railings, and it seemed that it was watching me. That's why I remember it so clearly. I pulled the curtains closed and it flew away."

"Midori, watching over your dreams," Horatio stated. Emma had to nod. It did make sense – now. Her hand strayed to her abdomen, and a tiny frown creased her forehead.

"There was something else I discovered out there," Horatio went on. "It is talEbol who is blocking the Ether. I don't know if I'll be able to break through. But I will continue to try until the block collapses. In the meantime we will just have to believe that Deveron is on the case."

Chapter 13

Loren gave Milo's duelling rapier a last wipe with the blue cloth as the duellists arrived in the Great Hall for the bout. The sharp-pointed rapier was double-edged, a light and fast weapon belonging to the King who had insisted on Milo's use of his own weapon in the duel. Shorter than a conventional sword, and heavier than a foil, the rapier was perfectly balanced, with a jewelled cross guard. More useful in a cut and thrust situation rather than a slash and maim one, Milo noted as he took the sword from Loren. It was a beautiful weapon, but one he'd little experience in wielding.

Loren said nothing as he sullenly handed him the cross-hilt weapon. Milo merely smiled and thanked him.

"Tell Horatio I have done my part," Milo told him as he took his sword and swung it in a left and right, experimentally testing its movement and flexibility. Ser Loren dodged involuntarily and scowled at his back as Milo walked away.

"Beware, my Lord, he means you harm," he whispered to the Prince as he ran the white cloth over Hamnet's rapier and handed it to him.

The two duellists faced one another across twenty feet of flagged stone. To the onlookers, it seemed like an even contest – both were of slight build, though Milo possibly had the longer reach. But the Prince had more experience, and everyone in the Great Hall knew this. Neither wore a protective vest. Milo had refused at the last minute, hearing that the Prince had decided against wearing one. "I don't want it said that I had an unfair advantage," he had retorted when Maggie and Jeff had tried to persuade him.

Then Maggie had tried a different slant, reiterating her previous misgivings. "I don't think you should use the King's sword, Milo. Remember the Play. Why not use one of Horatio's?"

"Hamnet demanded a rapier, Maggs. Horatio does not have a rapier in his rooms. I have no option but to use the King's sword."

So now he stood alone in the vastness of the Great Hall, a bejewelled cross-hilt rapier in his hand, watching his opponent as he began his preparations. For a moment, Milo wondered why he was here, but instantly a picture of Olivia's cold drowned body rose up before his eyes, and his resolve strengthened. He walked across the hall, raised his sword into *en garde* position, and taunted the Prince who stood waiting, twenty feet away.

"You bested me the last time we crossed swords, but you will not this time!"

Hamnet put up his hands. "I have no wish to fight with you, Master Milo. Can we not settle this matter another way?"

"No. The time for talk has passed. This time you *will* act! *En garde*! Raise your sword!"

"And if I refuse?"

"Then, Prince, I call you a coward as well as a murderer." He took a step forward.

"I have done no murder." Hamnet's voice was less calm now, as Milo began to circle round him, flicking the point of his sword at him and continuously passing vicious comments. Finally, Hamnet's calm shattered. "Very well, Master Milo. You will have your duel!" He stepped back and raised his sword into *en garde* position.

Milo wasted no time. He lunged and caught Hamnet's sleeve near the shoulder. "That's for Olivia, whom you killed, as surely as you did Polon!"

"She took her own life!"

Milo's voice was a snarl. "She loved you and trusted you." He lunged again and a rip appeared in the Prince's jerkin. "But you? You scorned her," he lunged again, "rejected and reviled her and then you murdered her father!"

Hamnet brought his sword round swiftly catching Milo off balance. For a moment Milo was pinned against the wall while the Prince, his face inches away from Milo's, spoke through gritted teeth. "Polon's death was accidental." Milo twisted sharply and swung himself out of range.

"Tell that to the jury!" he called mockingly.

"And you would be the Judge? Why so? You barely knew her!"

With a leap and a lunge, Hamnet knocked Milo's sword out of his hand, and caught at his ankle as Milo threw himself on the floor after the weapon. Before he knew it, Milo was pinned to the floor with Hamnet's sword at his throat.

"I do not wish to kill you," the Prince said, his voice low and precise. "You are a visitor to my world, and it is not right that we should fight. Take back your harsh words and go home in peace."

Milo's face twisted in fury and he kicked upwards viciously, catching the Prince off-balance and sending him sprawling across the flagstones near to where Milo's sword lay. The Prince's own rapier lay at Milo's feet. He lifted the Prince's sword, and admired the basket-hilted weapon. "Nice balance," he said, as the Prince lifted himself to his feet and picked up Milo's sword.

Standing at the side of the King, Maggie saw him start forward and then suddenly stop. He began to raise his hand, but this gesture too was aborted.

They began circling again, each wary of the other's moves. Then almost simultaneously the two moved in a furious exchange of blows. Then Hamnet, gripping his borrowed weapon hard with both hands, brought it round to cut across Milo's jerkin. Leather and linen undershirt split, but Milo managed to spin away.

Balanced on the balls of their feet, the two protagonists faced one another. Milo began once more to throw insults at the Prince. "She was pure and gentle," he said bitterly, "and deserved better than you!" He lunged once more, but it was mistimed and Hamnet parried it easily.

"I did love her."

"Fine way you showed it!" He feinted and followed it up with a reverse thrust that took Hamnet off-balance. During the Prince's frantic defensive parry he managed a cut to Milo's lower right arm. Blood oozed from the wound, colouring the shirt with its brilliant red.

"First cut!" called the King. "Put up your swords."

"No!" yelled Milo. "I will have my revenge!" He lunged once more, and this time succeeded in getting through the Prince's guard, spilling royal blood.

Panting, he pressed forward, hoping to continue his advantage, but Hamnet fought back, trading blow for blow. They broke and circled for a time, while each attempted to catch his breath. Milo's right sleeve was saturated with blood and he was losing his grip. Then when he lunged, he found himself staggering, unable to keep upright. Suddenly his legs gave way and he collapsed in a heap on the stone floor. Hamnet stood over him, panting and watching him.

"There is something here that is not right," he stated. "He is not badly injured. His arm wound is not deep enough to cause him to pass out. A mage! A spell is needed!"

Deveron was already half-way across the floor. He knelt down in the cold stone beside Milo's body and quickly checked his pulse and breathing. Both were faint, and very erratic. He turned to find Maggie beside him.

"This is more than a sword cut," he told her. Just then a convulsive shudder wracked Milo's body. His eyes opened. Pain-dulled eyes.

"What is wrong with me?" he whispered, just as his body began to shudder violently. Deveron lifted him into his arms, pouring healing power into him, but to no avail. His breathing rapidly deteriorated into shallow gasps as he fought the spasms in his muscles. Then as suddenly as they had begun, the shudders slowed and stopped.

There was no responding heart-beat, no inhaled breath.

Milo's head fell back, lifeless. Deveron lifted shocked eyes, and met Maggie's uncomprehending ones.

Tell Horatio that I have done my part.

For many heartbeats, no-one moved. Then Deveron gently laid Milo's limp body down on the cold stone and closed Milo's eyes for the last time before turning to Maggie. His pitying eyes pierced her flimsy fog of disbelief and she screamed Milo's name into the silence.

Jeff came up behind her and turning, she fell into his arms. Her harrowed sobs rent the air. Deveron turned back to the body on the floor, puzzlement written on his face. As he examined the wound on Milo's arm, Hamnet stood nearby, gazing blankly at his sword. "His cuts were minor," the Prince repeated, "and his blood loss was insignificant."

"It was not blood loss that caused his death. Look here. The wound is infected. The blade you cut him with was poisoned, my lord." Hamnet's fingers loosened from the hilt and the weapon clattered to the floor.

"And I? Am I also about to die? I too am cut."

"You changed swords. Remember? When you both were disarmed, you took Milo's sword and he, yours. Neither of you was cut before the exchange of swords."

"So Milo's sword was poisoned. He intended to kill me, by fair means or foul." All at once, his legs gave way and he too staggered. Deveron steadied him with a hand below his elbow.

"I did not mean him to die. He was angry and filled with grief, and I know I would have bettered him, and then perhaps he would have let me explain. But instead – he is dead. Dead, Deveron."

Deveron looked round as Loren came forward. He glanced over towards the King, then back at Milo's lifeless body. "May I speak, my Lords? Unwitting, I have done a great wrong." He cast a glance over his shoulder in the direction of the King, who had taken a step forward. It all fitted, and made horrible sense. He looked back at Milo's lifeless body and his face crumpled.

"Tell us, Ser Loren. Do you know who is responsible for Master Milo's death?"

The boy took a deep breath. "I am. But unknowingly. I did not intend harm. Do not blame me, good sirs."

"Tell us Loren!" Prince Hamnet's voice was hard and cold as the steel he had lately held in his hand. Loren's voice dropped to a whisper. "When preparing Master Milo's weapon I cleaned it with this blue cloth. So I am to blame for this tragedy. But I swear this – I did not know the cloth contained poison!"

"Where did you obtain the cloths? Who ordered you to do this?" Hamnet was barely keeping his temper under control, and as the boy's eyes shifted in the direction of his uncle, he knew the answer. Milo had used the King's rapier.

Loren stammered, "It was at the King's command. He gave me the blue cloth that contained the venom."

Hamnet wasted no time in thought. He snatched up Milo's sword from the floor, and sprinted across the room to where the King stood motionless, as if grown from the flagstones.

Hamnet! NO! Deveron tried to shout but the words echoed uselessly inside his head. He was unable to speak. He tried to move a hand. He couldn't. A paralysis numbed his limbs and held him totally immobile.

Claude tried one meaningless entreaty to the boy whose throne he had usurped, as the young Prince ran at him, sword point aimed at his heart. He gave a guttural cry of pain as the envenomed point pierced his chest and blood stained his velvet doublet.

"King-killer!" Hamnet yelled as he rammed the sword home. "Brother-killer! Now it is your turn to die! Let your venom do its work! Die, *Uncle*!" As he ripped the sword out of the body the dying King grabbed for a chair, missed and crashed to the ground to lie still, blood gathering in a pool beneath him. He looked at his brother's son and his last words were a pathetic entreaty. "Mine was the hand, but not the will. Never the will. Forgive… "

Hamnet stepped back, and gazed at his would-be murderer's corpse. Then with a wild yell he threw the blade away from him as far as he could. Its sharp clang as it hit the stone wall and clattered to the floor filled the horror-struck and deathly silence. After an immeasurable moment, the lonely young King lifted up his head and spoke.

"Thus is it ended. We will honour Master Milo Diaz, for he was a true friend to the Serra Olivia, and though misled, defended her to the death. A fitting memorial will be made in appreciation of his sacrifice. However," he paused and glanced once more at the bloody body at his feet, "my uncle's body will be taken from here and after due mourning time will be buried in the deepest crypt and forgotten, for he was guilty of regicide and fratricide."

A stunned silence followed his words. The queen let out a mournful high-pitched wail of grief. Her ladies ran to her, and led her away from the Great Hall. As her grief-filled weeping faded, a lone voice broke the silence, ushering in a new reign. "The King is dead!" he cried. "Long live the King!"

**

Loren, standing near to Deveron, frowned and wondered at the Antriantara's utter immobility until he saw his anger-filled eyes. He looked over at Hamnet, and at the body of the dead King in its pool of blood and instantly recalled an overheard conversation between the other-worlders a few days ago. One of them stated that an evil spirit possessed the King. Now the King was dead, and Deveron… His intuitive certainty of what had occurred was rapidly followed by sheer blind panic. He turned on his heel and almost ran from the Hall.

The courtiers, still stunned at the appalling turn of events, lined up to pledge themselves to the new King Hamnet II, but Maggie and Jeff remained crouched beside the body of their friend. Deveron remained as if rooted to the flagstones, his eyes flashing anger. At his ear, he heard a voice – an old, cold voice. *TalEbol!* he whispered inside his head.

Very clever, the voice of talEbol remarked from somewhere nearby. *I am unmasked, it seems… oh well, it had to happen, I suppose. Now we will just wait for young Horatio to arrive. I do so hope you are not too uncomfortable, my dear Antriantara – immobile as you are…*

Chapter 14

"We have to find a way of breaking through talEbol's block," Horatio said. "I don't know what he's done but it is something that I cannot breach. Until I find out, I cannot break through to reach Elsynvaal."

"But your new powers…" Mhari said. "Surely there's something you can do to open it."

Horatio ran a hand over the stubble on his face, and sighed. "It's very strong. I barely had the strength to return that last time. In fact I probably would not have managed it if it hadn't been for what you did, Emma. And the support you three gave her. Coming after me was foolhardy, but also very brave. You have extraordinary powers."

"Well then," Rian's voice was quiet in the silence that followed Horatio's words. "How about harnessing Emma's power, and Mhari's and mine, and co-joining them with yours, Horatio? Like you did with Alain in the Forest, and I did with Mhari to contact Deveron?"

"Mindmelds are dangerous, Rian. Twinning two minds is difficult enough, but to try and forge links between four," he looked at Duncan, sitting silent on one side, "or five untrained minds could be suicidal for all of us. Anyway, even if we did manage a mindmeld, I do not know if raw power would break through the barrier."

"But isn't it worth a try?"

"Rian, I realise that you want to get back home. So do I, but if we fail we would all be stranded in the Ether. Can you imagine that? Trapped for ever in the nothingness? I cannot allow you to do such a thing. The blockage was removed before. It will again. We only have to wait until it is. TalEbol cannot keep that intensity up for too long. When he weakens, I will break through." He struggled to stand up. "I need some rest. Tell me. Is there anywhere that I can sleep apart from that paddling pool?"

Worried about the blockage, Horatio did not fall asleep easily. His own words to Emma came back to haunt him. *"Next time I will be prepared."* But a sixth sense warned him that there was little or no time left – talEbol was moving towards his ultimate goal. He remembered Hamnet's dilemma after the visitation of his father's ghost, and his procrastination as he waited for proof. He, of course, needed no proof. The personality in the Ether had been clear enough. As was his path now.

He had to utilise his powers.

He had to get to Elsynvaal – somehow.

And he had to keep the others safe…

While Horatio slept, Emma and Mhari experimented with their newly discovered powers, trying to find out what they could do. Rian sat for much of the time in silent contemplation, while Duncan volunteered to go for some pizza for them all.

After a while, Rian came out of his meditation and addressed the two girls. "Horatio referred to us as *largely untrained* minds. Well I think we should get him to remedy that. We should get Horatio to teach us Human magic. I have been a Sylvan magicand for many years. And despite my age, my brain is not so decrepit that I cannot learn anew. And you, my dears, are young, intelligent and resourceful. Additionally, Mhari, it is possible that your brother Duncan may have sufficient power to anchor us. What say you?"

"What say who?" Duncan's deep voice made them all jump. None had heard him come up the stairs. Rian smiled and repeated his words. Duncan shrugged. "We can talk to him. Sound him out. Someone want to wake him? Pizza's getting cold."

Horatio was not easily persuaded. The pizza was devoured and the coffee mugs emptied long before he succumbed to their arguments.

"This is not my world," Rian said. "I have no option but to attempt to return to Elsynvaal. As for helping quell the Renegade, I would be privileged to stand by you."

"I'm coming too," Mhari said. "Once Midori is taken care of, I want to see Elsynvaal."

Duncan volunteered to act as anchor, if it was feasible.

Then Emma spoke up. She'd said little so far. "My mother and my grandfather are in Elsynvaal. It is my grandfather who is causing the blockage. It is right that I should help unblock it, if I can."

Eventually, and with significant reservations, the Mage tested each in turn to determine their raw power levels, and started working on a plan of lessons which he thought would give them some protection in the void and afterwards in Elsynvaal, if they made it that far. Mhari was a natural telepath, and had some potential as a healer. As for Rian, his interest in magic was more than theoretical. The Sylvan had power of their own, unknown and all too often misunderstood by Humans. Power that Horatio now hoped to utilise.

Emma was another story. Horatio's calibrations were rough and ready, but early indications showed Emma to have strong potential in at least three of the major metafunctions, and quite possibly more. But would she be able to hold it all within her?

"The power within each of us," he told them, "comes from the core of our being, where it lies, even now, quiescent. To raise a power, you must learn to *harness* that power core, *channel* it through your body in the form you require. Some of your Powers we are already aware of. Rian, you must build on your own ability as a Sylvan magicand, using the new tools I will give you.

"Powers are often hereditary and believe it or not, Mhari, Duncan, you both have strengths in di'speak. Mhari could not hold an Ether Crossing open without that ability. So I will teach you, Duncan, how to anchor the Ether strands.

"Emma, you have the potential to be very strong indeed, but as a grand-daughter of talEbol I would have expected that."

Emma looked up, a haunted look in her eyes. "And if I do have these powers?"

"Then I will teach you to find them, to learn their qualities, to control the power."

"But it was her powers that made Midori go mad, wasn't it? Will they do the same to me?"

Horatio tried to soothe her. "It is likely that Midori allowed herself to be used by the Power, instead of learning to control and use it. You've got to be strong, Emma. You cannot go back to how you were before, even if you would. The Power is within you, and it is yours to use, yours to control. The only thing you can do is to learn how to control and use it."

"Can I do it, Horatio?"

"You can do it. I know it." She looked away, only half-convinced.

Before beginning to teach them, Horatio would, he told them, first cast a spell of remembrance, the *sleep-awake* spell he used on Emma that first night when his arrival through the void had panicked her. This spell, he explained to them, would allow them to rest while taking in the information directly into their subconscious and their long-term memories. Horatio had thought hard about what spells to teach them, matching ability to difficulty.

"In effect you will see with your mind's eye, rather than your physical eyes," he told them. "But there is danger in teaching spells in this way. Normally, a novice slowly builds up his awareness and knowledge as the spells he learns become more complex, but we don't have time for the luxury of learning through practice. Instead, you will learn theory only. So in a crisis, it is possible that you will be unaware of the ultimate scope or limitations of a particular spell. Especially, be very wary of trying to use coercion. Spells such as those are too easily turned back on the caster."

"Why are you teaching us spells?" Emma asked. "I thought we were to learn a mindmeld."

"That too, Emma, but when we break through, talEbol and Midori will become aware of the fact. We have to be alert and prepared. And that means having spells available, especially defensive ones. It could be very dangerous. You will all learn several spells, and once you know the words of the spell and its accompanying hand sign or *sigils*, you must use what time we have left to practise them."

He looked at each of them in turn, aware of how he was about to change their lives, because once they had tasted the use of magic, there was no going back. Ever. For a moment his mind fled back to Deighford University, where he had lectured on these same subjects to his students. But back then, they'd had time to investigate each Power in detail. Now, when it actually mattered, he had to force-feed them...

At Horatio's command, they settled themselves comfortably and waited for him to cast the initial spell. Gathering his strength from his inner being, Horatio drew the sigil for the *sleep-awake* spell and his four companions immediately felt their lids grow heavy. Within a minute, they were breathing the smooth rhythm of a deep sleep, while simultaneously being aware of all that was going on.

Then he began to teach them the elements of Elsynese magic.

Horatio spoke clearly and succinctly. As he spoke his words were punctuated by the hologram appearance in mid-air of the main points, much in the manner of a College lecturer using a whiteboard.

Mhari, though deep under the influence of the *sleep-awake*, saw with her mind-eye and was fascinated as the words appeared floating in as Horatio described the Five Powers, or Metafunctions:

Telekinesis, Healing, Di'speak, Mind-control and *Creativity*. Most of the major powers had sub-powers with *Healing* as the exception. *Levitation* was a sub-power of *Telekinesis*; *Ether Crossing*, an advanced form of *di'speak*; and *Artefact Creation* and *Illusion* the sub-powers of *Creativity*. Taking each in turn he explained and demonstrated each of the five metafunctions, showing how each raw power can be used.

"*Inanimate telekinesis*," the holographic words leaped into the air and shimmered above their heads, "is used both defensively and in attack. It is in its most basic form the ability to move things around by will-power alone. *Levitation* is usually used as a defensive mechanism, but it has been known to be used in attack. It can have severe limitations.

"*Di'speak*, also known as *far-speaking*, as you all know, is the ability to converse over distances with another mage, as you do here in your world by means of a telephone. Neither di'speak nor *Ether Crossing* can be used as a weapon.

"*Mind Control* is often referred to as *coercion*, and is a basic offensive attack. Some spells use a modicum of coercion diluted by Healing, such as the *sleep-awake* spell laid upon you now.

"*Creativity* is one of the most potent of the Powers. With *Creativity* one can basically order the universe to one's own liking. It can be used equally well in attack and in defence. *Artefact Creation* is the making of real and lasting artefacts that will not disintegrate like the flower illusion I made in Kelvingrove Park. *Illusion*, Creativity's poor relation, is mainly a defensive mechanism, but can be used effectively as attack under certain circumstances.

"*Healing* is the blessed power. Most mages have the ability to heal – it seems to be the most essential to any potential mage, and together with telekinesis, is the one most easily spotted."

He paused and the words circled round in the air, dipping and swooping around their heads, before dropping towards the floor and disappearing.

He paused in reflection for a moment, trying to quell the slight unease he still felt. Then with a long indrawn breath, he began to teach them a number of spells, mainly defensive, that could be used if they were cornered by either the Renegade or 'The White Hawk', the nickname Emma had bestowed on her mother. He taught them how to draw out the power from within, which words to use to form each spell, and the hand-signs – or sigils – that would finalise it and empower it.

Finally Horatio wrote a sigil in the air, a movement too fast for the eye to follow, and the *sleep-awake* spell dissipated. The four novice-students of Magic opened their eyes, stretching their limbs and yawning. Horatio went round checking each in turn.

"Horatio," Emma said reflectively, "in Kelvingrove Park you told me that your creativity was low. Is it still the same?"

"No, I don't think so. More likely that it is vastly improved. Pain brings its rewards. Midori did not do herself or her father a favour by skinning me."

"What are your powers now?" Rian asked. Horatio smiled.

"With time and the opportunity to train myself, I believe I will be as powerful as talEbol himself... But I'm very afraid that time is something we simply do not have."

"What of us?" Rian asked.

"I cannot emphasise enough how dangerous this could be. There is still time for you to decide whether to come with me or not."

In the pause, Mhari looked towards her brother. Then Horatio spoke again. "But, a caution. If you decide to pursue and develop your powers, you must always remain aware that the more you learn, the more dangerous it becomes for you. Ineptly-managed magic can easily kill. I fear for each one of you, even as I ask your help. Think deeply about all of this. I will not ask for more than you wish to give – any of you."

For an hour, he helped them while the four mage-novices practised their hand-sigils and spell incantations, then Horatio moved away to one side and tried once more to quantify his own increased powers.

When he returned, Emma was standing by the window, looking down at the street below, no doubt wondering if she was doing the right thing. Rian was watching a chat show on TV. Duncan was flicking through a magazine of some kind. Mhari was sitting in her armchair, wandering the void. He stood watching them, uneasy once more about what he was asking them to attempt, and thought about the next thing he had to do to them. A mindmeld, which would involve exerting significant coercion over them. They would have to trust him implicitly. Did they? The unease intensified. Had he taught them enough? Or too much?

And would these few skills be enough to protect them from either talEbol or Midori?

A sudden movement behind him startled him and brought his mind back to the present. Mhari was sitting ramrod straight, a grin on her face. "You'll never guess, guys," she said gleefully. "It's down, Horatio. The blockage has disintegrated! The Ether is clear."

Horatio stood stock still and immediately began an Ether search for Deveron's signature. Emma turned from the window. Her face was pale. Duncan put his magazine down, and walked over to his sister. "I suppose this is it then, Sis. Take care."

Duncan took his place in the armchair as Mhari, Rian and Emma prepared to leave – to cross to another world. They took their places beside Horatio as he stood with closed eyes in his search for Deveron.

***

Deveron stood immobile, held transfixed by talEbol's power. Blood puddled beneath the body of King Claude as the courtiers lined up to pledge loyalty to their new King, Hamnet II.

Close to Deveron's ear, talEbol's cold, dead voice continued to spaek. *Unfortunately I will have to decide what to do with you, my dear Antriantara. You knew of my possession of Claude's body – yes I was aware of that – but you chose to do nothing. I wonder why, for it is an inept action for the Leader of the Wizards' Council. Indecisiveness is not an admirable trait in one so highly placed.* Deveron felt a movement of some kind in front of him, and glimpsed a shimmer in the air as the entity that was talEbol moved from his left side across to his right. *I have lost the use of a body,* the cold voice continued, *so I must search for a new host. Yours, perhaps? Yes, it appeals to my sense of humour, because the position of Antriantara should have been mine anyway.*

Deveron struggled against the bands tightening on his mind. *I will fight you all the way – every step. Even if I have to die!*

If you die, you die to no purpose. It is inconvenient changing bodies, but I have done it several times before. It will be easier for you if you relax, Deveron.

The master-mage fought with every ounce of his willpower, but one by one the synapses were sundered and his mind agonisingly invaded by an uninvited and unwelcome predator. Bitter pain grew into unbearable agony as talEbol staked his claim on his new brain and body.

***

His flight had been instinctive. Loren escaped from the Great Hall and up the stone staircase to the balcony above the Great Hall. There outside Prince Hamnet's library, he came upon Master Will leaning over the balcony, avidly watching events. The poet's face was pale and he barely acknowledged Loren's arrival. For once, the ink-stained fingers were empty. Paper and scribing pen lay unnoticed on the floor by his feet.

Down below, King Hamnet II looked across the heads of his courtiers towards the Antriantara, who had remained standing immobile since Claude's death. "Come, Antriantara Deveron," he called. "Will you make your pledge?"

Deveron did not move so much as an eyelash.

"Deveron?"

The Mage's hand rose unsteadily to his brow, and he took a hesitant step forward, reaching out as he did so. Hamnet waved to men-at-arms near Deveron. "The Antriantara is unwell. Help him to a seat!"

But the mage refused the men's help. He haltingly moved forward heading across the hall towards his new King. One foot shuffled forward, followed by the other. Left foot, right foot, left foot, right foot until he stood before King Hamnet, who watched in bewilderment.

Then Deveron raised his eyes to Hamnet's, and the King was taken aback at the pain he saw there. The mage's mouth worked, but no sound issued forth.

"Do you pledge allegiance?" Hamnet asked. "You need merely to incline your head, my good Antriantara." Slowly, the mage's head lowered, and rose again in a savage jerk.

"Thank you, Deveron. Now, as you seem to be ill, you may take your leave. We have matters to attend to."

Loren, watching from above noticed that as Deveron turned to leave, his movements became much more fluid – it was as if he'd had to *force* his body to cross the Hall to Hamnet's side, to overcome some great reluctance... Loren replayed the events in the Hall prior to his panicked departure. He saw again how suddenly the mage had become totally immobile and realised someone must have used an *Immobility* spell on him. A very powerful one, too, to overcome the Antriantara! The anger Loren had seen in Deveron's eyes confirmed this idea.

His blood chilled in his veins as he realised that his first panicked deduction had been correct. *The evil one had left Claude's body in the moment before The Prince's attack, and had used an Immobility spell, had taken over* Deveron's *body!* The shuffling, halting walk forward; the pain in Deveron's eyes; an evil entity would have been very unwilling to pledge allegiance to Hamnet, but Deveron *had forced his body* to move. Leaving the Hall there would have been less resistance, thus the movement of their shared body was more fluid. *The Gods help us!* Loren thought. Panic seized him once more. He laid his head in his hands and cried out to the only mage he knew he could trust.

<HORATIO! HORATIO! We need you!> he screamed into the Ether.

***

Hamnet walked over to Milo's body and stood, looking down at Maggie and Jeff kneeling beside him. In sad tones, he told them that Milo's body would be given a decent burial, with a headstone telling of his valour. Only live material can cross the Ether, he told them. Maggie's tears began flowing again as she realised that when Jeff and she left Elsynvaal to go home, they would be leaving Milo behind.

Laying his arm around her shoulders, Jeff led Maggie away from the bloody scene as the new King issued orders for the removal of the two bodies.

Chapter 15

After some time Horatio opened his eyes and looked round at each in turn. The Ether was clear, he told them, but he could not locate Deveron. He frowned, puzzling over the oddity.

"Try deeper," Mhari suggested.

With a smile, he closed his eyes again and sent out further. In the dank silence, he eventually found a glimmer of a thought. Homing in on it, he heard his name frantically called. *<Horatio! Horatio! We need you!>*

Locate the voice: *<Who calls?>*

<Ho Horatio! It is I, Loren! You must return! Now!>

Loren? How can it be Loren? What has happened? Horatio's mind flew back to that dreadful day as he sat on the grass at Deighford University and received a mental hail from this same boy. A cold chill ran down his spine. He sent a shaft of healing across the void to strengthen the link between them, and asked Loren to hold tightly onto the connection. Then he sped back to the attic.

"Something has happened," he told their anxious faces. "I cannot locate Deveron, but Loren has somehow managed to call through the Ether to me. He can only do this under extreme stress, so I fear that something dreadful has taken place. It would be best if I crossed alone."

"No," Emma said. "I am returning with you, no matter what!"

"We will all cross, as planned," Mhari said, looking to Rian for confirmation. He nodded.

Horatio inclined his head in acknowledgement. His promise to Emma the previous night came back to him: *Next time,* he'd said, *I will be fully prepared...* He shuddered momentarily, but then tuned his mind to the work in hand.

Duncan took hold of the threads of the Ether with his mind and looked at his sister. "Goodbye, Sis," he murmured as she and the others vanished, the only sound being the slap of clothing hitting the bare attic floorboards. Several long moments later, Horatio's voice echoed in Duncan's head. *We're across. Thanks, Duncan. The god be with you.*

***

Jeff and Maggie, arms wrapped around one another in sympathetic support, took their time returning to their rooms. Both were reeling from the shock of Milo's horrible death. But when they reached the door Jeff paused, his hand on the great door-handle. There were voices coming from inside the room. What now? Beside him, Maggie looked up at him, fear in her eyes. He placed a warning finger on her lips and gripped the door-handle with both hands. With a single movement, he turned the handle and pushed the door open.

"Who's th…" he began, before stopping in the doorway in astonishment.

"Close your mouth, Jeff dear," Mhari said as she walked forward to hug him. "You too, Maggie. God! But it's great to see you guys!"

After the euphoria of the reunion passed, Horatio grilled Loren over what had happened in the Great Hall. Loren described the duel, and Horatio felt a cold fury on hearing of Milo's unnecessary death. Maggie sat silent, tears not far away. He kneeled down on the floor beside her, and took hold of her hands.

"I'm sorry," he said. There was little more that he could say. He looked at Emma, who sat stunned. Yet, as he watched, he saw a change come across her face, and recognised the healing spell she'd used on herself.

"Well, that's another death lying at Gheron talEbol's door. I suggest that we do all we can to find out where he is."

"I know where the evil one is," Loren said, and told them what he'd seen happen to Deveron in the Hall.

"You're certain that's what you saw? Loren, it would be best if I can see for myself. Close your eyes and relax, please. I will be as gentle as I can."

"All right, Horatio," the boy said and closed his eyes.

Horatio too closed his eyes and laying his hand on Loren's head murmured the words of the ream. The pictures he saw were clear and well defined. He removed his hand and opened his eyes once more.

"I fear, Loren, that you are correct. TalEbol may have taken over Deveron's body, but Deveron, I am sure, will fight the invasion as long as there is breath left in his body." Horatio closed his eyes momentarily and a shudder ran through him. "This could kill him. He is not young, and has had much laid on his shoulders recently."

He turned to Jeff and Maggie and asked if they'd seen the leather-bound book that Deveron had brought back from Midori's cabin. Jeff said he thought he'd seen it in his rooms.

"Did he talk to you about its contents?"

Jeff frowned, trying to remember. So much had happened since Deveron's return.

"He said it was in the main a journal about the places Midori travelled to over a number of years. It also listed some spells, I think."

"We have to find that book," Horatio said.

He sat down to try to locate his old teacher. He ranged through the Castle but could find no trace of Deveron, nor of the mage he found and fought in the Ether.

"I'm going to Deveron's rooms to check them out. Loren, you check the Hall, library and so on. Jeff, Maggie, if you feel up to it, help him as you can. Mhari and Rian – you should stay here. We don't want anyone finding out I've returned. Not yet."

"But if you're seen?"

"I won't be." A flickering sigil and his appearance began to change. Soon a manservant stood on the spot where Horatio had been a moment before.

"An illusion," Loren said. "But if you see Deveron, talEbol will see through it."

"Not this one, Loren. I'm much stronger than I used to be."

The search through Deveron's rooms was fruitless. Deveron obviously travelled light, and no book was found among the meagre possessions. *I wonder what he did with it. If he had it on him when talEbol took him over, there is no way we'll get it.*

Then Horatio remembered something from his time as a student in Deveron's Tower. He reached in and pulled power from his inner being, and began searching for a magical artefact that Deveron told him about, an invisible trunk. The main clue he had as to the whereabouts of the trunk was that he knew it had to be here, somewhere. He strained his newly enhanced senses, marvelling at how easy all felt now. Power of this calibre was indeed intoxicating.

He focussed on one section of each of the rooms at a time, and eventually he found an anomaly. The colour of a small section of the wall near to the clothes chest seemed a paler shade than that adjacent to it.

"Gottcha!"

As the involuntary exclamation left his lips, Horatio felt a stab of regret over Milo's death, remembering his quips and his mind 'like a cesspit'…

He clenched his jaw, and crouched down in front of the invisible chest. Hands out in front of him, he felt round the edges of the small chest and found the handles. It was heavier than he imagined it would be, which led him to assume that it was bottomless as well as invisible. He smiled. Deveron liked his artefacts.

Mhari opened the door and watched, bemused, as Horatio struggled in carrying the invisible chest. "Luckily I did not meet anyone on the way," he said.

He laid his burden on the edge of a small table and the others watched as a long scratch appeared on the table when Horatio pushed it further across the surface. "It has iron bands around it," he said. "Now we have to open it… Ah, a simple padlock. I had a fear that it would be spell-locked."

"Interesting," Rian murmured, as Horatio's hands felt round the chest loosening the padlock and opening the lid. The first item he took out was a metal alloy casket, which he laid carefully onto the floor beside him. Then he seemed to rummage around inside the chest, his arm disappearing inside right up to his shoulder. Then he murmured something and withdrew his arm. In his hand he held a small leather-bound book.

"Deveron thinks this book's binding is made from Human skin," he said. His jaw clenched. Memories.

"That's the book Midori gave Emma?"

"It would appear so. Now give me a few minutes while I read it." He settled himself and opened the book at the first page, then rapidly turning over one page at a time, hardly seeming to glance at any page. At one point, a gasp escaped him, and the word 'Saravaal' formed on his lips before he continued his 'reading'. The door opened, and Jeff, Maggie and Loren came in. Seeing Horatio, they remained silent until he reached the end of the written pages. He looked up and smiled.

"Yes. That will do it."

The others heaved a collective sigh of relief.

***

"Remember - once we begin, you must all remain inside the pentagram. He could use any of you when we force talEbol from Deveron's body." Horatio leaned back in his chair and momentarily closed his eyes while sending a self-heal through his body. He was still physically weak, despite his returned and expanded internal powers. Their plan should work, as long as they were able to entice the Renegade to the dungeon. The only question was: Would Emma be strong enough emotionally to set the trap for talEbol – her own flesh and blood? No way to know until we try it. He pushed himself upright.

"It's time. Let's go downstairs."

They approached the dungeon from the Western staircase, a dark room below ground level lined with stone. Maggie recognised it from her first Crossing, when Lord Polon, Ser Loren and Serra Olivia had met her and the others. She glanced at Ser Loren behind her, wondering if he was thinking the same, but his thin young face was unreadable. Sometime during his talk with Horatio, his panic had evolved into stoic resolution. This was to be his initiation into the realms of magery – something he had apparently long desired. Mhari looked around the shadow-filled room with keen interest, holding her burning torch closer to the walls the better to see the curious runes and sigils carved into the stone. Not all had been made by the same hand – there seemed to be a number of languages here. One bore a similarity to stylised pictograms, while another looked more like an Arabic script. A third script an uncanny resemblance to one of JRR Tolkien's Elvish scripts.

Horatio and Rian had begun their preparations. One by one, the spells in the walls were animated, until the walls were a mass of glowing symbols and sigils. The ethereal light from the glowing walls illuminated Emma and Mhari as they measured out the pentagram on the floor. Smudged markings from the aborted crossing on the night before Claude's Coronation Day had still been visible when they started. Periodically, Jeff, Maggie and Loren went upstairs into the Castle to keep a check on the whereabouts of Deveron/talEbol and the new King. Silence lay heavily in the room, each bowed under the weight of his or her tasks and the possible danger of what they were trying to do. Gheron talEbol was ultimately responsible for all of the deaths within the walls of Elasyn; Milo's death was but one of them. This had to work!

The door opened and Loren, Maggie and Jeff entered with the news that Deveron/talEbol was in his rooms in the north wing, and that the new King, Hamnet II was holding a meeting with the nobles in the audience chamber adjacent to the Great Hall.

297

Horatio looked up at that news. *I should be there, at his side in his first days of rule! Forgive me, my liege!* But it was important that his return should remain a secret.

Horatio and Rian completed the last of the wall sigils and turned to the floor pentagram. Soon, there was, laid out on the floor, a large pentagon with a star-shaped pentangle within. At each point of the star a candle burned in a small jar. Beside each candle was a phial of liquid, each a different colour. At the apex of one of the points lay a plain casket. Horatio walked round, inspecting the Pentagram, and gave the girls a nod. "Well done, both of you. Now all the preparations we can make are complete. I pass over to you, Emma. It's up to you now. Are you sure you can do this?"

Emma looked at Horatio and smiled grimly. "I will do what I have to," she replied. She walked sedately to stand in the arm of the pentagon directly opposite the doorway, and lifted the green phial. The others silently took up their positions. Horatio and Rian flanked Emma; Mhari and Loren were on the far side of the pentagon; Jeff and Maggie back-to-back in the centre. The varicoloured liquids in the phials that each now held up glinted in the ethereal light emitted by the wall sigils and runes. One last glance at the intrepid group and Horatio said, "When he comes, make sure you all keep the spell in your head." Then he nodded to Emma. "Go."

Emma raised her phial of ocean-green liquid high into the air and sent out a cry: "Gheron talEbol! Hear me, Emasiyo! It is I, your granddaughter who calls to you! I have read the book my mother gave me. I understand it all now. I want to be with you and learn from you! I am here in the Castle, in the dungeon room. Come, Grandfather Gheron, come to me, and take me away with you! Come, Grandfather!"

Horatio raised his hand. The glow from the walls faded and a shimmer appeared in the air, gradually thickening into a solid wall that split Emma off from the remainder of the group. She seemed now to be standing alone in a chalked diagram with a candle at her feet and a stone wall inches from her back. The door remained closed. She called again, repeating the same words.

From the other side of the illusionary wall, Horatio could hear the desperation and panic creeping into her voice. Long, interminable minutes passed. Within the room, on both sides of the wall the tension rose as doubt entered their hearts. It was not working. Horatio sent a calming wave round the circle to bolster flagging energies.

Then a shuffling sound was heard outside the great oaken door. The door opened inwards towards Emma and she saw Deveron standing on the threshold. He leaned heavily on a staff and looked at her.

"Emasiyo?" he queried. "At last we meet!" His voice was like yet unlike Deveron's – it had the same tenor, but with deeper, darker overtones. "You are the very image of your mother, Midori."

The Renegade Mage shuffled forward towards her, but at that moment, Horatio, still hidden behind the shield wall, made a pass of his hand. The door behind talEbol slammed, and a shiver of light snaked round the edges of the door opening, sealing it tight.

You'd better survive this, Horatio my lad, he thought wryly, *or none of them will get out of here!*

Deveron/talEbol glanced behind him at the sealed door, and back at Emma in front of him.

"Why did you do that, granddaughter Emasiyo?"

But at that moment, Horatio collapsed the illusionary wall and a tight smile fleetingly lit up Deveron's eyes, as if the Antriantara recognised the trap. So simple. Emma looked away, strange emotions warring inside her.

Gheron talEbol directed Deveron's gaze towards Horatio. "What are you going to do with us?"

"Kill you." Horatio calmly replied. Emma gave a start.

"Horatio, Horatio. Deveron is, or was, your patron. I doubt if you have the temerity to cause his death. See Emasiyo doubts you too. Isn't there a small part of your mind that wonders if I'll not just leave Deveron's body and find one more complaisant? He is hard work, you see. He fights me continuously. But worry not – none of you here is suitable. I would prefer a male non-mage body, but the only one here is hideously disfigured. Though," his head tipped to one side, eyes fixed on Jeff, "I suppose the scars could be dealt with at leisure. Hmmm… a strong young body would feel good…"

"I'm lame!" Jeff called out. "And I would fight you all the way!"

"Oh bravely spoken, young man. But believe me, you would have no option. I commanded Prince Claude for more than two years, and before that…"

"Prince Torven." Horatio's voice was icy. "You were on Saravaal three years ago. It was you, masquerading as Prince Torven, who repealed the anti-mage laws. Why? How did you know he would not reinstate them once you'd left?"

"Ah, Horatio the Saralese mage, of course. It is so long since you left your native land I am surprised that show such concern. But to answer your question, a little mind control set in his brain. He will change nothing that I put in place. Mages will be free to practice in Saravaal. You should be happy at the news, Horatio. You can go home now."

"I was never prevented from going home. Why did you do it, talEbol? How could you possibly benefit from having Saravaal open to mages?"

"The mage-born are the true rulers of this land and the lands of Cheam and the Sunset Lands beyond the Eastern Sea. And of the mage-born, I am the most powerful, the greatest mage there has ever been in the history of this world. It is my destiny to rule, and that of my heirs – Midori and Emasiyo – and her unborn child. Your child, Horatio. Join us."

Horatio glanced at Emma, and realised that she had slowly been moving forward towards talEbol.

"Emma! Don't move. Stay in the pentagram!" But it was too late.

She stepped across the chalked line.

"Emma!" he yelled again. And she lifted her head and looked over her shoulder at her lover, the father of her unborn child.

"Come back, Emma. Come back." Horatio's gentle voice finally seemed to break through to her. Her eyes widened as she looked down at her feet on the wrong side of the chalked line. Her hand flew to her mouth, and she stepped back, narrowly missing scuffing the line, just as Deveron's hand reached out for her.

"Boldly tried," Horatio told the Deveron/talEbol creature. "But you know now how weak you are, bound in that body. Deveron is fighting you, sapping your energies. You cannot fight both Deveron and me, talEbol. You are too weak."

"We will see about that!" Slowly, Deveron's hand rose, the index finger slowly straightening to point directly at Horatio. But no powerful spell followed. The hand shook and trembled in the silent battle for dominance. Gradually, the hand dropped.

Horatio glanced over his shoulder. "Ready, my friends?" he whispered. Then he raised his red phial. "You cannot enter the pentagon, talEbol."

"And you can do nothing to me without leaving it!"

"No?" Horatio's arm flew up, shifting in a confusing blur.

All at once the walls burst into flame as the quiescent sigil elementals embedded in the walls awoke and responded to Horatio's command. TalEbol/Deveron crouched down, his arms attempting to ward off the multi-pronged attack. But to those watching, the flailing arms worked slowly, half-heartedly.

Deveron was actively working towards his own death.

Light flashed as elemental after elemental was absorbed into the Antriantara's body. The two entities entwined within Deveron's skull fought once more, but this time it was an unequal battle. TalEbol, the interloper, struggled futilely as the elementals' invasion combined forces with Deveron's consciousness.

Finally, with a hideous cry, the spirit of the Renegade flew from its host. The elementals flew with it, encircling the disembodied spirit and compelling it into the small casket that Horatio, stepping now from the safety of the pentagon, now held raised in his hands. Though his mind was screaming in agony, talEbol emitted no sound as his ghostly spirit, bereft of any autonomy, collapsed in upon itself.

As he snapped the casket closed, Horatio called over his shoulder to Rian and Mhari. "Go to Deveron!"

Horatio stepped back into the pentagram and opened the casket. The shadowy spirit flowed in the bottom of the casket, sigil elementals preventing its escape. Horatio poured the red liquid from his phial into the casket, and then swiftly moved to where Mhari had left her phial with its violet liquid. This too was poured into the casket. Next, Loren poured in his amber liquid, followed by Rian's blue, Jeff's magenta and Maggie's pale green. Finally Horatio turned to Emma, who was watching Rian and Mhari's efforts with Deveron.

As he did so, he noticed a small rodent near Emma's foot. Before he could do anything, the rodent grew in size and transmutated. Emma stood safely within the pentagon, but only two feet away from her, Midori the Murderer stood in all her terrible fury. Her black eyes flashed with insane anger.

"Daughter! Daughter! How dare you betray your own blood with such treachery!"

Emma looked at the vial in her hand, and then at the small woman standing in front of her. In that second, something within her snapped, and all the dammed-up feelings against her mother welled up. She focussed her will on the phial and then her hand jerked forward and she threw the contents of the phial into her mother's face.

For a moment nothing happened. Midori stood still, green viscous liquid dripping from her chin, her eyes fixed on Emma.

"I see we were mistaken in you, daughter. Curses be upon you!" Then… she began to transmute. But instead of gaining a new form, she began to – dissolve. Her features began to run together like wax melting in a flame, and her beautiful hair, so like Emma's, fell in clumps to the ground. Her grotesquely misshapen mouth opened in ghastly scream as the horrible spectacle continued. Her clothing shredded and fell as rags. Then her skin split, exposing rotting flesh and then bare bones that slowly fell clattering to the stone floor.

Finally, it was over.

Midori Campbell dalEbol was dead.

Emma stood staring in shock at the pile of white bones and rags at her feet.

In the shocked silence that followed, Mhari whispered to Horatio. "What was in that phial?"

Horatio blinked as if coming out of a dream or nightmare. His face was pale. "It was Hate," he murmured, looking down at Emma shocked at what she had inadvertently done. "Emma transmuted the contents, changing them into hate. Her creativity quota must be massive…"

Emma's scream rebounded from one wall to another, but instead of decreasing in volume, it continued to reverberate interminably around the stone dungeon. The remaining sigil elementals, playful now that their work was done, bounced the scream from one wall to another until the sound reached unbearable intensity. It continued until Horatio raised his hands and cried out in a powerful voice none of them had ever before heard him use: "Enough!"

The scream died. Silence fought ringing eardrums. Emma collapsed in a faint. Horatio cradled her in his arms, but Emma pushed him away as soon as she opened her eyes. "I killed my mother! You didn't tell me what was in the phial!" she cried out. Horatio stepped back, and Maggie moved over and put her arms around Emma's shuddering form. Horatio backed away from the terrible accusing look in Emma's eyes and crossed to where Deveron lay on his back on the floor. Rian and Mhari were still working on him.

"How is he?"

"Breathing."

"Well that's one thing to be thankful for."

Rian shifted a little and Horatio crouched down, running his hands gently across his old mentor's body. Sigil elementals were fickle creatures, as well he knew, and there was a grave risk that Deveron might not survive the shock of their attack. His recovery, in the end, would depend on how much control he had retained over his mind and brain and whether he had been able to prepare himself for the onslaught in the moments before the attack. Had he been able to do anything at all to defend himself? Horatio tried to console himself with knowing that talEbol had left his host very quickly after the onslaught had begun. Perhaps enough was left of Deveron's personality to survive this rape.

He looked down at the casket on the ground beside him. The simple metal alloy box, two feet long and one wide that he had found in Deveron's invisible chest, was now bound with such spells and wardings that even talEbol would not escape its bonds. The combination of liquids and the elementals remaining inside the casket would ensure his imprisonment until the judgement of the Council of Wizards at Rowlan Gayts decided his fate.

Chapter 16

The deliberations of the Wizards' Council were complete. For three long weeks they had argued and fought over the crimes of Gheron talEbol, and now his fate was sealed. The decision was far from unanimous for one faction had declared for total annihilation, a second for imprisonment, while a third called for rehabilitation.

TalEbol's transgressions were examined and weighed. While the spirit of talEbol lay immobile, incarcerated in his casket, the wizards pored over his former Misuses of Magic – gross misuses that had long ago earned him the soubriquet 'The Renegade'. The Council was determined that he should not escape as he had done on a previous occasion. *Disembodied Possession* and *Mage Signature Subjugation* were his chosen methods of 'disappearing' and each was a gross transgression of the Wizard's Code. Even had he not been guilty of the regicide of the King Hamnet and the attempted murder of Prince Hamnet, now Hamnet II, he was still guilty of Gross Misuse by the possession of both Claude's body and Deveron's.

The Council ruled for Interment.

Three days later, a small group of mages accompanied the casket of Gheron talEbol to his place of entombment. The casket had been further weighted by various spells and wardings, and been declared inviolate. The place of Interment was to be a cave in a rocky hillside at a point where no ley-lines passed. The tomb would be marked on no map – a lonely hillside far from any habitation. There in a small cave in the rocky hillside, indistinguishable from any other, the casket was left, sealed with spells and wardings, and there Gheron talEbol was interred – his only companions the three sigil elementals remaining inside the casket.

The wizards left the cave and sealed it from the exterior with an avalanche of rock and icy snow.

As they made their way back across the uneven ground to where the horses were tethered, Horatio talMerios lent an arm to his old Master-Mage, Deveron di'Caledon, Antriantara of the Council as he settled himself on the hover-chair Horatio had created for him. In his other hand the old mage still clutched his Staff of Office.

"Will it be enough?" Deveron murmured, as he turned the chair to take a last look. "Is talEbol removed from exerting his influence on our land for ever?"

Horatio smiled and shook his head. "No-one could break the wardings on that casket, Deveron. He is powerless. Believe me and fear no longer. He is buried in that hillside and will remain so until he is forgotten."

"I hope so, my boy. I hope so." He turned the hover-chair and set it in motion, Horatio keeping pace at his side.

"And now that this has been completed, have you completed the arrangements for your other-worlders? I understand that you are leaving Elasyn and coming with us to Rowlan Gayts."

"Yes, I am. Marcus will remain with the King in Elasyn and take up the position of Chancellor, at least temporarily. I have been given leave to attend to other things."

"The other worlders?"

"Yes. I have promised to take the four of them to Rowlan Gayts where the work I have been doing on Jeff can be completed. After that I will return Jeff and Maggie to their own world, though Emma and Mhari will remain in Rowlan Gayts to begin their studies. Mhari has voluntarily chosen to remain and it is essential for Emasiyo to be taught how to control her powers." He paused, thoughtful. "She is of talEbol's blood, and is still very much an unknown quantity. She must remain here in Elsynvaal."

"I am glad that Mhari is to remain with us. She has the makings of a fine healer," Deveron said. "But I was sorry to discover when I regained consciousness that Rian had already returned to his people in the Northern Forest. I would have liked to say goodbye to him. He has a good mind."

"He has new skills too, Deveron. Remember that. I doubt that we have heard the last of him. He will keep in touch."

"And you, Horatio, what are your plans after you return from Earth?"

"I will be returning for a time to Saravaal. I am concerned about some of the things I read in Midori's Book about talEbol's doings in my homeland. I intend to visit my family on my home estate and to go to Court to speak with Prince Torven."

"Ah yes. But what of the child – your child, Horatio?"

Horatio looked away, into the far distance ahead, where the first of the Wizards had already reached the tethered horses. Eventually he spoke.

"Emasiyo has agreed to remain in Rowlan Gayts until the birth. After that I hope that she will consent to remain here. I do not want to force her to stay, but she is too powerful to be allowed to return to Earth. She must be given the chance to learn control.

"My son will be brought up in Elsynvaal, and when I return to Saravaal to take up my duties, he will come with me to my family's estate. He will be brought up in the full knowledge of his inheritance."

Deveron nodded, his head moving slowly up and down like a marionette's. "Horatio, will you take the advice of an old man?"

"You are not old, Deveron."

"Perhaps a month ago I was not, but now? Now I am old. On my return to Rowlan Gayts, I will resign my position of Antriantara, and retire to my Tower of Illusions and take on a Mage Apprentice or two. But before I go, dear boy, may I offer you some advice?

"Beware arrogance, Horatio. Your powers have grown so vast and so quickly that you are in grave danger of that very vice. Just as Emma must learn control, *so must you!* Take care, Horatio talMerios!"

For a moment, Deveron sounded just like his old self. Horatio stopped and looked closely at his mentor. "Have I grown so arrogant, old friend? Then if I have it has been totally unintentional. Believe me."

"Often it is so, my boy. Often it is so."

"Then I offer my thanks to you for your words. I will take note and remember your advice."

When they reached the tethered horses, Horatio helped the Antriantara from the hover-chair and on to his horse. Then he disassembled the chair and turned to mount his own horse, Starfleet, who had unaccountably returned safely to the stables at Elasyn Castle from the North.

As he gathered the reins, Horatio turned towards the rocky hillside, to set in his memory the exact position of talEbol's Interment. Some wished to mount a guard over the cave. Perhaps it would have been wise to do so for a while at least, but a guard would attract attention to this lonely spot. Better to leave it as it is – one indistinguishable and buried cave among so many other piles of rock. The matter had been dealt with quietly. Few beyond the Council knew of talEbol's dark deeds. And even fewer of Emasiyo's. The Renegade would be forgotten quickly enough.

Horatio turned Starfleet and urged him into a trot. Deveron and the other mages were already far ahead.

Behind him, the setting sun played with shadows. Much of the hillside it painted in beautiful hues of red and orange and shadowy brown. All except one small area – a new rock fall that remained obstinately dark.

Epilogue

The car pulled up smoothly to the kerb and the three friends sat for a moment listening to the gentle purr of the engine. Maggie looked up to the third floor of the tenement building where Jeff shared an apartment with Martin. There was a light on in the living room, but the curtains were pulled closed. Still keeping her eyes on the window, she called over her shoulder to Jeff in the back seat. "Are you sure Martin's ready for all of this?"

It was Duncan who answered as he switched off the engine. "Yes, well as ready as he'll ever be. He's been calling the house regularly since he found out you'd all crossed over to Elsynvaal. He's desperate to know what has happened to Emma."

"Let's go then. No sense in sitting here!" Maggie opened the door and stepped out into a slushy puddle. "Ugh! How could I have forgotten the rain and the puddles? We've not been away all that long."

"It's only two weeks till Christmas," Duncan reminded her. "You were away for almost two months."

Maggie smiled as Jeff leaped across a puddle and ran for the tenement doorway. "Amazing, isn't it, the difference it's made to him. He's like a little boy!"

"It's incredible what Horatio was able to do with his leg. I'll tell you – when Jeff stood up after the Crossover through the Ether, I hardly recognised him. To see him with his clear skin and purposeful walk – you could have blown me over sideways!"

Maggie looked at his bulky outline and laughed. "Somehow I doubt that, Duncan. Come on. Jeff will be at the top of the stairs by now. By the way, did I tell you that he started phoning round for a driving school this afternoon? He's taking driving lessons! He'd never bothered before because his bad leg meant he'd only be allowed to drive a specially adapted car. Now there's no stopping him!" Both were smiling as they followed Jeff into the building.

By the time they reached the third floor flat, the door was open and Jeff was inside the hallway with Martin. The intervening two months had not been kind to Martin Patterson. There were shadows under his eyes and his hair was lank and listless. The brightness of his eyes made Maggie wonder if he'd been using drugs. They followed him down the hallway to the living room and tried to find somewhere amidst the squalor to sit down.

"I see you didn't bring the sorcerer with you," he said. Jeff and Maggie exchanged a look.

Jeff lifted his beer glass with a scar-free hand and smiled. "Horatio crossed back to Elsynvaal this morning," he said. "He remained here only long enough to speak with Milo's parents before returning to his world. Without his powerful coercion they would probably have become convinced that Milo had been murdered, and called in the police."

"Yes, the sorcerer would be very good at coercion, I'd guess."

"If only we'd been able to return Milo's body to them." Maggie's voice was quiet. "But it was impossible. Anyway, Milo'd probably prefer to be where he is." She looked across at Duncan. "He is buried next to Olivia."

Duncan toyed with his glass, swirling the beer inside till it threatened to over-spill onto the table. "It seems so unlike him. I didn't know him well at all, but he didn't strike me as the type to go overboard for a girl."

"There was much more to Milo than we all thought."

Martin peered into the whisky glass he was holding, trying to give an impression of unconcern. "What of Emma? Is she happy with her sorcerer?"

Maggie reached forward and took his hand in hers. "She's trying to come to terms with what she's discovered about herself; not an easy thing to do. She did something that she's having problems accepting."

Jeff was more brutal. "Emma has changed, Martin. She's dangerous. She killed her own mother for deserting her when she was a baby."

Maggie tried to stop him, but Jeff ignored her entreaties. "This is hard for you to hear, I know, Martin, but you need to know the truth. She put all the hate that's been boiling up inside her all her life into a phial of liquid and threw it at her face. Emma's mother died a horrible death. Doing that kind of thing affects a person." He shook his head. "She's changed, Martin. You're better off without her."

Martin pulled his hand away from Maggie and stood up. He made his unsteady way to the drinks cabinet where he poured himself another whisky. As she watched him stagger away, Maggie re-lived in her mind the last conversation she had alone with Emma.

309

For once they were alone, sitting by the fireside in their room.

"I had another dream Maggie," Emma said. "How I wish they would stop, but they won't. They just keep coming." She pulled herself more upright and looked straight into Maggie's eyes. "But it wasn't the usual one about the White Hawk this time. It was about you, Maggie. You and Jeff. Tomorrow both of you are going back. Back... home. But I'm not, not yet."

She paused and looked into the fire as if trying to see the future there. "Horatio insists that the child must be born an Elsynese and be brought up knowing his power and his heritage." She looked back at Maggie. "And he is right," she said. "Otherwise he will never find happiness. So, until my son is born, I will remain here and learn to control this power – or it will control me – again..."

She stretched across the gap between them and took Maggie's hands in hers. "What I did with that vial was unforgivable. I killed her, Maggie. And in the most horrible way imaginable. And that is one thing I can't ever allow myself to forget."

She turned away laying her cheek against the plush fabric of the upholstery. Maggie shifted across to the opposite seat and laid a comforting arm around her shoulders. "You did not know what you were doing."

"And I should be forgiven because of that?" Emma broke away from her friend's embrace and walked over to the window, gazing unseeingly down into the courtyard, and into the air for a flying speck that would herald the coming of the White Hawk.

"She was mad, Emma."

"Yes, she was insane, but should that necessitate her death? Especially the one I gave her! She should have been imprisoned or something, like my grandfather."

"She was a monster. She skinned Horatio to make book-bindings!"

"And what I did was more humane?"

"Horatio explained what happened, Emma. You have got to accept that it just happened, and start to forgive yourself. It was unintentional on your part. You were scared. You were angry. You didn't know your strength."

"Neither did my mother at first, and when she discovered her heritage it drove her insane. She was dangerous, and so am I. Horatio knows it. That's why he is so afraid of me. He thinks I could go mad also. Sometimes I think he's right."

"I don't. I think you will study and learn what your powers are, and how to control them. Mhari will remain here too, remember. She will help you, as well as being someone from home!"

Emma laughed, but it was humourless. "Mhari? She is but a child. Everything for Mhari is black or white. How can she understand what I am facing? All her life she has played at magic. Ouija boards, tarot cards, horoscopes, séances… You name it, she's tried it. Now she's discovered a mediocre mage power and is utterly enthralled with it. She hangs on Horatio's every word…"

Maggie cut across the torrent of words. It was as if once Emma had begun talking she could not stop. "Why do you think you'll never come home?"

Emma cocked her head to one side. "But I will come home, Maggie, but not with you tomorrow. You see, Maggie, I can see futures. But I cannot see my own, or anyone whose life touches mine. Horatio could not see Master Will's fame because somehow their lives are still entwined. I cannot see *your* future, or Jeff's or… Martin's, which means after you return home… at some point our lives will touch again. But I *can* see Horatio's future – so we are not meant to be together. And I can see our son's future life. He will be a very powerful mage, Maggie, but, and this puzzles me, I can only see him until he is in his teens – not when he's older. I don't know why that is. Does it mean I'll return to Elsynvaal? Or it just that I can see only so far into the future?"

"I don't know," Maggie started to say, but Emma was still talking.

"I see Mhari's because she'll stay here in Elsynvaal to become a mediocre mage who will harbour no doubts about her destiny. The thing is… " she looked away out of the window again, but this time she wasn't searching for any specks in the sky. "The thing is in some ways she's right. Lucky Mhari… Everything for her is straight-forward and clear." Emma's voice faltered and Maggie had to strain to hear her next words. "I wish *I'd* known…" Then she shrugged and looked over at the window, once more scanning the skies for the White Hawk.

Silence fell again, and Maggie lay back, thinking about what her friend had said. After a while Emma spoke again, her voice quiet and full of sadness. "My mother cursed me, Maggie. She cursed me with her dying breath. I researched it in Horatio's books and it's not good. I shall never be happy in Elsynvaal, and I can only hope that things will improve after the child is born, and I can leave. So, when

311

you go home," she said, "I want you to take a message to Duncan from me. Say nothing to Jeff and especially not to Horatio. Ask Duncan to open the Ether for me 360 days after you cross over. By then I will have given birth and can leave. Will you do this for me?"

"Of course I will. But what about Martin? Is there anything I should tell him?"

"Tell him what has happened. And tell him I'm sorry, and that things could have been different had others not intervened. Tell him that he was right – that what I felt for Horatio was magically induced. Tell Martin that I *did* love him. Tell him I wish him a good life. A happy life."

"What about you and Horatio?" Emma merely shrugged. "I know he loves you, Emma. It's only this fear he has of your parentage and powers that is holding him back. I'm sure of it. Give yourselves time. Forgive yourself, Emma. Study, learn, and find your new self, Emma. *Then* decide."

"Then decide... Then decide..."

***

The memory faded and Maggie once more became conscious of the men's voices.

"I just find the whole thing incredible," Duncan was saying, "I mean, you all being part of Shakespeare's *Hamlet* scenario! Meeting the bard himself... Is he still in Elsynvaal?"

Jeff stretched his legs out in front of him and pushed his hair away from his clear skinned face. "Yes. He decided to stay a while longer. I'd have thought that one good story line would have been sufficient for him!"

"What of Emma?" Duncan seemed oblivious to Martin sitting silent on the floor, his back against a sofa, his head thrown back and eyes closed.

Maggie threw a glance at him as Jeff answered.

"She's going to learn about her magical powers. She's also trying to come to terms with her parentage, and what she did. Not easy, I would think. I don't think it will be plain sailing for either of them. One thing is certain," Jeff went on, "she is one confused little lady. She's unsure of who she really is. She wants to be known as herself, and not as Midori's daughter or Gheron talEbol's granddaughter. But I think it will be a long time before anyone forgets that little snippet. Least of all Horatio. Theirs would not be a marriage made in Heaven. Poor kid. I hated to leave her like that, her being pregnant and all that."

"Ah!" Martin's exclamation came as a sigh. Maggie thumped Jeff's arm. How insensitive could he be? She continued to watch Martin's face. It was becoming paler by the minute. Would Jeff ever shut up?

Maggie roused herself. "It will help Emma to know that Mhari is with her. They're studying together."

Duncan looked down at his almost empty glass.

"My sister – training to be a mage in another world. Do you really think she'll ever come back? Will we see her again?"

"Who knows, Duncan? With time running faster here, who knows?"

"Emma won't be back." Martin's voice was ragged.

Maggie took a deep breath. "She may," she said quietly. Martin sat up and opened his eyes. "When we left she was adamant that she would return."

"She's coming back? When?"

"She asked if Duncan would oversee an opening in the Ether in early December next year."

"Next year?"

"Time differential. By then the baby will have been born. She says she will leave it there with Horatio and come home. At least that's what she said three days ago in Elasyn. Martin, she said to tell you she was sorry. And that you were right all along."

Martin turned to Duncan. "Will you do this? Will you open the Ether to give her the chance to come home?"

Duncan shrugged his shoulders. "I suppose."

Martin stood up and walked over to the window. Down in the street a grey cat was sitting atop Duncan's car, grooming itself. Up above the roofs and chimney pots and TV aerials, the stars were coming out. It was a cold and crisp winter's night. And tomorrow the sun would rise.

He could live with that. Indeed he could. For the first time in two months, Martin Patterson allowed himself to hope. A smile crept across his lips.

It felt strange.

$\mathfrak{The}$ $\mathfrak{Tales}$ $\mathfrak{of}$ $\mathfrak{Elsynvaal}$

continue in

"$\mathfrak{The}$ $\mathfrak{Crystal}$ $\mathfrak{Mage}$"

www.chrisdavidson.info